A Love Undercover series

In Perfect Timing

A Novel

BOOK ONE

Bev Powers

Disclaimer

This book is a work of fiction. Names, characters, businesses, places, events, and incidents are either the products of the author's imagination or used in a fictitious manner. Any resemblance to actual persons, living or dead, or actual events is purely coincidental.

ISBN-13: 978-0998253602
ISBN-10: 099825360X

Dedication

I dedicate this work to the women who are broken from abuse, rape, and the stain of abortion, and life's disappointments, or whatever it may be that causes you emotional pain. No matter how long ago or recently it may have happened to you, just know that your Father God has given you His love and grace for you to overcome anything you may go through. I sincerely pray for your wholeness and wellness. May you experience God's loving arms wrapped around you, His love for you in a deeper way. I pray that you would experience His healing, a heart to forgive, and restoration by His Holy Spirit through the words on these pages.

The thief cometh not, but for to steal, and to kill, and to destroy: I am come that they might have life, and that they might have it more abundantly.

John 10:10 KJV

In honor of my late, but dear sister and forever friend, Peachie, you have made your home in heaven, now. I thank God for your inspiration, prayers, and encouragement while you were here with me; you shall forever have a special place in my heart.

Acknowledgements

Thank you, Heavenly Father, for your immeasurable love and guiding me to fulfill my purpose. Without You in my life, I would have given up. You are the wind beneath my wings.

I would like to express special thanks to the following:

My daughter, Jevonia, what can I say? You are a true gift from God. Even while I carried you in my womb, I knew you would be a treasure. Not only are you my daughter and the mother of my grandchildren, whom I adore, you are also my friend. Your honesty, encouragement, face-to-face *tell it like it is* talks were the very words that set me on this journey. You are a beautiful soul. I love you, always.

My son-in-law, Phillip, again, I'm speechless. You are more than a son to me. Your kindness, gentle words of encouragement, and checking up on me to make sure I'm still on course have not gone unnoticed. Your hugs and all the other things that only a wonderful son like you could do gird me up with strength. I so appreciate you. Love you for always.

My editor, Karen H. Rodgers, of Critique Editing Services, your eagle eye, guidance, and excellence of service fueled my confidence to push forward past the obstacles during this project. Your support and encouragement is invaluable. I look forward to the many projects ahead of us. Thank you for being part of my team!

Donna Bond for your encouraging words and feedback. It wouldn't have felt right without you being on this journey with me. Thank you for your wisdom and insight.

Barbara Billups for your dedication and unprecedented diligence in this project. God placed you in my life for such a time as this. Thanks for being my lifeline during this project.

My business coach, Darnyelle Jervey of IFU, you helped to keep me focused on my priorities. Thanks for all you do!

Sandra Frisbey, my prayer warrior who helped me birth this book. You helped push me across the finish line. Thank you!

Pastor Keith Echols, of WOFCC-PA. You are a true shepherd of God. One who cares that his flock gets it—that we may live and thrive in the presence of our Mighty Lord and Savior, Jesus—Who is the Christ. May you continue to be rewarded richly here on earth as in heaven. Thanks for teaching the unadulterated Word of God that has caused me to grow in order to do the work of the Lord as He has designed.

Min. Riena Echols of WOFCC-PA. Not only are you our First Lady, a woman who is a perfect example of a kind and meek spirit, and Godliness, but you are also my friend. Thanks for all your encouraging words and support during this project. You are always there when I need you.

Pastor Marq Echols of WOFCC-PA. It brightens my heart to see such a young man of God on fire! Your passion for God transcends not only in your teachings, but also in demonstration of the life of Christ, which you live. God bless you and your family.

Thank you to my Welch family siblings, Mom Greta Yorkman, my WOFCC-Pa family, the women who mentored me, and a host of many more. Thanks for being here with me in spirit and prayers through this process. Your kind and encouraging words were felt and very much appreciated. I love you all.

Part One

And Isaac brought her into his mother Sarah's tent, and took Rebekah, and she became his wife; and he loved her; and Isaac was comforted after his mother's death.

Gen 24:67 KJV

Prologue

Tyro Hernandez Simmonds became an instant hero. It happened on a Friday evening in mid-fall. The sun had just nestled in for the night and the moon beamed brightly in the starless sky.

The traffic light had just turned green. As he proceeded to turn left onto Limestone Road he suddenly had to swerve his 2015 Land Rover. Only by a few inches did he avoid ramming into the side of the Shrek-looking contraption.

The truck had two trailers hitched to the back of it making it as long as an 18-wheeler. The putrid lime-green motif made it look as if it belonged in a circus. Without warning, it had jutted into the middle of the intersection like a raging elephant, heading directly toward his brand new vehicle.

"WHAT AN IDIOT!" he shouted as he maneuvered to get out of the way. "What *is* that?" His car swerved in a full circle. After he managed to regain control, he stole a brief glimpse of the driver as he pulled his vehicle to safety. "Is that a woman driving that thing?"

A myriad of loud brakes from other cars meeting the same fate squealed in the background. It was a disaster bound to happen. Images of gruesome injuries and damage resulting from a multiple car pile-up, and worse yet, bodies sprawled out in the street bombarded his mind. As he sat for a moment to still the adrenaline pulsing through his body, he silently prayed no one got hurt.

Voices escalated in obscenities from impatient drivers who were laying long and heavy on their horns. Was she blocking traffic? Tyro hopped out of his car and looked toward the growing commotion. The unsightly jalopy had fishtailed as it turned aside.

Spinning completely around, it halted abruptly right in the middle of the intersection. Sirens blared in the distance.

Tyro wiped his forehead as he grimaced at the reality. His gut feeling warned him, compelled him to leave it alone. He thought to just walk away and be grateful he was unscathed by the incident. Why should he get involved? he contemplated. But for him, not to get involved wasn't who he was. The woman was in trouble.

He charged forward. He could only surmise it was the rush of hormones still surging through his veins. As he got closer, he noticed the brown-skinned woman feverishly pumping the gas pedal. The driver side was open. It had no door. Her leg was exposed, protruding through the split fashioned on the side of her skirt as she pumped up and down. She mindlessly shifted gears, repeatedly scraping them as the sound filled the air like a chainsaw raking over a heavy sheet of metal.

It was obvious she had no idea what she was doing.

Sirens were closer... too close!

Fire trucks and other emergency vehicles barreled down the road. Alarmed bystanders yelled desperately... screaming as their arms flailed like octopuses urging her to get out of the way.

Sirens were much closer now whirling and blaring warnings of the urgency. They were coming through. Even if the drivers wanted to, there'd be no stopping the momentum of the powerful, heavy equipment, soaring her way.

Smoke billowing out of the restaurant on the adjacent corner caught Tyro's attention. It confirmed his suspicion. The emergency vehicles weren't coming on her behalf. It was of a more urgent matter. Her ridiculous monster-looking vehicle was in the line of fire. And she was still in it.

The fact that she hadn't gotten out of the truck baffled him. Doesn't she hear the sirens? Doesn't she know she's in the way? He watched in disbelief as her foot continued to pump the pedal. Her hands yanking the column shift from gear to gear. Why doesn't she get out of there? Thoughts of terror seized his mind as he continued running her way.

Within a split second, his disbelief turned into horror. The first of the fire engines was rocketing around the corner. Its driver had no way to see what lay in the middle of the intersection and hadn't slowed down. Once it turned the corner, it would be too late.

If somebody doesn't do something, she will be killed, he reasoned.

He couldn't explain it, nor make any sense of it if he tried. Something rose up within him propelling him forward. Within a split second he found himself pushing harder, flying through the air. It was as if his feet never touched down.

She turned in his direction and saw him coming. The world around him melted as their eyes met. Her fear-stricken face quivered beneath a faint smile as if somehow, she knew he'd come for her. Death had to loosen its hold. Her prince, her savior had come to save her.

His steel gray eyes pierced into her hazel browns. His heart pounded in light of the situation, within a fleeting moment his mind had calculated her beauty. Her fear. Never had he seen anyone as exquisitely breathtaking as she. His feet still barely touched the asphalt as he raced toward her. His sandy brown locks flailing like Flash Gordon's. Would he get there in time?

The first fire truck was barely twenty yards away now. It was at that very moment she'd seen it too. He lunged forward and darted up into the truck through the opening on the driver's side. His eyes locked onto her hazy, panic stricken stare.

***

He cradled the woman he'd just rescued in his arms as he searched for a safe place to set her down. Everything prior to this point was a blur. How he had gotten the vehicle out of the middle of the intersection just nanoseconds from being hammered by the double engine careening around the corner was muddled in his mind.

Her reddish-brown locks bouncing beneath her shiny sequined cap brushed lightly against his face as he carried her to the nearest curb. He turned her aside to shelter her from the rowdy spectators who were still enthralled with the vehicle she had been driving.

Her body quivered in the reality of what just happened. She held her arms around his neck. He steadied himself as he stole a moment to gaze into her lovely face. He was mesmerized, captivated as the moon illuminated her beauty. Her eyes pulled him in deeper as he searched her face. *Who is she?* he wondered.

"Thank you, " she muttered barely above a whisper, her body still trembling.

Her voice soft as velvet rippled through his heart. A pulse of life soothed his aching heart. And there he saw it. A glimpse of what could be. The sparkle in her eyes pierced through the darkness in his soul. The heaviness from the recent loss of his mother lifted. For a moment in time, he was free of the antagonizing grip of his grief.

As their silhouette illuminated under the full moon, it cast the picture of a perfect couple. He was uncertain. Is she the one? His heart drummed. He remembered his dream. It was a dream of hope… comfort… a promise of peace.

In his reality, he had been too late to save his mother. But in the dream, he had come just in time to save the mysterious woman. Just like tonight, he had saved her. In the dream he never saw the woman's face, but now, here he stood holding her in his arms just as he'd dreamt.

His expectancy rose. In anticipation of a tender kiss, his lips drew slowly closer to hers, barely touching. Numerous people had started to gather around, speculating on the event that just occurred.

"What a hero!" one onlooker chimed.

"He's a very brave man!" another cheered. The crowd swelled, heralding his heroism as wild cheering erupted. It was at that moment the attraction between the hero and heroine was instantly broken. Still nestled in his embrace, he swerved their backs to the crowd as he delicately placed her down. He handed her his jacket to shield her face as he saw the swarm of paparazzi heading their way.

And within an instant, their magical moment was gone — *Poof.*

The reality of what he had just done, the risk he took seized his nerves reminding him of his lunacy. "What *is* that thing?" he gasped under his breath. Within seconds the whole ordeal tumbled vividly through his mind as he looked at her vehicle.

Its front wheels still teetered over the curbside rail. The utility bucket on the end of the long crane tilted haphazardly in the air. Tyro peeled his eyes away, refusing to look at it any longer. He shuddered at the reality he could have been killed.

He needed to take his mind off of the whole nightmare. He turned his attention back toward the woman who had gotten him into the predicament in the first place.

She was gone. Only the jacket he had given her remained. In the few moments he had taken his eyes off of her, she had slipped away right from under him. Vanished without a trace. Had they been two strangers destined to meet— if only for a moment? Would he see her again?

Onlookers pointed his way. He turned to make his escape when something shiny near his foot caught his eye. It was her hat. He stooped and discreetly shoved the silver cap she had worn in his pocket. It was all that remained.

Like the prince in Cinderella—whose life had not been in such danger, yet—he too held the only remains of the magical moment shared.

And he didn't even know her name.

Chapter 1

Tyro awakened abruptly. His seventy-five-pound Shepherd, Sheba barked ferociously at someone banging on the back door. Their persistent knocking had jarred him from his fitful sleep. Although the reality of his foolish heroism last night plagued him, it was not as haunting as someone now hanging heavily on his doorbell.

He bolted upright in bed and rubbed his hand through his hair. He contemplated not answering it. The relentless pounding against the mahogany door, and sharp peals continued to resound throughout his house as if the world was ending. He knew it could only be one person. His dad.

A peek through the door's side window confirmed his speculation. Soughing loudly, he paused before he opened the door. Living on a private island with your dad has its advantages. But such times of inconvenience, like now, warranted second thoughts. Is he out of his mind? The sun isn't even up yet.

"Have you been watching the news?" Quincy spat. Storming through the door he slammed a bunch of papers on the counter he had printed off the web.

"I have been calling you for hours." He gave a disgusted grunt and spun around, not giving his son the opportunity to answer. "You should have at least had the decency to call me back. I am your father. Or have you forgotten that fact?" he said matter-of-factly as he spewed out a few choice words.

"Are you kidding me?" Tyro muttered after squinting to see the time on the iPad nestled conveniently on the black marble counter top. "It's 4:45 in the morning," Tyro said plainly as he rubbed at the stubble on his face.

The coffee timer was set for 7... *I need coffee. NOW.* Tyro picked up the tablet, punched in a few digits to reset the timer for the coffee to start to brew while he kept his back to his dad. "I got in late. Thought it'd be too late —"

"Tell me this is not you," his father interrupted as he snapped one of the pictures he'd printed off of the Internet at his son's back. Tyro kept busy with what he was doing.

The picture depicted a woman cradled in the arms of her "hero." The shot was taken from a side view. It was the only view anyone had been able to get as he stealthily concealed both of their faces. The paparazzi and the onlookers had gone wild taking pictures on their personal devices.

"What are you talking about?" Tyro retorted as he poured himself a cup of coffee. He didn't bother to look at the crinkled sheet of paper in Quincy's hand. He already knew the deal. Pictures of the hideous green truck were everywhere.

The exaggerated tales raised questions such as who were they, where did they go? Did he swoop her away to his castle? Where is his castle? How did they get away? Was it magic?

The headlines were incredulous. He snorted just thinking of them. All of them were pretty much the same. From the news on the television, eNews tribunes, on-line news, too and all the other cyber articles and videos, he'd already scoured through them all. And quite frankly, he was sick of it. What was the big deal? People need to get a life. So what, he'd rescued some chick? Big deal.

"Do you see this?" His father flailed another print out in his face.

To appease his father, he took the picture and held it up to look at it.

The woman's leg dangled between the long split in the side of her gray spandex skirt. Her warm chestnut skin tone radiated under the moonlit sky. The ankle boots she wore matched her gray leather jacket perfectly. Her reddish brown hair curled up from under the shimmering cap snugged on her head. What could be seen of their

16

faces as their lips barely touched was like the swirl of French vanilla crème in mocha coffee.

Tyro thought they were the perfect blend. Out of all of the photos he'd seen, this was his favorite. He sipped his coffee and handed the paper back to his father. "Nice legs," he said, knowing it would get him fired up more.

"Nice legs...?"

Here it comes...

"Are you out of your mind, son? How can you be thinking about sex at a time like this?"

For the life of him, Tyro couldn't understand how his father thought he'd ever share his interest in a woman with him, or bring any woman to his house. Not with the way his father was always ranting and raging about practically nothing. His attitude was impossible for him or their staff to bear. And frankly, Tyro had grown tired of it.

However, he and his dad were scheduled to meet with the detective on Monday. Up until now, there had been no positive leads on who'd murdered his mother. It had been six months. He was skeptical that this meeting would be any different than the last. Even with the new leads that might possibly shed some light on the case, Tyro would not get his hopes up.

"Are you listening to me?" Quincy spat, leaping off of the stool at the counter.

He assured himself, now would not be the time to confront his dad's tyrannical behavior. He'd have to deal with it later. He looked away from the pictures sprawled over his counter. There would be no end to this. He was sure of it.

"Dad... please..." Tyro rubbed at the bristles on his face repeatedly. "I need to shower."

After pouring his dad a steamy cup of coffee he set the java down, since Quincy refused to take it. A glimpse of one of the latest updates Quincy had printed off and laid on the counter caught his attention.

Brave Knight in Shining Armor Saves Damsel in Distress from the Abominable Ferocious Green Monster.... Where did the hideous green mobile come from? Is it for sale? Bids on eBay soared to over a half million dollars for the mysterious green vehicle.

"Great articles." Tyro smirked as he headed up the back stairs.

"Oh...," Quincy said sarcastically as he and Sheba treaded on his heels. "You think this is funny?" He displayed a different printout from the eTimes Post, capturing the overnight craze as he followed him into his bedroom.

"PRINCE or SUPER HERO?"

> *"Prince Saves Princess from Abominable Green Monster. Be sure to text us your vote today for a chance to win a free weekend getaway at the Prince's castle.*
>
> *TEXT PR123 to vote he is a prince.*
> *TEXT SH456 to vote he is a superhero.*

Tyro disappeared into his master bath without responding as Quincy's intense pacing echoed off of the Brazilian floors.

Chapter 2

Tyro showered and came out of the bathroom dressed in a pair of pajama bottoms and a tee. Quincy had raised the TV in the footboard on Tyro's bed and was watching the latest events. The news thundered in great force as the story grew even larger.

The photo of the mysterious Prince Charming with his princess cradled in his arms as they were about to share a kiss, was taken by one of the bystanders. It had gone viral within minutes.

"Senseless," Quincy bellowed. "The whole situation is nonsense and unnecessary." He scowled. "Why did you have to get involved? Now the whole world knows what an..." His hands exploded upward in idiotic motions for the lack of finding the right words to say.

"Do you see my name mentioned anywhere? Are you able to see my face?" Tyro took the remote, turned off the TV, and pressed for it to descend into its resting place. He already had determined not to watch television until this whole matter blew over.

"Turn that back on!" his father snapped.

"I'm not watching the news. It's depressing," Tyro gritted through clinched teeth. As soon as he'd said the word, "depressing," he cringed. He faltered under the weight of the insatiable presence as depression weighed down on his shoulders. Tugging and grasping at his sanity, determined to pull him back into its lonely, dark hole.

Quincy had felt it too. He'd stormed out of the room and barreled down the steps. The door slammed announcing his departure, although Tyro had already seen the tears swelling in his father's eyes. He was sure he had tried to hide them.

He felt the guilt of losing his mother swallowing him. He lay on the bed with his hand behind his head. Sensing the feeling of despair overcoming her master, Sheba leapt onto the bed and nuzzled her nose in his side. As she had done numerous times since these spells started, she'd lain next to him until it passed.

Tyro stared at the ceiling as memories of the horrible day ate at his mind. The thoughts threatened to devour his soul in one gulp. In his mind, he heard his mother's voice crying out to him for help. He saw her face.

Her contorted, blood stained face. Her lifeless eyes were wide open as she reached for him. "I failed you, Momma… I'm sorry. I should have been there. I should have saved you." His words cried out into the darkness enveloping around him.

Tyro wished he could turn back the hands of time to when he still lived with his parents. His dad was not the tyrant he is now. After he had learned of the horrid death his wife suffered, it was as if he— the real Quincy—had died along with her.

Tyro hadn't always lived with his parents. He'd moved in with them while his home was being constructed on their private island. After his home was finished, he continued to live with them. He couldn't shake his gut feeling something wasn't right. Last winter, they'd hired his mother's private helicopter pilot and chauffeur. Within three-month's time, he'd been fired.

Mario, his mother's brother, had blamed himself for bringing the disconcerted employee onboard. Twenty years ago, Casillas and he had served in the same Navy Seals platoon. They'd survived many dangerous missions together. They'd fought side by side never leaving the other behind. Because of the trust and bond they'd developed, although it had been many years ago, Mario overruled the normal protocol Laino had set in place.

Mario revered his sister and loved her dearly. Tyro adored her and she'd cherished her son. Quincy loved his wife. He'd given her the nickname, Laino twenty-seven years ago when they'd first met. Her full name was Malaino Sofia Hernandez Simmonds. Born in

Venezuela, her family owned a Mahogany tree farm. From a young age, her Latino heritage taught her what it meant to work hard.

She was the office manager to the Hernandez-Simmonds family business, known as Laino Enterprises. Laino ran a tight ship. She had been the driving force behind it being the multi-billion-dollar establishment it is today.

She had written all of the company's policies and procedures in compliance with state and federal, as well as FCC and aviation laws. She ensured that everyone followed them to the "T." No exceptions.

It was during one of their Sunday family/business dinners she'd learned protocol had not been followed with her new pilot. Just before dessert was to be served, Mario had let him go. Tyro didn't like the way the former pilot looked at his mother as he was escorted off the property.

After her death, Tyro, Quincy, and Mario each had his own way of grieving. His father chose control, dominance, and drinking. Mario chose denial, while Tyro anesthetized himself on prescribed meds.

None of their methods brought any solace or healing. Instead, they were estranged; their three-cord bond had been broken. The family business Laino had charted into a billion-dollar conglomerate was suffering, hemorrhaging to death. And although Tyro couldn't bear his father's intolerance for much longer, he still loved him. He needed his father as much as his father needed him.

In his impatience, Tyro took a third pill after the first two hadn't taken effect fast enough. Why hadn't he gone back to the office earlier that night like he'd planned? He'd never forgive himself for ignoring the sinking feeling he had in his gut. If he had followed his mind, it would have been the perpetrator for whom the coroner had come. Not his mom.

As he waited to fade off into a world of nothingness, he thought of the tender moment he'd shared with the woman he'd rescued last night. He removed the hat she had left behind from his nightstand. He breathed in the mixture of fragrances lingering from her hair and perfume. It soothed him. Placing it back in the drawer, he vowed he'd stop at nothing until he found her again.

Remembering how he felt as he'd held her under the moonlight, there was no getting around it. Something special had happened between them. What it was, he didn't know. A good feeling washed over him as he thought of her. The guilt and regret he had carried over the past six months diminished enough for a sliver of hope to come. And with that glimmer of light he knew someday he'd find his way back to being himself.

In his newfound salvation, he realized thinking of her, the way she smelled, and how she felt in his arms caused a smile to form over his face. Tyro slipped into a peaceful realm of sleep.

Chapter 3

"Oh my God!" Moriah Styles cried as she bolted straight up in bed. Drenched in sweat, she'd had the same nightmare three times in a row. *Did I really almost kill myself?* It was so real. As pain shot through her ankle, there was no denying it. It had been real.

Unable to go back to sleep, she turned gingerly to allow her feet to dangle over the bed for a few moments. The circulation slowly returned. "Ow!" She winced.

"You okay?" Moriah's roommate and best friend, Nettie asked. She reached and turned on the lamp screwed into the wall above the nightstand separating their double beds. The residential hotel they occupied was temporary. Its yellowing wallpaper décor in faded fleur-de-lis and matching drapes carried the tales of the elegant folks who had long ago graced its presence.

The dated motif and lingering stale aroma by far screamed anything but the luxurious lifestyle Moriah had been used to, but at least it was clean. For now, it would have to do.

"I can't believe I almost got myself killed driving that thing!" Moriah shuddered at the thought of the whole nightmarish event. She knew she should have followed her mind and walked away from buying the hideous truck when she had the chance.

But her desperation got the better part of her judgment. The hydraulic bucket lift at the back of it piqued her interest and caused her to override common sense. Having a marketing business that hung large signs and billboards, she needed a truck capable of handling her clients' requests. And besides, Junkman, the owner of the junkyard where she'd bought the vehicle, promised he'd give her a "sweet" deal.

"Gurl...You don't have to tell me about getting killed in that thang," Nettie complained as she retightened the scarf around her silky black hair. "I can't believe I let you talk me into going back there to help you move that thang at some two in the morning," Nettie said, stressing every syllable at each point while rolling her eyes and popping her neck.

"You're crazy. You know that?" Moriah chuckled looking at her friend going through the motions and exaggerated antics. Nettie was as educated and eloquently spoken as any of the others in Moriah's business circles. But she could be straight up "ghetto" when she wanted to. When they were together, she was just plain, down to earth, Nettie. It's what Moriah loved about her best friend.

"You? You calling *me* crazy?" Nettie chuckled. "But still, you know Larry's not going to let you leave that beast of a truck of yours in his garage for too long. These twins might work miracles," Nettie said, pointing to her well-endowed bosom, "but 'All good things must come to an end,' as my grandmother used to say."

"How am I supposed to service my clients without my truck?"

"You should have thought about that before you bought it. If you'd asked me, I would have told you straight-up, 'No!' and would have dragged your behind off to the looney bin somewhere if you still insisted on buying that death trap." Nettie picked up the Veterinary Anatomy Concepts textbook she'd been studying and flipped through the pages.

"There's no way you or anybody in her right mind should be in that thing, let alone driving it. You're lucky your prince... dragon slayer... whatever you want to call him, came along in the nick of time." She sighed as she closed the book and tossed it toward the bottom of her bed. She reached for her tablet to browse through her notes.

"Yeah," Moriah said dreamily. Her mind drifted back to how he'd swooped her into his strong arms, lifting her out of the truck when he saw she had injured her ankle.

Nettie looked down as Moriah rubbed her ankle. She helped her to lift her leg back onto the bed and stuffed several pillows under it. "He must be a blue collar worker. Too bad he's not rich," Nettie said.

"Nettie! Being rich isn't everything. But he sure was a good-looking man." She stared mindlessly into nowhere. "Something happened between us. It was as if the whole world had disappeared. As we stared into each other's eyes, for a moment I thought he was going to kiss me. It was like we made a connection, you know?"

"Yeah, right!" Nettie snickered. "He was probably thinking how crazy you were to be driving that death trap. That's what he was thinking."

"I'm just glad he knew what he was doing. I had no idea the transmission would give out on me," Moriah added, ignoring her roommate's reprimand. She moaned as she struggled to get comfortable with her leg being propped up on too many pillows.

"How'd you say you did this again?" Nettie pointed to her ankle as she removed one of the pillows and tossed it back on the dinky sofa sleeper in their makeshift living room area.

"I think when he shoved me..." She held her palm up to ward off any comments Nettie was about to make. She could see it in her eyes.

"There was a metal toolbox or something on the floor between the two front seats. I must have hit it or something... I don't know. Everything happened so fast." Moriah looked far away. "I've never been so scared in my life."

"You should have been. I hope it serves as a lesson to you." Nettie got up and placed some ice she removed from the small hotel frig into a plastic bag. She wrapped a white towel around it. "But knowing you, Ms. I Am Woman, Hear Me Roar," she said as she trekked back to Moriah's side and wrapped the ice pack around her ankle, "I seriously doubt it."

"You never told me where you got that contraption from." Nettie propped herself back against the dilapidated headboard, laid her open notebook over her lap, crossed her arms, and waited.

"When I tell you, don't be going off on me. Okay?" Trying to crook her neck, Moriah rolled her endearing hazels at her friend. They burst into laughter at Moriah's awkward head movements. She never could get it right.

"I officially ban you from ever doing that again," Nettie teased. "Now come out with it." She was bent on hearing the whole story.

Moriah grabbed two generic ibuprofens, popped them in her mouth, tilted her head back, and swallowed them without any water. "I got it from a salvage yard."

Chapter 4

"The junk yard? And you paid somebody for that... that thing?" Nettie retorted incredulously.

"Are you going to let me finish?" Moriah narrowed an eye at Nettie and leaned her shoulders back. She watched Nettie as she zipped her lip with her fingers.

"I hadn't intended on it. I went to look for a piece of scrap metal to make a sign for one of my clients." Moriah fidgeted with her bedspread. She stole a quick glance at her friend's piercing eyes. "He said it would only need a tune up later and that he'd make me a good deal."

"Un huh," Nettie couldn't resist as she crossed, uncrossed, and crossed her arms again. She fumed on and on about her friend's mindless decision.

But Moriah's mind drifted as she thought about her four-year-old niece, Amelia. She had recently lost custody and was forbidden any unsupervised visits. *Oh God... What if I had been killed? Who would take care of Amelia... my little Rosebud?* Moriah shifted uncomfortably on the bed as reality set in. *Petra and Parker? No way.*

Moriah drew a deep breath and let it out in a long sigh. Petra and Parker were Amelia's father's parents. They already had gained full custody of her after they'd fired Moriah. They had loads of money from their successful marketing firm. The company she helped grow into the multi-million-dollar business it had quickly become.

Now, thanks to them, Moriah had no decent place to live. She'd sold her condo, her car, and all of her stocks and investments and had spent every penny of it on legal and court fees. The custody battle had been brutal, a battle that she had lost. But she would not give up. Even with the ridiculous trumped up charges and allegations of her being unfit, along with "child endangerment," she was a fighter. She had too much at stake to give up now.

She was determined to get her career back on track and make the money she was used to having before she was unfairly terminated. Then she would get the courts to give her back full custody of Amelia as she once had. After that, she planned to have the judge to drop those insane charges and clear her record. Getting Amelia back would mean the world to her, more than anything.

She thought of her current episode and possible trouble with the law — she had left the scene of an accident. *I don't need another setback.* "God, please help me. What was I thinking?" she whispered. Parts of a scripture from the third chapter of Ephesians, the twentieth verse tugged at her heart. She looked up the verse in the app on her cell. *God is able to do exceeding abundantly above all we ask or think according to the power that works in us.*

After writing it on a sticky note, she slid into her slippers and hobbled to their tiny kitchenette. She placed the note on the refrigerator next to the others reminding her of God's unfailing love.

She got a drink of water. As she sipped from her glass she wrestled with thoughts of the man who'd saved her. *Is it destiny? What will come of it? Will I ever see him again? Why haven't I been able to get him off my mind?* She sighed.

"Gurl!" Nettie yelled ecstatically as she turned up the TV. "You're on the news!"

"The news?" Moriah frowned as she limped back into the bedroom, combo living room area. She gestured for Nettie to turn the volume down. She didn't want the neighbors to hear through the thin walls.

28

"They probably already know about it," Nettie rebutted. "I'm sure everybody knows. It's been all over the Internet ever since it happened." She turned the volume down just a tad. "Remember how I had to distract the camera crew looming in the shadows, how they were waiting to see what 'fool' would return to retrieve the monstrous vehicle of yours?" she added before turning her attention back to the TV.

Nettie nervously flailed her fingers at it. "Look!" A caption in boldface letters scrolled repeatedly across the bottom of the screen: *** NEWS UPDATE*** $100,000 REWARD FOR THE *SHINING KNIGHT...DAMSEL IN DISTRESS...*

"...And there you have it, folks, a $100,000-dollar reward if you can identify either of the two displayed on your screen."
This is APN – All Peoples News – reporting live here outside of the Delaware Courthouse in downtown Wilmington.

The picture contorted in and out on their antiquated television screen. Moriah sat frozen. Staring in disbelief at what they were able to catch at the end of the news report, she felt sick. The fairytale picture of a man with a woman cradled in his arms and the "Green Dragon" in the distant background unsettled her nerves. She'd seen enough.

Moriah knew for sure if Petra and Parker found out that was her in the photo, she'd never get Amelia back.

Chapter 5

Tyro awakened several hours after getting the sleep he needed. Thoughts of the beautiful woman he met caused him to smile again. Realizing the media may be the only clue to lead him to her; he reluctantly raised the TV up from the footboard and clicked it on.

Just as he had suspected, the story was still going strong. His personal chef and confidant, Roy, knocked on the door. "Come in, man." Tyro called knowing the familiar knock would be him.

A lankier, Louis Gossett, Jr. looking character cruised in the room and set a tray of food on the bed. He pivoted as he marched over to open the French doors leading to the balcony. "Ya need some fresh air. You want lunch on the terrace?"

"I'm good right here." The TV blared with the latest updates arresting both men's attention.

This is PNN, People Need News reporting live here outside of the Delaware courthouse in downtown Wilmington. We have just been advised the DA, Dankiel Lodgeport has filed charges against the alleged Prince, John Doe and the alleged Princess, Jane Doe for reckless endangerment, and leaving the scene of an accident."

The news reporter shifted to the man standing to his left and pointed the mic toward him.

"So tell me, District Attorney Lodgeport, why criminal charges?"

"Well, the world might think it's a cute and dandy fairytale, but actually, leaving the scene of an accident is a crime," the DA spewed. "Therefore, under TITLE 21, the State of Delaware has issued—"

"What do you think of the $100,000 reward Mr. Quincy Simmonds, the multi-billionaire of Laino Enterprises has offered for anyone who can positively identify either one of these folks?" The reporter said, interrupting him as he held up a photo for the viewers to see. "Can you get a close up of this shot?" the reporter asked.

The cameraperson zoomed in for a close up. The photo enlarged across the screen. It blocked the person behind it who had reached in to gently tug the DA out of view of the screen. As the reporter put the photo down, a new face surfaced.

"So, tell us, Mr. Simmonds, is it $100,000 for both alleged criminals, or is it $100,000 for each of them if convicted?"

The man looking like an exact replica of Virgil Earp in Tombstone played by Sam Elliot stared into the camera. *"Correct,"* the man said without flinching. The reporter recoiled at the man's ambiguous response and faced the camera.

"Well, there you have it folks, $100,000 will be paid to the person or persons who identifies either of the people shown here." He held up the picture crookedly of the mysterious man and woman. "It might be a little difficult because the woman, as you see here..." he straightened out the angle of the photo, "she's wearing a head covering of some sort that obstructs a clear vision of her face."

31

"Why he go and do something like that?" Roy said as he shook his head. "He running for mayor or something? I don't — "

Roy stopped mid-sentence as Quincy burst through Tyro's bedroom door. "Do you ever answer your phone? Why do you have one if you are not going to use it?" Instantly, the air evaporated out of the room at his presence.

Roy excused himself after bidding a good day to Quincy. "I'll check you out later, man," he said, giving Tyro a sympathetic slap on the shoulder.

All of the news channels were broadcasting their own rendition of the story repeatedly. Tyro, weary of it clicked the television off. When he'd tossed the remote, it bounced off of the extra-fluffy Egyptian cotton comforter. Quincy quickly nabbed it as it rebounded and turned it back on in one swift move.

Tyro turned to his father and stared in disbelief. "Why'd you do it?"

"You need to watch, keep your eyes open. See what's going on."

"I'm talking about the reward money? Why did you have to put yourself out there? What sense does it make?" Tyro set his food tray aside and climbed out of bed. He traipsed to his dressing room. A few minutes later, he emerged fully dressed in a navy blue sweat suit.

As Sheba saw him emerge, she let out an excited whine and leapt to her feet. Her tail wagged rapidly as she made her way to the bedroom door. She sat and waited. Her tail thumped rapidly against the hardwood floor.

"Don't play dumb with me, son." Quincy started pacing. "I know it's you in those photos. You are my son. I would know you anywhere," he barked as he snatched the remote from the night table and turned the television back on for the third time.

"What's all this hoopla have to do with me?" Tyro signaled for Sheba to go downstairs. The Shepherd bounded through the hall

32

and down the stairs in front of him. Tyro followed and Quincy trailed after them ranting in his normal manner.

"Well, look at that!" his father said sarcastically as another news flash scored across the TV someone had left on in the kitchen.

Tyro swore each time he heard the story, it became more and more embellished. Now, it was being reported they'd flown off to Paris on a honeymoon. "There is such a thing as 'True Love at First Sight,'" the caption read.

"America has gone fairytale crazy!" Quincy furrowed his brow. "This better not have any negative impact on the business, son. You know we don't need another lawsuit—" He stopped abruptly in mid-sentence.

Tyro spun around. Sheba's leash dangled in his hand as she waited near the door in the mudroom. "Why? Because your son wasn't smart enough to save his own behind the last time?" He thumped his chest before sweeping his fingers through his sandy-brown hair.

"You got that right. So, what is the plan?" Quincy sat on a stool at the kitchen island. He peeled a banana and jabbed it in his mouth.

"Plan, what plan?" Tyro stabbed his hand in his front pocket. "There is no need for me to do anything. The whole thing will blow over in a few days. You know how it goes."

"What if somebody got a good view, a picture of you and her? It could be looming out there waiting for the perfect opportunity."

Tyro raised his eyebrows. *Humph. And you offering a hefty reward helped the matter?* he mused to himself. "I slipped away before the paparazzi caught up to me," he muttered in his father's direction.

"And the girl?"

"What about her?" Tyro said more forcefully then he intended.

"You'd better get ready for a lawsuit. The last thing we need is her slapping a civil suit against you for —"

"For what? Saving her life?"

"You of all people, Mr. *I got my law degree in five years, but flushed it down the toilet...* you should know how these kinds of things can turn out. Just like the last time." Quincy stood and mindlessly shook his head. "You should have let things be, son."

"She would have been killed," Tyro gritted through his teeth. He curled and uncurled his fist and wiped his sweaty palms on his pants. He snatched his jacket off of the hook. Unable to put up with his father's belligerent behavior any longer, he turned to walk out the door, but spun around instead.

As he was about to put an end to his father's shenanigans, the weariness draining his father's face caused him to pause. For just a short moment, he felt compassion for him. He did lose the love of his life and hadn't been able to move on.

Tyro's shoulders lowered as he dropped his hands to his sides. "Dad. Is this whole"—he flailed his hands in the air—"thing about Mom?"

Chapter 6

Moriah's heart was heavy. She'd gotten up early to pray. Leaning over the back of the sofa, she peeked out of the curtains just as the sun was peeking over the horizon. She smiled at the majestic colors announcing the awakening of another day. She enjoyed the cool breeze blowing over her as she opened the window and breathed in the fresh air.

After spending time praying and listening to her favorite worship CDs, she felt better. Stretching like a kitten waking up from a good nap, she smiled and decided she'd cook breakfast.

She removed her headset and placed her bible on the coffee table and eased off of the sofa.

She looked over at Nettie who was snoring after working a double shift at Tata's Restaurant and Bar. Unable to resist seeing his face again, she scrolled through the photo log on her cell. She ran her finger over the photo she'd taken of the handsome face of her hero. She'd snapped it just as she was getting away. For the hundredth time, or so, she just had to look at it again, one more time. Not wanting to get Nettie all riled up over the matter, she quickly closed it when she thought she heard her waking up.

Gingerly, she lumbered into the small kitchenette and fixed eggs, frozen waffles, fried apples, and chai tea. Although she preferred to have made homemade waffles, their space was limited so she kept her major commercial grade appliances packed away in storage.

The savory aroma wafted through their compact living quarters and awakened Nettie. They sat, ate, and chatted at their cramped, two-chaired wooden table.

"So, how're you doing?" Nettie asked spearing eggs, waffles, and apples with her fork and shoveling them into her mouth. Moriah looked at her, amazed that she could cram so much in at one time. She figured with Nettie having to study all those hours to become a vet, she was used to eating like that.

Moriah, on the other hand, did not attend college right away. During her junior year in high school, she'd landed a work-study job at Thomlin-Smythe Marketing Agency, known as TSMA. The owners would later become grandparents. Amelia's. She sighed. How that ever came to be was a story within itself.

Moriah remembered she had always worked hard for the company since the day she started. She was a quick learner and her ability to think on her feet intrigued them. For being such a young student starting out in the field, the firm was greatly impressed with her skills.

In addition to the work-study program, she'd work for them a few nights after school as well as all day on Saturdays to earn some cash. That same year, they'd hired her for the summer and kept her on part time during her senior year.

By the time Moriah graduated high school, she was hired full time with an impressive health benefit and investment package. It included a paid education for as long as she worked for the firm, two years for every equivalent year of college credits.

By Moriah's first year anniversary with TSMA, she was promoted as an assistant to the manager of advertising. By her eighteenth month, she was the advertising lead. Her creativity blossomed. She had pulled herself up by her bootstraps and the long hours and hard work paid off big time for Moriah. It wasn't too long before she was landing the company some pretty impressive clients with her savvy marketing skills.

Now, she was their archenemy through no fault of her own. Moriah sighed. Working there had been bittersweet. They were like family, until —

"You haven't heard a word I've said," Nettie said, finishing off the rest on her plate. She looked down at Moriah's plate. Eggs and pieces of waffle had been skated around her plate. She'd been in deep thought.

"Ew," Nettie complained. "I was going to eat those." She pointed to the soggy tidbits that had once been waffles. She reached for Moriah's bowl of apples left untouched. "But, no thanks!" she said as she scrunched her nose at Moriah's plate. It now looked like it belonged to a two-year-old. "What're you thinking 'bout anyway?"

"I just don't get it!" Moriah's hands shot in the air. Her fork was still clutched between her fingers. She sighed as she leapt up, avoiding putting weight on her weaker leg. She hobbled over to dump her breakfast in the trash. She spun around, eyes fuming. "I worked hard for those people. If it weren't for me, they would have never landed those government and mayor election campaigns, which were their first million-dollar clients, thank you very much," she said sarcastically.

Moriah knew she shouldn't allow herself to become bitter. God had blessed her to start her own marketing firm. And she'd allowed the hurt and disappointment of their deceitfulness drive her into becoming a force to be reckoned with. She wouldn't purposely go after their clients, but neither would she turn any of them away who sought her business.

"Get over it!" Nettie whooped, bringing Moriah's thoughts back to the present. "So what, they screwed you. Screw 'em back."

"Nettie, that's not a 'Christian' thing to do."

"You may be right 'bout that. But, don't be crying over spilt milk." She reached tenderly to touch her friend's arm. "I know it hurts after all ya'll been through together. But, you can make it. Keep reminding yourself that you're blessed and highly favored."

"Look at you!" Moriah said, leaning her shoulders back applauding her friend's use of a scripture.

"You go prop your leg up. You can finish telling me about how you got bamboozled into buying your Shrek mobile while I clean up this mess!" she teased her roommate. "I sure hope he's a true prince cause Lawd knows you gonna need you a cook and two maids," she teased, shaking her head at the mess Moriah had made.

Moriah limped out of their makeshift kitchen and settled on the bed. The whole truck incident was taking its toll on her. She lifted her legs on top of the blanket. If it came out that she was the one responsible for the vehicle and had left the scene of the accident, it could set her back for months… possibly years. Exhaling long and slow, she kept her tears from spilling. If she cried at that moment, she would fall to pieces.

Moriah had too much on the line. Maybe she should just come clean and turn herself in. Get it over with. Remorse over her brief moment of insanity seized her as she told Nettie the whole story.

She told her everything, leaving nothing out, no matter how foolish she felt. Nettie was her closest friend and she was tired of carrying the burden and shame alone.

She told her that she hadn't heard Junkman say there was a problem with the transmission. It was now as she looked back she remembered. She looked off into the distance as she continued on to say that neither did she realize the second trailer hitch was part of the deal. His conniving crew hooked it up after they drove it out of the yard and parked it on the street while she finished the money transaction.

"No need to tell you he refused to take it off. 'You bought, now you own it.'" Moriah shifted her eyes to see the reaction on her friend's face. She felt comforted as she saw the look of compassion and understanding on her face

"But still, I was excited," she had to admit. She had just bought her very own commercial truck!

"Moriah. Moriah. Hey… Hey..." Nettie snapped her fingers toward her face. "Are you listening to me?" She had tried to interject several times as Moriah rambled on

"What?"

"I said," she turned toward her friend to make sure she was listening this time. She wrapped Moriah's ankle in a fresh ice pack as she continued. "He should be arrested for selling you that death trap. If it weren't such a hot topic right now, I'd march right down there and tell him," Nettie said, popping her neck and rolling her eyes like the expert she was at doing so. "I can't stand the thought of you driving around in it," she said on a more serious note.

"Yeah. Getting that truck was stupid. But it did lead me to the bravest man I ever met. I mean, who would do such a thing, and for a stranger at that? He didn't know me… yet, he came anyway." She stared off into the distance.

Nettie listened all dreamy-eyed as Moriah retold the whole scene. She told her she'd wished it had been her who had been carried out of the face of danger by such a charming man. "Even if he isn't rich!" Nettie just had to add.

"Okay, at the time, I may have been a little dramatic about my ankle. But when he carried me out of the truck, I felt like I really was a damsel in distress. He saved my life, Nettie." She turned toward her confidant with tears in her eyes. "He was my angel."

"Was it worth you almost getting yourself killed?"

"I guess not. But the whole thing happened like it was right out of a fairytale." The smile quickly disappeared as the consequences she faced rose to haunt her.

She may have gotten herself in a "little" trouble with the law, but she thanked God no one had gotten hurt. She closed her eyes and breathed deeply.

She smiled, thinking how she felt as if his eyes had pierced right through her. She couldn't help but wonder if he had been thinking of her. Would he someday try to find her?

Chapter 7

Neither of the men had moved. Tyro stood at the back door waiting for his father to answer his question. Quincy had rose to his feet. The empty haze that remained plastered over his face depicted his deep thoughts. The banana peel still rested on top of the island where he'd placed it several minutes ago. Tyro finally agreed to let Roy take Sheba for a walk. She shot out the door like a rocket.

He wondered if his dad's latest bone of contention was because he'd saved some stranger... but not his mother? He had to admit he had questioned his motives himself a few times. Had he jumped in to save the woman to redeem himself? Did his actions have anything to do with him not being there that night with his mother... could he have saved her? Tyro couldn't answer any of them. He turned and faced his dad.

The two men stood in silence looking hopelessly at each other. It was a tender moment of unspoken words. He walked over and hugged his dad. Quincy held his son while he nervously clapped him on the back.

"Your mother did have a point." He pulled away to break the awkward moment. It had been a long time since they'd embraced. Tyro knew it had felt as good to his father as it had to him. Tears filled his father's eyes.

"About?" Tyro asked as he removed his jacket. He waited for his father to go there. He already knew where the conversation was heading.

"Going undercover. You know, to see what is going on in the field with our crews."

His shoulders relaxed as he let out the long breath he'd been holding. He wasn't expecting his father to talk business. Laino Enterprises was divided into three divisions.

Tyro managed the Package and Express Mail delivery trucks. His uncle Mario managed the fleet of commercial trucks, which included the waste disposal services, while Quincy handled the division for local and long distance moving. His mind drifted to his mother's last order of business. To this day, he still heard her words clearly in his head.

"You boys need to get out there and work among your crew. Find out why it's taking twice as long to do the same jobs as our competitors." She'd laid the respective reports down in front of each of them containing the statistics to prove it.

There could be no denying it. Even though they repeatedly underbid the other companies by significant dollars, they had lost numerous jobs to competitors who projected shorter spec times. Bottom line, they had been out bidden on significant jobs because Laino Enterprises would take too long to get the jobs done. "I bet you'll find there's a lot of unscheduled coffee breaks and long lunch breaks going on," she had said.

Tyro hung his jacket on the hook as he brought his mind back to the present. He eyed his dad. "Everything's fine in my—" He'd stopped mid-sentence, fully aware of both his and his dad's struggle to go back into the office.

It was where Laino had been killed. Neither of them had been back there since. But maybe what his dad was saying was a plea for help. Maybe he needed encouragement, motivation to get back into the swing of things so he could move on.

The manner in which Tyro had set up his department to run had been brilliant. Even in his absence, his division was closer to their yearly projections compared to the other two. But, he was losing money in corporate deliveries. He'd read the reports his foreman emailed him every day. Sales were down. Deliveries were not making their destinations on time and they were losing to their biggest competitor, big time.

He knew of his neglect. Not that he would suffer financially if he folded his sector. He'd invested his money well when he'd sold his law firm to become a partner in the family business. Even before his mother had left him a hefty inheritance, Tyro had become a multi-billionaire.

He truly knew what it felt like to be stuck. It wasn't until he'd met the woman of his dreams — through happenstance — that he felt like he'd been given a lifeline. The feeling of being pulled from out of the muck was liberating. Although it was slow, at least he was moving forward.

"Dad," he turned to his father who had been leaning on the counter, his face buried in his hands. "Let's do this… together."

Quincy removed himself from the high back stool. He walked over and clapped his son on the shoulder. "I can't, son." He squinted his bloodshot eyes at him. "I just cannot." He strolled out the door, closing it slowly behind him.

***

Sunday morning was the first time Tyro had stepped into his home gym in several months. He had walked into the room countless times only to turn around and walk back out. Since his mother's tragedy, he rarely visited this part of his house.

He lacked the energy and he had no motivation. There was no joy in doing any of the things he used to love. He no longer enjoyed watching a movie. He couldn't care less about taking a swim, or working out. Although he missed the ragging with the guys while they'd played basketball at the Yard, he just couldn't bring himself to go back there. And he'd lost all inspiration to work on any of his creative inventions. Nothing was the same anymore.

He had always loved to tinker around with electronics and create gadgets ever since he was a kid. Just last year when it came time to build his own home theatre and gym, the architect was fascinated by his brilliance, to say the least. Even the contractors had marveled at the doggie bathroom Tyro had built for Sheba. They'd said it was over the top and unlike anything they'd ever seen.

Sheba's bathroom contained all of the amenities of any five-star hotel. It had a flushing toilet, shower, paw and face washbowl, and a full body dryer. The fixtures were designed to accommodate her and were operated by a gentle push of her paw.

He had equipped his gym with the latest technology and exercise equipment any man — or dog — would desire. Adding his personal modifications, he didn't need to go anywhere else to get a thorough workout.

The 30 by 40 square foot room sat behind a wall of frameless windows overlooking the pool. On the other side of the wall was his home theatre. It was just as large and impressive. These two rooms took up an entire wing of his 12,000 square foot home.

As Tyro walked into his gym the lights instantly came on. The orange-yellowish glow indicated that his energy level and mood were mild with moderate apprehension. A female avatar instantly appeared on the twenty-foot screen and obtained his workout and music preference.

His mind raced faster than his reps as he lifted the 100 lb. bell. He was not pleased that his stamina in lifting weights had decreased so drastically. He wouldn't have been as disappointed if his endurance had dropped by 20... 30 pounds maybe, but 50? He was humiliated, to say the least.

After his workout, Tyro agonized to finish his four-mile jog on the beach surrounding the outskirts of the island. He vowed to get back into his normal routine as he heaved for air. His chest was killing him. Sheba was winded too. Her profuse panting reminded him of another area of his neglect.

During his jogging... slash, running... slash, walking... his mind kept rewinding to what Quincy had said. Although it had become increasingly difficult to have a decent conversation with him, this time his father made perfectly good sense.

Tyro's motives to work as an undercover boss in his division might be selfish, true, but it would serve his purpose. Finding the vehicle would possibly lead him to her. Just the thought of seeing her again caused his heart to skip a beat.

Suddenly, it dawned on him. She had taken a picture of him, but why? What was she up to? Tyro was now convinced his father was right. It was time to get back to work. He needed to find her.

Chapter 8

"Criminal charges?" Moriah was appalled. It was the fifth day since the incident. The severity of her mindless action of buying that truck had gotten out of hand. Her angst grew daily over the potential charges she'd face for leaving the scene of an accident. And the fact that someone named Quincy Simmonds — whomever he was in the first place — offered a $100,000 reward to identify her had become a real nuisance. She clicked the television off.

Lately, she couldn't go anywhere without someone getting up in her face staring her down. She was tired of having to duck and dodge, and sneak around to get from one place to another. Having to look out for people who were following her, snapping her picture without her consent was beyond ridiculous.

"Don't you people have a life?" she yelled, as she had to get off a city bus several blocks before she reached her destination. A group of relentless passengers blatantly insisted she was the woman they'd seen on TV. Even the bus driver chimed in his two cents.

She wondered if the man who rescued her was facing the same dilemma. Thinking of him made her heart ache although she hardly knew him. Truth was, she missed him. She just couldn't dismiss the connection they'd made.

This past Monday, she made the mistake of wearing her gray jacket to the grocery store. Suddenly, a woman had literally bum rushed her and pinned her up against the freezer door in the frozen meat section. The woman used every bit of her 400 lbs. to hold her there as she hollered for someone to call the police.

When the store manager realized what was going on, it took him a good seven minutes or more before he could get her to let Moriah go. Only after he threatened to have her arrested for badgering his customer did she relinquish her hold.

He saw Moriah reach for her swollen ankle. The owner feared Moriah would file a lawsuit after getting hurt in his store. He'd banned the perpetrator from entering the store again. The disgruntled woman protested as she marched out the door making threatening remarks. She wanted her reward money. After all, it was she who had seen "the Princess" first.

"People do strange things nowadays with no regard for how it affects others," the manager said as he gave Moriah free rein to grab as many grocery items as she could carry. Too bad she didn't have a larger refrigerator and freezer at home.

He paid for a taxi to get her home. She managed to bring enough food to give to some of the families in the surrounding neighborhood. But now, she couldn't even walk to the bus stop without someone hollering, "Hey lady, you got any more of that food?" This was not good when she was trying to keep a low profile.

Moriah had become paranoid and decided to handle her business as much as she could from her tiny abode. She and Nettie would move in a few months, as soon as she could get a steady line of clients. Nettie would be finishing up her internship soon and could work more hours at her night job. She was on target to become a licensed veterinarian by next spring.

The sun had just risen. The pain in her ankle had awakened her earlier than she'd planned. She didn't want to go to an urgent care facility or the doctor's office for fear of being recognized. She figured if she'd just stay off of it as much as possible, it would heal much sooner. She crawled from the sofa to the kitchen to get something to eat when she noticed a strange envelope lying by the door.

Someone had slid it underneath the door. But who? When? She fidgeted with it as she studied it. How long had it been there? she wondered as she labored back onto the sofa. She moved one of the dingy drapes aside, opened the window, and peeked out. If someone had just left it, perhaps she could spot who it was. It was too early for someone from the front office to have put it there.

For a moment, her heart skipped a beat thinking that maybe, just maybe, her hero had found her. Thinking of his woodsy scent as he held her in his arms made her blush inside.

As she started to raise the envelope toward her face hoping she might get a whiff of his cologne, she stopped mid-way. It was not the kind of package she imagined someone wanting to impress a lady would leave. If she hadn't been on her hands and knees, she never would have noticed it.

She examined the strange package further. The exterior was cruddy and a faint odor rose from it. Her expression changed to horror as she turned it over. Someone had marked a large "X" across the back of it with a strange substance. Dried blood. At least that's what it looked like.

Moriah panicked as she flung it across the room. "Oh God!" She shut her eyes and squeezed her head between her hands. "It can't be…." Landing on the coffee table, it teetered on the edge. A morning breeze blew it to the floor.

THUD

The sound echoed as it hit the hardwood. Moriah froze. The seams had rippled and the edges were slightly torn from being forced to fit underneath the door. She wondered how she hadn't heard anything as someone forced it into the room.

Her sweaty hands caused her fingers to fumble as they raced over the dial pad. She'd tried to reach Nettie. The call went to voicemail. She looked at the time. It was 7:05. Nettie would be making her rounds at the clinic with her mentor.

"God has not given me the spirit of fear," she repeated to herself as she braved to retrieve the daunting envelope. She reached for the package and stopped just before her fingers touched it. Quickly, she pulled her hand back. She stared at it strangely. What could it be? Hands trembling, she reached again.

A lump lodged in her throat as she felt its contents whoosh between her fingers as she held it. She gazed at the duct tape that sealed it. Her gut feeling told her what was inside wouldn't be pleasant. As she stilled her nerves to open it, what she found inside made her wish she hadn't.

Chapter 9

Nettie rushed home after hearing Moriah's frantic voicemails. Her words made no sense. Something about a scarf... a rat... and someone not being dead...? No matter how many times she played the messages, she still had no clue what she was talking about.

When she opened their hotel door, she found Moriah sitting in the fetal position in the far corner, dazed. A baseball bat lay at her side. A small package with a dark red "X" across it had been ripped open. It lay as if it had been tossed across the room.

She rushed to Moriah's side, anxiously calling her name as she approached her. She got no response. Moriah's lips were moving but no sound was coming out. She'd been crying. Her mouth was smudged with a dried white substance. At least she'd taken her anxiety medication.

Nettie slid to the floor and gathered Moriah into her arms and held her. She rubbed her back and consoled her, saying that everything was okay. She had no clue what time Moriah had taken the medicine; she could only guess it may have been twenty minutes ago. She'd ride it out with her until the medicine kicked in.

She rocked her gently, slowly in her embrace assuring her she was safe now. "Not safe," Moriah muttered repeatedly. "He's not dead."

Nettie shushed her as she consoled her. "It's okay... everything is okay, Nettie's right here with you." She tried to get her cell to call Moriah's doctor. It was in her back pocket. The awkward position she was sitting in made it impossible for her to reach it without having to move. Moriah was drifting off to sleep.

Finally, she fell asleep. Nettie gently lifted her head off of her shoulder and positioned her to lie on the floor. She didn't want to leave her there for too long and had texted a colleague from the veterinary clinic to come over.

While she waited for him to come, she walked over and picked up the envelope. It had been ripped open and she got a good whiff of the putrid odor of what had been in it. She dropped it. Nettie searched around as she tried to find its contents. She couldn't find it.

She'd searched under the bed, behind the sofa, and in the bathroom. Still nothing. "Where is it?" she mumbled as she heard a car door close. She hurried to the door and looked through the peephole. She flung the door open and waved for her friend, Brad to come inside. As he entered, she took another look both ways outside of the door before she gently closed it.

"What's that smell?" he asked. Nettie put her finger up to her mouth for him to lower his voice. She pointed to Moriah sleeping on the floor.

"I need you to help me move her to the bed. I don't want to wake her." She nodded in the direction they needed to go. "She's not feeling well and took a sleeping pill," she added as his face puzzled at the odd position in which she was lying in the corner. Nettie was glad she'd cleaned her face before he'd gotten there. She really didn't feel up to explaining anything further.

Brad gently moved Nettie aside. He kneeled down and lifted Moriah into his arms. Her body went limp as he carried her. "That must be some kind of pill!" he mused. Nettie glared a warning at him not to wake her.

As he lay her on the bed, she snuck a quick glance over to where Moriah had been laying. Nothing. She thanked Brad and told him she'd call him later. She gave him a gentle peck on the cheek and was relieved he wasn't expecting more.

"Going to hold you to that," he said as he smiled and left.

Nettie continued to change out the cold cloths over Moriah's head. She seemed a little warm. Her pulse was normal and her breathing was shallow as she slept. Surmising Moriah was okay, she'd put off calling her doctor. This would be the fourth spell she'd weather her through within the last three months.

She knew something horrible had happened several months ago while she was away on a business trip, although Moriah wouldn't talk about it. Nettie would give her the time she needed. She would be there for her whenever she was ready to talk.

Figuring she'd be hungry when she woke up, she looked in the mini freezer for something to eat. She pulled out two frozen fish TV dinners, popped them in the toaster oven, and tossed the containers in the trash. That's when she saw it.

She instantly mashed on the foot pedal for the lid to pop open again. Her hand immediately went to her mouth as she gasped. She pulled a pair of vinyl gloves from her medical bag and covered her mouth with a mask as a precaution as well.

She spread a kitchen trash bag on the floor and deposited the items as she removed them from the garbage. Using two fingers, she lifted a small zipped sandwich bag in the air. It was filled with decaying blood. She stared at it. She'd found the source of the odor.

A white scarf that appeared to be recently stained with the same blood dangled at the end of it. As she laid them on the garbage bag she'd spread out on the floor, the remains of a rodent of some sort swished lifelessly in the blood.

Nettie couldn't tell which kind of a rodent it had been. She suspected it had been a rat although its tail and paws had been cut off. She pulled another item out the trash that baffled her. Four cable ties intertwined together contained a note that was taped around it. It looked like a five-year-old had written it with a red crayon.

It read, *FOR THE NEXT TIME...*

After Nettie composed herself, she took pictures on her cell of the items. Using another bag, she left them in place as she covered the display. She tossed her gloves and mask in a small grocery bag and threw it in the trash.

She checked on Moriah. "When you wake up, you've got some explaining to do, whether you're up to it or not." Not that she blamed her for anything; she just wanted to know exactly what her best friend was facing.

Chapter 10

On the fifth day since he last saw it, Tyro kneeled on a hill looking down at the vehicle. He was relieved that working as an undercover boss had paid off so quickly. He'd spotted the Green Monster two days ago as he delivered several boxes of car parts to Larry's Auto Repair.

He'd been back to the garage numerous times waiting, discreetly watching to see if the mysterious woman would turn up. He didn't want to raise suspicions by asking questions. Not just yet.

"Can I help you?" A gruff voice boomed from behind him.

"That's an interesting vehicle you've got there," Tyro said, turning around addressing the man who had deliberately snuck up on him.

"Oh, that thing?" He rubbed the knots on his beard. "How much you talkin'?"

"What makes you think I'm interested in buying?" Tyro lifted himself off the ground. He stared straight into the man's greedy eyes.

"Ya been over here the last few days lookin' at her. Gotta be worth somethin' to ya." He grinned eagerly.

Tyro suppressed his startled reaction. He hadn't intended for anyone to see him. He'd deliberately parked his delivery truck a mile or so up the road and treaded through the back woods each day as he waited for her to show up.

No need to continue playing 'cat and mouse' games with this dude. Tyro figured one hundred grand to match the reward money plus an additional twenty for him to keep his mouth shut was worth the investment, as long as he'd agree to follow one small stipulation.

Chapter 11

Moriah shot straight up in the bed. "What time is it?" She'd awakened just as the timer on the toaster oven dinged.

"How you feeling?" Nettie asked, pressing her palm against her forehead.

"Fine!" Moriah said as she hopped out of bed. She was relieved to see her ankle had gone down, allowing her to sprint around as she searched for a change of clothes. "What time did you say it was?"

"I didn't. But it's eleven."

"In the morning?" Moriah asked with a look of panic on her face. "Oh God... please... please tell me it's still the same day... I can't miss my deadline," she said as she hurried to get dressed.

"And where do you think you're going?" Nettie held her friend by the forearms. "You need to take it easy..."

"Shoot!" Moriah complained. "I just missed the 11:05 bus." She turned to Nettie, "Can I please, please, *please,*" she asked shamelessly, "use your car?"

Nettie walked over to the items she had covered up with a kitchen garbage bag. She crossed her arms. "Moriah." She turned and looked at her friend.

Moriah trailed over to her. "Why you standing there looking at me like you're my mother? Like I done did something wrong?" she teased. "Whatever it is, I ain't do it!"

Nettie was amazed how Moriah could always spring back from difficult situations like nothing ever happened. She could shake it off like nobody's business. And that worried her.

She pulled back the top trash bag that she'd used to cover the items she removed from the garbage. "Something you want to tell me?" She studied Moriah's face. "Isn't that your favorite scarf? I thought you said you'd lost it?"

A look of horror seized Moriah as she eyed the contents laid out in that manner. She rubbed at her wrist as her eyes fell upon the note. She quickly dropped her hands as she felt Nettie's relentless eyes on her.

Earlier, when Moriah had seen the mutilated rat immersed in blood along with the other items, she immediately hurled them into the trash. Now — after she'd quickly composed herself — she shrugged as if there was nothing unusual about having a dead varmint wrapped in one's favorite scarf. She spouted out the words, "Whatever," spun around and walked away.

"What's that you cooking? It sure smells good, but I just don't have time to eat right now," she spouted a few seconds later.

"Do you have time to call the police?" Nettie retorted, still standing over the evidence with her arms folded into each other.

"Call the police?" Moriah questioned. "What for?" She saw that Nettie had her 'girl, don't play with me' look on her face. She walked over to her.

"It's a long story —"

"I got all day," Nettie said without cracking a smile. "Look, I know you might not be ready to tell me everything. But I care about you. I love you like my own sister. We've been friends since first grade. I know you're scared, but you got to tell me something… or I'm calling the police. *Right now.*"

"No!" Moriah insisted. "Please don't call the cops." She sighed. "There's nothing they can do."

"You mean to tell me that somebody slips a dead rat in here and there's nothing the cops can do?" She began to tap her foot against the floor. "I ain't buying it, Moriah… something ain't right."

Moriah looked at the time on the microwave. "Look, I really need to go, but I promise you, I'll tell you later. Just not right now. Now can I please..." she folded her hands as if in prayer, "borrow your car. I'll have it back in no time. I promise!"

"Providing you tell me just this one thing before you go." She walked over to her friend. "What're you gonna do?" She nodded toward the gruesome sight that was spread out like it was evidence in a crime lab.

Moriah sighed. "Don't know. All I know is that we can't call the police. Please Nettie, promise me that you won't call them."

Nettie stared in disbelief.

"I promise you I'll explain everything later. We just got to get out of here. That's all. We just need to move from this rat hole." Moriah grabbed Nettie's keys from the end table, kissed her on the cheek, and bustled out the door.

Chapter 12

"What's this?" Moriah screamed when Larry's assistant mechanic handed her the sticky note with the stranger's cell number scribbled across it. She could barely decipher the numbers through the grease marks. "You got to be kidding me... right?" She stormed through the open bay area of the garage until she reached the dinky back office and yanked opened its grimy door.

The missing top hinge caused the door to fall to the side. She jumped back, almost landing within the assistant's grasp who had trudged up behind her. She swerved her shoulders to avoid his filthy hands.

"I told you, Larry ain't here. He's out to lunch," the lanky guy said to remind her. He smiled as he gave her body another onceover with his eyes. His grin displayed dark gum spots where his top two front teeth were missing from long ago.

Moriah glared back into the office. She cringed as she peeled her eyes away from the greasy fingerprints smeared over a half-eaten sandwich. It lay awkwardly on top of the filthy, cluttered desk.

She spun around. "Of course he is. He swindled my truck right from under me. He knew it was the only means for me to handle my business."

"Err..." Moriah marched over to a door she assumed was the bathroom. A sign with some of its letters not visible through the oil smudges dangled on the door. It read "M PLOY ES ONLY."

She snatched one of the blue grease-removing cloths out of the towel holders and wrapped her fist in it. She banged on the door.

Once… Twice… The third time she kicked the door as hard as she could. "Larry, I know you're in there."

The toilet flushed. The door immediately flung open, shifting as if it too were about to fall off. A stocky man whose work jumpsuit was just as disgusting as the smell wafting out of the bathroom. Moriah sidestepped as he squeezed his way out of the tiny hole in the wall.

Apparently it didn't matter to him that he had bypassed the sink and hadn't washed his hands. She watched in disgust as he meandered over to the office, picked up the remains of his sandwich, and stuffed it in his mouth.

"What's the problem, little lady?" he asked with his mouth full.

"You know good and well what the problem is," she spat. Moriah was getting nauseated just being in the despicable place. It gave her the creeps, the heebee jeebees, and everything else. If she didn't hurry up and get out of there, her skin would crawl right off of her.

Her truck was gone. No need wasting any more of her time arguing about it. "What's the use?" She threw her hands up, spun around, and stomped toward the closest exit. "You'll never get any of my business!" She reeled, slamming the door behind her.

A series of "oohhs!" and "aahhs!" chorused from several mechanics as they circled around something on the side of the building. Curious, she held her distance and peeked between two greasy suits as they gawked longingly at the center attraction.

A fully loaded, convertible Mercedes — fire engine red — glowed within their midst like a blazing fire. "You can look at 'er, but don't touch, boys." Larry walked up behind the crew. "No need in getting her pretty little shine all smudged up. Now back up!" The men cowered backwards at his bark.

"Well, it goes to show you, money talks," she complained as she marched away.

Her ankle was beginning to throb. She rolled her eyes as she limped away from the grungy establishment. Nettie had brought her there last week to hide her truck. She had assured Moriah it would be well hidden and secure there. She couldn't get mad at her. At the time, she had no choice. Where else could she have parked it without drawing attention to it?

She turned and glared at the thief as he backed his "baby" into a separate garage connected to an odd looking house. If she wasn't so ticked, she would have been amazed at how neat and clean the garage was.

She was sure somehow the fully loaded luxury came at the expense of her truck. Guess she should have told him it wasn't for sale when she first dropped it off.

Nevertheless, she had a bigger fish to fry and a deadline to meet. She peered at the sticky note. She was desperate. Her client's sign had to be hung in place by four o'clock. Today. It was already one-thirty. The two college students she hired would be at the graphic shop by two to pick up the sign. She didn't have time to play games. Moriah needed her truck.

She punched in the numbers from the note. Before the person on the other end could fully answer, she'd spat into the phone. "I don't know who you think you are, but you better get my truck back to me right now!" She rubbed the back of her neck. It was as tight as a ball of rubber bands.

"Ah. Your voice is just as lovely as your face," the masculine voice on the other end remarked. "And feisty too!"

"What… Who is this?" she spewed, placing one hand on her hip and shifting off of her sore ankle. "Look, I don't have time to waste playing games with some freak who—"

"I didn't look like a freak when I rescued you out of that stubborn 'Green Dragon' of yours…" He paused. "…did I?" His jovial tone annoyed Moriah. But before she could interject, he continued. "Now. Now that you've calmed down, please tell me your name?" he said after her brief moment of silence.

Moriah froze. "Are you... Is this..." she stammered.

"Your Prince. Yes."

The alarm on Moriah's cell chimed. She glanced at her watch. *1:45.* She didn't have time to play these games. She had a deadline and potential bonus if she finished by three. With her hotel rent and college students to pay, she needed every penny she could make.

"Look, Mr. Casablanca..."

He laughed at her candor.

"I'm not kidding with you. I have a sign that has to be installed by three... *today.*"

Her voice quivered in frustration as if she were near tears.

"Where's the job?" He relinquished his toying with her.

"What? Why do you care? Just give me my truck so I can do what I need to do."

"Now, now, Mrs.... what did you say your name is?" he said teasingly.

"Pissed off!" That's what my name is. Now either you give me my truck back or I'll—"

"What? Call the bluecoats?" He paused after interrupting her. "As I remember, you were there as well, and *you* left the scene, first."

"I'm sure this call can be traced." Moriah quickly moved the phone from her ear to take note of the number. *Private caller. Ugh!*

"Just give me the address and I'll meet you there," he said.

"I first have to pick up the sign from Dango's Studio. Fifth and Broad."

"Be there in fifteen minutes," Tyro appeased.

"Could you please make it in five.... I'm really on a tight deadline," Moriah said, practically begging.

"Where to?"

"What?"

"Where does the sign belong?"

"Mario's Grill... Main Street."

"Really?" He paused.

"Yeah, I was hoping to finish ahead of time. I need the bonus." She cringed as she realized she'd given too much information. She rubbed the back of her neck, a third time.

"Don't worry, it'll get done," the anonymous voice promised as he ended the call.

She pulled onto the interstate and drove toward her destination without turning the radio or CD player on. She needed a clear head to think, and pray.

Moriah had no choice but to trust the nameless caller as she sped down the highway. "Lord, please... Please don't let this be some kind of a prank."

The more she thought about the childish shenanigans of her so-called "hero," the more the pretentious image she held of him waned. Her good feelings for him were quickly evaporating. Any hopes of what could have evolved between them vanished. If she hadn't been in such a hurry, she would have already deleted his picture from her phone.

Chapter 13

Around 2 p.m. Moriah pulled in front of the graphic designers to pick up the sign, and her truck. When her truck was nowhere in sight as he'd promised, she was furious.

"Err!" What was she going to do? She snatched her cell and punched the "dial back" feature. No answer. She waited a few minutes more, thinking perhaps he might be circling around the block trying to find the place. After five minutes, she stormed inside.

"Have you by chance seen a large... umm, green truck?" She fidgeted with her hair remembering she had planned to park the truck out of view in the back of the lot behind the trees.

The students she hired were strong enough to have carried it through the back door and loaded it on the truck. She'd worry about them keeping the mobile a secret later and vowed to herself she'd get it painted. Soon. But for now, she couldn't afford to be without it for the three days it would take to get it done. Nor, did she have the money.

"No, ma'am." The part time student responded without looking up from what he was doing. He continued stacking the shelves with new art supplies. She doubted he had even heard what she'd said. As she thought about it, she was grateful he hadn't.

"Moriah!" A friendly voice called. A woman dressed in eclectic clothing glided her way. They embraced. "I see you got yourself a set of new hired hands. Eh?" Dango said as she pulled away and took a friendly, but suspicious look at Moriah. "No, no dear. Those go on the top self," she called to the new hire as she turned her attention from Moriah for a few moments.

"I do," Moriah replied as Dango faced her. "They're part time... students from UD and they're right on time," Moriah said, turning toward them as they walked through the door.

"Oh, not them," the woman said, positioning her hand to her neck as she nodded her head towards the door. "I'm talking about the handsome tiger that came in with a small crew and picked up your sign for you."

"What... who... what are you talking about, Dango? They are my crew." Moriah nodded to the two jocks waiting by the door, her face quickly turned from puzzled to panic.

"*Oh*," Dango murmured.

When Moriah worked at TSMA, it wasn't uncommon for her to send a crew to pick up the signs to take them to the client's establishment.

Moriah would normally be at the job site by now to ensure everything was in order for the enormous fixtures to be installed properly. She was meticulous. Every little detail had to be perfect. But for this job, she specifically told Dango that she'd pick it up herself. At least she thought she had.

Dango cocked her head, eyeing Moriah from a side view. "You didn't send anyone to pick up the sign for Mario's...?"

"No," Moriah sang worriedly. "That's why I'm here." She tried to control the impatience trickling up her spine. "Did you give him a receipt? Did you get his name? What did he look like? What was he wearing?"

"Whoa, whoa. Slow down," Dango encouraged her as she reached out to touch her arm, but immediately pulled back as she realized the array of paints on her hands were still wet.

"Did he say where he was taking it?" Moriah asked after she'd pressed the dial back button to no avail for the third time.

"Why no... Mario's Grill, I assume?" She made a tsk sound with her teeth. "I'm sorry if I've made a mistake, Moriah."

"No, no... It's okay. It's not your fault."

"He was a very handsome man, though," Dango said as if it would make the matter better.

"What?" Moriah said, lifting her head up from deep thought. If some pervert had stolen her sign playing some idiotic game with her livelihood, she was sure this would ruin her reputation. She needed this job to get done on time and she needed for it to be done correctly.

She cringed at the very thought. Her business hadn't gotten off the ground... nobody hired an incompetent company... word of mouth gets around very quickly.

She wondered if good ole Petra, her former boss from TSMA was behind this. After all, they'd like nothing more than to see her fail. Which would definitely work favorably for them since Moriah had appealed the ruling in their custody suit for Amelia.

"Moriah, why don't you ride over there and see what's going on. Besides, I can't imagine anyone spending that amount of cash just to be spiteful."

"Thanks." Moriah sighed as she hugged her good friend before dashing toward the door.

Chapter 14

Tyro stood in the shadows and watched as Moriah's face lit up. She had barely stepped all the way out of the car, when he saw her eyes twinkle as they were drawn to the work of art.

"Mario's Grill." *Perfect.* She mouthed as she snapped a picture with her cell of the red and gold sign. *And on time for a bonus too!*

As she stepped up on the curb, she twisted her nagging ankle and stumbled as she struggled to catch herself. A strong but gentle arm grabbed her just as she was about to fall.

"Thanks, you sign and truck thief!" she said as he helped her up.

"How'd you know it was me?" he asked charmingly.

"The shoes," she said plainly. "Are they your normal work shoes?" she asked, peering down at the pair of Surface to Air suede shoes adorning his size tens. She was familiar with the brand; they had been one of her clients while she worked at TSMA.

His brows rose. He looked at his shoes as it dawned on him. They didn't go so well with his work uniform.

"You were wearing those very shoes the day of the... the incident," she spouted for lack of a better way to put it.

"Ah! Very observant," he commended her as he helped her to sit on a nearby bench.

"And now you think I have reason to thank you twice, I suppose?"

"No. Actually it's three times," he stated, correcting her as he playfully flashed three fingers."

"Three times?" she repeated. "For what?"

"One." He put up one finger. "I saved you. Two." He put up a second finger. "I saved you," he said, turning to indicate the perfectly hung sign as he handed her an envelope from his back pocket with her name on it.

"How did you—?"

"And three," he said, interrupting her as he put up the third finger. "Moriah Styles, I saved you from going to jail and your beautiful face from being plastered all over the Internet."

Moriah winced and reached down toward her lower leg.

"I'm sorry," he said. "I didn't get a chance to introduce myself properly, but why don't we do the formalities over lunch?" he said, tilting his head toward Mario's restaurant.

Moriah looked at her watch. "Actually, I'd like to get my truck back." She scooted to the edge of the bench. "Besides, it's getting late. Their grand opening starts at four. That's why I had to get the sign up right away. And, in case you've forgotten, you're supposed to be giving me my truck. I'd like to get "the thing" out of the way before the customers get here."

"All right," Tyro said. "But could we please get something to eat?" Tyro was not about to let her get away from him again. He'd worked too hard to find her.

Although he now knew her name, he didn't have a valid way to contact her, other than her cell. Her business address was listed at the graphic arts location, although the young employee there had no idea who M & A Marketing Company was.

"You don't know, do you?" he asked.

"I don't know what?" she asked in a more no-nonsense tone than she had meant. "Look, it's been a very long day and I'm just about spent — " She stopped mid-sentence as his eyes met hers. A nervous smile crossed her face.

66

"Moriah." His gaze remained locked onto hers. "I'll be honest. I've waited so long for the chance to see those lovely eyes of yours again. I really don't want our time to end right now."

Moriah nodded. She lowered her head as her smile brightened.

"Please dine with me, Moriah. Have dinner... lunch... whatever you want to call it, just be with me for a little while longer. Please?" he said playfully.

"I want to be upfront with you." He brushed aside the kinky lock of hair cascading onto her face. He lifted her chin with his finger. "I was the one who called you at the last minute for the job." He nodded toward the newly hung sign above the restaurant door. "I had no idea that it was you... you... although I am pleased that it is... you."

Moriah chuckled at his use of words. The sun beamed over his shoulder as it descended across the horizon, allowing just the right amount of light for her to see the depths of his steel gray eyes. The same ones she melted into the first time she gazed into them. They still held a small peek of sadness that pricked her heart. She gave in to his request.

"I could use something to eat."

Chapter 15

"'Use something to eat'?" Now it was his turn to chuckle. "I've never heard it put like that before," Tyro said as he stood and held out his arm for her to grab hold to. She struggled to hold her balance as she tried to put weight on her throbbing ankle.

"I could carry you, you know," he offered as he waggled his eyebrows like Groucho Marx.

"Oh no you will not! I don't think so," she said in a singsong tone. "The last time you 'whisked' me off my feet, it was plastered all over the news and still hasn't let up."

"Yeah. I've noticed it myself." He chuckled as he guided her inside.

"I have your table ready, Mr. Simmonds," the hostess immediately announced as he stepped in the door.

"Thanks," he responded as he escorted Moriah on his arm to where they would be seated.

"I don't find it funny at all." She frowned. She sat gracefully in the chair he held out for her. The table setting was intimate. A lit candle illuminated their shadows on the wall as the flame flickered in the middle of the table.

"Yeah, I don't either, but what can you do about it? People will be people," he said, searching for words to quickly change the subject.

"Do you know what it's like trying to shop, or walk down the street or... or whatever"—she raised her hands in frustration—"with somebody staring, I mean really staring you right in your face?" She sighed. "Then, they have the nerve to whip out their cell and try to snap pictures of me."

"You're kidding me, right? What do you do? How are you handling it?"

Moriah shrugged her shoulders. "I get through it somehow, depending on the situation."

"Come on, you're telling me you weren't flattered, not one bit?"

She leaned back and narrowed her eyes. It was the most asinine thing he could have said. "Were you?"

"Too much attention would annoy most people," he offered, as his mind raced for a better topic. His family had just come through their share of being in the headlines. Twice. He definitely knew.

Moriah told Tyro what had happened to her at the bus stop and the grocery store. She was glad to see he had a better understanding of her frustrations. She glanced at his watch. It wasn't a Rolex; at least she didn't think so. But looking at the exquisite piece of jewelry told her it was just as expensive if not more.

She stared at the white linen cloth. She couldn't help but wonder what it would be like being with a man who lived a life of luxury. His brash personality was sexy and just looking at him at first glance you wouldn't know he had money, if that was indeed the case. Other than his shoes and watch he fit in like an ordinary guy, only he was extremely attractive, of course.

Still, their worlds would clash. How could a man like him be interested in a woman who lived in a run-down hotel? And then, there's the issue around her depleted finances. But under no circumstances would she be somebody's charity case, money or no money.

Moriah looked him in the eye, "You still haven't told me who you are"—she leaned back—"or do I have to call you Mr. Mystery Man?"

He took her hand into his, locked eyes with her and pronounced, "I am Tyro Hernandez Simmonds. I'm pleased to be with you, again." He placed a gentle kiss on her hand.

Moriah melted as chills ran up her arms. She had never met anyone so debonair.

Chapter 16

"So, you know the owner?" Moriah was eager to keep her mind off of her personal drama. Another reason it could never work between them. She wouldn't be seeing him again after tonight.

"This Mario guy must be well off," she quipped, turning her head in every direction to admire the array of sculptured chandeliers. "Wait… this is not you… you're not …" She stammered at the thought he could be the owner.

"Nope. Not me," Tyro said, gesturing at the establishment. "What makes you think he's well off?" he said as he kept an even expression.

"Must be," she continued looking around. "Opening up a restaurant of this magnitude… and on Main Street at that."

"Does it intrigue you?"

"No, not really. Going into business nowadays is tough, especially a restaurant."

"Oh?" He gestured for her to continue.

"Before starting my own company, the agency I used to work for had installed signs for numerous new businesses." He noticed the sorrow as she lowered her gaze and paused. "Unfortunately, too many of them had called back within two years' time to have it removed." She faced him. "It got to be disheartening. No matter how hard the owners tried to succeed, a lot of them just didn't make it." Her eyes fell to her hands. She hadn't realized she'd been fidgeting with her napkin. She placed it on her lap.

"I can tell it bothered you." He longed to touch her hand, but they remained on her lap. He forced his mind back to their topic of conversation. He wanted to ensure what she spoke about the failing business wouldn't be the case here. He couldn't imagine his uncle's restaurant failing.

The food was excellent; the service was warm and friendly and it had a touch of sophistication and class. Mario's love for what he did and his savvy management skills were topnotch, right up there with his mother's. In fact, it was Laino who had suggested Mario become a partner in their family business.

So he did. Several years ago, Mario lived in Venezuela and managed the tree farm he and Laino had inherited from their grandparents. When Quincy asked him to become a partner in Laino Enterprises, he sold the farm and moved to the states. He became an equal partner, making the business a family trio.

The waitress set their drinks on the table. Moriah squeezed the lemon wedge into her water. "You have to run a pretty tight ship, know who to trust and strategically put people in the right skillsets in order for your business to succeed." She stirred her drink with a long spoon.

She looked up at Tyro whose mind had trailed off into deep thoughts once again. What she'd said made him think of his mother. His mother indeed ran a tight ship, not only in business, but in their home life as well. She was the one who helped him to map out the rigorous course study to obtain his law degree in an unprecedented amount of time.

She knew her son. They worked out his course of classes together. The counselor and dean had initially forbidden him to take on such an aggressive course load. Nonetheless, he'd completed his undergrad studies mid-way through his junior year.

Although he wouldn't be allowed to graduate in his junior year, he delved into his core law courses. He'd spend the next two years doubling up, taking online classes in addition to day and night classes. Tyro had finished law school two years ahead of the normal time it took. He graduated at the top of his class.

A flutter of sadness flew over and perched on his shoulder. She'd gotten to see the fruits of her son's labor. He'd become a well sought after defense attorney and soon he'd opened up his own firm. But Laino never got to see her brother's dream come alive. She would have been thrilled. His mother knew all the sacrifices Mario made, the risk he took to become a partner in Laino Enterprises.

Tyro suspected Laino's sudden death made Mario realize life was too short to keep putting off the things he desired to do. And "Mario's Grill" had been his longtime dream.

Moriah's silhouette dancing upon the wall in the flickering candlelight brought his mind back to the present. Seeing her made him think of the night when he first held her in his arms. The warm feelings tugging at his heart assured him he'd soon grow to love her. He chuckled at himself. He may not have been a believer in love at first sight, but being here, consumed in her presence, made him question his own beliefs.

His brows furrowed as she excused herself to go to the ladies' room. He didn't care how awkward it might have seemed, he insisted on escorting her, although he used her ankle as an excuse. There was no way he'd let her get away from him again. Ever.

Chapter 17

When Moriah came out of the restroom, she was relieved Tyro hadn't stood there waiting for her. It was a good sign. Thinking of her past six months assured her she wasn't being too cautious in keeping her guard up. Unbelievable — if she had to explain it in one word. She closed her eyes and breathed in deeply, slowly and exhaled.

When she returned he stood and waited for her by the table. Pulling her chair out he placed her napkin over her lap as she took her seat. When he sat, he leaned forward. "How did you do it?" He studied her as he awaited her response.

"What?" she asked softly as she leaned her shoulders back.

His gaze intensified. "Are you going to tell me?" As she reached, he moved the basket of warm bread away. "Or not? I turned my head for one second and you were gone. *Vanished!*" His hands imitated one of the reporter's gestures.

"How did you get away?" He was more than curious. Since that night, he hadn't been able to come up with any logical explanations. He knew better than to believe it was magic as the crazed media had implied.

"When you turned your head, I just melded in with the crowd," she said plainly. "You and everyone else were still gawking at the truck. I then removed my hat, fluffed my hair out, and started snapping pictures with my cell."

She sighed. "I lost my hat though. Must have dropped it. I loved that hat." She leaned back and peered in his face. "With all the crazy things going on, I'm surprised no one has found it. I was sure it would've been another hot item on eBay by now."

"And then?" his gaze was relentless.

"I kept my head down as if I was fooling with my phone. As the police cleared the crowd, I shuffled along with everyone else as they headed back to their cars. Fortunately, a bus happened to come along and there was my way home." Moriah sipped her lemon water to hide her nervousness. She prayed he wouldn't ask where she lived. She wasn't ready to tell him everything, not just yet.

"Ah, clever."

Moriah smiled warmly. She loved the way his chin tilted upward when he'd nod and say "Ah!" when something intrigued him.

"I'm surprised you didn't draw anyone's attention. Didn't your ankle hurt when you walked?"

"Don't get me wrong, it hurt really bad, but I managed. I think because I tried to walk as normal as possible it made it worse. It hurt much more the next day."

"And just how did you hurt it?"

"I didn't."

"Oh... I thought you — "

"Actually, you did it."

Tyro narrowed his eyes. "Me? How? When?" Just then the waiter arrived with their meals.

"That's a story for another time." She looked at the scrumptious food as steam curled up from her plate. The presentation was unlike anything she'd seen and she had eaten in many a fine restaurant. "Superb!" she praised as she clasped her hands together in delight.

Tyro sat back and watched Moriah as she closed her eyes. She bowed her head and uttered a few words over her food. She must have felt his eyes on her as she immediately stopped and peeked one eye over at him. She raised her head and reached for his hands to pray with her.

"Nah, I'm good. You go ahead, do your thing, girl," he said in an awkward attempt to be cool.

The next time Moriah closed her eyes, she was savoring each of the a la carte items she'd selected. She enjoyed the caramelized lobster nuggets with roasted garlic, creamy garlic mashed potatoes, and the sautéed tomato spinach soufflé. It also contained garlic.

"I get the hint."

"What?" she said sweetly.

"I take it you like garlic."

"I do," she chimed.

"Garlic's not good for kissing," he unabashedly stated. "And it upsets my stomach." A cunning smirk crossed his face. He was about to say something devious as he leaned toward her.

Moriah stopped him as she tilted her fork at him. She warned him as she forbade him from saying what she assumed he was alluding to. "That's too bad," she cooed.

He adored the way she held her fork between her two fingers as if it were a part of her. As she talked, she'd wield it this way and that way, like a baton. He guessed she was so used to doing it, she probably didn't realize it.

"Well, that's only if I eat too much of it." He laughed out loud. Her demeanor was charming. It felt good to laugh. He gazed over at the mysterious woman he was getting to know. She had qualities he appreciated. She was cute, witty, and quick on her feet.

When Moriah finished chewing, she leaned toward him and pointed her fork at his plate. "Looks to me like somebody wasn't as hungry as he said." The lemon seared swordfish, roasted red potatoes, and avocado soufflé on his plate were barely touched.

She took another forkful of mashed potatoes and closed her eyes, relishing the smoothness of the whipped potatoes as they delighted her palate. Moriah put her fork down and squinted an eye at him.

"What?" he asked teasingly.

Moriah shrugged.

"Okay, Ms. Moriah Styles. Come out with it."

"Nah. You'd probably get mad and get all defensive on me."

"That bad, huh?"

"Bad is not the word I would have chosen." She picked up her fork and nabbed a piece of swordfish from his plate. "'You can't handle the truth!'" she teased, using a line from an old movie being the movie buff she was. She squinted her eye at him again while she chewed.

"Hey!" he complained blocking her fork as she came after another piece.

"Ah hah! See... you are a momma's boy. I bet you live at home." She pointed her fork at him in the cutest manner.

"That doesn't mean I'm a momma's boy. It could mean that I was going to eat it... or take it home to my dog... It doesn't mean—"

"I bet she washes your shorts for you and irons them too!" she teased, cutting him off in her cute manner of slight chortles.

Her laughter made him laugh. He didn't want their time to end. They bonded so quickly, like two magnets being drawn together just as they had the first time they'd met.

The truth was, his mother *had* ironed his boxers and tees. Well, she used to. It wasn't one of the first things he thought about when he thought of her. But now that Moriah mentioned it... He did miss the joy on his mother's face, the tune she'd hum as she'd placed his neatly pressed undergarments on the designated shelves in his master closet.

He felt the familiar sadness lurking in the distance. He missed his mother, to say the least. But now wouldn't be the right time to bring up her death. It would spoil the momentum... especially after she'd made the remark about her ironing his shorts. And, she had been right. Still, he couldn't chance rippling the waters by bringing it up. Not just yet.

As the evening began to wind down, he reasoned it would only be appropriate to introduce her to Mario. The expression on her face when she learned he was his uncle was priceless. The resemblance between them was strikingly undeniable.

Tyro looked like his mother, except for his sandy-brown hair. Even as he told her that Mario and his mother were twins, he still didn't mention her death. He also left out the part that they were partners in a multi-billion-dollar business. He'd save that for a more appropriate time.

As they ended their evening, he knew he wanted to know more about this Moriah Styles, the woman who made him laugh so much. The mysterious woman who made his sadness go away whenever she was around. He was determined to see her again. Soon.

Chapter 18

Early Thursday evening, Tyro stood gazing out the kitchen window into his back garden. He loved the fall with the color of autumn splashed over the trees. Pink and orange clouds stretched like fingers across the sky as the sun melted into the ocean.

And just as seasons bring change, he'd witnessed Moriah's sudden shift as he offered to take her home last night. Well technically, it was earlier this morning although he hadn't meant to keep her out so late. It was just that he enjoyed being with her.

He remembered the fear that rose in her face. Why had she been afraid for him to take her home? Maybe it was because she barely knew him. Maybe it wasn't a good idea he'd offered. He should have called for one of his chauffeurs to take her.

Still, he wanted nothing more than to pull her into his embrace. To hold her, let her know he'd let nothing happen to her. He could see himself wrapping his world around hers, protecting her while she learned to trust him. He could only hope that one day, she'd want the same thing too.

He'd met her friend Nettie when she came to pick her up from Mario's. She seemed like a good friend, although a little rough around the edges. He sighed. He didn't understand why she had her drive all the way back there to get her. She had already come by earlier that evening to get the car. Whose car was it anyway? Did Moriah not have a car?

The unsightly truck she was driving the first night he met… rescued her, crossed his mind. He was glad he'd taken care of it.

Sending it to its long overdue death, he had it crushed at his company's yard. Seeing forty tons of steel swallowing the unsightly beast in its hungry jaws ensured that neither she, nor anyone else would ever drive it again.

He hoped it wasn't her only means to take care of her customers. He hadn't thought about the repercussions of her not having a vehicle. At the time, he hadn't cared. She had no business being in it. It had to go. As long as she didn't bring it up, he wouldn't either. Although he knew it would only be a matter of time before she did.

Roy swaggered into the kitchen interrupting his thoughts. He turned and watched as his chef and most trusted confidant removed the cream-based dish from the refrigerator. He'd placed it there giving it time to set. He pureed the rice and poured it on top of the base.

"I know dat look," Roy accused.

"What are you talking about?"

"Mmm huh," Roy said, placing several bowls, plates and dishes needed to serve the meal on the island. He placed a tray in each of the double ovens. He looked at Tyro. "You done gone and fell yourself in love, ain't ya," he said matter-of-factly rather than asking a question.

Tyro looked back into the garden. "I just can't get her off my mind, man."

"Ain't nothin' wrong with a little love... c'est la vie!" Roy held his hands in position and swayed as if he were dancing with someone to a slow, snazzy tune.

Tyro sighed. "She's different. I've never met anyone like her." He wondered if this was the time to bring it up. Should he tell him or just let him find out when he meets her?

"She has the most beautiful almond shaped eyes." Tyro's own eyes twinkled. "Her hair matches them perfectly. It's soft and..." He tried to think of how to describe it. "It's kind of wiry and twisted...curled all over her head.

"AW NAW! Don't tell me she be that girl I seen you with on TV?" Roy asked incredulously.

Tyro paused. He wasn't about to lie. He adored her for who she was. And that was that. "Yeah, she was... I mean, she is."

"WHOO WHOOO, WOOOH!" Roy sang. "You really heading yo self for some trouble now." He shook his finger at Tyro as he spoke. He paused only for a moment before he resumed delicately slicing thin slits into the leg of lamb.

"Trouble, what trouble?" Tyro defended.

"You, Mr. White Billionaire. Your dad, Mr. Said Billionaire's father..."

"You're Black," Tyro snapped, cutting to the chase.

"Yeah, but I ain't no hoochie mama trying to get all up in your bank account either. And you know dat's exactly what your father gon' think. Who you think gonna pay to get ya'll out of this mess you done caused?" Roy wiped his hand on a towel.

"Is that what you think? That because she's Black all she wants is a 'White man's money?'" Tyro said, emphasizing the last four syllables.

"Black. White. Hispanic. Korean. Asian... you name 'em. Don't make no difference, a woman is a woman. All she want, eat, sleep, dream, and poop, is a man with some money. And baby... you got money, money, money!" Roy sang the famous 1970's O'Jays' hit "For The Love of Money" while he did his rendition of the mashed potatoes.

"Yeah, but you got money, money, money too," Tyro repeated back, but less melodramatic and with less rhythm than Roy. "Is that all your Athena wants?"

"She don't know how much money I really have... You kiddin' me? Shoot, half the time, the stuff I bring home, I tell her you gave it to me!" Roy chuckled. "I tell her you be going through one of your moods again. You know how you do, be throwing stuff out."

"No you don't!" Tyro chanted in disbelief. "That's what you tell her? And she believes you?"

81

"Sho do! Maaan..." Roy sang as he normally did when he was making a point. "If she knew I had the money I do, she'da been done gone and bought her own island somewhere before you could say 'hallelujah.' And that's a mighty long word. She be watching all them shows on HGTV and gettin' dem big ideas..."

"How you get around it when she asks you for something more than you want to spend?" Tyro slid a stool from under the island and took a seat as he asked curiously.

"I tell her, baby, we can't afford that right now, but one day, I'm gonna buy you the moon." Roy stopped wiping down a goblet and he stared in mid-air as if he was contemplating that one day, he really just might buy her the moon.

"And she falls for it?" Tyro was astonished.

"As long as I keep promising her...and givin' her a lil somethin' somethin' to hold on to, she'll back off. She be's right fine."

Tyro's eyes rose. "A lil somethin' somethin'?"
"You white boys don't know nothin' 'bout that," Roy said as he put the finishing touches on the evening meal.

"You see this ri here?" He held out the oval serving platter full of delicacies. "Now this is what I call a lil somethin' somethin'.

"These are some of her favorites." Roy showed off the array of rotisserie duck with hoisin baste and grilled oranges, stuffed mushroom caps with crab, and a spread of goose liver pâté set on top of a broiled lobster tail.

Roy gestured with his hands. "Dis here is what I call my magic potion." He looked at Tyro to make sure he was following what he was getting at. "I'm gonna take 'em home, set out some candles, pour a little wine, and serve it to her like she's a queen and let her eat till her heart's content."

"Once she get done with eatin' these... man... Mmm mmph!" He blew a kiss in the air and watched it disappeared as if it were magic dust.

Tyro stared at his chef. He didn't know how to take him sometimes. He was in no wise prepared to do all that.

"Hope, man," Roy said after seeing the confusion on Tyro's face. That's all I'm talkin' 'bout. I give my woman something to look forward to. That's hope."

Roy set a succulent crab creole dish in front of Tyro along with garlic red potatoes and asparagus tips with his secret Hollandaise sauce. The savory aroma made his mouth water.

"Smells good!" he said, grabbing his fork and digging in.
"Now ya eat up." Roy patted Tyro on the shoulder twice. "Enjoy!" he said as he emptied a container of lamb, a little somethin' somethin' for Sheba in her bowl. He lifted his platter, and whistled a happy melodic tune as he carried it out the door.

Tyro thought for a moment. There was something about the contented look on Roy's face. "Hope, huh?" Tyro's spirit rose as he decided he'd give his newfound ray of hope a call later after he and Sheba finished enjoying their meals.

Chapter 19

Friday morning, Moriah lay on her back holding the check for $4,500.00 Tyro had given to her in the envelope Wednesday at Mario's. She held it in the air. Her first check from her first client, and the hefty $500.00 bonus included made it an impressive earning for her first job. M & A Marketing definitely was on the right track!

She was amazed that he had been her first client; well technically, it was Mario who was her client. But Tyro had gotten the sign for him as a gift. So, technically, it made Tyro her first client, she bantered back and forth to herself.

"Oh who cares!" she mused, realizing her silliness. The fact that they'd been right under each other's noses without knowing it, amused her. "God, you sure know how to do!" she praised in a singsong manner.

She sighed in relief. She calculated her total funds adding the payment to the installment Tyro had initially made through PayPal. She'd now be able to pay her portion of the rent for a few months in advance. She prayed they'd be out of there by the time the next payment would be due.

She looked at the seal on the business check and thought it odd that an "H & S Law" had signed it. But with all she needed to take care of, it was a blessing and at this point, she didn't care who endorsed it— as long as it was legit.

Moriah put the check in her purse to deposit later that afternoon. She snagged her cell and perused her photos, stopping as she reached the snapshot of her hero who she now knew as Tyro Hernandez Simmonds.

She scrolled her finger gently over his face and smiled. "What is it about you, Mr. Simmonds?" she said, taking note of a quiet sadness surrounding him. It was obvious, although he tried to do it subtly, whenever she'd mentioned his mother, he would change the subject.

Mario had a spark of heaviness about him too. She picked it up right away as Tyro introduced them at his restaurant. It led her to wonder about his dad. Now, she was a little concerned about what she might be getting herself into. No matter what it was, it was too late now. She had already agreed she'd see him again. And beside all that, she loved being with him.

Her cell buzzed. It was Tyro. They had spent all evening and into the wee hours of the morning talking and laughing at Mario's the other night. They'd spent two hours talking on the phone together last night as she soaked her ankle in the tub. She was delighted to have heard from him again this soon. She closed the photo files and answered his text.

"How's the ankle?"

Moriah grinned as her fingers typed, "Better."

"Hungry?"

"Little bit."

"Lunch at my place? I have one of the best chefs around... but don't tell Mario I said that LOL."

"You mean @ your place?"

"Yes. Problem?" Tyro must have noticed the ellipse appearing, fading and reappearing on his end as she was hesitant, not sure what to say. He waited. The three dots pulsated in and out as she took a long time to respond.

"Ms. Styles, we can go somewhere else," he typed.

"No, your place will be fine. Time? Address?"

85

"Think it'll be better if I pick you up. Bring your bathing suit for the pool. Meet you at Mario's in half hour. Is that good? Or, I can pick you up at your place."

"Oh no u don't! I'm not telling u where I live. U might be a stalker." They both texted, "LOL."

"I have errands 2 run... 2pm fine?" Moriah sighed in relief as she ended their chat. She wasn't ready for him to see her current living conditions. It would breed too many questions. And shame.

Moriah rolled up her swimming suit, long white cotton pants, and a white cover up and tucked them into a small carrying bag. She stuffed her flip-flops in along with them.

She checked her purse to ensure she'd put the check to deposit in there. She bounded out the door to catch the bus to Main Street. In her rush, she had forgotten to bring any make-up or hair products to tame her full head of kinky curls for after her swim.

She had less than an hour to take care of her deposit and dash over to the restaurant. She didn't have time to go back. She was already praying the buses weren't running late.

Chapter 20

Moriah had put too much weight on her ankle and had agitated it as she rushed around. She headed toward the bench near Mario's. She stopped suddenly when she saw a homeless man sitting off to the side near where she'd planned to sit.

"Hi, Mr. Willie," she said, surprised to see him. "What brings you on this side of town?"

"Oh you know. Gotta go where He leads me," the wrinkled-faced man said with reverence twinkling in his eyes.

"That's right, Mr. Willie. You keep going where the Lord leads you, you can't ever go wrong doing that." She fished around in her purse and pulled out the last $5 bill she had on her. She gave it to him.

He grabbed her hand and held it tightly between his for a few precious moments. "God bless you, chile." He smiled a big toothless grin. "Not ever'body has a heart of gold like you, Ms. Riah. I sure do 'preciate it." His smile never wavered as he stuffed the bill into the pocket of his well-worn blazer. She was sure it had been a great find from one of the Salvation Army bins, many years ago.

She sat on the bench with her legs propped up and she said a little prayer for him as he shuffled down the street. He smiled at anyone who would pay him any mind. Very few did.

She waited for Tyro to drive up, which reminded her she didn't know what kind of car he'd be driving. Ten minutes later he poked his head out of Mario's. "There you are." His brows rose. "Why are you sitting out here?"

"Waiting for you, my prince," she teased as she pointed to her propped up ankle.

"Ah," he chimed, tilting his chin upward. He paused as he gazed into her face. His eyes danced at the sight of her. She took advantage as he walked toward her to get a good look at him.

The two buttons were undone at the top of his stylish, fitted shirt. She didn't know if it was his sculptured physique, or the slim style of his shirt hugging him in all the right places that made him look like he'd stepped right out of a GQ mag. *Man, was he sexy!*

She allowed her mind to *go there* and linger for just a few moments. How could she not, as gorgeous as he was? "Did I tell you I have a surprise for you?" he asked.

"What...?" she responded, half dazed as his words took a few seconds to catch up to her mind. "Surprise?" She leaned back and looked at him. He stepped closer to help her off the bench. The mixture of wood fire and jasmine fragrance flirting with her nose wasn't helping her keep her mind where it should be.

"Yes, a surprise." But it'll have to wait until —" Just as he was about to lift her into his arms, they both turned as they heard a commotion heading toward them from a distance.

"There they are... Cinderella and the Prince!" a woman yelled as she and several others charged toward them.

"I spotted them first... It's my reward," another person yelled as he shoved someone out of the race.

Moriah pulled her hoodie over her head and shielded her face from view. Tyro quickly swept her off her feet, cradled her in his arms, and bounded in through the restaurant. Whisking her into his Land Rover parked in the back, he sped away.

They arrived to their destination within fifteen minutes. The drive time was definitely cut in half with him driving 100 mph. Moriah caught her breath as he helped her out of the vehicle.

Several of her wavy twists had unraveled and were sticking out from under her hoodie. "Thanks for getting me... I mean getting *us* out of there." She peered up into his face as she removed the hood and smoothed her hair back into place. He smiled at her as their eyes locked.

"I'm your prince, remember? It's my job to rescue you, you know." He tugged playfully at her chin. His hand brushed against her face as he moved his hand away. She tingled inside. *Lord, You got to help me with this one!* she mused as the fine specimen reached in to retrieve her carry-along bag.

As Moriah looked around, she had no clue of where she was. It was an enormous fleet service area of some sort. Heavy duty and commercial trucks were neatly lined up under rows and rows of bays in every direction she could see.

A signed posted on the door of a two-story commercial-looking building they had parked in front of read "Laino Enterprises." A basketball court sat off in the distance on the right. She peered back in the direction of the gated entrance they just drove through.

As they walked, she contemplated her options if she needed to get away in a hurry. She brushed off her thoughts as she told herself she was being silly. *What harm could possibly come to me?* she thought, until she saw the huge German Shepherd bounding her way.

Moriah measured the distance between her reaching the building or the car. Just as she decided to head back to the car, Tyro snapped his fingers twice.

To her amazement, the Shepherd trotted over to him and sat obediently next to his feet. The dog sniffed toward her direction. Tyro walked over to Moriah. "She's just curious… or jealous," Tyro teased.

"Not funny," Moriah said, seized with caution not to move suddenly.

Chapter 21

Tyro immediately noticed the apprehension on Moriah's face. "Sheba, you be on your best behavior. Say hi to Moriah." He turned toward Moriah.

"Moriah, this is Sheba. You be on your best behavior too!" he teased. Sheba wagged her tail low as she walked over to Moriah. She sat near Moriah's feet, looked up into her face, and whined.

"Aw, aren't you the cutest!" she said as she rubbed the dog behind her ears. Tyro was pleased to see they liked each other. Sheba meant the world to him. He needed for them to get along.

A commotion rising at the gated entrance caused Moriah, Tyro, and Sheba's heads to snap in that direction. The media and a mob of people crowded around the security entrance. They'd trailed them from the restaurant.

Voices yelled through the gate, cameras and a few other people attempted to climb over the fence further down from the mini security station. A low, menacing growl came from Sheba's throat as one of the intruders was almost over the fence.

"Look this way," Tyro said to Moriah as he turned his back toward the crowd. He placed his arm around her shoulder. "Can you run?"

"I think so…" She snatched the hoodie back onto her head.

"Sheba, to the back." The dog looked from Tyro, to Moriah, to the growing excitement at the security gate. She rose and trotted toward the back of the building turning her head periodically to look back at her master.

Although the Yard was enclosed inside a gate, he knew their one security guard would not be able to hold off the number of people rattling the gate to get in. He made a mental note to update their security.

Tyro lifted Moriah in his arms to relieve her agony from having to hobble along. There was no way she could run in the gravel surrounding the building. He felt possessive of the woman as she wrapped her arms around his neck.

He could feel her breathing, taking him in. He hurried toward a sleek black craft. It rested on one of the landing pads tucked away in the back of the building.

"Do you trust me?" He panted as he scurried around the building with her securely in his possession.

"What choice do I have?" She heaved in and out between breaths. Her bag and purse, strapped over her shoulder, bounced along as he ran.

As she buried her face in his neck, he hoped the fear of being arrested for leaving the scene of an accident had been erased from her mind. He'd stop at nothing to protect her.

Moriah hadn't seen where they were headed until he stood her on her feet. As he reached to open the door, her eyes grew wide. She touched his forearm and leaned her shoulder back to look in his face. "You fly this?" she asked as her eyes shifted from him to the helicopter they stood beside.

Without answering, he popped his shades on his face and grinned a sexy smile. Heat flushed her face. He whistled. Sheba trotted next to her master's side. Moriah looked down at the Shepherd as she panted. The dog looked up at her. Moriah smiled.
Sheba whined and lowered her head as she came toward her.

Moriah bent slightly to rub her head. "You're a smart dog, aren't you, girly-girl!" she stated as she rubbed her with more gusto behind her ears. Sheba closed her eyes and enjoyed the moment until they heard footsteps quickening their way.

Moriah turned and looked over her shoulder. A reporter somehow had gotten through and was hightailing it straight toward them. A security guard and another Shepherd were hot on his heels. Still, he was close enough to get a clear picture of the two of them. Too close! If she had any doubts about flying in the helicopter with Tyro, it was too late to turn back now.

"Get in!" Tyro insisted as he helped her climb up into the back seat of the helicopter.

"Good girl," Moriah heard Tyro say as he closed the door after Sheba lunged in and took a seat in a place designed especially for her. It was located behind where Moriah sat. He closed the door and ran to the front of the craft and hopped in the right-side pilot seat.

Moriah had flown in helicopters many times. She scooted over to sit in the left seat so Tyro could have easier eye contact with her as he piloted from where he sat.

Flying in choppers had been a necessary means of quick transportation in order for her to keep up with the many demands of her clients when she worked at TSMA. She'd fly over cities and remote areas to view some of their billboards from the air. Riding a helicopter also made it convenient when she had to meet with clients in DC in the morning and New York in the afternoon.

"Don't I get any ear protectors?" she yelled up to Tyro as he placed a set over his ears. He was too preoccupied to hear her. His fingers moved feverishly as he worked the controls, turning on this, switching on that...

She looked at the smoked glass window at the back of the building several yards away. She was amazed to see by the reflection the rotor blades were in full rotation. She could feel the vibration, but the quietness within the cabin was unlike what she had been used to.

An automatic double seat belt retracted over Moriah's shoulder. She was impressed. Locating the lap belt, she tightened it around her waist. She threw her purse and carry-along bag in the seat beside her.

A flashback coursed through her mind of the many times she'd flown, particularly the last time, which had been with Fletcher. She quickly swiped the horrible memory from her mind.

Chapter 22

As the chopper rose, Moriah relaxed and removed her hoodie. The windows were tinted so she could see out and surmised no one could see in. She fashioned her shades on her face. She could see that an intruder in pursuit of filming their craft had been apprehended. He was now being handed over by a security guard to the city authorities for trespassing. She assumed the one in the tan and green uniform was Laino's security enforcement.

Peering at the ground, she saw the swelling crowd of people gazing up at them. She looked down at their awestruck faces as if a real princess was being swept away. She chuckled as she imagined how she would write the headlines. *Damsel in distress saved again by her Prince Charming from a crowd of blubbering fools.*

Once in the air, Moriah was able to see the yard in its entirety. The roof of each bay was color-coded and strategically aligned.

"Glad to see you're relaxed." He repositioned the mouthpiece as he spoke into the radio. "Roger. Will let you know when we're ready to touch down."

"I am," she responded as she waited for him to program his landing coordinates. She nestled back in the soft leather seat. "The moment you closed the throttle before you cranked the engine, I had no doubt you knew what you were doing."

Tyro's eyes swept over her as he looked back. "Is that right."

"Yep," she said as she popped her lips. She marveled again at the quietness inside the cabin. It was unlike the ones she traveled in before. She remembered having to wear those cumbersome headsets, and talking on the phone was virtually impossible with the noise from the rotor blades. Here, she could hear Sheba's slight snoring in back of her. She rested her head on the soft cushion. She wanted to close her eyes for a few seconds to clear her mind. "I'm definitely in good hands," she cooed.

**

"So — " Tyro said, but paused suddenly as she jumped. He'd startled her.

Moriah hadn't realized she had dozed off. She shuddered as her eyes popped open at the sudden dip in altitude. Had she heard Tyro's voice close, as in being right beside her? Couldn't be.

"What..." Her eyes shifting from the pilot seat to where he sat next to her. "Are you crazy?" she yelled incredulously. Gesturing with her palms turned up she motioned toward the pilot's seat as if she was dumping something into it.

"Auto pilot." He grinned.

"Auto pilot or not, don't be playing with my life in your foolishness. You know that someone should always be at the controls." She bolted upright in her seat as much as the safety belts allowed.

Tyro climbed back into the pilot's seat and reset the alarms after he ascended back to the appropriate altitude.

"I didn't mean to scare you, Ms. Styles," he said as if he were surprised at her reaction. When she didn't respond, he peeped over his shoulder. "You're afraid?" he said, amused.

"Yeah, I'm afraid. I'm afraid of being a thousand feet in the air... with a lunatic. Now, if you would please turn your attention back to what you need to do"—she pointed to the controls—"before you get us killed." Moriah took a deep breath and let it out slowly.

"As you wish," he responded, trying to hide his embarrassment.

She was having second thoughts about letting her guard down. One moment she'd been smitten, thought he was a keeper. He had been charming and very protective. The next she was convinced he was a senseless moron. *Was he trying to kiss me?* she wondered.

Why would he do such an irresponsible thing? *He must have lost his mind,* Moriah mused after seeing a side of his arrogance. It brought back the horrible memories of a similar incident that was the demise of her career with TSMA. Her unprofessionalism had cost her her career and her dignity.

Since then, she'd been determined to regain her standard of living and clear her name. But the thick knots she felt beneath her pant leg reminded her of the price she'd paid. The cost of one simple kiss would haunt her for the rest of her life. She quickly folded her hands and positioned them in her lap.

She looked up and was relieved to see Tyro wasn't watching. She hadn't realized she'd been rubbing her fingers over the twenty-inch scar that ran down the inside of her right leg. Slipping her shades back on, she fought back the tears swelling in her eyes.

Chapter 23

Tyro was disappointed that Moriah's attitude had changed. Her shoulders slumped as she stared off into the distance. Her usual bubbly demeanor had solidified into a lump of clay. She was right. That was a stupid thing to do. Tyro scolded himself. "Um… I'm sorry. I shouldn't have done that."

He glanced at her briefly as he spoke. "You've been through enough already today," he said remorsefully, thinking of their recent getaway. He took another glimpse. He saw her slightly nod as she forced a reserved but nervous smile.

Tyro hoped Moriah believed his sincerity. Now, he'd have to find a way to get her past his brainless action and get her back to her normal self; although, he could see she wasn't as tense as she was five minutes ago.

He really liked being with her and needed to find a way to amend the error of his ways. After all, they would be spending a lot of time together over the weekend and they needed to figure out the best way to handle their escalating predicament regarding the criminal charges.

Moriah leaned forward. "If you ever do that again…," she warned, gritting her teeth through every syllable as she jabbed her finger in the air.

"All right, all right," Tyro said as he raised his left hand in surrender. He smiled.

Tyro sighed in relief. She was back on board. He watched as she relaxed and enjoyed the view of the colorful landscape as they coasted along. Although he had the fuel to do more sightseeing for several hours, he noticed clouds were brewing ahead.

The sun was beginning to dip behind the horizon. He smiled as she removed her sunglasses to admire the splendorous burst of yellow and orange colors mellowing across the clouds. The sun had surrendered its goodnight kiss to bid the closing of another day.

Indeed, it had been a beautiful day. Tyro couldn't have been more pleased that the woman whom he couldn't get off his mind was enjoying it with him.

The chopper made a slight ninety-degree turn as it whisked toward the secluded peninsula just off of the Chesapeake Bay. Moriah leaned forward to take in the scenery. "Breathtaking!"

"I'm glad you're enjoying the view." Tyro pushed a few buttons and clicked several switches in the down position. It was time to land.

"Is this where we're going?" she shrilled. Her lips curled upward as she looked over the island. A vast array of tall vegetation and exotic trees were bending in the wind.

The sun hadn't fully set. Its lingering illumination allowed her to see some of the sights below. She imagined the sound of the waves as they rolled up onto the private beach just below her. She watched as they playfully pulled back into sea and quickly raced back to the shore again.

He passed over an elongated two-story beach house that looked like a five-star resort. It sat toward the far end of the beach. "Mmm hm," he crooned a few minutes later as he maneuvered the cyclic stick to glide the craft toward a clear patch. "Home sweet abode."

Chapter 24

"Home?" Moriah asked, turning to watch as he guided the helicopter toward the landing pad. Moriah got a better view of her destination. Three houses positioned in a triangular formation dominated the right side of the island. After she'd met Mario the other evening, she had asked Tyro if he lived near his uncle. She remembered the awkwardness of his response when he'd told her they all lived in the same area.

"Which one is yours?" she cooed.

"You'll see soon enough." He tilted his head enough for her to see his smile.

Moriah surmised that the more modern, industrial-looking house with a row of solar panels splayed across the roof was his. It was positioned on the lower left end of the island and faced eastward. The other two homes were spaced equally apart.

A two-story colonial with four large columns adorned the back of one of the houses as it faced the garden. The third home was a one-story octagon. She guessed it was his uncle's. It fit his dazzling personality.

Her eyes shifted back to the colonial. She gathered that one would be his father's. She huffed. She'd be sure to stay far away from that house. She remembered the nasty look he'd shot at her from across the room the other night at Mario's. Tyro had gestured for him to come over. He had wanted to introduce her.

From a distance, she thought he'd looked familiar. Oh well, she'd worry about that later. But she would certainly try at all costs to avoid running into him. Although Tyro seldom talked about his mother, she could only hope that she was more amiable than his dad.

Moriah turned her attention back to the scenery below. An expansive garden sat in the middle of the courtyard that intertwined and connected the three homes. The meticulous exhibit of greenery and blooms morphed into distinct and unique styles as it bordered each home.

Colorful lights illuminated the numerous pathways. It was too dark now for her to really appreciate the entirety of its beauty. Moriah looked forward to coming back, possibly on another day, to explore the private oasis.

Water cascaded over a boulder-type cliff into a lighted pool that sat off to the distant right of the garden. "So much to see!" Moriah called up to Tyro who was in the midst of revising his landing coordinates. There had been an increasing change in the weather. "Sure feels good to get away from all the hoopla for a minute," she stated, sitting back fully in her seat.

When he didn't respond, she leaned forward to be sure he could hear her before she spoke this time. She wondered what they would do the short time they'd be there. They could have gone for a late swim if only the weather would cooperate. Which she highly doubted since they had just flown through the cluster of storm clouds looming over the area.

She gazed back out the window and frowned. Even the chance of a walk through his garden was out of the question as drops of rain splashed against the window. She reasoned that after they would eat the meal he'd planned, he would probably just want to show her around, stretch his legs before they returned.

"How long do you think it will take to refuel and get back to Delaware... one hour? Two?"

"What's that?" he asked, turning his head slightly as he continued alternating his plan to descend. Tyro needed to maneuver the craft to a different position to achieve a smoother landing. The wind gusts had steadily begun to pick up momentum.

Occupied with talking to his control tower, he hadn't heard her question. "I'll take you up tomorrow, so you can get a better view in the daytime," he quickly assured her.

"Tomorrow... you're not planning to take me back tonight? I wasn't planning on—" she stammered.

"No can do," Tyro interrupted in a chipper mood. He hated the fact the weather had changed so suddenly as he flew over his peninsula, giving him no choice but to land earlier than he'd liked. He had risen to the top of his game by giving her an A-1 sightseeing tour and had regained her confidence. "Storm's coming, Mo."

She looked out the window into complete darkness. She felt the chopper shift as it changed course. "I... I... can't stay... where are you taking me?" Moriah sat up in alarm. *Mo? Did he just call me...Mo?* Moriah could never bring herself to say that name. She would cringe anytime someone did.

Now, she feared she was in a situation similar to the last. The air suddenly evaporated out of the cabin. Fear clamped its ugly talons around her throat. Tiny shards of the vicious attack from the last time someone had called her by that name clouded her reasoning. Unbuckling her seat belt, she clambered to her knees.

She couldn't breathe. The memories she'd been suppressing since she'd entered the craft flooded in like a tidal wave. Sheer terror took over any logic or self-assurance as the craft descended.

Her heart raced as negative thoughts poured in. How could she have allowed herself to be placed in this predicament again? This time, she was sure she would die as Fletcher's face flashed before her just as everything fell quiet.

Unaware of Moriah's dilemma, he called back to her. "You'll be fine; my staff will take good care of— MORIAH!" Tyro yelled after taking a quick glimpse of where she was seated just a moment ago. His eyes trailed downward. She was doubled over on the floor. Her chin was tucked between her knees. Her knees were tightly pulled to her chest. Her arms buried her head.

Not able to leave the controls until he radioed the controller to take over from the ground, he called her name repeatedly as he alternated his attention between landing and yelling out her name.

In his desperation he pulled up and hovered the craft around 1000 feet. The air pushing against the sides of the helicopter made it hard for the controller in the tower below to hold it steady for too long.

"I got you, buddy," the controller announced after receiving the distressed call from Tyro. "Holding steady for sixty seconds."

Tyro snatched the headset off and rushed for the few seconds he had to check on Moriah.

Removing her arms out of the way, he lifted her head from between her knees. She was breathing, but shallow. He propped her up against the seat and placed an oxygen mask over her face. He shook her face, determined to make her open her eyes.

Moriah's eyes flickered open.

"It's okay. It's me, Tyro." He glanced up at the controls before turning back to her. "Are you okay? What happened? Don't move... stay right there...," peppering her with questions and commands at the same time.

"I don't know... but I'm okay... I'm... I'm fine... are we still in the air?" she asked, looking at him dazedly.

"Uh... sort of," he said as he doubled back to the front and plopped the headset back on. He shifted his attention from his landing coordinates to Moriah a few times as she struggled to get back into her seat. He released a sigh of relief as her seat belt clicked.

After advising the controller, he manually took the craft over and proceeded with his landing. He started a gradual descent. He wasn't sure what happened with Moriah; although, he surmised it stemmed from anxiety. He recognized the symptoms similar to those his uncle suffered with from time to time.

"If it was something I said... or did..." He got no response as he glanced back to see her staring blankly out the window. The alert on his radar beeped urgently. A wind gust of 100 mph pummeled the side of the helicopter.

He quickly shifted his eyes towards the back as Sheba let out a nervous whine. Moriah continued to stare as if unmoved by the shaking. "Easy, girl," he said out loud as if to soothe both his Shepherd and the craft he was skillfully able to recover.

Moriah was embarrassed by her recent outburst. Well, it wasn't an outburst per se, she reasoned to herself. Blood had rushed to her head as she had internalized her fear before she'd momentarily lost consciousness.

She pulled herself together and put on her facade. She tucked her fears back deep in her mind from where they tended to escape on occasion.

Chapter 25

It was pitch black out by the time the aircraft touched down on one of the five helipads. The aerial lights illuminated their surroundings enough for her to see there was quite a distance between where they were and his house.

Tyro had powered down the 'copter. After he'd let Sheba out, he waited patiently beside the open door for Moriah to finish pulling herself together.

"Well, are we going to sit here all night?" she teased after a few minutes, as if nothing happened. Tyro knew to leave well enough alone, for now. He'd soon have a bigger issue to deal with for bringing her there.

She accepted his hand as he helped her out of the chopper. As she looked up, she saw the man she hadn't formally met last night, marching toward them. He reminded her of Sam Elliot. His white hair thrashing in the wind told her he carried his own storm.

She watched as Tyro stuck his hands in his front pockets and sheepishly lowered his head. His left foot kicked at nothing on the ground.

She was shocked at Tyro's sudden change in demeanor; he was not the same confident man who'd just flown her through great turbulence to get there. The place from which, without him, she had no means to get home. A storm may have been brewing in the distance, but a bigger storm was thundering right toward her. *He's afraid of his dad... I don't believe this.*

"How do you want to handle this, son?" he barked through his thick white mustache. His eyes shifted coldly from Moriah to Tyro as if she was a street merchant. Tyro stood there continuing to kick at nothing, now with his other foot.

What? This is bizarre. Moriah peeked up at the clouds billowing across the sky. Her hair flailing wildly in the wind depicted her emotions.

Quincy's eyes stayed on Tyro. "Either you take care of it— or I will. Right here. Right now," he barked. "For God's sake, Tyro. Why did you have to bring her here?" Emphasizing heavily on the "her," his upper lip curled. "*Why?*" he repeated tersely.

Moriah wrestled with her internal rage. *Why doesn't he say something? Defend me?*

"We're heading to the beach house where she'll be staying," Tyro said, having had enough of his father's tyranny.

"Oh, no she will not. You brought her here. Now either you get back on the helicopter and take her back where she belongs, or she stays in your house. Your mess, you take care of it."

A wind gust pushed Quincy backwards as Moriah and Tyro stumbled back toward the helicopter, causing the man to change his tune. He looked up at the clouds rolling in. "I gather you have enough sense not to be flying around in this weather," Quincy said as if it wasn't him who had been ranting about taking Moriah back.

Did he just call me a "mess?" Moriah glared at Tyro.

Quincy turned toward the woman standing there. "No offense to you, little gal. I am sure you're a nice person. But my son knows we do not tolerate him bringing—"

"Moriah," she said, interrupting him as she walked toward the lanky white man. She held her hand outward to shake his. *Alrighty... since Tyro is obviously too afraid to handle this situation, then I will.* "My name is Moriah Styles. And I would appreciate it if you'd call me by my name." Her voice trembled, but she was not going to stand there and be belittled like that.

Quincy looked at her hand as if it were a rattlesnake. He didn't budge. Moriah kept her hand extended. As long as he would stand there and look at it, she was determined she wouldn't withdraw it.

Stepping closer, she stabbed her hand forward further. "It won't rub off," she said as she used her other hand to brush back a patch of hair that had blown in her face. "Tyro," she called as she retracted her hand but kept her eyes trained on the red-faced man. "Radio TSMA 123.650. Give them the flight and landing coordinates to come pick me up. Their H-65 can weather the storm to get me out of here quite well."

She walked gingerly back toward the helicopter. Her ankle throbbed, sending a sharp pain up her leg. But she dared not limp or show any sign of weakness. Both of them were out of their minds. "I just need to get my stuff," Moriah said as she prayed desperately Tyro would ignore her bluff. With TSMA's pending lawsuits against her for 'Unprofessionalism," and "Misuse of Company Property," "Disorderly Conduct," and all other charges their lawyers had trumped up, the last thing she needed was for them to know where she was.

What was she saying? For her to even remotely consider having Petra and Parker come to get her was totally asinine on her part. They'd be the first to go to the media. With the media's recent fairytale craze, and the $100,000 bounty out for the two of them, she wouldn't put it past them to try to collect it themselves.

As Moriah tried to hide her sudden nervousness, it came to her. She remembered now. The man standing before her was the same person who offered the generous reward for someone to identify... his son? But why... what kind of sense did it make?

The more she thought about it, nothing was making sense. Moriah's mind churned. Something was not right about this picture. *Of course... that's it!* Quincy Simmonds, owner of Laino Enterprises, the multi-billion-dollar conglomerate. *So all of this is his dad's? Is that why he lets him talk to him the way he does?*

106

Dad or no dad, rich or not, she was not going to let him talk about her as if she wasn't standing there. If Tyro wasn't man enough to do something about the situation, then she certainly would.

"No you will not, little lady— Ms. Styles," Quincy said, breaking her tantrum of thoughts. He quickly corrected himself and addressed her by her name.

"I will not have your life on my conscience with you flying off in this weather. It is supposed to storm through the night. You can leave in the morning. Tomorrow morning, early would be soon enough." Quincy emphasized heavily on the "would be soon enough" part.

"Dad." Tyro stepped into his father's space. "Enough! Moriah is my guest and I'll be the one to determine where she'll stay and how long she stays," he said as he thumped his chest. He reached over and retrieved Moriah's belongings from the cabin.

He'd noticed Moriah shifting uncomfortably to take the weight off of her ankle. He handed Moriah her purse, heaved her other bag over his shoulder and immediately swooped her into his arms. He whisked her away, leaving Quincy standing there with his fists jabbed into his hips.

Sheba trotted alongside Tyro as he disappeared with Moriah cradled in his arms. He stepped onto the lighted path leading to his world, his own private oasis on the island he called home.

Part Two

There is no fear in love; but perfect love casteth out fear:
because: fear hath torment.
He that feareth is not made perfect in love.

1 John 4:18 KJV

Prologue

Six months ago, it happened like so...

The wheels on the gurney charged forward. The victim, a forty-four-year-old woman, was whisked from the ambulance into the medical Trauma Center of St. Francis. She was drenched in her own blood from multiple stab wounds. The machine she was connected to sang a continual, elongated, high-pitched sound as three men burst through the door. They were rushed from out of the midst of the chaos just as quickly.

Two of them stepped backwards as horror seized upon their faces. But the other man cursed uncontrollably; he was instantly restrained and forced away. His demands to save his wife went unnoticed as the medical team continued to work tirelessly.

The three men smeared with the woman's blood from when they had tried to stop the bleeding, stumbled into the waiting room and huddled hopelessly in a corner. Their arms intertwined and locked as the life of the woman they all loved slipped through their fingers. Their heads lifted simultaneously as footsteps padded their way. Prayers of desperation stuttering from each of their lips, their eyes pleading for the doctor to give them good news... something... anything to hold on to as she approached them. Had she been able to save her? Their eyes twinkled with a sliver of desperation but suddenly darkened in inevitableness as she began to speak.

"I'm sorry," the doctor told them. "We did all we could." She placed her hand gently on the arm of the husband of the deceased. "She had already lost too much blood," she said. Quincy stumbled backward as her words pierced his heart. He had just lost his best friend, his lover… his wife.

She shifted to address the brother of the deceased. She shuddered briefly at the resounding resemblance. "I'm sorry—"
Mario fell lifelessly into the chair as her words sucked the very breath out of his body. He had just lost his twin sister, his only sibling… his world.

The doctor pivoted to address the son of the deceased. His eyes reflecting disbelief in what he just heard. Even though she'd spoken of the same woman, he prayed she'd have something different to say to him. "If you need anything…" Her voice trailed off as reality gripped his soul. He fell to his knees. Tyro had lost his mother, his champion… his life.

She was gone.

Chapter 1

Tyro stepped onto the lighted path with Moriah cradled tenderly in his arms. Despite the confrontation he'd just had with his dad, he was relieved. The situation didn't get too far out of hand, this time.

Gazing into her eyes, he felt his contentment resurfacing. He shifted her weight to steady her more securely as he headed home. She was in his world now, and he was eager to share a part of it with her.

He peered into the sky. The storm had gone out to sea. He was glad to see the weather cooperating with his backup plan. It was going to be a great evening. Instead of the pool, the night called for a cozy outdoor fire, a warm soak in the Jacuzzi, and a platter of Roy's delightful specialties. Pleased with himself, his hope soared as high as an eagle.

He had arranged everything by the push of a few buttons on his smart watch. In anticipation, he'd done so as he waited for her to pull herself together on the helicopter. She seemed to feel better now, another thing he was pleased with.

Tyro felt Moriah frequently squirming in his arms. "Are you all right?" he asked, noticing her restlessness. "Is your ankle—"

"That was interesting," she said, getting right to the point. She cringed as she jutted her head back toward where he had landed the helicopter. He knew exactly what she meant—Quincy's rudeness. Suddenly, the wind died beneath his wings.

Why doesn't she leave the matter alone? He narrowed his eyes before quickly looking away. She was right, though. His father's actions were inexcusable. But Tyro had given his word.... Why had he agreed to his mother's request? How could he not; she was dying. Tyro remembered it vividly.

His mother had called for an urgent, last minute business meeting between the four of them. As they reported to the office that evening, his uncle Mario had spotted her first. His mother was lying face down, drowning in a pool of her own blood. She'd been stabbed in numerous places.

The grueling sight had paralyzed his dad, rendering him useless. He was forced to ride along with Mario to the hospital. Tyro clutched the lifeless hand of his mother as he rode beside her in the ambulance. She forced her eyes open. Her fading stare pleaded as she mumbled her final words in desperation. Caught up in his own emotional turmoil and the fear of losing her, Tyro had given in to her plea. He made a promise he was sure he could never keep.

His mind snapped back from deep thought. Because of the promise he made six months ago, things were out of control with his dad. His mother's words, still resonating in his mind, plagued him. *Take care of him*, Malaino Hernandez Simmonds had commissioned her son as she breathed her last. *Take care of your father*.

He glanced at the woman he carried in his arms. Until recently, he hadn't seen the need to do anything about his dad's constant badgering. He'd merely stayed out of his way, and his dad avoided him. He realized now the consequences of letting things go too far, but he had no idea what to do about it.

He also suspected his dad had changed his mind about allowing Moriah to stay on the island purely for his own selfish reasons. Another thing Tyro would have to deal with. He restrained his face from revealing his inner turmoil.

Absorbed in her own thoughts, Moriah shifted anxiously in his arms. If she were to be in a relationship with this guy, would she have to compete with his father? Would it cost her her peace of mind?

Dignity? Her sanity? Just thinking of it made her fidget more. But there was nothing she could do about it at the moment.

She gazed into Tyro's face and smiled. When he smiled back at her, she melted deeper into his arms. She closed her eyes and breathed a sigh of relief and determined she'd enjoy the time they'd spend together. She'd worry about his dad later. She looked up into his eyes. He was still staring at her.

"What's the plan, my prince?" she asked as she gently jostled her fingers against his shoulder.

"Plan? What plan?" His spirits rose. "You'll just have to wait and see. Since I was the one who rescued you—four times, may I remind you—you owe me. I should at least have time to decide." A playful grin spread across his face. "But whatever I say, there's no turning back, no escaping. Deal?"

She laughed. "You have no idea what to do, do you? You're just winging it."

"Winging it?"

She chuckled at the puzzled look on his face. "I knew it! So now I'm your guinea pig, huh? Left to your thoughtless whims."

"You have a problem with it?" He kissed her forehead.

"Oh," she sang. "Maybe I do… maybe I don't," she teased. "It depends on what you have in mind." She felt his heart beating in rhythm with hers. She rested her head on his shoulder. It would be a night of promise. She'd take the opportunity to know more about this Tyro Simmonds, the man who'd been knocking at her heart's door since they met.

Chapter 2

Moriah had no other choice than to stay overnight on the island with the man she'd met just last week. She considered the opportunity and assured herself there'd be much for her to do and to see. Her anticipation rose, thinking of the endless things they could do tomorrow, if the weather would only hold out.

Moriah closed her eyes and enjoyed the evening breeze blowing off the ocean. As it swept over them, she thought of the night they first met. Her shoulders relaxed until Quincy's disgruntled face popped back into her head.

Her eyes flung open. *He's so belligerent and such a hypocrite!* She fought to contain the thoughts that kept creeping up in her mind, to keep them from spilling out.

Oh how she hated hypocrites! She'd seen Quincy Simmonds on television numerous times. He had been ranting about the preposterous mystery couple that had fled the scene of an accident. Never once did he consider no one had gotten hurt, and that a life, hers nonetheless, had been saved.

Visualizing the timeless picture of her hero carrying her to safety, she smiled. It had been the perfect shot: just as they were about to share a lover's kiss, her hair was swept up by a sudden breeze and concealed most of their face. It was that sexy snapshot that had gone viral, sending Quincy over the edge.

Although everyone else had idolized the romantic moment and wanted to know who the couple was, Quincy deemed the incident a "travesty."

"Travesty!" She was appalled. *The nerve of him! How dare he.* It had been Quincy who had offered a hefty reward for anyone who could identify the couple.

All along, he had known it was his son. *Who does such a thing?* Moriah fumed. The more she thought about it, the more sure she was that the man couldn't be trusted. And the fact that he was Tyro's father, which she'd just learned tonight after landing on the man's private island, unnerved her even more.

She looked in Tyro's face as he continued to carry her toward his home. *Who are you? Who is this Tyro Simmonds? Too late to be thinking of that now.* She couldn't help but wonder if he was anything like his dad. She grimaced at the thought.

An undeniable sadness peeked from Tyro's eyes. Had her foul mood caused it? Already she realized the effect his father could have on their relationship, if they'd let him.

"You can put me down now," Moriah blurted after Tyro rounded the bend out of Quincy's sight. She imagined the man was still standing on the landing pad with his fists jabbed into his side, scowling. Cursing.

She glanced around at her surroundings. She closed her eyes and breathed in the soothing mixture of earth and foliage that filled the air after the rain. It was different on the island than what was found in a polluted, industrialized city. *Tyro lives on an island.* Her eyes popped open. It was his father's island, no doubt. Her body shivered as a cold chill pierced through her.

His family was wealthy. She was not. Currently, she was living in a run-down motel, barely able to make her half of the weekly rent. Moriah hadn't always been so destitute and neither did she plan to remain that way. She was on track to turn her finances around and get back to the comfortable lifestyle she had once enjoyed.

She breathed deeply. It felt nice being with Tyro until his father came to her mind again. There had been no reason for him to let his father berate her like that. Now that she had a clearer picture of their family dynamic, she had to determine how she'd deal with it.

Would Tyro remain in his father's control because of his money, status? Would he be willing to sacrifice it all for a relationship with an independent woman like her?

She prayed she wouldn't see Quincy again—at least not tonight. Meeting him under the circumstances and the awkward treatment toward his own son hinted at the dark secrets that lurked ahead. *What in the world am I getting myself into?* She thought about how his dad refused to meet her at Mario's the other night. Had he even said that the man was his dad? She couldn't remember. Maybe she'd missed that part of the conversation.

His grip tightened around her as he continued toward his estate. She shifted uncomfortably. The more she thought about it, the more appalled she became at how his father had talked to his own son. Even worse, he had the nerve to treat her like she was a street urchin. She remembered the look on Tyro's face as he kept his head down while his father blew over him like a tornado.

One thing was for sure, she didn't have much respect for a man who couldn't stand on his own. A little help and guidance along the way, sure, but to be under someone's thumb like that was totally unacceptable.

Chapter 3

"I can make it on my own," she said again. She felt the change in his demeanor. He hadn't acknowledged her first request to put her down. His grip tightened as he trudged forward. She peered into his face. It was solemn. A shadow of unrest seemed to cloak him. With each step, he continued to stare mindlessly into the night.

She looked at the moon. It swept behind the gray clusters floating aimlessly by. The perfectly rounded sphere slipped again from its hiding. Sheba returned from out of the shrubberies that aligned their path. Sniffing cautiously, she trotted closely alongside her master. Sheba raised her eyes and whined as she peered into his face. Her trot fell in place with his intense pace.

Moriah noticed Tyro's eyes were now deep blue instead of their normal steel-gray. His distant gaze and lack of response confirmed he had disconnected from the world around him. He was barely aware of her presence.

She'd seen this behavior many times in her father who had suffered with depression. She was told that his episodes became less frequent after she and her twin sister, Anaya were born. But right after her sister had passed, the despondency in her father began to raise its ugly head again. She remembered the times they'd be in the midst of a vibrant conversation and within a matter of moments, he'd become detached, distant, and withdrawn.

She recognized the same behavior in Tyro. *Why haven't I see this before now?* But she had. That first night as he held her in his arms after he had saved her. She'd seen the sadness peeking from behind his eyes.

As he walked on, she nudged his shoulder with her hand as he slipped further into a distant gaze. "You okay?" she asked.

"I'm fine." His eyes narrowed and swept over hers before shifting away. Her heart beat faster as he kept her pressed against his chest. As if something grabbed his attention, he suddenly loosened his grip, perhaps just noticing he'd been holding her so tightly. "We're practically there," he said in a more amicable, but solemn tone. His hint of a smile was forced.

"You miss her, don't you?" she asked softly as she brushed a few strands from his eyes. She caressed his face with the back of her hand. "I know," she began gently, "you lost your mother to a tragic death."

Tyro stopped abruptly and stared at her. She shivered from the cold daggers that pierced through her. He pulled his gaze away. *Bingo.* She had identified the reason for his sudden despondency. She twisted her lips as her mind raced. She'd been down this road many times with her own father. Was she up for the challenge of delving into a relationship certain to be unstable? Rocky?

"I heard one of the reporters offer Quincy her condolences."

"What do reporters care?" Tyro retorted.

"Why didn't you tell me?" her voice trailed in uncertainty. After all, she hadn't been fully honest with him about her own pain. The way he had studied her as they talked at Mario's, she suspected he saw her brokenness and that she was holding back as well.

He began walking without answering her. His face fell, more solemn as the familiar gloom gained more leverage. Grief had swooped in and secured its claim on his soul, his emotions.

An unsettledness of being alone with him nipped at her nerves. She sighed as she chastised herself. After all, he'd saved her from being in a fatal car crash. His act of bravery had earned him a special place in her heart. Why would he want to harm her now? Was she just being paranoid?

She determined that Tyro wasn't at all like his father. Nor was he disoriented like her former pilot had been. Up until now, Tyro had been kind and compassionate, and gentle, not to mention that he was *so* debonair.

He made a sudden right turn as he carried her toward a flagstone pathway. As promised, she could see his house in the distance. It was much grander than seeing it from the air. Translucent blue lights continued to pave the way. Bird of paradise, exotic flowers, and a mixture of colorful ornamental grasses seemed to sway in greeting as they passed by.

The calming fragrances quieted Moriah's uneasiness. She relaxed. Burying her head into his neck, she inhaled the fragrance lingering on his collar. It reminded her of the night they'd first met. She cuddled without a care in his arms.

He carried her up the two large steps that led to a door on the side of his home. She instantly felt the sensation of warmth and coziness as flames danced in the fireplace. She cooed as the sweet aromatic bubbles foaming in the Jacuzzi teased at her nose. The lingering tension she felt oozed completely from her.

She was delighted that the remaining storm clouds had finally drifted out to sea. The ambiance was perfect and promised a relaxing and enjoyable evening.

Chapter 4

Weariness had completely drained Tyro by the time he'd set her down on the retaining wall. She dangled her feet over the edge as her circulation slowly returned. Just as she poised herself to stand, he reached and flipped off the outside switch on the wall above her.

Instantly, the fireplace died. The bubbles in the hot tub ceased churning, and a sudden stream of bright lights burned her eyes. It was as if a giant pin had burst her bubble. She shivered as disappointment quivered down her spine. Her mood quickly deflated. Only the residue of cedar and jasmine lingered in the air.

He reached for the door handle. "You can stay in my house with me," he paused, "or you can stay at the beach house. One of my staff will escort you to your suite." His tone was aloof.

She could see the inner turmoil churning as his eyes drifted to the ground. "Hey, what's come over you?" she asked, reaching out to touch his arm. He kept one hand on the handle. He swerved as he jammed the other in his front pocket, moving himself from her reach. His back remained toward her. His shoulders slumped while he waited for her answer.

"Which is it?" he turned slightly as he glared at her. "The choice is yours." She shuddered at his indifference.

Maybe he is ruthless like his dad. But as she watched him, his glumness reminded her of her own father's behavior whenever depression took over him.

"It's late, Moriah. I need to sleep," he said when she still hadn't responded. He spun around. "What do you want to do?"

"I don't mean to be a bother or an inconvenience."

"I brought you here, didn't I?"

She stammered at the dark haze in his eyes. "And what's that supposed to mean?" If she hadn't been there, she wouldn't have believed he was the same guy who had just flown her across the Delaware River, along the Chesapeake Bay. In their haste to get away from the media, and the mob of fantasy-crazed people, he had whisked her away in his private helicopter. He'd shown her the most spectacular views. He'd constantly leaned back from his pilot seat to make sure she was comfortable and enjoying the flight.

Now she found herself on the doorstep of a man whose coldness toward her gave her second thoughts about being there with him. She wondered where the thoughtful and attentive man was she'd been with less than an hour ago. *Where did that kind and considerate man go?* She sighed as she mused within herself.

His demeanor had completely transformed. His stare was cold and he had turned aloof toward her just as quickly as more storm clouds barreled across the darkening skies.

Lord, please give him peace and rest in his soul, she prayed silently. A heavy sigh escaped her.

Despite her unrest, she knew that being there with Tyro was totally different than when she had been around Fletcher. It had been the latter part of last year when Fletcher had been hired as a helicopter pilot at TSMA.

She had just become the Executive Director of Marketing. Within a few months of his employment, he'd become her personal pilot. Shortly afterwards, his behavior became strange and he'd become inexplicably possessive of her.

When she told her employers that she felt uneasy being alone with him, they accused her of inciting his behavior. They told her they had pictures to prove it. *What pictures?* she had wondered.

She'd known of the one photo. It was the only time she had allowed him to kiss her but stopped it immediately when he put his hand where it didn't belong. It happened while their helicopter hovered in midair. He had eased himself into the back seat and sat beside her. Within a flash of a moment, he'd taken a quick selfie of them while kissing her—just as he *touched*.

Only as she stood before the judge in her custody battle over her niece, Amelia, who was also her bosses' only grandchild, did she learn of the video camera. It had been secretly installed inside the cabin of the helicopter she often used. Unbeknown to her, they'd also hired a P.I. All of it was a setup and played well in their custody battle.

Their insidious allegations that she'd broken the "no fraternizing between company employees" policy leaned in their favor. They painted a picture of incompetence, citing her inability to balance her personal and work life while being a full time parent. The photo had misconstrued her character. She had not been *making out* with the subordinate employee. Still, the allegations that she had been carrying on with inappropriate conduct sealed her fate.

The Smythes had won. Amelia had been immediately removed from her custody and placed with them. She was ashamed of the picture they'd painted of her. She didn't know what she'd do if her best friend, Nettie, wasn't there to help her through it. Nettie always gave her the support she needed and Moriah was determined to get the situation turned around in her favor.

Moriah was devastated over the loss. She couldn't focus on her work and her clients' accounts soon were in complete disarray. Surprisingly, it was Fletcher who had snapped her out of it. There was something different, odd about how he rallied in her corner. Still, what he'd said made sense.

She'd learned of their plans to dismiss her. Fletcher encouraged her to become a force for them to reckon with. She strengthened her rapport with her contacts, worked hard to regain the trust and confidence of the clients she had previously neglected. And it was only a matter of time before she'd landed the most lucrative marketing contract ever.

Not only in her career but it was the largest contract the agency had ever had, as well. The company's first million-dollar commission, an astonishing $1.5 million to be exact, had come about because of her hard work and savvy business skills.

Fletcher had been acting strangely again. His rationale was bizarre and he was extremely paranoid, and hostile. She'd determined after the last time that he'd never fly her again.

She was stunned that the company had sent him to fly her home given their history. She had just spent a long three days negotiating with a new client in the Keys. She was exhausted and desperate to get home. Taking a long hot bath and sleeping for a few days was foremost on her mind. The full moon had nestled in and out of the clouds as it scampered across the daunting sky. The summer evening was hot and muggy. The flight back to Delaware from the Keys had been rocky.

The helicopter sputtered at various times and the AC hadn't been cooling fast enough for Moriah. Without thinking anything of it, she unbuttoned a few buttons at the top of her blouse. Just as fast as she could wipe the sweat away, it continued to roll down her chest as if she were in a sauna.

She had leaned forward toward the cockpit to ask Fletcher what the deal was with the air. "What...?" she remembered stating as his eyes gawked at her chest. "You never seen boobs before?" she had said jokingly as he continued to stare. Thinking back, she should have held her blouse closed before she had leaned. She'd never forget the ominous look in his eyes.

"We can't stand here all night." The curtness of Tyro's tone jolted her from her thoughts. Her attention met his cold gaze. She froze. He shifted his eyes away from her pensive expression.

Did she make the right decision to not go to the beach house and to insist he take her home in the morning? She considered his demeanor. He was in no condition to fly her home. She thought of her dad.

From her experience with her dad's bouts with depression, she considered the facts: Tyro could be in this dark state of mind for days, and it was unfathomable for her to even think that Quincy would consider taking her home. Period. Not that she would want to be flown across the peninsula with that tyrant in the first place. Moriah felt a sudden chill course through her veins. *Lord, what have I gotten myself into?*

Chapter 5

Moriah fought the temptation to cave in to fear as she stared into the face of uncertainty. She studied Tyro's demeanor, noting his shoulders remained slumped. She was familiar with the faraway look in his eyes and felt assured she wasn't in any real danger by being there with him. Even during the times her father had refused to take his medication, he had never once become violent.

She considered her situation further. She knew Tyro's melancholy was due to his grief. He'd lost his mother. It was not the same as Fletcher—who had been delusional, and manic. Even though she'd realized the difference, her mind fought back the horrors of when Fletcher had attacked her.

The memories of that evening and the days that had followed were still raw in her mind.

Moriah's eyes fought back the tears. She heard Tyro's voice piercing through her thoughts once again, bringing her back to the now. She hadn't realized her mind had trailed down the rabbit hole twisting and weaving through her dark memories. She shook the haunting thoughts away as tears stung her eyes. She peered over at Tyro.

Her emotions were all over the place. Yet, an unexplainable, overwhelming feeling of compassion overrode her emotions. She looked at Tyro, her new friend. Somehow being there with him was where she was supposed to be. Although she trembled with uneasiness, she knew he needed her just as much as she needed him.

She stood unsure of what to do. His hands remained drooped at his sides, his gaze distant. His grief resonated deeply within her. Sheba licked his hand a few times as she sat beside him. He remained unresponsive, even toward his Shepherd.

Shoving her own horrible memories aside, Moriah reached for his hand again. "He's going to be just fine," she said to Sheba as she rubbed behind her ear. Both of them kept their attention fixed on Tyro.

She folded her palm over his and placed her other hand on Tyro's shoulder. "Hey, everything's going to be all right," she said, touching him lightly to console him. He was hurting. Perhaps helping him through his pain would help her to heal from her own.

Without releasing her hand, he turned slowly and opened the door. He stepped over the threshold. Turning to look at her, their gaze held. Sheba, anxious to get to her food bowl, squeezed herself between them to get inside. Sniffing the air, she trotted toward the back of the house.

The moment the door closed, he fell into Moriah's arms. He couldn't stop his chest from heaving as his turmoil raged inside of him. "It's okay... let it out," she consoled as she held him tightly. By the grace of God, she was able to stoop along with him as his body slumped to the floor. She held on to him as if she were his parachute. His lifeline.

His head lay still in her lap as she stroked his hair. His shoulders began to relax. The light shining from the perfectly round sphere brightened the foyer only for a moment as it waltzed across the sky. She brushed gently down his arm. Sweetly, she hummed a timeless melody as she felt the slow rise and fall of his chest, watching the tension ease from him. A comforting sleep took its place.

The moon spilled its light again through the nearby floor-to-ceiling windows and kissed the wetness on his face, the evidence of his tears. Its illumination quickly sashayed behind the blanket of gray, sending the foyer into darkness again. Moriah wondered if this was a sign… an indication of how their relationship would be if it were to go anywhere: in and out… on and off.

It was a chance she was willing to take, at least to give it a try. She knew there'd be no turning back. It was the unspoken commitment she made the moment she took his hand and followed him willingly over the threshold.

Chapter 6

Tyro awakened several hours later. His back, neck, and shoulders were stiff although his head rested on something soft. Shifting himself upward, he peered into the face of Moriah. Her head lay crookedly to the side against the door. Her mouth was slightly open. He chuckled at her cute whimpers and gurgling sounds as she slept.

Without warning, a sudden rush of fear seized his mind as his recent melancholic episode crashed through his mind.

She knows.

He couldn't remember all of the details, but he knew that he'd acted indifferently toward his guest. And yes, for a while there, he wanted nothing more than for her to leave him alone, so he could wallow in his sorrow. But she hadn't.

He studied her longingly as she remained asleep. *Who are you?* She hadn't run off and locked herself in a room. She stayed right there, comforting him through his darkness. He remembered her stroking his hair. His heart softened as the sweet melody she had hummed played in his mind. It was a tune he remembered his mother singing to him when he was a boy. "Jesus Loves Me."

Since his mother died, his relationship with his father had been strained. And any course of relations with God had been far removed from his mind. Of course he blamed God. But for the first time since he'd given up believing God cared, he'd felt a peace rising within him. He was pleased that he had drifted into the sweetest sleep he'd had in months. More so, he was relieved to know that such a sleep still existed.

Without his parents, he felt lost. Without God, his hope was all bound up and he felt forsaken. No matter how hard he'd fight it, he couldn't find a way to stay out of his darkness. He shifted his weight in order to lift Moriah, careful not to awaken her as he carried her to the upstairs quarters.

After Tyro laid Moriah gently on the guest room bed, he stepped into the adjoining room and made a call. Twenty minutes later, a quiet knock on the door caused him to place a gentle kiss on the cheek of the woman he'd returned to watch over. The room she was sleeping in was a room he had prepared for his mother. He had built it with her in mind for whenever she would have wanted to stay over. It was a "whenever" that never came.

As Tyro patiently waited in the next room while his female staff took care of Moriah, he felt the familiar dolor pecking at his heart. He missed his mother. He thought back to the conversation he'd had with her as he was building his house over a year ago.

"You'll need to design the "Queen's" room, you know," he'd told his mother as they stepped over the slab into the open framed area.

"There will be no such thing," she had said. "Why do I need a room? Have you forgotten in that smart head of yours I'm only a stone's throw across the garden?" she said, pointing towards the direction of the three-story colonial as she patted him lovingly on the cheek.

"What you need to do is find a beautiful woman, marry her and give me some grandbabies... I say that's what you should do with these two rooms." She stepped onto the backer boards freshly lain in the bathroom that awaited the slab of black marble that would soon cover it.

Laino looked around. The plumbing had been roughed in. She squinted her eyes up at her son. "And what is this?" She pointed to where the elongated soaker tub would go.

"Aw, Mother, you know how you love your baths." He hugged her shoulders.

"And this?" she pointed to the framed exact replica of an adjacent room.

"Now you know if I build a room for you, Dad's going to want his own room too. You can share the adjoining bathroom." He grinned, knowing she was pleased, despite the fact that she would protest. She had loved the thought of rocking her grandchildren to sleep.

"Listen to me, papito," she lovingly held his face in her hands. "You give me some grandbabies and I'll stay over to take care of them anytime you want." She wagged his face, slightly squeezing both cheeks. She smiled widely. "Until then, don't expect me or your dad to stay overnight." She kissed his cheek and exited out of the 900-square-foot framed room.

Just as she stepped over the threshold she stopped, turned and faced her son. "I'm sorry it didn't work out between you and Glorieta," she smiled humbly. "Be patient, my son. Love will come. You just wait and see. Love will come soon."

Tyro's heart felt heavy. He thought about the sapphire necklace his mother had given him on the morning after he had announced his proposal to Glorieta LeVogue. He was to have placed it around her neck on their wedding night. She would then pass the necklace on to her firstborn son once he got engaged, keeping the tradition alive.

Mario, being the firstborn son, had inherited it when their parents died. He'd never married and had given the necklace to Laino when Tyro was born.

Remorse gripped him. Because of his mindless act, the necklace was gone. Right after his mother's burial, he'd tossed it into the ocean.

When Tyro heard the bedroom door to where Moriah was sleeping close, he was soothed. His staff had taken care of her without

130

waking her. He could hear the gentle wisps of her breathing through the bathroom door which was slightly ajar.

Again he'd found solace in the mysterious woman who had given him a glimmer of hope. Unlike the night they first met, she hadn't run away. The heaviness that had threatened to swallow him lifted as Moriah's beautiful face danced in his memory. His head sank into the fluffy pillows in the bed he'd prepared long ago for his dad. His eyes closed as he drifted into a peaceful sleep.

Chapter 7

Moriah awakened with sunny rays tickling her cheeks. A warm smile crossed her face. She lifted her arms above her head and stretched like a kitten waking from a nap.

As pieces of last night floated into her remembrance, her eyes flung open. She bolted upright in bed. Jerking her head around, she felt better as she saw that the other side was empty and hadn't been disturbed. *Whew!* They hadn't slept in the same bed. She let out the breath she'd been holding.

Or had they? She wasn't worried whether any physical activities had happened; for some reason, she trusted him. She mainly was curious where he'd slept. She thought of the despair that had overtaken him last night.

Someone shuffled behind a closed door off to her right. She jumped. A shower suddenly came on. There was whistling. If that was Tyro in the bathroom, he definitely sounded better. She sighed, relieved.

She gazed around, taking in her surroundings. In her many travels, Moriah had stayed in plenty of extraordinary hotels, but this room was the most exquisite of them all. The satin royal blues, fuchsias, oranges, and various shades of green were trimmed with braided bronze. Surprisingly, it all blended in well. The various textures and patterns complemented each other. The grandness of the room was fit for a queen. As her eyes lingered over each of the exotic furnishings, she became even more eager to see the rest of the house.

She pulled herself out of bed and couldn't remember all of the details of getting there, not exactly. She sighed contentedly to find she was fully dressed. The two-piece silk loungewear fit her well. It was then she remembered the two ladies helping her get into them. It showed more curves than she would have liked, but most of all she adored the fluffy slippers that sat by the bed.

She slid her feet into them. Immediately, she closed her eyes and cooed. *These are the most comfortable slippers I—*

A knock at the door startled her. Who could be knocking at her door? Should she answer it, let whomever it was in? If Tyro was in the shower—which she'd assumed, then she didn't want whoever it was at the door to think she'd slept with him. She was not that kind of girl.

The third knock caused her stomach to jitter. This time, it was louder. Were they annoyed? Probably. She should have answered it before now. Surely they had gotten the hint that someone didn't want to be bothered or either it was that they were not used to waiting. "Oh God, I hope it's not…"

Moriah stood there contemplating whether she should jump back in the bed, pretend she was still asleep. But then Tyro dashed from the bathroom and headed toward the door. He was wearing only a towel around his waist. Moriah gasped. Her eyes widened as he opened the door.

"Perfect timing," he said as he hustled back into the bathroom. He stuck his head back out. "I see you're awake. I hope you're hungry."

"I… I…" Moriah couldn't get her words out before he disappeared back to where he'd come from.

A tall, dark-skinned man, casually dressed, waltzed in carrying a tray of covered food. "I figured you'd like breakfast on the terrace," he said as he set the tray on a table by the window. As he opened the French doors, he swiveled to pick up the tray. His eyes caught a glance of Moriah looking bug-eyed as she stood there clutching the top of her fully buttoned-up loungewear. Her curly, reddish-brown hair was matted against her head on one side and splayed wildly on the other.

As he caught another glimpse, he turned and shook his head. Moriah could see the grin he tried to suppress before he burst into a hearty guffaw. His attempt to apologize for his rudeness was muffled as he tried to contain himself. After he'd left, Moriah marched over to the floor to ceiling mirror leaning against the wall and took a good look at herself.

What did he say? *Buckwheat*? Moriah knew exactly what he meant. If there was anybody who was an old movie and TV show buff, she was surely staring right at her. At first she was appalled by his comment. But she had to give it to him as she took another look at herself. Her bedhead did resemble the "little rascal!"

"Did I miss a joke?" Tyro asked, bounding out of the bathroom fully dressed.

"Buck...wheat..." was all she could get out as she heaved for air in between her laughing. The more she looked in the mirror, the harder she laughed.

Tyro chuckled more so at watching her bowing over in stitches. She'd point at the mirror and laugh hysterically each time she looked. Tyro honestly didn't get it. He'd Google *Buckwheat* later to refresh his memory. Or, he'd ask Roy. There was no doubt he'd been the one that had instigated the matter.

Chapter 8

Moriah felt refreshed after she had showered and washed her hair. She used coconut oil to smooth her hair up into a tight, high ponytail. It would flair out into a curly-pouf style as it dried.

She had enough make-up in her purse to highlight her features. She dusted a small amount of bronzer to accentuate her cheekbones. Leaning back, she took a good look at herself in the vanity mirror. Being pleased with her natural look, she lightly misted herself with a sweet-musk spritzer she also carried in her purse.

As Tyro and Moriah ate breakfast on the balcony, she took in the scenery overlooking the garden. It was gorgeous and serene beyond words. The intricately designed bistro was just enough for an intimate conversation.

After she'd met some of the staff earlier, she was able to relax and enjoy herself. But just as she was beginning to really feel comfortable, she'd *accidentally* run into Quincy. Literally. Tyro had been on the phone and she wanted to take a quick look at a sculptured bush that sat just below the terrace. Big mistake! She wasn't paying attention to where she was walking and bumped right into him.

She noticed a great sadness in his eyes. He'd grunted and cursed after seeing that she was still there. She felt pity for him—well, a little. Although it took a while for her to calm herself down, she wasn't going to let him ruin her day.

"Moriah!" Tyro called her several times to get her attention. "Your episode... what was that all about?"

"What, you never heard of Buckwheat?" Moriah asked as she squinted her eyes at him.

"Sure I have. Billie Thomas, known as Buckwheat—"

"Oh no you don't." She pointed her fork charmingly at him. "Don't give me the version you probably just looked up on the Internet."

"And don't try to act like you don't know what I'm talking about," he said in a tone sharper than he had intended. Relaxing his voice, he repeated himself. "When I told you that I wouldn't be taking you home last night, you came unraveled." Tyro put his fork down and waited for her to respond.

"Oh. That," she said plainly as she used her fork to dab a piece of waffle into the freshly made strawberry syrup. She plopped it in her mouth and closed her eyes as she pointed her fork at her plate. "This is so good," she said after taking her time, savoring every chew.

He had leaned back in his seat and stared as he waited. His eyes remained locked on her. When he realized she was avoiding looking at him, he reached out and touched her hand. "Moriah, is there something you need to tell me?" When she didn't respond, he lifted her chin with his finger until their eyes met.

He waited as he searched her face. She shifted her eyes to her plate. "I like you, Moriah Styles...." His charm lit the air as she breathed easier. He continued. "I like you a lot. You're smart. You're funny, and very sexy." He narrowed his eyes in a playfully seductive manner. "And, I want to know you. The real you that's hiding inside your invisible cage."

He searched her deeply. Her eyes found his and held them captive. "I want you to know something." He paused. "Honesty is very important to me. Being able to trust the people I let into my world is important. Very important." He leaned back without taking his eyes from her gaze. "Once that trust is broken, it's gone and there's no coming back."

Moriah's fork slipped from her hand and clattered on her plate. She lifted her shoulders and gave him her signature glance. "That's it? If somebody does anything to hurt you, you're done?"

"No. That's not what I said." He steepled two fingers under his chin but immediately dropped them as she narrowed her eyes in disbelief. He leaned forward in his chair. "Not telling the whole truth by withholding information is the same as lying. I don't trust—"

"Trust takes time," Moriah said without stammering. *No he's not about to call me a liar.* "I don't know you. You don't know me. So, what are you getting at?" Her eyes absorbed his no nonsense demeanor.

"You panicked last night. Why?" He studied her as she shifted several times in her seat. He softened his tone. "Something horrendous happened in your past." His gaze held hers as he waited for her to respond. "What was it, Moriah?"

What does he expect of me…? What does he want me to say? Does he think this is a Kodak moment? Am I to spill my life out all over the table and he gets to sift through it, and determine… what, that I'm damaged goods?

This time, she purposely clanked her fork on her plate. "I just felt a little overwhelmed, that's all." She shrugged and excused herself from the table.

Chapter 9

Moriah walked over to the glass railing. Anxiety nibbled at her soul. Wrapping her arms around her shoulders, she breathed in the sweet mixture of fragrances permeating from the garden below. Despite what Tyro wanted, there was no need to talk about it. She needed to leave her past behind her and that's exactly what she intended to do.

She focused her attention on the panoramic view and took in the pleasantries of the lush greenery and various flowers on the island. Her eyes trailed over the numerous paths intertwining throughout the garden. She was delighted that some of them led to walking paths, or bike trails around the outskirts of the peninsula.

The sun beaming over the ocean captured a picturesque view of birds frolicking in the wind. She could have basked in its tranquilities forever. It took her breath away. It reminded her of a mural she'd loved at the institution where her parents had once lived. Her mother's sister, Rachel, had raised Moriah and her twin because of their parents' mental challenges. Her parents lived close enough for them to visit often.

A feeling of warmth enveloped her as she thought about the enormous painting on the wall at the end of the long hallway. She smiled as she remembered the numerous times her aunt had had to pull her away. She could have stood there all day lured into its majestic pull.

Tyro's tender touch upon her shoulders returned her attention back to the present. She trailed her fingers along the rail as she gracefully moved away from his intrusion. Her thoughts were her own. She stared into the distance as she considered her dilemma.

Her family was something she wasn't ready to discuss. How could she tell him about them? What was she to say about her parents' mental challenges…her deceased sister… or Amelia? How was she supposed to get around the questions that would follow? His expectations of her were too much. She was not who he thought she was. Things between them were moving too fast.

And then there was that nagging question—the one he'd been so adamant about. It weighed heavier on her than she had realized. Of course she knew why she'd panicked. She just wasn't ready to discuss it with him. She couldn't.

Moriah knew there was no comparison in being there with Tyro and with Fletcher. But the things that happened to her the last time she had been swept away in a helicopter were terrifying, too unbearable to think about. And although she lived with the torment of it every day, somehow she managed to keep it buried beneath her busy life.

She closed her eyes and breathed deeply, wishing the reality of her past would go away. All of it. Forever. She assured herself again. No way could she tell him what had happened to her. Not just yet—if ever.

The sound of a helicopter off in the distance caused a wave of anxiety to rush over her. Immersed in the murkiness of her deepest fear, she felt herself drowning in her sea of shame. The mere thought if anyone were to find out… She hadn't even told the investigators all of it. What would Tyro think of her? She could never tell him what she had to do to survive. He wouldn't understand.

Suddenly, relentless undercurrents sucked her into a world of unforgettable memories. She was held captive by the things she wanted to forget. Her fingers rose to her neck. She rubbed along the indentations where powerful hands once squeezed the breath out of her.

Her breath now caught in her throat as she remembered. Her chest tightened. Her lips pursed as the taste of seawater vividly rose to her mind. She groped for the railing. She struggled to ward off the memories thrashing inside her like a whirlwind. Unable to stop her soul from raging, the storm unleashed.

She remembered the night. It had been dreary. She felt the doom lingering from behind scattering clouds. Fletcher had taken her to a deserted island against her will. Just before landing, he attempted to drug her while they hovered in midair. Her body went limp.

When he thought she was unconscious, he hurried to lower the helicopter to land. Before he had touched down, she jumped out. She'd escaped, but only for a moment, and for that, she knew she would pay.

Fletcher's eyes were dark and empty, void of any human compassion when he caught up with her. Unmercifully, he'd dragged her by the hair across the deserted island. Fists full of sand slipped through her fingers as her nails dug into the tiny granules. The fragile stubbles and briars sticking out of the sand snapped in her desperate grasps, leaving her nothing to hold on to.

A crippling pain shot up her leg as he dragged her over a sharp rock. She choked at the smell of her own blood as her flesh ripped from her thigh. "God, please... help me," she cried as she slipped hopelessly into darkness.

A sharp, clanking sound caused Moriah's mind to snap out of her deep thoughts. Someone had dragged a metal chair across the patio below her. She gripped her head as the memories of her past lingered.

"What is it, Moriah?" Tyro's voice calmed her as he glided her into his arms. She felt cold chills piercing through her, although the weather had been pleasant all morning. She tried to shake it off, but it had not come easy for her this time. Her fear swallowed up her reasoning. This time, her present state of being couldn't outweigh the reality of her past.

140

His comforting arms continued to hold her as he assured her everything would be okay. But it wouldn't. She knew this wasn't the end of it. She would be tortured by her past, as she had many times before. When it would come she had no control. At the sound of waves crashing on the shore... the smell of the ocean... the taste of salt, the warmth of a sunny day... anything, at any time could trigger it.

He removed her hands from her head. "You're trembling." He pulled her tighter into his embrace. He assured her she wasn't alone. "I don't know what happened to you," he lifted her chin, forcing her to face him, "but you're safe here with me." He soothed her with tender care as he gently caressed her tears away.

Although she knew that was a tall order that only God could keep, she needed the tangible assurance of feeling safe. She hadn't been able to fight the emotional attack this time on her own. She allowed him to rock her delicately.

Her shoulders began to relax. She pulled from his embrace. Her fingers sprang up, but she quickly restrained from twirling her hair again. "I'm not feeling well. I need to lie down for a little while." She forced a smile. Her hands were still quivering.

"Okay, but don't be gone for too long. I don't want you to miss the tour over the peninsula that I've planned for you." Tyro paused as her sudden smile reflected his. "The helicopter is fueled and ready to go." There was something about the way he caressed her cheek that assured her. She breathed deeply. She had nothing to fear. She felt relieved as the remaining anxiety fluttered away.

Her eyes brightened and she nodded. "I'd like that very much." Her smile widened. Turning to take another glimpse of the mountains, her joyful expression dissipated as Quincy stepped out into her full view.

Chapter 10

"Tour?" Quincy snarled. He grunted as he raised his drink to his lips. He squinted his eyes, and they burned right through her, sending a sudden chill in the air.

The way Quincy stared up at her, she knew he had been standing beneath their balcony for a while. He lifted his cup in a sneering toast toward her.

Tyro stepped forward and saw his father glowering at Moriah. "Go rest now," he said as he placed a tender kiss on her forehead. He kept his gaze on Quincy, watching the manner in which he sipped from his mug. No doubt it had been full of coffee laced with liqueur.

He had the audacity to spy on them. How else would he have known about his plans for the day?

"I hope you heard whatever it was that you were listening for." Tyro's words flung over the railing like a poisonous dagger. Charged as his words were, they had fallen onto a man of staunch indifference. He didn't even flinch.

Quincy kept his stare trained on Moriah as he sipped from his coffee mug. He pointed it directly at her as he spoke to his son. "Oh, by the way," he retorted ominously, "you are mistaken, son. There will be no helicopters flying off of this island, today.

"Necessary maintenance," he smirked. "Whatever you want to call it—or do with *her*—suit yourself." His upper lip curled. "Guess I will have to put up with her another day." He drained his mug. After slamming it on a mahogany bench, he trailed off down the path through the garden that led to his home.

"You don't have to be so mean!" she yelled, unable to resist the urge.

She sauntered back into the guest room where she was staying. She turned to face Tyro as he followed behind her. "I think I will stay another day, that's if the invitation is still open?"

She folded her arms over her chest as she stared out the double doors and over the balcony. There was no sign of Quincy. "I like seeing him all riled up," she said as she watched Tyro's brows rise in curiosity.

He was amused at her look of determination. How quickly she was able to bounce back from whatever had caused her anguish just a few moments ago. He didn't know whether he should be concerned or pleased that she could shake it off so quickly.

And the way she handled his dad's disapproval of her intrigued him. He felt perplexed as he headed toward the door leading to the hallway. "I won't be too long," she promised. "I just need to close my eyes for a few."

As he walked through the door, she resisted the urge to latch onto him to stay a little while longer. She needed him. She longed to feel his assurance wrapped around her in a tender embrace. He hesitated before opening the door to let himself out. "Are you sure you're okay?" He waited for her to respond.

Her voice caught in her throat as she opened her mouth to speak. She nodded instead. Her lips quivered as she forced a tight smile. She felt like melting as his eyes smiled back at her. She broke their eye contact as her eyes shifted to the floor.

Her body quivered as he gently closed the door behind him. Although she'd put up a good front before him and his dad, her nerves were all jumbled up inside.

The way Quincy looked at her made her feel uneasy. But there was no way she'd tell Tyro that or let Quincy see he had gotten the best of her. She'd meet the tyrant head on if she had to and deal with the aftermath of it later.

Chapter 11

Tyro charged down the back stairs. He would not tolerate Quincy's despicable behavior any longer. His dad must have lost his mind to treat his guest like that. Regardless of what he'd promised his mother, he was going to put a stop to it. Right now.

As he bounded down the spiraling stairwell, his mother's last words seized his mind. His pace slowed as he reached the bottom stair. He sat on the last step. *What did she mean 'take care of him?'* *Why?*

He could hear his father's voice escalating through the kitchen. He leapt to his feet. A sudden burst of voices exploded louder as he stepped into the room. He was surprised to see Quincy trampling behind Roy out of the butler's pantry. His dad's hands whirling in the air like crazy as he spit and spat about something *preposterous*. The feud ended abruptly as soon as they saw Tyro heading toward them.

"What's going on?" Tyro demanded as he looked back and forth between his dad and Roy. Roy shook his head and removed a covered dish from the refrigerator. He headed back toward the butler's pantry, turning as he narrowed his eyes at Quincy and then at Tyro. "The way you two be carryin' on...." He shook his head in disbelief. "It ain't none of—"

"That is exactly right!" Quincy retorted. "Since 'it *ain't* none of your business,' you stay out of what goes on between me and my son!"

"Whoa, whoa—Dad!" Tyro moved quickly as he stepped in between the two of them. "You got to stop this!" He lunged into

Quincy's space. "What's going on with you? Why're you talking to him like that?" He walked over to his chef and confidant and placed his hand gently on his shoulder. "Sorry, man." Tyro tugged his shoulder in a kind gesture before letting his hand fall away.

Roy hunched his shoulders before disappearing through the double doors and continued on with his chores.

Tyro spun around and faced Quincy. "Mom would have never tolerated you——"

"You think you know that girl?" Quincy brows furrowed.

"What?" Tyro's face puzzled.

Quincy glared at his son before he marched toward the back entrance. He whirled around, his face contorted in an awkward twist. "I thought I knew your mother." His eyes shot fire. "I gave your mother everything. I trusted her. I knew she was having an affair." He reached for the door. "I am no fool. You better think twice about whom you trust. Quincy narrowed his eyes. "And you have the audacity to bring *her* here?" His jaw clenched as he spat every syllable.

"An affair? What are you talking about? Mom wasn't seeing anybody and you know it. And if she were, though you and I both know she was not, what does she," he jabbed his finger toward the stairway, "have to do with Mom?"

Quincy snatched the door open. He jutted his chin upward. "As soon as this fairy tale crap blows over, I don't ever want to see her on my property again." He stormed out.

After his run-in with his dad, Tyro took a brisk walk. He never got to say what he wanted... needed to say. Quincy was out of control. But now his dad had thrown a monkey wrench in the midst of everything. *What did he mean by thinking twice about whom I trust? What does he know that I don't?* Although he wanted to deny it, his gut told him his father knew something about Moriah. Even he had his own suspicion of her.

He trekked up the steep incline and followed along the wavy yellow path that led to where his mother was laid to rest. Thinking back, he should have just let his father keep walking as he stormed out the door. But there was no way he was going to let his ridiculous accusations about his mother go unchallenged.

Tyro reached the top of the hill. He stood for a long time outside of the tall, elegant mausoleum. After all this time, why did Quincy decide now to bring up these insinuations that his mother had been having... *an affair*?

His mother would have never cheated on his dad. Would she? Why was his dad so adamant that she had? Could it be true?

He sighed as his mind whirled with a billion thoughts. *What did he mean for me to ask Roy? Ask Roy what? What would he know that he hasn't told me, he wouldn't have kept anything about Mom from me, would he? Does he know something about who killed her? And Moriah—what does she have to do with any of it?*

None of it made any sense to him.

Chapter 12

It had been an hour since Tyro had challenged his dad to come out with it. Whatever had been eating at his father needed to be dealt with right then, right there. But Tyro would have never been prepared for the words that flew out of Quincy's mouth. Still shaken to the core, regret at what he had just heard writhed relentlessly up his spine.

On the day his mother died, Quincy had argued with her before he'd stormed out of the house that morning. He'd had the nerve to say such horrible things to his mother, threatening to leave her if she didn't tell him the truth about her love affair. What affair?

He ran his fingers through his hair. His other hand trembled as he pressed on the door handle. The exquisitely carved door opened slowly. Instantly, he dimmed the automatic lights after he stepped inside where his mother rested. "No way... No way you would have ever cheated on Dad, Mom," Tyro cried out into the empty atmosphere. His effort to assure himself was futile. Still, he reasoned, there had to be a logical explanation.

His mind raced back to the months just before she had died. He slumped down on a cold bench and buried his face in his hands. "No! No!" he sobbed. He remembered now. She had been gone away from the business and home a lot, which was totally unlike her. Laino had always poured her heart and soul into her family and the business, as well as her son.

She had been there for Tyro as his engagement fell apart. And it was she who supported his decision to sell his prosperous law firm to buy a third of the shares of the family's business. She had always been his champion. But still, he couldn't deny the facts staring him right in the face.

Before her death, she would disappear for hours at a time. At the time, he hadn't thought anything of it. He was so buried in his own woes over the break-up with his fiancée that he'd barely noticed. If Quincy hadn't said something earlier today, he would have never thought about it.

"Did you even notice how happy your mother would be when she returned from wherever she had been?" Thinking of Quincy's words rushed over him like a fifty-foot tidal wave. Tyro leapt up, his mind was in a terrible flux. His hands flailed, expressing his anguish as his thoughts tumbled into place.

He remembered clearly now. He sat lifelessly back on the cold surface and faced the white and gold marble sarcophagus. There had to be a logical explanation. "There has to be!" He yelled into the darkness as he bolted off of the stone bench again. The lights popped back on after going out from the absence of any movement. He flicked the switch off and plopped back down and clasped his hands together. He waited as if an answer would surely come.

As Tyro headed back down the path, a feeling of heaviness weighed on him for his father. His dad wasn't just drowning in a sea of loneliness and grief, but of regret. Tyro recognized that now. He couldn't imagine what he'd feel like if his last memory with his mom had been an argument.

Quincy never got the chance to tell his wife he was sorry for his irrational and jealous behavior. It was later that evening that he'd found her stabbed multiple times and left to die. And now he's living with the stench of it all every day of his life.

He sighed. His mind raced back to his recent encounter with his dad before he'd climbed up the hill. Quincy had swung wildly at him, cursing profusely for him to leave him alone before stumbling away. He could still see the anguish in his face. The memory of it tugged at his heart. Suddenly, his mother's dying request jolted him.

Tyro then knew what he needed to do. He would get to the bottom of his father's absurd accusations that his mother was having an affair.

Chapter 13

Moriah's mind churned from one thought to another, as she lay curled up on the bed. She fought to block out the negative thoughts of her past and forced her recent encounter with Quincy out of her mind. In doing so, she hadn't realized how fixated she'd become on Mickey, who had been assigned to make her visit in Tyro's home comfortable.

She was pleased with having her to assist her versus the redheaded one. Maybe it was because of Mickey's gentle mannerisms and sincerity as she'd waited on Moriah. She was always pleasant and ensured she had everything she needed, even though she had already left her an abundance of clothes and shoes to wear.

She'd also learned that the garments had come from the free commissary that the *Misses* had set up for the employees to use. "The Misses." Moriah gathered Mickey was referring to Mrs. Simmonds. All the other staff referred to her as "Miss Laino... God rest her soul," whenever they'd spoken of her. She had given the entire staff the freedom to take whatever they needed from the island's store. Moriah was touched by Laino's heart of kindness and generosity.

"What's the use?" Moriah said as she sprang from the bed after tossing and turning for over an hour. She neatly folded the afghan and placed it back over the blanket stand.

Tyro had already assured her during breakfast that she was free to explore the island as much as she liked. She changed into one of the leisure suits that Mickey had hung in the closet specifically for her.

As soon as Moriah stepped outside, she breathed deeply of the salty breeze blowing off of the ocean. This time, it comforted her. She smiled and began walking along a path paved in canary yellow. She purposely avoided the three-story colonial sitting up the hill toward her right, assuming it was Quincy's house.

She also thought about how Mrs. Simmonds had once lived there. She couldn't imagine how she'd tolerated the man's obnoxious demeanor. *No need to drink of his poison,* she thought to herself as she allowed her negative thought to fly away just as quickly as it had come.

The wonderful stories she had heard about his wife caused her to think of her as a kind and elegant lady. Perhaps her stature was that of Lady Eleanor Roosevelt. Her staff seemed to have loved her so much. Everyone spoke very highly of Mrs. Simmonds. She couldn't imagine why she was met with such a horrible tragedy. Tyro wouldn't talk much about it, but she'd learned that she had been murdered at their office complex.

Moriah continued along the yellow path until it led her to a very steep hill. Her eyes followed the path as far as she could see until it spiraled around a large tree. Unable to see around it, she couldn't tell where it led. She wanted to explore it further, but the soreness in her ankle outweighed her curiosity.

Resting on a bench outside a small chapel, she decided she'd tackle the hill another time. She sensed the tug on her heart as she observed the small building. *Pray.* Immediately, she felt the undeniable barrier rising between her and God. But wasn't she the one who had placed it there? She now realized it had been a long time since she'd had an open and honest talk with God.

She studied the gorgeous stained-glass artwork in the top portion of the door. The mother holding her child, who seemed to be sweetly smiling down at her, caused Moriah to smile back. She was amazed how God used the simplest thing to remind her of His love for her. She bowed her head in shame. Even in her mess, He was reaching out to her.

She gazed again at the chapel's door. She wanted to go in; she just couldn't bring herself to do it. How could she?

The shame of what had happened to her caused her to accuse God of forsaking her. She had ignored going to church numerous times. But now, something deeper than her inner turmoil sparked within. Her anticipation ignited. She sensed what she desperately longed for waited for her inside.

Chapter 14

Moriah had barely turned the knob when the door eased open on its own. As she stepped inside, the lights came on. The chapel was quaint and the warm ambiance welcomed her. Reflectively, her hand clutched her chest as its beauty captured her breath. The tall stained-glass windows lining the entire room drew her in. Quietly, she closed the door behind her.

The meticulous handiwork in each of the windows told its own unique story. Yet the biblical story from Genesis to Revelations displayed as each connected to the other. She walked slowly as she admired each rendering and hadn't realized she had wandered to the back of the sanctuary. In deep thought, she sat on one of the pews.

She turned her attention to the window depicting the woman touching the hem of the Savior. *Thy faith has made you whole.* Her lips moved silently as she thought of her own life. A familiar pain pricked at her heart.

She wasn't ready to relinquish… trust Him with her pain. How could she? Her wounds were too deep. The stitches created the barrier she needed to keep her emotions from getting out of control. What would happen if it came undone?

But Moriah knew the burden was too heavy for her. She needed the Lord's help on this one. Overwhelmed with emotion, she cried out into the room full of colorful lights streaming through the windows. "God. Are you there?"

But the truth stared her right in the face. What did He think of her? She had abandoned His care for her and she doubted His love for her. Oh yes, she would pray, and spend her quiet times in personal devotions. And not to diminish any of it, but a lot of it had been superficial…going through the motions as she resisted His call for her to trust Him.

Trust Him? Moriah shifted in her seat.

She thought about the times when she used to feel His presence—before she was damaged. There was no denying it, since the attack, her time with God hadn't been the same. Nothing had been the same. Moriah considered her feelings. What had happened to her left her broken. Ashamed. She had been forsaken.

She looked around at her surroundings. It had been a while since she'd been to church. "Going to church doesn't mean you have a relationship with God," she remembered her parents telling her. Her parents… she missed them so. It'd been several months since she'd been to see them.

With all that had been going on, she couldn't bear to face them to tell them the truth. Everything had happened so fast. For so long she'd put off telling them about losing Amelia and her job. It had become too painful for her to tell them now. But still, she knew it was the right thing to do. As the reality that she no longer had custody of Amelia pierced her, she thought back to how it all happened.

It had been three years since her sister, Anaya died. She had suffered with postpartum depression after Amelia was born. Amelia's father, Kenny, had his own emotional setbacks from her death. She had been his first and only love, despite the fact that his parents, Petra and Parker, had been against their relationship.

After Anaya's death, he'd been too grief stricken, and depressed to properly care for his child. He had given full custody of Amelia to Moriah before he'd succumbed to suicide. She learned later he had stopped taking his medication.

Becoming an instant parent had been bittersweet, but to have it snatched away so quickly was disheartening. Her former bosses' sudden change of heart toward her—once they found out their son had granted her custody of their grandchild—had turned her world upside down.

When she visited her parents, they would stretch their necks to see if their granddaughter was with her. They adored their precious rosebud very much. She couldn't bear the thought of going to see them without having Amelia with her. Petra and Parker would close up shop, move away before they'd even consider taking Amelia to see her other grandparents. Moriah closed her eyes as she prayed for guidance.

And then there was the attack: the brutal, debilitating, senseless assault that had left her scarred and empty. How could God have let something like that happen to her? Hadn't she been faithful? She'd been keeping herself untouched for the man she hoped to marry someday.

All of it weighed heavily on her shoulders. Tears streamed down her face. Something, a yearning deep within propelled her forward until she found herself standing at the altar. "Oh God," she cried aloud. Slowly, she climbed the mahogany steps up to the small edifice. She wept bitterly. Endlessly.

All of the pain and anger she had pent up inside of her gushed out. The stitching had come undone. She fell to her knees. Sprawling herself over the plush carpet, she dared to allow the words… the questions she'd been holding reverently inside to blurt out of her like a dam. "I've been faithful… How could You…? I thought You loved me—God, *where were you?*"

"*I've been with you all along.*" The quiet voice of tangible strength assured her. "*My Word is true, daughter. I will never leave you nor will I ever forsake you.*"

"Oh God," she sobbed. She remained prostrate across the altar for an unspeakable amount of time. His love enveloped her as she poured her heart out to her Savior. After shedding tears until she had no more, she felt the assurance of forgiveness and she repented for doubting Him.

Since the attack, God had given her the strength and courage she needed to carry on. Yet something still nagged at her soul. There was something more she longed for. Moriah forced her mind past the shame. For once, she pushed past it. She felt the courage, the strength to admit it. She had been raped. Why had He allowed something as horrific as that to happen to her——His baby girl?

Moriah felt paralyzed. She could no longer go on carrying this burden of not knowing. Determined to get closure on the matter, she'd wait right there for the answer to come, even if it meant she'd stay there all day and night. She was at a place where she just couldn't get past it.

She gazed up at the statue of The Giver of Life. He indeed had given His life for her. It was then that she realized, she hadn't given Him all of hers. How could she? Ever since *that* day, her life hadn't been the same and she wasn't sure it would ever be.

Her constant awareness of what happened and never letting the reality of it go, kept her in control. Safe. Yet she knew, living like this was killing her on the inside. No one should have to live like that. Still, she waited for her answer to come.

And then God's answer came. *"My grace is sufficient for you, Moriah. My love is rich and sovereign enough for you to overcome anything you will ever go through."* She ceased from her uncontrollable sobbing as His Presence enveloped her like a mother's arms.

"Remember how you held on to Amelia as you were teaching her to ride her bike?" Moriah's face brightened just thinking of it. She remembered it clearly. *"As she pedaled along, do you remember the moment when you let go of her?"*

"Yes. I do, Lord. When I thought she could hold her balance." Moriah remembered it vividly. How could she not? It was on the Thursday evening, the night before she had lost custody of her. That evening, Amelia had pleaded for her to remove her training wheels. "I can do it, Auntie. Really, I can!" Moriah smiled as she remembered the excitement and brightness of her face.

Amelia had been so eager to ride without the training wheels just like all the other four year olds at her pre-school. She wanted to be able to tell her class of her accomplishment during their Friday

"Celebrating Your Achievements" time. She had already decided she'd choose the big red balloon as her reward.

"Did she fall?"

Moriah lifted her chin as she recalled the moment. She remembered the look on Amelia's face as she helped her off of the ground. Pained with confusion, the question rang out louder than the cries from her minor scrapes and bruises—despite the knee and arm pads she wore. "How could you have let me fall?" Amelia's tear-filled eyes asked in unspoken words.

Moriah wrapped her arms around herself just as she remembered holding Amelia that day. "She wouldn't have ever learned to ride if I'd never let go."

"But, you knew she might fall."

"Yes."

"Did it make you a bad parent? Did you love her any less, or more?"

At the time when Amelia had fallen, Moriah hadn't considered whether she loved her any more or less than before. She just knew she loved her with everything within her.

"You did not cause Amelia to fall." A palpable silence filled the room as she drank of the words. *"I do not cause bad things to happen."* Moriah felt a warm presence as the Lord continued to speak to her heart. *"The world you live in is a place of unrest and selfishness. Evil exists and bad things are bound to happen while it is in such a state. Nevertheless, I have overcome evil with my good. With my love, Moriah."*

157

Chapter 15

A glorious light shining brightly through one of the windows awakened Moriah. She hadn't realized that she had fallen asleep. She glanced at the image etched in the glass as she lifted herself from the altar where she had been laying. Peering through the light as it beamed through the window, the illustrated story grabbed her attention. The illustration of God's love as He offered His Son was the greatest gift to mankind.

Life. He had given His life. Not just for those whom *she* judged worthy to receive it. His love and forgiveness is extended to all. The truth of that fact caused her to wrestle with God right then and there regarding Fletcher.

Moriah never wanted to see that animal… that beast again. For all she was concerned, he could burn in the embers of Hell forever.

A sudden breath of wind rustled through the pages of the large bible that sat on the long table beneath the statue. Her eyes grew wide. She spun around searching for an open window. All of them were closed.

"What's going on?" she cried out through stammering lips. She looked around the room again, this time she took notice of the door. No one had come in. Bewildered, she trembled as she eased her way toward the open book.

She ran her fingers over the deep, rich red letters that had caught her attention. "For if ye forgive men their trespasses, your heavenly Father will also forgive you:"

Forgive him.

Moriah clamped her eyes shut. She had heard the undeniable voice speaking to her heart. "He doesn't deserve my forgiveness— I don't want to forgive him, *ever!*" she bellowed into the empty room.

Surely You can't mean... Her eyes looked back at the passage again. It was at the end of the Lord's Prayer in the book of Matthew, sixth chapter, verse fourteen. She swiped the few locks that fell over her face and tucked them quickly behind her ear. Her eyes raced back over the passage again.

Her lips sputtered and her finger moved quickly as she scanned the verse over and over again. She moved to the fifteenth verse. "But if ye forgive not men their trespasses, neither will your Father forgive your trespasses."

Moriah looked up. Her gaze was afar off. She knew the passage very well. Her eyes swelled with tears. Her former pastor had preached from the very same passage. She had determined that it would be the last time she'd step foot in that place. She had been appalled. Offended.

"Did they expect me to forgive him, let it go just like that?" she yelled incredulously.

Yes.

"But what about me? What about what..." Her words caught in her throat as she remembered the pastor's closing words: "The forgiveness is for you," he had said as he looked over his congregation. He'd closed his bible. "God can," he paused, "and He will do more in you forgiving than He could ever do with your bitterness."

At that time, Moriah wasn't trying to hear it. She had gone to God's house that day to be healed, made whole, and to feel justified for wanting revenge. What did forgiving a monster like Fletcher have to do with what he had done to her? How could *they* have been so inconsiderate with her feelings?

Now her pastor's words resonated with her in a new light. The wounds of her soul pulsed open, exposing the lie. She had no right to hold on to the hate she held in her heart. God's love washed over

Moriah, slowly and methodically rinsing away bits of her bitterness, piece by piece.

She felt peace and a strange closeness wooing her, comforting her, assuring her. A great love swelled within her. She grasped at the curtains of her heart to cover her nakedness and shame. How could she let Him see the ugliness that lay within? But love melted her resistance.

God's acceptance rose within her, tugging at the fabric she clutched so guardedly. She was tired of fighting. Overwhelmed, her eyes spilled the remaining tears she'd been holding back. She released the curtains shielding her heart. In a fainting wisp, they flew away like the wings of a dove. It was right there that she surrendered her life back into the hands of the loving Savior.

She knew that surrendering her pain completely would be a process. She could only hope that one day she'd find her pain had been all washed away. God's presence permeated the air and she realized that His love was more than she would ever comprehend.

Moriah eased down the steps of the altar thanking God for His goodness. She felt clean, relieved. Whole. She tucked the words and the encounter she'd had while in the chapel in her heart. Although she had lingered longer than she intended, she was grateful for the serenity of His Presence that had vitalized her.

She quietly closed the door as she left the chapel. Her heart was still tender. But for now, she had other issues to deal with. She thought of Tyro and silently vowed she'd leave that matter in God's hands, too. Come what may between them! Who can control the matters of the heart? *Right God?* She looked up into the blue sky. After appreciating the beauty of the gorgeous Saturday morning, she smiled.

Chapter 16

"There you are," Tyro said when he saw Moriah. "I see you're enjoying the walking path." She nodded as her eyes avoided his. "Hungry? Lunch will be ready shortly," he said before spitting out what he really wanted to say. "Mind if I join you?" He held his arm out to escort her.

"Maybe after lunch?" She managed a slight smile as she thought of the things she still needed to settle within herself. Alone.

"All right," Tyro said dejectedly, dropping his arm to his side.

A sudden breeze caused a few locks to fall over her face. She immediately tucked them behind her ear as she noticed him reaching to do it for her. Exotic fragrances wafted past her. She shifted slightly to view the pleasantries of the garden behind him. She was eager to be on her way to finish exploring. Alone. As she looked in his face, his disappointment caused her to look away.

The moment felt awkward. Neither of them moved out of the other's way. His eyes pulled her in. She wanted nothing more than to fall in his arms. She longed for him to hold her, to feel the physical strength that would assure her that everything was okay.

But she wouldn't allow it. Not right now. The nagging feeling intensified. She shifted her weight off of her weaker leg. If she could just get going, she could make it without his help. He reached for her. "Please," she whispered as she pulled away. Focusing on the ground, she pulled the light jacket she wore closed.

"What is it, Moriah?" He gently tugged her arm. "Have I done something wrong?"

She lowered her head. "No. I just need some time…" She remained speechless as she studied the multiple colors under her feet. Each color spiraled off into a separate path. *Why is he still standing here? Does he think I'll change my mind?*

"That path goes around the outskirts of the developed portion of the island." He pointed to the yellow path spiraling out from the rainbow-colored pavement. "The blue path," he pointed behind her, "leads back to my house."

"I wondered where each of the colored lines went. Where do the red lines lead?" Her shoulders relaxed. He wasn't going to press the issue.

"My dad's." Tyro studied her face.

"Mmm. I'll be sure to avoid going that way," Moriah playfully muttered. They laughed simultaneously. She shielded her eyes from the rays peeking from behind the clouds as they drifted away. She turned in the direction of the sounds of the waves crashing along the beach.

"How big is this place anyway?"

"So far, we've developed almost a thousand acres. We still have another 2,000 acres to work with. This island is a branch off of one of the Poplar Islands just off of the Chesapeake. We're not too far off coast from Baltimore." He pointed toward the back of the mountains in the distance.

"Wow," she said, amazed.

Moriah's cell chimed. She was surprised she had gotten a signal in such a remote location.

"We have our own optic service and tower," Tyro offered after seeing her expression of surprise.

"I better get this." She forced a smile as she moved away.

"Remember the blue path leads back to my house." He turned and headed toward the direction from which Moriah had just come.

She watched as he veered left and up a path marked in yellow. It was the same one she saw before she went into the chapel.

Although her curiosity beckoned her to go along with him, she answered her call instead.

Chapter 17

Before Moriah could say hello, her best friend Nettie's voice bellowed through her cell. "Where are you?"

"I'm... I'm okay." Moriah sighed.

"I didn't ask how you were; although, I'm glad you're okay. But gurl... you're all over the news again," Nettie's voice trilled. "So, who's this multi-billionaire who has swept you off your feet?" Nettie didn't wait for Moriah to reply. "...And in a helicopter too? Your Prince Charming has his own helicopter?" she sang.

Before she could respond, Nettie had taken a deep breath and peppered her with her other concerns. "Gurl, I can't even go back to the hotel. My friend Joe's been driving me around all morning hoping these people will leave soon. The place is still swarming with reporters, cameras, and nosey neighbors. I stayed at his house last night. He slept on the couch, of course... Are you okay?" She took a breath after noticing Moriah's quietness.

"Sorry."

"I'm going to lay low at my brother's for a while till this *thang* blows over. You sure you're okay?"

"Yeah. I'm good. I'm on his private island." She hesitated. "Well, his dad's island, that is." She shifted to her other foot.

"Island? What island... where...? You know I don't like you being away somewhere where I can't get to you."

"If it makes you feel any better, I'll send you a picture of the place."

"And what's that supposed to do? You better send me a map or flight course or something. Don't let me have to fly over there and

164

set things off. You know you's my girl. I ain't playin' with him—prince or no prince."

"Nettie, you're funny," she said as a smile crossed her lips. "Don't worry about me. I can take care of myself." Moriah's smile broadened. It felt good to hear her voice. She sighed. Nettie always knew how to make her laugh and she loved her for it. She could always count on her being Nettie. Lately, she was the one constant she could count on being in her life. Besides God...

"Okay... but you better call me every day or I might just have to collect me a lump sum of $100,000 and send the authorities after your behind."

"You worry too much." She watched as the sky suddenly became overcast, and then the clouds drifted by. She was glad they had moved on just as quickly as they came. She didn't want any storms to ruin the gorgeous weather.

"Okay, Ms. Shrek-mobile driver ... 'Oh save me, my prince,' 'Oh, wait a minute... I don't know where the heck I am.'"

"I'll be fine. Really," she interrupted her friend before she dragged her through more of her lengthy, exaggerated antics. Although Nettie teased her, she could tell she was worried. She tried to disguise her melancholic mood. "I have to go. We'll talk soon."

"Promise? You know I'm worried about you, Moriah."

"Scout's honor. Call you tomorrow, first thing. Love you."

"Moriah." Nettie paused. "I saw Amelia today." She waited for Moriah to respond. When she heard her take a deep breath and hold it in anticipation, she continued. "She's so beautiful. She needs you. *I* need you. Take care of yourself, you hear? You're all she... you're all we have. I hope you're remembering to pray."

Moriah let out the breath she'd been holding. "Will you do me a favor?"

"Sure, I'd do anything for you," her friend chirped.

"Would you please check up on my parents for me? Assure them I'm... we're okay. Tell them I'm away on a business trip or something."

"You want me to lie to them?"

"It's not a lie. Tyro, he is… I mean…he was my client. Mario's, remember?"

"Oh yeah… that's right." Moriah hoped she felt better after hearing it from that perspective.

"Tell them I'll be back soon and Amelia and I will visit then."

"You know you're lying now! I'll go see them to make sure they're okay. But I ain't gonna lie to them." She huffed. "Lord knows I hope they don't ask about their precious lil' Rosebud."

"Well, if they do, just tell them she's with Petra and Parker for a while. They'll understand. After all, they're her grandparents too." But as far as Moriah was concerned, their custody of Amelia would be short lived. She would soon file a countersuit for their wrongful termination of her. Her lawyer assured her that the evidence she presented against their claims was in her favor. She planned to leverage her position to regain custody of Amelia.

"Hel-lo, are you still there?" Nettie spoke several times into the phone, bringing her attention back to the present.

"Okay, I gotta go," she said after Moriah finally responded. "You behave yourself now, ya here," Nettie teased, using a silly southern accent. Hearing her friend saying it like that made her smile.

"Bye!" Moriah chuckled as she disconnected the call. She realized that while she was talking, she had wandered off onto the turquoise-colored path. She remembered Tyro telling her it was the color that led to the beach.

What a gorgeous Saturday morning! She followed the path for a while until she could hear the waves washing up on the shore. They soothed her.

She smiled as she thought about the wonderful time she would spend with Tyro once she got back. This time she really meant it as she promised she wouldn't be too long. She hoped he hadn't been offended by her aloofness. She had needed this time alone.

She wondered what his *surprise* would be. Perhaps the helicopters had passed their inspections, maintenance... whatever they needed to go through. She was going to get her tour after all!

And maybe they would have their lunch on the beach first. She hadn't been on a picnic in a long time. She thought of his handsome face. Just thinking of the possibilities made her want to twirl in her excitement, if only her ankle would allow it.

Thinking about him made her anxious to get back. She just wanted to take a peek at the beach and then she would head right back. She stepped off the trail onto the sand. Following the sounds of the waves, she came across a large rock. Its monstrous size reminded her of a small mountain. It obstructed her view of the ocean.

She trailed around to the front of it and froze.

Her smile dissipated as she stared in disbelief. Her heart raced and she stumbled backwards. Her breathing increased. A salty mist caught in her throat. She choked at the memories of when she had encountered such a place as this one before. It was a place where she had been tied up, tortured and abused in a cave just like it.

Although she knew it was not the same place, seeing it caused dreadful, crippling thoughts to flood her mind. With all her might, she resisted giving in to fear. Only her knees didn't listen. "God has not given me the spirit of fear," she cried, gasping for air.

Moriah's eyes fell upon the white sand where she had collapsed. "Oh God," she bellowed, "please help me!" She feared she'd live with her skeletons for the rest of her life no matter how hard she'd try to get rid of them. "He's dead. I can let it go... forgive...," she told herself.

But she couldn't let it go. Deep in her heart, she wanted revenge. She wanted him to hurt like she hurt. Suffer and struggle to live a normal everyday life without physical pain, the torments of fear, anger, and hatred!

But the vision of his helicopter engulfed in flames as it crashed into the ocean caused her to come to her senses. There was no one to exact her revenge on. Fletcher was dead.

Chapter 18

Moriah's heart fluttered as she thought about the package she'd received the other day. It contained a dead rat. She could still picture its beady eyes staring lifelessly through the plastic bag. It floated in fresh blood. Her heart beat rapidly just thinking of it. She knew within her heart of hearts, there could have only been one person to do such a thing. Fletcher.

"But he's dead!" she yelled louder as she grabbed fistfuls of sand. She desperately tried to convince herself. "He's dead... I saw him die!" Fear gripped her. Flashbacks rained over her mind like pieces of shattered glass. She had been stranded and left alone to die by that man. He had kidnapped her. He'd brought her to that desolate place for his selfish and evil advantage.

She had watched him die right before her very eyes. There was nothing she could do to save him, even if she'd wanted to. Neither had she tried. She'd watched him fly away in the helicopter. She saw it sink into the ocean... she saw when it exploded.

The peaceful churning of the sea lured her to its presence. Moriah tried desperately to snap herself out of the grisly memories only to have them drag her back into their womb of devastation.

The sun waltzed from behind the clouds and beamed over her. A warm sensation wrapped itself around her.

Talitha Cumi! She heard the Lord speaking in her spirit. *Cumi. Daughter, I said for you to arise.*

Moriah did arise. As she lifted herself from the ground, she felt the cloak of heaviness, brokenness, and death fall from her. She lifted her hands to the heavens and declared that she would not live a life of fear. She felt free. Moriah twirled as she basked in the sunlight. She was free!

She could only pray that Tyro hadn't been following her. Watching.

Shuddering as she stumbled away from the ghastly sight of the cave, she forced the memories trying to reclaim her soul out of her mind. When she reached the shore, she removed her sandals and stepped into the liquid warmth. She allowed the waters to caress her ankles as it pulled back to sea. It calmed her. Being at the beach always helped her find serenity.

The granules left between her toes as the water receded were the finest of sand she'd ever felt. As if large chunks of guilt, shame, and feelings of hopelessness were being forever plunged into the sea of forgiveness, a feeling of wholeness filled her heart.

Her soul had been cleansed, her stamina renewed. "I will not live in fear!" she declared boldly. Any residue of brokenness that remained, she tucked back into its hiding place. She'd have to deal with it at another time. For now, she found solace in being free of the tantalizing grip of fear.

Feeling refreshed and renewed, she closed her eyes and breathed deeply. She allowed the air to escape slowly from her lungs. Tyro came to mind. Had she been drawn to him because she could identify with his pain? Did she think she'd find redemption in helping him through his dark times while she drowned in her own? Was that why they were drawn to each other? But she knew deep within, even if it had been the case, it wouldn't work.

She had a new perspective on her life. She wasn't going to put some unforeseen spin on the matter of their relationship. She liked him. It was as plain and simple as that!

Besides his sudden mood swings, things had been perfect between them. She thought about how he had laughed and joked about her quirky mannerisms. She had to smile. She took a few moments to pray for his healing, peace and closure over his mother's death. She prayed for his father too, although she didn't know exactly what to say, but still, she was sincere in her prayers for him.

Moriah thought about how much she'd prayed for Tyro since meeting him. She hadn't meant to care for him so deeply. There was just something about being with him that made her feel safe. Appreciated. Alive. There's no denying it, she was falling in love with him. In fact, she fell in love with him the first night they'd met, if the truth were to be told.

As she turned to head back, she felt something caught between her toes. A sudden streak of light reflecting from it caught her eye. She stooped and unwound a gold chain from her toe. She marveled at the gorgeous blue sapphire that dangled at the end of the necklace.

She heard the sound of laughter heading her way. She looked toward the children running along the beach as she tucked the jewelry in her pocket. She would give it to Tyro as soon as she caught up with him.

She waved back at the woman following the group of elated students as they ran toward the water. The guardian turned her head to warn the children not to go too far out into the water. Moriah used the opportunity to slip away. As she trekked back up the beach, she could hear joyous laughter as they splashed giddily in the crystal blue water.

Moriah wondered whose children they were. Who was the woman? She looked along the direction of the long stretch of beach from which they had come. A building resembling a resort peeked over the hill-like sand dune.

Moriah found her way back to the turquoise path. She tried to remember the way she came to find the blue path. She wasn't sure if she was heading in the right direction so she veered off onto the first trail she saw since leaving the beach. It led her to a red path. Thinking she might have come up the back way, she groaned at her choice of paths.

She followed the trail until a lofty colonial came into view. She stopped to admire the stately edifice. As tempting as it may have been to peek around a little, she happily trailed off onto the blue path as soon as she saw it. She knew she was getting closer as she stumbled upon the large pool. She remembered seeing it from the helicopter as they circled the island last night.

For a moment, she thought she heard voices escalating beyond the 20-foot diving area where the water cascaded into the pool. She watched as Tyro stormed further away on the blue trail while Quincy quickly headed in her direction. He carried some sort of hedge clippers in his hand.

Within a split-second, she thought about hiding behind a large topiary. It had been intricately cut into the shape of a mermaid. Feeling silly, she decided she'd face the tyrant head on. She didn't feel he'd do anything to physically harm her. She was relieved when he deviated to the left.

Several steps later, she heard a series of repeated snipping, snapping, and clipping. A few choice words sailed along with each snip. Numerous pieces of shrubbery flipped, flopped, and tumbled high into the air. She was sure Tyro had been the reason for Quincy's apparent tiff. Most likely, it was because of her being there. Whatever the reason, she felt sorry for the gardener who'd have to clean up behind his mess.

Chapter 19

For lunch, the redheaded servant, Tempa, seated Moriah at the far end from Tyro. The thirty-foot exquisitely hammered steel table could have easily seated twenty-two guests. A mixed arrangement of exotic and tropical flowers sat in the middle and at both ends of the table.

Although she was impressed with his modern taste and industrial styled furnishings, she pouted as it stifled the cozy and intimate conversation she wanted. Looking down the long table, she eyed the empty chairs on both sides of where Tyro was sitting.

With disappointment, she scrunched her nose in response as Redhead offered her samplings of the finest cheeses from around the world. At the time, she hadn't cared that she had offended her, although she quickly thought better of her actions and immediately apologized.

Tyro laughed out loud as she pouted and picked at her salad.

"What's so funny?" she scoffed, pointing her fork at him.

"You are." He headed to where she sat. Standing next to her, he nodded toward the kitchen. "Come on. I have a feeling you'll be more comfortable in there."

Despite her sore ankle, she leapt from her seat, grabbed her plate, and scuttled behind him. Once seated at the island, Redhead gave her a tight smile as she placed his plate before him. She then lifted her head and plumed from the room. Moriah sheepishly smiled back at her, although she had already left from the room.

"This is much better," she cooed. She smiled as she melted into the high-back Italian leather stool seated at the island next to him.

Occasionally, she'd lean back to steal glimpses of him as they talked. They joked about old movies and TV shows in between the courses of their meal. She was surprised he liked the *I Love Lucy* shows as much as she did.

He used his phone to search through his video library displayed on the TV. After searching his library, he stopped at his favorite episode. They shared hearty laughs at Lucy as she trampled over grapes. Lucy's big mouth had gotten her into trouble once again.

"My mother loved this show," Tyro said, surprising Moriah that he'd mentioned her without her having to ask about her. "Believe it or not, so does my dad." He peered out the corner of his eye as he mentioned him.

Moriah broke off a piece of roll. "Your father doesn't like me," she said matter-of-factly. She smothered the freshly made butter over the hot bread and plopped it in her mouth.

"No. He doesn't," Tyro said, smiling.

She kept her eyes closed as she savored the smoothness as the buttered texture slid down her throat. She wasn't going to let on that she had been taken aback a little at his candidness about his father's dislike of her. His straightforwardness was another thing she'd have to get used to, although she definitely appreciated knowing exactly where he stood.

"My father doesn't *like* anyone at first. He has to warm up to you, check you out. He needs to make sure you're not out to tear down his empire."

"I'm sure all this media hoopla isn't helping." She rolled her eyes. "But I'm not buying that it's the only reason why."

"Well, since you brought up the subject…" He reached for the remote and started surfing through the various channels. He wanted to catch up with what was being reported regarding their fairy tale event. The last time he'd checked, there had been over fifty alleged sightings of the two. People claimed to have spotted them in places as far away as Paris and the Amazon.

He vowed he'd do something to squash the whole Cinderella-

Prince saga. But exactly what, at the time he had no idea. He turned off the electronics. "Nothing much has changed," he said, watching Moriah let out the breath she'd been holding.

Between her constantly twisting her hair around her finger, shifting in her chair, and rolling her eyes away from the television screen, he realized she was as fed up with it as he was. He'd forgotten that she had told him so while they were at Mario's.

"Why did you leave?" he asked as he placed the media control down.

"What...?"

Their eyes connected. "You are a very pretty woman, Ms. Styles." He restrained the urge to shudder as his heart skipped.

She blushed. Nervously, she refilled her glass with water. A few tresses fell over her face as she leaned. Tyro tenderly placed them behind her ear. He cupped her chin, lifting her face to his. He relished the moment as their gaze held.

"Are you going to tell me?" Tyro asked, watching as she pulled away. He released her face and he leaned back and waited. "All right," he raised his hands in surrender, "it's a story for another time. Speaking of which, your ankle... how did you hurt it?"

"I didn't," she teased. Her shoulders sprang back to life. "You did." She grinned as she tried to make light of the situation.

"Oh come on now." He leaned forward. "Ms. Styles, come out with it," he said as his eyes smiled at her.

She shrugged.

"Don't give me that cute shrug of yours," he said, toying with her as Redhead placed another one of Roy's famous French cuisine creations before her. Moriah smiled gratefully and thanked her.

The woman nodded. She told Moriah it was her pleasure. The woman was less tense as she graciously served Moriah first. "I don't know how you do it." Moriah commented on having to be served his meals all the time. She watched her return with such poise back to the butler's kitchen, and admired the look of humbleness on her face.

"All of our employees are grateful for the opportunity to work here. You'll see what I mean tomorrow." He waited for Moriah to finish saying her "grace" thing after the main course had been served. "I hope you're up for a picnic before our adventure later," he said, resisting the urge to ask why she'd waited until then to pray. He looked at the serving dishes containing half of the amount of breads, rolls, and cheeses it had before.

"A picnic... today?" Her eyebrows rose. She looked at the amount of food sitting in front of her. As delicious as it was, even if she'd only eat half of it, it would be a long time before she could eat anything else.

"Well," he teased, sliding her plate playfully away from her as he threatened to give it to Sheba, "since you're watching your girlish figure and, you're not answering my question, I know someone who doesn't mind the extra pounds since she's going to have pups soon. Isn't that right?" he said, playfully leaning Moriah's plate in his Shepherd's direction.

Although she continued to sit obediently in her place away from the island, Sheba gave a quick bark as she cocked her head. She whined before she let out another bark just to let him know she'd gladly take him up on his offer.

"Oh no you don't, Mr. Simmonds!" Moriah pulled her plate back to her place setting. "And you, Girly Girl," Moriah said as she leaned toward Sheba, "you have your own food. Now go over there and have at it, Missy!" She waved her fork in the direction the dog was to go and watched as she trotted into the mudroom. Sheba wasted no time devouring what was in her bowl.

"Ah! I see who's the boss between you two," Tyro said, amused. "She really listens to you."

"That's because you've trained her well." Moriah smiled warmly at his "Ah" gesture that she'd grown to love so much.

"Well?"

"Well what?" she asked responding to the curious look on his face. "You sure have a lot of questions. What do you want to know first?"

"Uh huh. Don't think you're going to get away with not answering them either," he said. Playfully, she pointed her fork toward his fingers at his last attempt to come after her plate.

His face grew solemn. "All right." His voice resonated with displeasure. She constantly avoided his questions. "Let's finish our meal, and then we will talk." His eyes remained on her as he emphasized the word "will." It was his way of letting her know he was tired of her evasiveness. He wanted answers and would accept nothing less.

Moriah had already resolved within herself that she wouldn't have any discussions with him regarding her feelings. Not at this point in time in their relationship. Both of them had their issues to work through. Although she had been delivered from a big chunk of her own pain earlier that day, discussing her feelings prematurely would surely end in disaster.

Moriah settled her chin in her palm as she looked up. She smiled as she stared at him. She had to admit she was glad to see his *alpha* ego raise its dominant head again, although she was taken aback that it had been directed toward her. Now, if only he'd channel his testosterone where it needed to be, at Quincy and not her.

But she'd let him have his *growl*, for now.

Chapter 20

"Alrighty!" Moriah chimed right after she'd returned. She was glad she'd been allowed to help clear away the dishes. She had insisted. "Since we're laying our cards on the table, tell me something," she said as she returned to the kitchen for the final time.

Tyro had relocated himself at the far end of the island away from where they had initially sat. The expression on his face as he scrolled rapidly through a text, alarmed her. She had heard it chime when she'd first left the room with a handful of dishes.

Absentmindedly, he returned to sit back next to her. His hand fumbled as he tried to put his cell away. Something he just learned had stunned him. Disbelief was etched all over his face. There was no denying it, whatever it was had shaken his world.

"Is everything okay?" She reached out to touch his arm. He carefully moved out of her reach as he got up from his seat. His eyes were darkening by the minute. *Not now...* She knew she had to do something quick to get him to snap out of whatever it was that was threatening to pull him under.

Although she had a strange feeling the message had been about her, she rose slowly and walked to where he stood. Her hands trembled, but she reached for him just the same. She steadied him by the arms. "Hey. Talk to me." She waited. "What is it?"

Their eyes engaged each other's for what seemed like a long time. She caressed his face with the back of her hand. She was pleasantly surprised when he reached and cupped it over his face. His face mellowed. He planted a gentle kiss in her palm before pulling her in a warm embrace. She closed her eyes in relief as she drew in a breath.

"Let's just say that I hope it's not true." He gave her a tight smile as he released her. "Now, what were you saying? Sorry about the interruption." He pointed to where he'd placed his cell.

"You want to talk about it?" she asked, shifting her eyes to where his cell rested.

"No."

She considered his demeanor and decided to leave well enough alone, for now.

He shook his head. "Not right now. I don't have all the pieces to know where to begin." He guided her back to sit. "Now, you first. What's on your mind?"

"Why didn't you defend me last night?" she asked as her eyes bore through him.

He soughed. "It's no secret, Moriah." His expression changed at her reaction to his curtness. "My father... at this point, we're only tolerating each other." His eyes deepened. "I found out something about him earlier. I'm not sure if what he said just slipped off his lips, or if it was his way of proving his point.

"And what does it have to do with you letting him disrespect me?" Tyro ran his fingers through his hair. "Since my mother died, we barely agree on much. He's hurting, Moriah. I don't know what else you want me—"

Oh, no he's not going to go there! If he thinks for one moment he's going to lay his issues with his dad on me . . . Besides, does he expect me to just throw my cards on the table for him to see all of mine and he's not willing to show his own hand? We might as well fold and he can take me home right now. Moriah didn't realize her mind had gone there. Still, she held her ground.

"—And you let him use it as an excuse to talk to you like he does? You loved her too, Tyro," Moriah needlessly reminded him. He needed to see things for what they were. She was willing to call a spade, a spade.

"I'm not a counselor, but what you two have going, it's not healthy at all." She eyed him. She fell a few words shy of saying what she really meant. They needed spiritual and professional help.

A wicked smile crossed his face as if suddenly he was amused.

"Are you taking me seriously? I mean it. It's not helping matters that you let him get away with treating you like he does." She arched her shoulders back. "I'm warning you; I will not let him talk to me or make derogatory remarks about me in my presence." She snapped to her feet. "The least you could do is stand up for me!"

"I thought you handled yourself quite well." He smirked. "You should have seen his face as you stood your ground." He reached to pull her into his arms.

She backed away. "It's childish. And it's not funny at all, Tyro. I was there. Or have you forgotten? My parents taught us—" She retracted her statement. "I mean that I was always taught to respect people."

"Well, I really admired your spunk last night, Moriah." He stared at her. "He's not happy about this whole Damsel in Distress... Green Monster... Princess fairy tale ... whatever the thing is that's sweeping across the country." He twirled his finger in the air. "And need I tell you, he definitely wasn't happy with me bringing my 'Cinderella' here." He flexed his fingers in air quotes.

"What's that got to do with me... how'd he know it was me... and so what if it is? It doesn't give him the right to treat me like I'm a derelict of some sort."

Tyro walked over and placed a gentle kiss in the palm of her hand. "You are a wonderful woman, Moriah. I will not allow you to be disrespected, by him or anyone ever again." He gave his 'scout's honor' pledge.

Moriah snatched her hand away. "Better not." There was no smile this time.

Tyro returned to his seat. "To answer your question," he said dryly, "he knew. He recognized me the moment he'd spotted me the first time it aired on TV. Or maybe it was those beautiful browns," he teased, trying to lighten the mood.

"But I thought… I thought our faces were hidden."

"They were. I did a pretty good job, didn't I? You owe me big time." He grinned.

Moriah leaned back. "Owe you?" She grunted at his sense of humor. He reached for her hand again.

She immediately pulled away. "Don't play with me. You should know I didn't think very much of you leaving me out there like that." She narrowed her eyes at his devious smile. She didn't see the humor in the matter. "Your dad is a piece of work."

"Ah?" His eyebrows rose. She was still ticked about his father's tantrum. "It's that bad, huh?" he asked. The smile eased completely from his face. "And exactly what did you think of me?"

She turned and faced him, looking him square in the eyes. "You're a coward."

Chapter 21

"Oh... those are strong words. My ego might not like it," Tyro teased as he rose and pulled her close. "Then again, it just might fuel my passion to show you how wrong you are."

He kissed her lips tenderly. He entwined his hands in the back of her hair. Its softness coiled around his fingers sending sensations through his body. Their eyes connected.

One tender touch from him caused Moriah's shoulders to relax. The tightness in her jaws melted away. She couldn't stay mad at him long. How could she? He knew how to turn on the charm and she couldn't resist.

He gently held a few tresses of her hair. Bringing her lips closer to his he paused. "I needed for you to know what you were getting yourself into," he said ominously, allowing their lips to brush before pushing his deeply into hers.

Nervously, Moriah pulled away. Wrestling with feelings of regret and vulnerability, she clasped her neck. She had promised herself to be more careful, selective before she'd allow herself to get emotionally involved.

She just had to. She couldn't help but think about the last time, how an innocent, tiny, little kiss later led to tragedy.

Secretly, she admitted she had had feelings for Fletcher, before his crazy side emerged. And she wanted to take her time before getting into a relationship with him, or anyone. She had told him so. She hadn't done anything to lead him to believe otherwise, as Petra had accused her of doing.

She tried to shake Fletcher out of her mind. The man standing before her was nothing like him. Tyro's kisses were soft. Sweet. Comforting. And she had welcomed them, even if it would be just this one and only time.

Would kissing him this one time cause her to want to do it again? She knew it would. Would breaking her own promise to herself be so bad? Was it a compromise? She could no longer deny it, she was falling for Tyro, and hard.

She realized her emotions were all over the place. Without thinking, she'd grabbed the remote, wielding it in numerous directions as she talked. She made herself refocus. She wasn't willing to let Tyro get away without answering her question. She had to know. She spun around. "What are you going to do about it?"

Tyro's cell chimed. He reached in his pocket. "Do about what?" he scoffed, looking at the display.

"Are you paying attention to me?" she asked. "It's like your dad owns you, or either you owe him something. It's so … degrading. I bet he talks to Sheba with more respect than he does you."

As if on cue, Quincy walked into the kitchen and snatched the remote out of Moriah's hand. Clicking on the television, Quincy scrolled over to PNN. The announcer was concluding the broadcast of the latest update. The DA was now walking toward the courthouse in the distant background.

From what Moriah had gathered, the Kent County Courthouse in Dover would remain open for the weekend for the alleged prince and princess to turn themselves in before midnight, Sunday. If they did as the DA had stated, some, if not most of the charges might be dropped.

Moriah was dazed. For one, she hadn't realized she had been holding the remote and had inadvertently picked it up.

"She should be arrested for being so stupid," Quincy said blatantly as if she wasn't standing right there, or he didn't care that she was. He turned toward Tyro only to find him pulling her away from his presence.

Every nerve in Moriah's body seethed. Screaming and scratching at her, they dug under her skin, begging to get loose. Her temperature rose so high, she couldn't think straight. And neither did she want to. She knew what she was about to say wouldn't make the situation any better, so, she quelled the fire blazing inside of her and submitted. She allowed Tyro to cajole her into moving to the great room, leaving Quincy to fume through his self-righteous orations. Alone.

Moriah knew the real issue lay with Tyro. He, if anyone, should have stepped in and put a stop to his father's lack of decency, as he'd promised. What happened to her rescuing prince, her knight in shining armor kind of guy? Slaying dragons might not be his thing; she'd give him that. But she swore that the next time he did what he'd just done, there would be blood in the water, and it wouldn't be hers. Definitely not!

As Moriah stood in the great room, she thought about her choices. She could let what just happened ruin her day by spiraling into a foul mood, or she could let it go and deal with it later.

Although her face flushed redder than the Hawaiian shirt Quincy had been wearing all morning, she chose the latter. She'd go for a swim as they had planned. Perhaps it would help her to mellow out and get this problem off her chest. She and Tyro definitely needed to talk. And talk, they would.

When she left to go change, Tyro's eyes were blue. They were not as deep in color as they had been last night; but still, she knew he was not in the frame of mind for a reasonable discussion.

Chapter 22

Moriah changed into her swimwear. She admired the iron staircase that spiraled to the main level as she carefully walked down. She stopped abruptly as she heard voices coming from the great room where she had left Tyro.

She peered around the wall as the conversation subsided. She saw the back of a bright red shirt, just like the one Quincy wore heading out of the room toward the kitchen.

Convinced it was he, a gnawing feeling pinged at the pit of her stomach. Suspicion churned in her gut. What were they up to? Their conversation seemed tense, very tense although they spoke in a hushed tone. Was he putting his father in his place? She doubted that much. Tyro sympathized too much with his dad for that to be the case.

Tyro's cell rang. She froze where she stood. He hadn't seen her standing there. It wasn't as if she was eavesdropping for the heck of it, she needed to find out what was going on. Could she trust this guy, or what?

"Tomorrow?" He sighed as he listened to his caller. "The sooner, the better. I need to get to the bottom of his nonsense." Tyro stared at his cell for several moments after he ended his call. She noticed the increased number of calls and texts he'd received since lunch. And she was annoyed that he hadn't changed into his swimsuit.

"Where's Girly Girl?" she asked, making her presence known as she walked toward him.

He shuddered as if she'd startled him from deep thought. He nodded toward the kitchen. "Waiting impatiently by the door," he said forcing himself to smile.

"Don't blame me for being the hold up. I'm ready." She felt his eyes on her as she took the liberty to browse around the room before he hurried up the stairs to get ready.

She wondered if he thought her attire was too inappropriate to swim in. He hadn't made a comment about it even though she expected him to do a double take when he saw it. She wore a one-piece, white swimsuit and a pair of matching cotton pants to cover her legs. It was perfect for lounging around the pool. She'd have to figure out how to get into the pool without him seeing the disfigurement on her leg.

A few times she'd wanted to tell him about the scar. It snaked like a winding river from the top of her inner thigh down to her knee. She longed to show him, get it out of the way. Perhaps they could move past it, or move on.

But thinking about it, reminded her of the times when she couldn't even bear to look at it herself. How could she expect for him not to be appalled at the ghastly site. And then there were the times that seeing it reminded her that she had survived.

She determined that one day, she'd get beyond the embarrassment and see it as a mark of victory of the great battle she'd won. She prayed the day would come soon.

But for now, she wasn't ready to expose this part of her. Not willing to chance seeing the look of disdain on his face, as he'd lay his eyes on it. She wasn't ready to go into the gruesome details from the questions she knew would follow once he saw it.

She decided it was best to keep the unsightly thing hidden. There was too much she needed to learn about him before she could trust him with her pain.

She turned her attention to looking around the room. She marveled at the twenty-foot-high ceiling arched together into a steeple as they touched. She admired the hammered-steel-faced fireplace that ignited instantly when she touched the digital panel.

She pushed another section and flames roared high. Another button made them burn orange, then red, yellow, purple... blue. Each button offered various settings, temperatures, and moods. Realizing she had become engrossed in satisfying her curiosity, she quickly switched it off, giggling that her inquisitiveness had gotten the best of her. She had wondered how the controls on the complicated computer screen worked. *"Really, Moriah?"* She chuckled at herself. It was only a fireplace, for goodness' sake!

She set the remote back on one of the accent tables. Seeing the fire glowing in the different ambiances made her think about Tyro's mood swings. When he was not in one of his melancholy states, he had such an alluring gentleness about him.

Nicely decorated, Moriah thought. She continued exploring her surroundings. The black and white macho-modern wasn't her taste. But how everything was put together made the room absolutely stunning. She decided she liked it. It fit him.

The expansive row of floor to ceiling windows beautifully displayed a picturesque garden off to the side. "What a gorgeous view!" She hadn't realized she had spoken it out loud as she craned her neck to see as much of it as she could. "Beautiful garden—"

Tyro immediately snapped his fingers. Moriah jumped as she spun around. Sheba bounded over and sat next to his feet. "Sorry to have startled you." She hadn't heard him come back into the room.

He had only been gone less than five minutes. *He couldn't have changed that quickly?* She was surprised at the swimwear he wore. She thought he'd put on a pair of skimpy black trunks to show off his physique.

Instead, he wore plain white swim shorts that resembled a pair of long boxers. For someone as wealthy as he was, she appreciated his ability to be practical. She smiled.

Moriah's face appeared puzzled. Sheba was sitting tall next to Tyro. "You mention the "G" word." Nodding his head in his dog's direction, he explained. "She gets a little crazy about going there."

Moriah thought it was strange. Didn't she get to go in the garden every day? After all, his section of it was practically outside of his door.

Chapter 23

"Allergies." Tyro responded seeing the puzzled look on Moriah's face. "I cut back on her antihistamines when I'm breeding her. Sheba let out a very loud bark as she bounded to her feet. She wagged her tail wildly as she pranced back and forth. Tyro snapped his fingers again and pointed toward his feet. Sheba obediently complied as she sat back at his side. She cocked her head up at her master, and whined excitedly.

"It'll be up to the lady."

Moriah was amazed as the dog instantly turned and gave her an irresistible puppy doggish look before giving her the cutest whimper. As soon as Moriah said she'd loved to see the garden, Sheba shot toward the kitchen before she could finish speaking. She instantly returned as her master gave one quick and loud whistle.

"You're too much, Girly Girl." She looked over at Tyro. "I think we should go to the pool and then we can do the 'G' thing, if it's all right with you."

"I think it's a great solution. Besides, she'll enjoy the pool just as much."

"You are something else, I tell you." Moriah rubbed the Shepherd behind her ears. Sheba began licking at Moriah's hand relishing the moment.

"Well, don't mind me, you two." Tyro chuckled, watching them bond in their display of appreciation for each other.

Sheba bounded into the kitchen and looked up at Moriah. She whined before heading toward a door Moriah hadn't noticed before.

"Patience!" Moriah called. The Shepherd kept leaping up at the door handle. "You got your master to blame for the hold up," she teased, turning to look at Tyro.

"Blame me for what?" he asked. He'd just popped back into the kitchen after being gone for another five minutes. "What…this?" he held his cell up. "Business," he lied, unless he considered speaking with his dad, business.

He smiled as he leaned to open the door. Sheba shot out of it like a bat out of a cave. She headed left and disappeared around the tropical flowers lining the walkway.

"Show off!" Moriah yelled after Tyro plunged for the third time off the 20-foot dive, displaying his skills at various diving positions. As he climbed up the high edifice for the fourth time, she removed her pants. Diving into the water, she swam several laps across the shorter width of the pool being sure to stay out of his and Sheba's way.

After his last dive, he played around with Sheba. He'd throw her doggie toy down the long end of the pool and would swim along with her as she retrieved it. After several fetches, Sheba soon grew tired of it and frolicked away to play with a stick that had fallen into the pool.

Tyro swam to Moriah who was wading in the middle of the pool. She playfully splashed water at him. "Oh, now that she's tired of you, you wanna come bother me, do you!" She splashed more water in his face as she laughed.

"Oh, you haven't heard, I'm the king of splashing!" he said as he drove his palm hard into the water. He caused a small typhoon to rise in the air and Moriah quickly dove under to avoid it. As if all their troubles were behind them, they enjoyed their time of laughing, and playing around in the water, stealing quick kisses in between like young school kids.

Moriah climbed out of the pool as Tyro went to check on his Shepherd. She would be having her pups in a few weeks and he wanted to make sure she didn't overexert herself.

Moriah rolled her eyes when Tyro's cell buzzed. If he had been there to answer it, he would have held his cell up to signal that he needed to *get this*, and would have hurried away. Each time he'd returned, he tried to ease her mind by claiming it was business, only making her more suspicious.

She couldn't put her finger on what was going on, but she strongly suspected it had something to do with her. One thing she was sure of, he had been adamant in drilling his last caller. "Are you sure it's *her*?" he asked repeatedly as if whatever he had just learned had been despicably horrendous.

And from the bit she'd gathered earlier, something was going on tomorrow, *but what?* She ran through her mind what he said he had planned for them. Other than giving her the grand tour over the islands after breakfast, he had given her the impression everything else he'd planned would be a surprise.

"Some surprise," she muttered. Something was going down and since it was obvious that it involved her, she was going to get to the bottom of it. She didn't like feeling like a fool but felt she had no right to say anything about his *business* calls. After all, she was his guest. Technically, she was his father's guest, to her chagrin, since it was his father's island.

She decided to give Nettie a call after she dried off. Redhead had just placed two glasses of freshly squeezed lemonade on the table. She forced a smile as she thanked her. Tyro's cell rang again. It was lying face down on the table.

She was tempted to see who was calling, but Tempa, the redhead whose name she couldn't remember until now, didn't budge after setting the glasses down. Moriah had made the mistake of commenting on her choice of hair coloring. She had no idea the woman would be so enamored of a measly compliment. After all, Moriah was just trying to find something nice to say to her.

Now her opportunity to see who was calling him had dwindled. Tyro was heading her way. "It was Mrs. Simmonds who suggested I wear this color. She said it would look nice on me… You agree, aye?" Tempa chirped.

"What?" Moriah said, restraining her annoyance watching Tempa as she continued to pat her hair.

"Oh…Absolutely!" Moriah said, wishing that *Carrot-top* would scurry herself back inside. By the time she had, it was too late. Tyro had reached the edge of the pool.

"Please?" He gave her his signature sexy smile as he nodded toward his phone.

"Sure." She thought about taking a quick glance at the display as she handed it to him. She changed her mind when she thought how tacky it would look. If she had been bodacious like Nettie, she would have answered his cell on the first ring and wouldn't have cared whether he liked it or not.

Nettie demanded all of her man's attention when he was with her. But she'd granted him the same courtesy. "It's why too many couples don't make it nowadays, too many doggone distractions," Nettie would have said.

Moriah knew that her and Tyro's relationship hadn't grown to that point. Still, she was tired of the constant distractions as his cell rang like crazy.

Whatever it was he had going on had escalated. One of the times as he was talking, he'd glared at her, as if repulsed, before he quickly turned away. The only way to get to the bottom of whatever was going on was for her to face it head on. Right now.

Chapter 24

Tyro finished his call and lifted himself out of the pool. After drying himself off, he held his arm out to escort Moriah to the garden. The scenery was absolutely breathtaking. She had had a chance to explore some of the grounds earlier in the morning but had no idea the garden would be of this magnitude.

She could spend all day there and still not see everything. "You have very talented landscapers," she said as she strolled along gliding her fingers over sculptured trees and topiaries.

"My father created them for my mother."

"Your dad did all of this?" She stopped mid-stride. Amused, she looked around at the various trees, and bushes that had been fashioned into cartoon characters, animals, sea life as well as other intricate shapes and figures.

She glanced over at a series of bushes clustered together. They had been shaped into the resemblance of a rock star band. Above it hung a string of strobe lights. Moriah was sure it was beautiful when lit at night.

"Every last one of them," Tyro said proudly.

"Even that one?" she pointed to the sculpture positioned at the top of the path that led toward the big red colonial. The cluster of trees and bushes had been shaped into a sandcastle.

"Yep." He glanced over at her. "It's actually a tree house. I made the bench inside of it. My father made it for my mother's birthday last year. It had become her favorite place in the garden." He guided her along. "You should see it. It's a garden within a garden."

191

She pulled back. "Some other time, okay?" She smoothed her hair behind her ear. It had blown out of place as a gentle wind breezed by. She smiled back at his lively grin. He hadn't felt like running into Quincy at the moment either. Her eyes thanked him for understanding.

Simultaneously, Sheba caught their attention. She had been racing back and forth along the grass like she had just been freed from prison. They laughed as they watched her frolic around with bunnies before darting off to chase butterflies.

"Sheba sure is enjoying herself." She was tickled as her furry friend joined them and trotted alongside of her instead of Tyro. Moriah beamed as the Shepherd barreled off to catch the stick she threw for her to fetch.

"Nice arm," Tyro said. "I think she misses my mother." He stopped short after letting the words slip. Every time she'd mention her before he'd quickly change the subject.

Moriah lightly tugged his arm. They stopped walking. This time, there'd be no getting around it. He sighed. "The garden was her favorite part of the island."

Moriah's ankle had swollen so they chose to sit on the plush grass below a pair of sculptured guardian angels. As he helped her to sit, a gentle breeze ruffled through the leaves above them. Looking up, she smiled as she admired Quincy's handiwork.

The manner in which the cherubs had been positioned, Cupid's arrow was pointing right at them. She got caught up in the moment thinking of what could possibly become of their relationship; if only she knew what was going on. Until she found out, how could she trust him?

Just as she turned her attention back to Tyro, several baby foxes romping around a few yards ahead of them had caught her attention before they disappeared into the bushes. She would have loved to follow them, but she felt the heaviness around Tyro growing. Playing around with the foxes would have to wait.

"Tyro," she began, "I know it's hard for you to talk about her." She caressed his back. "It's not good to keep it bottled up inside." He kept his head low. He forced a smile as he mindlessly milled a twig between his two fingers.

She waited patiently as he searched carefully for words. Reaching over him, she petted Sheba. Moriah realized the dog had sensed his darkening mood by the way she had laid herself attentively next to her master.

"You ever lose someone and it hurts so much you can hardly breathe?" he asked.

She turned her head and stared in distant thought. "Yeah, I have." She thought about the last picture she'd taken of her sister and Amelia. It was picture perfect of mother and daughter in matching spring dresses on Easter.

It had dawned on her. She hadn't seen pictures of his mother anywhere in the parts of the home she'd been. It had taken her a long time before she could look at her sister's photos, or listen to old voicemails of her. Anaya had left her one a few days before she had passed. Hearing her voice had pierced her heart when she finally braved herself to listen to it.

Tenderly, she squeezed his arm, drawing his attention to look at her. Their eyes held with the same uncertainty as the first night they'd met. Tears swelled in her eyes. An overcast of sorrow filled his. Their tender embrace captured the other's sorrow and pain in the depth of their silence.

He was well aware of the source of his pain. But he didn't know Moriah's story. Not all of it. Only what he had gathered today from the phone calls and texts he'd received. He had wondered why she was being so secretive. He'd seen the scar on her leg, although he suspected she hadn't known he had. Whatever happened had to have been a terrifying ordeal. *How brave of her,* he thought.

However, bravery or not, his newfound information caused suspicion of her to swim around his head. He couldn't ignore the facts. But was Quincy right? How could Moriah have any connections to his mother's murder? Did she know his mother's killer, or had she just been another victim? Maybe what happened to her didn't have anything to do with his mother at all. Quincy had told him that the detective investigating the crime was sure she was the missing link, although none of it made any sense.

Tyro felt selfish for thinking it. He just couldn't help wondering why *she* had lived and not his mother. *Why did it have to happen in the first place? God... why?*

The thoughts overpowered his mind. He leapt up from the ground. His emotions were out of control. He really cared for Moriah. In fact, he was falling in love with her. But until his questions were answered, and his suspicion would prove otherwise, he vowed to keep his feelings in check.

And now, the guilty feelings of having to string her along in order to get to the truth, ate at his soul. He was torn. Should he follow his heart and throw caution to the wind? What could she possibly have to do with his mother's death? The whole idea was insane and irrational.

But for now, his desperate need for closure would have to outweigh his feelings for her. He wasn't willing to compromise the case. He'd keep quiet and go along with the plan—for now. He returned and lay his head in her lap. But still he vowed that every touch, every look into her eyes, and every tender kiss they'd share would be from the pureness and sincerity of his heart.

Chapter 25

Moriah took a deep breath and let it out slowly. *Oh God, why can't I shake this feeling? Why do I feel guilty for not telling him? Please God... show me what to do... what to say.*

Her heart was heavy. Her mind clogged with fears of what might happen once she opened Pandora's Box she kept hidden inside. Stroking Tyro's head as he lay in her lap, she decided she'd tell him. Now. Before she could talk herself out of it, she closed her eyes and methodically spoke the words that held her captive.

"Several months ago, someone tried to kill me. I was stranded... left alone to die."

There. She'd said it. There was no turning back and no beating around the bush. Lowering her eyes, she watched his reaction closely. She agreed with what he'd said earlier. They had a lot to get out on the table. Perhaps he would open up, tell her what was going on with all his phone calls and texts... give their relationship a fair chance to grow.

He shifted as he lifted himself to face her. "I know," he responded. Her eyes held fast to his as she searched him deeply, desperate to see his heart.

His cell dinged with a text. He ignored it as he continued to gaze in silence, giving her time to say more. His cell dinged again. And again just before it rang. "Must be urgent," she said with a tinge of annoyance in her voice. She couldn't shake the overwhelming fear that the calls were about her. "You better answer it," her voice trembled as she spoke. *Did he just say that he knew?*

He bolted upward in one swift leap after glancing to see whom it was. He was visibly shaken as he listened attentively. He turned to hide the incredulous look on his face, the redness in his eyes.

She walked over and hugged his back. After the call ended, he kept the phone to his ear while he composed himself. He remained still for several moments after placing it back in his pocket. He relaxed his shoulders, turned, and faced her. He had to pull himself together, to think straight... to be strong.

He considered the fact that Moriah had been through a horrendous situation. Her tragedy may not have anything to do with what he suspected. He felt in his heart of hearts she had nothing to do with it. He wished for it to be true.

He wanted to believe it. Desperately, he needed for her to be without fault. The turn of events secretly planned for tomorrow could be the demise of their relationship. But for now, even in the midst of the devastation the outcome could bring, he wanted nothing more than to be with her. Until then, he decided he would enjoy their time together.

He took his cell out and powered it down. He shut off the gadgets on his watch and pulled her into a deep embrace. She buried her head in his chest as her uneasiness melted. His head rested in her hair as they held each other. There was no denying it, their relationship had grown to a place he'd never known before.

He thought about his breakup with Glorieta. It was her loss. She was the one who had run off with someone else. When he'd caught them together, she'd told him she couldn't wait for him to reestablish himself after selling his law practice. It was then that he'd determined that he'd never let anyone get close to his heart again. That was, until he'd met Moriah.

He hoped she felt the same way. For the moment, their language consisted of no words, their future held no promises. Yet, even in their solitude they found comfort in each other. The sting of their pain melted away with the promise of what could be. They could only hope.

"I've got a special evening planned for us. Are you sure you don't want to rest before we go?" he waggled his eyebrows. "You're going to need it." He gently caressed her cheek. Before she could say a word, he told her it was going to be a surprise.

"You've got more surprises than anyone I know." Moriah looked at his mischievous grin.

"I'll send Mickey up to help you pick out something appropriate for the evening. And no *hitting her up* for any clues either!" Moriah chuckled at his choice of words. *Am I rubbing off on him already?* She smiled as she headed toward the guest room suite.

Moriah took Tyro up on his suggestion to rest. At least she'd get off her feet for a while. She thought she was too excited to sleep until Mickey tapped lightly on the door. She was surprised that she actually had dozed off. "I'm sorry if I awakened you," the petite woman said as she approached her.

Grinning widely, the servant held up two outfits for Moriah to explore. "Either one would be fitting for the evening," Mickey said.

"I know... I know; I won't ask." Moriah tapped her chin with her finger. She cocked her head as she examined each one carefully. "Lord knows I don't want to spoil his surprise," she teased. Although she figured Tyro would have loved for her to wear the red, above knee length with the sequins, she thought the color was too overpowering.

She chose the peach. It was more relaxing and subtle. Besides, it accentuated her warm-brown skin tone and was fitting for her personal style. She appreciated his thoughtfulness towards her in giving her a choice. After she had fully dressed, Moriah slipped on the pair of sapphire earrings she selected from the choices of jewelry Mickey presented to her. They dangled daintily.

"This would go perfectly!" Mickey said as she displayed a matching sapphire necklace in her palm.

"Where... how did you get—"

"It was in your pocket," Mickey said as she backed away. Her eyes quickly focused on the floor.

"Well, it's not mine to wear." She reached tenderly toward the young woman who obviously was bothered by her reaction. She touched her arm. "I didn't mean to—"

"It's okay." Mickey kept her eyes shifted away. "I just thought they'd go nicely together." She glanced quickly at Moriah's earrings before shifting her eyes away again. "I found the necklace earlier when I emptied your pockets. I placed it on the dresser." She turned briefly from where she'd just come.

"We always empty the pockets before we have the garments cleaned," she said, stammering as she glanced into Moriah's eyes. She couldn't resist smiling back at the compassion and understanding that met her.

Moriah had truly forgotten all about finding the necklace earlier. And it was odd that the earrings and necklace were a perfect match. But still she felt uneasy wearing it. She decided to leave her neck bare.

198

Chapter 26

Tyro guided the family's yacht, "Ms. Laino," away from the family island estate. Although Moriah had no idea where they were going, she basked in the tranquil atmosphere that danced with the promise of a splendid evening.

Cruising along, he gave her the grand tour. She stood at the bow admiring the various lighthouses, dolphin sightings, and other boats as their ship drifted effortlessly over the calming waters. Tyro pointed out a bank of colorful homes that looked like a cluster of polka dots sporadically burrowed in the craggy hills.

She took in the beauty painted across the sky as the sun nestled down for the night. It illuminated several of the small islands hidden in the distance that she otherwise wouldn't have noticed. "Thank you," she said as she turned toward Tyro. He smiled back at her.

Amazed, she was captivated watching a blue marlin put up the fight of its life. "Most likely they've been wrestling with it for several hours now," Tyro commented as he joined her. "Aw man!" he tsked in disappointment as it finally wrenched itself out of the fishermen's grasp. Moriah smiled at its escape. *Good for you!* she thought to herself as she watched it swim away.

Twenty minutes later, they were coasting along the estuary of Virginia. The light from the full moon exposed the golden flecks sprinkled in the midst of Tyro's gray eyes. An exceptionally warm breeze, for being the latter part of September, rustled in the air. She admired his brownish locks as they frolicked in the wind.

The sleeveless, peach floor-length dress fit her like a glove, hugging her every curve. The front of it swooped into a rounded series of folds, landing a hair above her cleavage. When she chose the dress, she'd hoped it would complement whatever he wore. She wasn't disappointed. Her eyes beamed at his choice of his usual preppy, casual style. *Man, does he look good!*

Her warm skin tone radiated as she stood under the glimmer of a low hanging moon. She reached up as if to catch its light. She turned toward Tyro who stood next to her and playfully pretended to pour it into his hands. Instinctively, he cupped his palms as if to receive it.

She closed her eyes and breathed deeply. For the first time since she'd been with Tyro, she felt completely relaxed, and appreciated the time away from her troubles.

Thinking of how good his arms felt wrapped around her waist, tugged at her heartstrings. For one moment, she allowed herself to imagine what it would be like to be with this man forever. A smile crossed her face.

"That's a mighty big smile you got there." He brushed away the tresses that had blown in her face. "I like it and I expect to see it for the remainder of our time together."

He pulled her close. "Deal?"

"Since you're making propositions, I want nothing more than to see those gorgeous grays of yours all evening. Deal?"

A passionate kiss affirmed and sealed the agreement. "Now remember, you gave me your word," he teased.

"Well then, it'll be your job to make sure you or nobody else ticks me off." She pulled her shoulders back and she stared pointedly at him.

"I can handle that," he promised as he pulled her back close to him.

"Oh?" She eyed him. "Is that right?" Moriah could see where the conversation could end up. But it was too perfect of an evening to let it go there. There definitely were some issues they needed to talk about. Soon. As far as she was concerned, Tyro needed to get his dad under control, and quick.

She turned again to take in the gorgeous views. He pulled her into his cocoon and held her as he rocked her slowly. She melted in his embrace. She leaned her head back on his shoulder as she folded her arms over his.

Basked in tranquility, they sailed in quiet bliss for twenty minutes. It was perfect. "Why can't it stay like this forever?" she whispered. Her voice trailed off into the atmosphere. Although he hated to do so, he had to excuse himself. He needed to check on their meal.

Roy had prepared their dinner and had set everything up ahead of time. The temperature in the warmer was set just right to keep their meals fresh and steamy for whenever they wanted it.

While Tyro was below deck, he turned on soft music. As Moriah continued to look out over the water, her body began to sway. Unable to resist, she closed her eyes, becoming more in tune with the smooth jazz mellowing from the sound system. Even the waves that lapped against the sides of the yacht seemed to fall in rhythm.

The sultry melody teasingly caressed her ears as he returned to the upper deck. She turned to face him. He smiled at the moonlight accentuating her features. Her lips were full and perfectly shaped like someone had actually drawn them on her face.

"You are lovelier than the moon," Tyro sang in a playful, salty tone as he walked toward her. He held a cocktail glass in each hand.

"You know I don't—"

"Uh, uh, aahh," he seductively crooned as he lifted the glass toward her lips, bidding her to take a sip. "I'm sure you'll enjoy this, Ms. Styles." He flashed a charming smile.

She leaned back and narrowed her eyes at him as she maintained a mischievous smirk on her face.

"Trust me," he insisted. As their eyes held, she lowered her head to sip.

"Mmm!" she cooed, delighted by the delicious, fruity taste. "What is it?" she asked, removing the glass from his hand and taking another sip. It wasn't as sweet as she'd thought it would be.

"Oh, just one of Roy's specialties. It's a pomegranate mojito mocktail."

"A what… mojo what?" she quipped as she set her eyes back on him. "Should I be concerned?" she asked with a smirk. "You and Roy into voodoo?" She laughed as she spoke the words "mojo mocktail."

"Mojito mocktail. It's a non-alcoholic cocktail."

"Okay, I get that part, but what about the mojo?" She chuckled.

"It's mo-he-toe, not mojo," he said, laughing as he enunciated it correctly for her. "You never cease to amuse me."

He removed the glass from her hand and set both of them on a table-bench near them. He placed his hand at the small of her back as one of the songs he'd preselected began to play.

Slowly, he lifted her other hand and intertwined it with his. He swayed her tenderly as Luther bellowed one of Tyro's favorite ballads, "Here and Now."

"I didn't know you *got down* with Luther like that," she said delighted, snuggling her head into his chest.

"Huh?" Tyro responded, trying to understand what she meant. She attempted to explain. He delicately shushed her with a gentle whisper in her ear. Not wanting to ruin the moment, she lowered her head back to his chest. He softly sang to her in between his tender kisses on her hand, her neck, her face, and her lips.

"And you sing too." *Lord help me!* "You have a wonderful voice!" she told him. He grinned proudly.

Chapter 27

Tyro guided Moriah to the lower deck after they finished their drinks. "Oh my," she exclaimed quietly as she clasped her hand over her chest while admiring the ambiance. The table was dressed with a melon colored linen, her favorite color. A Bird of Paradise adorned the center of the rounded table. The two candles flickering in the dimness provided the only source of light.

A Hawaiian orchid lay in the center of her empty plate. It matched her dress perfectly. She lifted it to her nose and breathed deeply. He admired how she appreciated the simplest things. He removed the flower from her hand and placed it in her hair behind her left ear. He smiled as it fit perfectly. Its delicate petals splayed outwardly toward her cheek.

He kissed her palm as she cupped his face. Guiding her to sit, he pulled her chair out and placed the napkin across her lap as she sat. Folding her hands, she said the blessing aloud over their food, their lives, and for his dad. He politely bowed his head but kept his eyes on her as she prayed.

Her prayer touched him. For a moment, he considered taking her hands into his. He wanted to, but he couldn't. He'd been avoiding praying. The whole *God* thing for him had gone awry months ago.

Her smile, as she finished praying, caused a warm sensation to course through his veins, ripping his heart open. He tried to squelch the feeling.

There was no getting around it. No way to escape the obvious. The woman he wanted to spend the rest of his life with was seated across from him. And God was a big part of her life.

But as for him, he hadn't surrendered to God's nudgings since they had buried his mother. As she was sealed up in her tomb, so was his need for any Deity in his life.

He thought of the scar on Moriah's leg, her anxiety attacks, her meltdowns. Although he didn't know the magnitude of the attack she'd suffered, he was amazed that she still held on to her faith in God. He thought of his own pain and wondered how that could be.

He knew of his neglect toward God, and why. His mind drowned in confusion. Guilt. It had been a long time… too long. But he wanted this woman in his life. She was a source of strength, a beacon of light through his darkness. He wondered if their differences could cause a gap between them.

For a fleeting moment, he turned his thoughts toward God, merely for his own selfish reason. But that was unacceptable. His mother had taught him better.

In the stillness of his mind he heard the pounding of his heart beckoning him to cry out to God. He desperately needed His help. His eyes fell from the woman staring at him, as if she could see his inner turmoil. She sat quietly. Waiting.

His heart melted for her right then. He knew before he could move forward, he'd have to settle his angst with God, and soon, before what little ray of hope he had left fluttered away completely.

Pushing his unrest aside, he smiled as he nodded toward the serving trays. "May I?" he asked as he rose from the table and began placing food on their plates. He filled their glasses with sparkling French water and took his seat.

"You, Moriah Styles," he began as he took hold of her hand across the table, "you couldn't have come into my life in more perfect timing."

Chapter 28

After their meal, Tyro gently journeyed the yacht down the Chesapeake canal. When they reached their destination, he skillfully maneuvered the vessel to dock at their private marina.

Moriah enjoyed their walk down the Chesapeake Pier and along the boardwalk. They held hands and stopped at various shops as gentle breezes blew their hair this way and that. "I love your hair," Tyro said as he planted a tender kiss on her head.

They walked amid other folks who were also out enjoying the evening. Couples moseying by, eating ice cream, chatting about this and that, or about nothing in particular. Just as she and Tyro, other couples enjoyed being in the company of someone they loved.

Other than hearing a few folks musing about the recent fairy tale craze, no one recognized or paid them any mind. She couldn't have asked for anything more. They blended in with the rest of the lovers walking along the pier. She breathed easier.

She wanted to stop at a small antique shop just off the main boardwalk. She had seen the sign several yards back. She loved to browse through art and antique shops.

Tyro led the way, holding her hand tightly. He was elated to see her enjoying herself as she cooed about various items. They spent countless minutes browsing, and admiring the various artifacts within the shop.

Her eyes trailed the jewelry case and stopped as she spotted a pocket watch. It was open and the lid displayed a place to hold a photo. "How much is this piece right here?" she asked curiously.

Tyro was across the room and turned as he heard her ask how much something cost. He wasn't used to having to do such a thing. If he saw something he wanted, he'd buy it. No questions asked.

"Wow... $200.00?" she haggled. "How about $150 and that's my best offer... for the both of them," she said sweetly pointing to a set of small picture frames that sat behind the watch. Moriah lovingly shoved Tyro out of the way after he whipped his wallet out and began peeling out several Benjamins. He'd only wanted to help.

She shot him a glare and made several odd facial gestures as she moved him further away. "You're ruining my surprise," she said, shooing him to the farther end of the counter. She didn't want him to see the small matching set of frames she was also purchasing. Their simplistic design would look great on the mantel in his modern styled great room.

He had no idea what was going on, but he quickly stashed his money away and plopped his wallet back inside his jacket pocket.

"Would you please wrap them as two separate gifts for me?" Her voice trailed off as she returned her attention back to the owner. "Those can be wrapped together in the blue and gold," she said in a hushed tone as she leaned to point at the set of frames.

"Of course," the owner responded. When she walked away, he mumbled beneath his breath. He moved her purchases toward the colorful rolls of metallic wrapping paper positioned directly behind the glass encasement. His eyes shifted from Tyro to the pocket where his wallet bulged, reminding him of the additional $150.00 he'd just lost. Begrudgingly, he wrapped the purchases as she requested.

She wandered back to where he was busy fussing with the packaging. Drawing a circle around the item lying on the counter as he removed the price tag, she leaned to speak so that only he would hear her.

"You and I both know that it's not worth half of what I'm paying you." She pointed at the winding stem and crown slightly off position at the watch's crown. She remained poised. "But I understand, business is business." The owner quickly focused back on the item as his eyes tore away from her astute smile. "Please wrap the Huntington in the red and gold print," she said as she pointed to the wrapping paper she desired.

She took a quick glimpse in Tyro's direction. Tyro pretended to be preoccupied as he looked at other items at the far end. However, her cunningness in getting what she wanted hadn't gone unnoticed. He rubbed his face as uneasiness pricked at his mind.

Moriah handed the storeowner her debit card. A few moments later, he placed it back on the counter for her to retrieve it after she had punched in her pin. She looked at the card he'd set back on the counter. "Excuse me, may I please have my card back?" Although she was within a hand's reach, she refused to pick it up.

In her mind, she had politely handed her card to him and she would accept nothing less but for him to hand it back to her out of respect, whether or not he was happy about what he let the items go for. He was a dealer. He knew how bargaining went. And boy, was she good at it!

A few minutes later, he handed her the receipt along with a small but exquisite looking shopping bag with her purchases. He avoided her eyes. She smiled sweetly and curtseyed. "Thank you," she said, adding extra "oomph" as she sashayed out the door with her arm locked into Tyro's.

"What was that all about?" he asked after they'd walked back to the yacht in complete silence.

"Oh nothing. Just a little *shoptalk*, that's all," she said.

"Yeah, I bet it was, 'just a little shoptalk.' You really ticked him off."

"Oh, so now you trying to get all up in my business… Tyro, you're going to ruin my surprise," she cooed, kissing his cheek lightly.

He straightened his shoulders and decided to let the matter go. Seeing her in action caused his mind to wander to what his dad had said about her earlier that day. Quincy had accused her of being conniving and a manipulator. But he refused to believe such a thing about her.

"I enjoyed myself tonight." She nuzzled closer to her six-foot hero. After kissing his cheek gently, she wrapped her arms around his waist.

"You'll have to wait until later... don't be getting any funny ideas in that head of yours!" She narrowed her eyes as she playfully pushed his head to the side with her hand.

"Surprise, huh?" he responded. "I can wait, the night's still young."

"What you got in mind, sailor?" she teased as he eased the vessel backward to clear the boat from the dock. Watching the stars as they twinkled in the night sky reminded her of the necklace she'd found earlier.

She'd forgotten all about it. She thought of how perfect the evening was going and determined it was best to wait for another time to tell him about it. She suspected that it may have belonged to his mother. She didn't want to put a damper on his mood with sad memories, although she wondered how it ended up in the ocean. She was sure it had sentimental value, but what or why, she couldn't put her finger on it.

"Are you up for watching a movie?" he asked, over his shoulder.

"I don't know, Tyro. It would be really late when we'd get back from a theater. I really don't want to be out on the boat when it's dark like that."

"Did I say anything about going to a theater? You worry too much. Let me handle my business, just like you handled yours at the shop, Ms. Negotiator, okay?"

Moriah leaned back. "Well... all righty then. Go on and handle your *business*, Mr. Simmonds." They laughed at each other's banter. But deep inside, she was glad to see this side of him. Now if only he'd stand up to his dad like that, she'd really be impressed.

Chapter 29

Tyro docked the boat back at the family's island. He recommended they watch Gone Girl. The night was still full of promise. Exhilarated from the time they'd spent together, neither wanted it to end. There was yet more to discover about one another.

She'd let nothing spoil her evening. It had been absolutely perfect. She could get used to being around him. Their relationship was growing. She felt both excited and scared.

Having the time to get away from the media frenzy, and his cell constantly going off, she was elated he had kept it turned off. It would have spoiled everything. *What a pity that would have been.*

She thought of Quincy. She could only imagine what he must be going through. She knew too well the pain of losing someone you loved dearly. Remembering her promise to herself, she pushed the crippling pangs of losing her twin aside.

Still, Moriah felt sorry for Quincy in a way; although she didn't understand why he snooped around like he did. It was disturbing to say the least. Every time she'd turn around, he'd be standing in the shadows, peeping and eavesdropping in on their conversations. Like when they were on the balcony, during lunch, when they were in the great room, and at the pool. And even when they were in the garden, she saw him peeping out of the third level window before he came out pretending he was doing his *gardening*. He just seemed so lost.

She had expected for him to pop out like Jack in the Box as they sailed in the middle of nowhere. Moriah wouldn't have been surprised at all. Disappointed and enraged, yeah. Truth was, she anticipated it happening, and Tyro wouldn't have done a doggone thing about it.

As they strolled along, she looked in the direction of Quincy's house. The lights were out. She surmised he was asleep. Still holding snuggly to Tyro's arm, they headed toward the entertainment wing of his home. The bag containing the gifts she bought dangled freely in her other hand.

Tyro had told her about the perks he had in his entertainment investment portfolio. "Being able to preview movies legally before they hit the Box Office in the comfort of my home is one I particularly enjoy." When he emphasized the word "legally" it brought a devious smile to his face as he glanced out the corner of his eye.

"I would enjoy seeing Gone Girl." She was pleased with the perks in his investment.

Just as they were a few steps away from the media room, he pulled her around to face him. "I hope I won't regret telling you this," he said as he beheld the loveliness of her face. "I want to spend as much time with you as possible." His hands jittered as they released hers to pull her close to his chest.

She relished hearing his rapid heartbeat. She wanted to be with him just as much. But she couldn't get around the nagging feeling there was something he was hiding.

"No matter what happens, or how things turn out between us," he stammered, "you have captured my heart in a way I never knew possible." He raised her chin to gaze into her eyes.

She felt the same way too. But the uneasiness pricking at her increased. *What does he mean, 'no matter how things turn out between us?' What does he know? What is he hiding?*

"Tyro. What is it you're not telling me?" She pulled back waiting for him to answer. Her eyes flashed at him like a searchlight, looking for answers.

She could see the resolve in his eyes. He was going to tell her! He was finally going to spill it out—all of it. She just knew it. As her hands cupped his face, the package slid from her fingers.

She steadied his attention from reaching for the bag as it cascaded onto the plush runner lining the hallway. Her eyes bore into his soul. She wrapped her arms around his neck, holding his gaze steady. "What is it?" she whispered, pleading with her eyes.

He pulled her into his embrace. She received his kiss as he pressed his lips passionately into hers. Slowly she pulled away. While tingling with excitement, her mind wrestled with suspicion, apprehension. Fear. He kissed her again. The guard around her emotions melted away. Her desire for him had awakened. At that moment, nothing else mattered. She longed to trust him.

But deep within she found the strength, a voice reasoning inside of her warned her as she pushed away. He avoided telling her what she had to know. "I can't do this." Her eyes fell to her feet. He lifted her chin.

"What is it?" he asked. "What is it you *need* to know?" His eyes shifted from her gaze.

Suddenly she realized he hadn't planned on telling her anything at all. She was the one who had been gullible by letting her guard down. And then the overwhelming feeling that something terrible was about to explode caused her to pull completely from out of his grasp.

Chapter 30

Tyro lifted the shopping bag from the floor as his other hand took Moriah's. As she wearily entered the media room, she stopped abruptly. She couldn't believe her eyes. Quincy had just finished loading the popcorn machine and had flipped the switch on. He looked up at them as they stood in the doorway.

"I've been wanting to see Gone Girl myself... Ben's starting to grow on me," Quincy quipped as he grabbed the controls to toggle through the menu on the screen.

Moriah leaned her shoulders back and stared a hole through him. Her eyes darted from Quincy to Tyro, and then back again. "Is he spying on us?" she asked Tyro as she yanked her hand from his. She faced him, looking him square in the eyes for an explanation.

"How'd he know we were going to watch a movie?" She darted her index finger in his face. She narrowed her eyes as she waited for him to answer. "How did he know we were going to watch Gone Girl?" she demanded more loudly.

"Tyro," she stepped back out of the room. He had not yet answered her. "What is going on? Why does he... how does he know what we're doing?"

"Please." He reached for her. "I can explain." She yanked away. Reality rushed in on her like the evening tide. "Whatever is going on with your dad's beef with me, you're in on it too." She shuddered as she stepped further away. "You're telling him aren't you? I don't believe... I can't believe this." She wanted to run away so far she'd never see the likes of him, or his dad again.

Tyro caught her by the wrist as she turned. She screamed as she banged on his chest for him to let her go. "You're using me. But why? Why? What do I have to do with anything for you to do this to me?"

"*You know who killed my wife!*" Quincy bellowed as he marched toward her.

"What?" Moriah couldn't believe her ears. "I know what?" She cocked her head to the side. "You've got to be kidding me. So... that's it?" She shot a look at Tyro. "You're telling me... You think I know who killed your mom? I don't believe this—"

"Enough!" Tyro yelled to his dad. "You've gone too far! Let me handle this."

"You got your nose too far up her skirt to—" Quincy's face turned beet red as Tyro interrupted him. "Dad, I said that's enough... Leave us. *Now!*"

Tyro delicately guided Moriah back into the room as Quincy simultaneously stormed toward the door. He had taken the liberty of turning on the news before he'd barged from the room.

A reporter was talking into a microphone standing next to a fair-skinned, heavyset woman. The volume was muted and Moriah couldn't make out what they were saying. She could only surmise the detriment from what was scrolling across the screen.

Pregnant woman alleged she was pinned under the grizzly teeth of the Green Monster; says she will file civil charges for an undisclosed amount once the perpetrators have been found...

Moriah stood there for a moment, dazed as she fought to collect her thoughts. She couldn't believe the gall of the woman, trying to take advantage of the situation. With the charges and allegations piling up, and Quincy's despicable attitude, she needed to get away from that place. But how could she? She was trapped on an island. She had no way to escape. Reality gripped her. She had been foolish to trust him. *Lord, help me... please.*

"Moriah," Tyro said pointedly. She stepped back.

"Get away from me. Take me home, now!" she demanded. "If you don't, I'll... I'll call the police and turn myself in. I'll tell them you kidnapped me and brought me here against my will."

Running down the hallway, she tried to find the bedroom she'd slept in last night. She got lost in the maze of entrances and exits to the various wings of his estate. Lunging around the corner, she ran right smack into the arms of a tall strapping man. She knew him from somewhere, but at the moment, she couldn't remember. Her mind was so flustered.

"Mario!" Tyro yelled from the direction she'd just come.

"Quincy texted me. Said things had gotten a little out of control." He looked down into Moriah's face streaming with tears. He looked back at Tyro who stood behind her restraining himself from reaching out to hold her. To comfort her and assure her everything was going to be all right.

"Oh, so, you're in on this charade too?" she snapped, now remembering meeting Mario.

He put his hands out. "No. I had no part in it and I told him to back off." Mario turned and glared at Quincy before he shot a disdainful look at his nephew. "I never believed in it and I don't condone their behavior."

"Can you get me off this island, please? Take me home," she pleaded.

"Believe me, Ms. Styles, if I thought it was best to do so, I would. The only thing I agreed to that made any sense was now that you are here, it is best to keep you here for your safety."

"So... you *are* in on it," she accused, pulling herself out of his gentle embrace.

"No, that's not what I said."

"Am I being held here against my will?" She tightened her lips and glared at him while she waited for him to respond.

"Please," Tyro said, stepping from behind her, "I... we can explain if you would allow us to. Please?" He raised his hand directing her to the great room. He was careful not to touch her. He needed for her to be calm, relaxed, and somehow in the midst of the fiasco, to feel safe. He then eyed Mario for help with his choice of words to point out to her that she was in danger.

Chapter 31

Tyro could only hope Moriah hadn't thought anything more about Mario's insinuation that she was in danger. The authorities feared Moriah's attacker was still alive. They found no evidence to prove he was dead, as she had reported during the investigation. Could the same guy who had attacked her and left her mercilessly to die be the same perpetrator who'd killed his mother?

Was her attacker indeed who they'd been looking for? Could it be that Moriah knew his mother's murderer?

The detective was unsure of her part in his mother's death, which left more questions to be answered. This was another issue that had caused Tyro to wane in his trust for her. Had she lied about her attacker's death to hide her involvement? If not, and he was still alive, she could be in danger.

He wanted to believe she had nothing to do with his mother's attack. He desperately needed for her to be innocent regardless of what the evidence proved.

He also questioned how his father had known about Moriah's ordeal? He had filled him in on some of the details earlier. But how had he gotten such classified information? How long had he known? Was that why he was so out of control when he'd brought her there last night and then suddenly changed his mind, allowing her to stay?

Moriah let out a long breath as she wrapped her hands around her arms. She walked slowly, reluctantly into the great room and sat on the sofa. Quincy slouched in the room like a puppy with his tail between its legs and sat at the opposite end of her.

No he didn't just sit his mean behind on the same couch as me. Moriah shot him a look that could kill. Tyro immediately sat between them. She wasn't at all happy with him either. She bolted out of her seat and moved to one of the twin armless chairs positioned by the window.

Mario trailed in as one of the servants followed behind him. She offered to serve tea. Nobody was in the mood for tea. She left the tray on the credenza. "It'll be here if you change your mind," Mickey said as she gave Moriah a compassionate look before leaving the room.

Sheba sat by Moriah's feet. She whined as she looked up into Moriah's face. She felt relaxed seeing the Shepherd had come by her side. She reached briefly to rub her ears. Sheba laid her head over Moriah's feet and flashed her big eyes over at Tyro.

Mario fixed a cup of Chamomile tea mixed with a hint of lavender and handed it to Moriah. "It'll help." He smiled. Moriah received the cup and sipped the steamy liquid. He was right. After drinking most of it, she felt calm, in control. She set the cup on the table and leaned back in her seat.

"Moriah," Tyro's voice trembled as he spoke, "I know this is no excuse, but please, hear me out in what I am about to say." She kept her gaze fixed on the floor. What could he possibly say to excuse the fact that he had used her? Her emotions. He'd taken advantage of her fears, her anxiety, and her love, for his own selfish means.

"When I met you that night, I had no idea you were who we had been looking for over the past two months." He paced back and forth in front of the fireplace. "We'd been trying to track down the clients of a former pilot of ours." He reached to touch her shoulder. She leaned away.

"After we had fired him, he'd disappeared without a trace. Then, we got word that he'd changed his name and may have been hired as a private pilot for the company you work for." He paused to gauge her reaction.

She narrowed her eyes at him. "Used to work for," she adamantly corrected him. "Go on." She folded her arms as she kept her attention fixed on him.

He stammered. "We weren't sure if you were the young lady he'd piloted. But I promise you," he grabbed hold of her hand, "as I raced toward you that night, all I thought about was getting you out of the vehicle. I had no idea who you were."

She snatched her hand away. "And you felt like you were redeeming yourself... as if you were saving your..." She didn't want to come off cold, like she was insensitive. But for him to have been stringing her along and not being open and honest with her was downright inexcusable under any circumstances.

"What happened to being honest?" she snapped. "You were the one who told me how important honesty is to you. Doesn't it go for you too?" She stood.

"I've heard enough." She headed out of the room and immediately spun around just as she reached the doorway. "I'm truly sorry about Mrs. Simmonds. I really am. But using me... causing me to have to suffer through your despicable acts to find answers... closure, was totally unfair to—"

"Now you just wait one minute, little lady!" Quincy barreled out of his seat, startling her. It was the first time he'd spoken since accusing her in the media room. "There is no one to blame for this whole mess, but me." His head bowed remorsefully, only for a moment.

"I can assure you neither my son, nor Mario had anything to do with... with... this whole...." Moriah watched in disbelief as he struggled to find the words to put the situation in the right perspective. His hands flailed about like a whirlwind. "Connivery," he said as the word finally flew out of his mouth.

"Even if that were true, he's a grown man," she said, looking momentarily in Tyro's direction. "He could've put a stop to it. Couldn't he, Mr. Simmonds?" she stared at the white haired man and waited for an answer.

Chapter 32

Moriah turned to leave. Neither Tyro nor his dad had responded. Sheba trotted next to her. Moriah stopped just as she stepped over the threshold. "In fact, you should have told me. Why did you have to go along with it in the first place?" she said, stepping back into the room. Her eyes blazed at Tyro. "It's my life you played with. That won't be happening again."

"He did not know," Quincy spat. "Tyro only found out when I sent the wrong text to him earlier today." He folded his arms and jutted his head toward his brother in law. "He then called Mario."

"And that makes it okay?" she asked incredulously.

Tyro sighed. "Moriah, in spite of what this may seem like, I need for you to finish hearing me out. If you don't believe me, or it doesn't make sense enough for you to trust me, I'll have Mario or one of our pilots take you home. Or at least to a safer location than your current residence until you sort things out.

"What's where I live have to—" He put his hands out as she spoke. He moved closer but kept an arm's length distance. "The night when I rescued you, I didn't know who you were. But the truth of the matter is," he lifted her head and gazed into her eyes, "it was you who saved my life. That night, I had been driving around aimlessly. Trying to drown out the pain, the voice that constantly told me I had failed my mother."

Mario walked over and gave his nephew an affirming hug around his shoulder. "I couldn't take it anymore. I had no idea where I was going, or what I was going to do... I just wanted to end the pain. The guilt." Tyro's eyes brimmed with anguish. He choked on his words as he struggled to continue to speak. "I just felt compelled to drive up that particular road." He couldn't hold it back any longer as he sobbed in his uncle's arms. The mere thought of what he may have done to himself if he hadn't run into her that night was unthinkable.

Quincy joined in as Mario and Tyro hugged. They hadn't shown each other such affection since they'd huddled at the hospital when they had prayed, pleaded for Laino to survive.

Now here they stood in the midst of Tyro's home with a chance to start over again. Moriah watched the three of them huddle as they reaffirmed their commitment to be a family again.

Mario was the first to break from their embrace. "It seems we owe you a big apology along with great gratitude." He gestured to the three of them. Their frustration, pain, and despair was evident. Desperate for answers. Closure.

Still, she wasn't excusing their actions for one minute. Neither did she trust them. Not any of them. No words would come as her lips grew tighter. She kept her eyes focused on her feet.

"It is what Laino would have wanted." Quincy's voice broke through the awkward moment. He looked over at Moriah. He was taken aback with the thought of losing his son, if it hadn't been for her. A tear formed in his eye. He cleared his throat. "Thank you, Ms. Styles," he said in a low and flustered tone. "Thank you for saving my son's life."

A tear trickled down her cheek. So what, they had apologized. What did they expect of her? Was she supposed to break out her pompoms and sing the *Hallelujah* chorus?

Moriah had her own pain to deal with. And now… this? The man she fell in love with was only using her. They accused her of having something to do with the murder of the woman they loved. They hadn't come out and said it, but they acted like it.

The weight of everything came crashing down on her. She felt queasiness in her stomach. She suspected there was something more they weren't telling her. She felt trapped. She slumped to the floor. With tears barreling down her face, she heaved in a silent cry.

It was Quincy who noticed her first. Tyro rushed to her side and sat next to her. He held her tenderly as she cried. He rocked her, stroked her hair, as he tried to comfort her. "I'm so sorry, Moriah. From now on I promise to be open and honest with you."

Mario patted Tyro on the shoulders as he and Quincy left out of the room. They left them alone to sort through their differences.

In Tyro's anguish, he promised to give her the time and space she needed to sort through her emotions and issues, on her terms.

They'd cried the night away, vowing to try again. They agreed to pull through the pain of their travesties together and to give their relationship a chance. They recognized the long road ahead of them, the need to earn the trust of the other. Although he made no promises to jump blindly into the *God* thing, inwardly he recognized the need for Him in his life.

Chapter 33

Late Sunday morning, Tyro tapped on the guest room door where Moriah was still asleep. He assumed. To his surprise, she was dressed and ready to go.

He glanced at the Bible lying open on her bed. Mickey slipped quietly out of the room. Holding her hand on the door, she turned back and smiled at Moriah. "Remember His mercy," she mouthed as she pointed upward before closing the door behind her.

"What was that all about?" he asked, shifting his eyes from her to the Bible.

She patted her bed for him to take a seat. He glanced at his watch. He'd promised her a tour over the islands and a romantic picnic off shore. They would get started much later than he wanted if they wasted any more time.

He glanced at the scripture outlined in yellow. Scanning over the words "mercy... new every morning... kindness," he was familiar with the verses found in Lamentations about God's mercies. He remembered the words very well. The priest had spoken them at his mother's funeral.

He felt bile welling up in his throat. *If God was so merciful then why*— "We should go now," he said, cutting through his own thoughts. Lifting her chin with his fingers, he gave her a gentle smile.

Although he promised, he wasn't ready to weave through his tangled web of confusion and emotions about God and faith. Just before he'd come to get her, he'd tried praying but had gotten nowhere. And right now, he wasn't up for the disappointment again.

In fact, he didn't think he would be able to resolve his issue with God until he got what he needed. The mystery surrounding his mother's murder had to be solved; justice had to be served. And that's exactly what he'd planned to do. He'd let nothing and no one get in his way, not even his heart. He walked to the door and waited.

"Okay, let's go then," Moriah said cheerfully. He watched as she set the Bible back on the shelf. He knew she'd sensed his perplexity. She smiled, and plopped on her shades, hiding the puffiness around her eyes. She'd poured her soul out last night. And although he had gotten a deeper understanding of her pain, she had been vague in the details.

What she had told him was meaningless. Void of what he desperately longed to... needed to know. The truth. How well had she known Fletcher? Had she been there with him and things had gone too far when he'd killed his mother? She was hiding something. He sensed it with every nerve in his body.

Still, he promised her what she asked of him last night as he held her through her turmoil. Truth. Honesty.

His heart still ached with pain, and disappointment. Nothing she'd told him increased his trust for her. He hated the fact she was holding back, still. Even though he cared deeply for her, he felt justified that what he had promised her would have to wait until after what he had planned for today was done.

Chapter 34

"I'm having one of our pilots charter our flight for us," Tyro announced.

"Oh?" Moriah questioned. He opened the door to the helicopter to help her in. She stretched her neck to peer into the pilot seat. The pilot was now strutting around to the side where Tyro was assisting her.

As Moriah was about to step up to get in, she felt butterflies fluttering in her stomach. She spun around and was met with a strange pair of eyes full of reserve, glaring over at her.

"Hello," the pilot said in a thick British accent. The lines around her eyes suddenly curled to match the smile on her face.

"Hi," Moriah responded as she did a double take of the woman, short in stature, who stood with her hand extended toward her.

"Sable," the pilot said as she flipped a crop of blonde hair away from her eye with a quick jerk of her head. She had introduced herself before Tyro had a chance to.

Moriah surmised the woman could have been about 45, but looked to be in her late 50s. Her skin had been aged from being in the sun a little too long, or either she had had her share of wine in the past. Even still, Moriah felt more at ease that their pilot was a woman.

"Moriah," she chimed back, introducing herself. She held on to the pilot's hand a little longer than she'd realized. She was mixed with emotions as she studied her.

There was something familiar, yet indefinably uncomfortable about her. Yet, she'd liked her. Maybe it was because she reminded her of her Foreign Language teacher from when she was in junior high. The class often used the stories she told about her wild adventures to create essays. Moriah had always loved her stories.

Most of the class claimed she made the stories up. But actually, Moriah had been able to picture her former teacher flying around the world. She used to imagine her in a two-seater plane with her scarf around her neck sailing in the wind like the Red Baron. And here was the living proof, right before her eyes!

Moriah composed herself as Tyro nudged her to climb in the helicopter. He seemed eager for them to be on their way. She shook her head and complied as she realized her imagination had gotten away from her.

Chapter 35

Tyro placed the picnic basket on the empty front seat next to Sable. Sheba had gingerly claimed herself a spot next to Moriah. As he entered the cabin, she looked at her master with pleading eyes, and whined. Tyro commanded her to sit in her designated place in the back. Moriah chuckled at the two of them. She let out a deep breath. She determined she was going to enjoy her last day on the island. It was such a beautiful Sunday afternoon.

As the helicopter circled around the island, Moriah appreciated it much more during the day as opposed to seeing it at night. The tropical trees were more vibrant and colorful. Looking down on them, she had no idea they grew so tall.

He pointed out the various highlights of their island estate as he sat near her. She saw the walking and bicycle path extending around the back end of the island. She admired the tennis and basketball courts that sat off to the left side of the beach. She hadn't gotten that far as she walked the paths yesterday.

She peered down at the beach and the homes, the same ones Quincy had been adamant about her not staying at when she had first arrived. It was a picture carved right out of a magazine. She admired the elegance of the mansion as he told her it was where their staff and their families lived.

Moriah leaned her shoulders back and tilted her head. "Their families live here too?"

"Yep. When we consider hiring our staff, we generally hire their spouses as well. It was my mother's doing. She said it would be a good way to keep the families together."

"And they get paid to work here and live in a luxury beach home for free too? Wow! Impressive!" She smiled at the folks bustling around in golf carts. He'd told her that's what they were, although they looked like matchbox cars from the height at which they had ascended.

"My mother had insisted that we hire families by lottery. Once a year, she'd put needed positions in numerous newspapers and on our website. Once they won, and passed their background checks, they would receive the proper training. The current staff provides the OJT they need. Once on board, they have a job and home for life." He looked out the window as he continued.

"They become like family to us as well as to one another." Tyro swelled with heartfelt pride as he spoke of his mother's vision and heart of compassion.

Moriah felt warm inside. Such a remarkable woman had raised the man she'd fallen in love with. Her heart fluttered.

"It was my mother's way of giving back to society." He smiled as he watched the tiny children splashing around in the water.

She mulled over his words in her head: *As long as they want to stay, they'll have a home and job for life.*

Loyalty! she mused to herself as she realized that loyalty was a big part of his family's values. *Is that why Quincy felt so threatened by me being here?* Then it dawned on her. *Background check... he had the nerve to do a background check on me. But how did he get so much information about me?*

"We have tutors, and educational mentors to assist with the children's home schooling. Our virtual learning center equips them with everything they need," he added proudly. Hearing the pride in his voice helped her focus her mind on what he was saying. He had no idea of the disdain toward his dad she was feeling at that moment.

Still, she was pleased he spoke freely of his mother. The atmosphere between the two of them became rejuvenated and devoid of any heaviness. No sadness threatened to creep in. She turned her attention to the beach below. She was reminded of the children she'd seen on the beach yesterday. It caused her to remember the necklace she'd found.

She'd also made a mental note to give it to him as soon as they got back. She didn't know why she kept forgetting about it. After all, she'd left it out on her dresser to remind her.

They had circled around the peninsula several times so that she could see the island in its entirety. This time, they hovered a little lower. She was pleased to see the diverse culture of workers and staff bustling around. "Your mother was quite a woman," Moriah mused.

"Whose house is that over there?" She pointed to a large multi-story home connected to the lighthouse. It was a good way to change the subject. She'd noticed his demeanor waning a little as he spoke of his mother.

"The head of our estates lives there."

"Roy?" she asked out of curiosity.

"No. You haven't met her yet. Her husband is our air traffic controller and maintains and operates our lighthouse."

"Is he the one Sable has been calling in our travel coordinates to?"

"Yep," he responded as he leaned in closer to look over her shoulder. "Ah, I see you know a little something about flying."

"Yeah... I know a lil' somethin', somethin' about it!" she teased. She turned to gaze into his eyes for just a few moments. The warm and fuzzy feelings she craved arose as she looked into his face. The way he kept his stubbled beard neatly groomed and close to his face was sexy as all get out!

Turning her attention back to the scenery, she noticed a small building with a steeple. It was the chapel she had visited yesterday. Leaning forward to get a better view, she located the yellow path Tyro had trailed off onto as she headed toward the beach.

Moriah was surprised that the path had led to a graveyard. She noticed Tyro had leaned back in his seat as they flew over it. Even from her distant height, she could tell that the man trudging toward the large mausoleum was Quincy. His head and shoulders remained slumped as he stepped up and entered into the darkened sepulcher.

She reached and grasped Tyro's hand without turning from looking out of the window. She thought of the last time she had visited the grave of someone dear to her. Now was not the time to talk about his mother's death.

A tinge of sadness overcame her knowing that such a tragedy had happened to his mother as well as her own perils she'd suffered. *Was Fletcher the one they'd been looking for…was he the killer?* She couldn't help but wonder.

As hard as it was for her to remind herself that Fletcher indeed had attacked her, albeit out of his perverted, deranged attraction for her, she wondered, *Why Laino?*

Laino had done so much for her family, and others. What reason would he, or anyone have to kill her? Although she felt great sorrow about his mother, she was grateful that she herself had survived.

Moriah turned her attention to the bluish-green waters below as they pulled away from the island. As they coasted over the water, she could see the island's shape in its entirety located just miles off the Chesapeake Bay. His family's island reminded her of two boots joined together at the calves.

Thirty minutes later after flying away from the island, they enjoyed their several patches of silence in between their conversations. Tyro would lean forward and point out various sceneries and sights for her to see as they approached them.

"Before I started my own business, I used to fly—" She stopped mid-sentence as a small patch of land several hundred yards up the coast came into view. She froze as her words caught in her throat. She sat back in her seat. Tyro leaned forward and studied her.

She blinked her eyes several times as turmoil began to cloud her mind. For a fleeting moment, the familiarity of having flown this way before burst through her memory. She stiffened. Her heart pounded heavily, threatening to explode. She shifted several times in her seat. *This can't be happening.* Her eyes snapped shut, her lips moved silently with rapid pace.

He turned her face to meet his. "Moriah. Are you okay?" Trying to swallow her fear, she turned her head aside. She stared in disbelief as the abominable place she'd vowed she never wanted to see again, drew closer into view.

Chapter 36

Sable flew the helicopter over the deserted patch of land. The tiny plot, about the size of one and a half miles, sat in the middle of nowhere. It was still considered an island, nonetheless.

"You can set us down over there," Tyro called up to the pilot, directing her to land a few yards away from the cavernous rock on the northern side of the island. She nodded to acknowledge his request.

She approached the designated spot with skill, and hesitation. Hovering, she waited for the command.

"That looks like a great spot to have a picnic, what do you think?" he pointed from his window. He turned and observed Moriah. She was staring down at a huge black rock; her muscles had tensed.

Suddenly, she bolted forward as they headed toward a small grave. She could see it clearly from her window although it was now covered with brush and wild flowers. As they descended, the wind from the rotary blades blew the brush aside. Her eyes raced over the grounds like a searchlight until she spotted it.

The shovel. It stuck out a few feet from the evidence. She wondered if he had seen it. Had he known she'd been here before? Was this a setup? She couldn't help but think about his father's accusations of her last night.

"We're not going to land here, are we?" she asked, unwilling to believe that Tyro would dare to bring her to this place. *How did he know?* Again, he had betrayed her. She held her breath, holding back the contents of her stomach from bubbling up.

There was no denying it. This was the same place that had ruined her life and scarred her forever. The memories of the whole ordeal burst through her mind.

It had been several months ago when Fletcher had flown her to the very same place. He had circled around the island several times. She had tried to pull her thoughts together regarding an urgent and disturbing text she'd just received before she suddenly lost the connection. He hovered the helicopter over the water for an extended period of time. As she'd wondered what he was up to, she was reminded of his strange and bazaar actions lately. Like the caged rat he had in the front seat next to him. She hadn't noticed it until she'd leaned forward to ask him about the air-conditioning when they'd first taken off.

If only there had been another pilot available, or a commercial flight she could have taken, she would have. But she had just closed the largest deal of her career. She was desperate to get home.

Frantically, her eyes scanned over the endless body of water beneath her. Fear seeped through her skin. It was then that she realized that her snap decision to allow Fletcher to fly her home had put her life in danger.

She turned from the window to ask him what was going on. She'd shuddered to find him sitting next to her.

His sudden attack with a cloth full of chloroform was too powerful for her to fight off. She struggled to keep from breathing in the chemical. Their helicopter started wobbling out of control. She knew he couldn't leave the controls unattended for too long; she made her body go limp. Holding her breath as long as she could, finally he released her.

Her mind was groggy as she squinted to see him hurrying back to the pilot seat. She knew if she were to survive, she would have to jump before he touched down.

She was terrified as she leapt out, twisting her ankle as she landed. Still, she got up and ran for her life. The words of the last text

232

she'd received raced through her mind. *He's dangerous...get away from him as fast as you can. We're coming....*

She fought through the sleepiness as she stumbled away. Despite the pain in her ankle, she ran as fast as she could. She had no idea where she was going. Hopelessness squeezed her lungs as she looked over her shoulder. The blades were spinning wildly, and he was now only several yards behind her. The cage with the rat dangled crazily in his hand.

Besides being out of breath, her stumbling and falling was no match for his agility and military training. She knew her survival now depended on her using her wits. And God.

Panting for breath, she held her hands up in surrender as she turned to face him. That's when she noticed his limp. His left leg dragged as if it were dead weight; he'd never limped before. As he got closer she saw the deranged distortion on his face. *Fletcher*? She hardly recognized him.

Her eyes strained to see if it was someone else, not him. He couldn't have been the same person. She scanned her surroundings for something she could use, a rock... a log... a broken shell... She would have grabbed hold of anything, but found nothing within her view. Within a matter of minutes, he caught up to her.

He grabbed her hair and snarled as he slung her to the ground. She caught a whiff of the foul odor on his breath. There was something eerie and frightening about him. He was not the Fletcher she knew when he was acting this weird.

Standing over her like she was his prey, he warned her, "If you run like that again, I will kill you." Each word was labored between deep, and strenuous drags of his breath.

She managed to lift herself from the ground. Trembling, she held her phone out; she had been recording. "They've been following you," she stuttered through her words as she kept her other hand extended, as if that would ward off her predator. "They're coming to get me, you hear me? They're on their way."

She thought he would back off, knowing that they were after him. But, it hadn't mattered. As she continued backing away from him, she screamed at him, telling him everything she knew in desperation to buy some time, to save her life. She wondered if they had gotten her last text. *Do they know where I am?* Her mind raced in desperation.

"The detectives told me you were under investigation." *They didn't tell me you were insane.* A debilitating feeling rushed through her as she kept that thought to herself.

Fletcher foamed at the mouth as he muttered useless words she couldn't decipher. He struggled to pull out a knife.

Oh God, please help me... Her mind fell blank. All she could think of were the empty promises the detectives made that they would protect her.

Suddenly Fletcher became confused, disoriented. As if he were hearing voices. He pivoted wildly in crazy half circles from his left to his right, wielding his knife as he turned. Various voices began to speak out from his mouth.

Slowly she backed up as she watched his erratic behavior unfold. She thought of Mr. Nowak from the facility where her parents once lived. She had watched him go through the same levels derangement as multiple personalities emerged. Sometimes it had taken longer than others before the faculty came to remove him from the communal lounge.

"They told me you killed that woman," Moriah said in an ominous tone. She hobbled to her left. His body jerked as he followed her movements, wielding the knife as he swiveled.

"No he didn't," she said in an amiable, sweet manner after she'd stumbled a few feet to her right. He pivoted. His eyes remained trained on her.

"I don't believe he'd do such a thing either," she said in a different voice as she slowly backed further away. She saw something shiny in the distance, and hoped she could use it as a weapon.

"Yes you do!" she announced in the original ominous voice she'd used. She moved back a few steps. She was only a few yards away from it. She could see it! It was a shovel.

"She's lying," she called as she hobbled back further to her other side.

"Enough of this!" Fletcher barked as another personality emerged. He'd grown tired of her antics. Panic gripped her as she watched his demeanor change again, right before her eyes.

He began wiping the knife off on his pant leg slowly, meticulously as he teased her. Horror seized her. She'd seen the dried blood on the blade.

In desperation, she looked off into the distance. She heard no aircrafts. There were no boats.... No cavalry. Would they get there in time before he'd kill her? *Where are the people who promised to protect me? Are they coming?* she asked herself again in uncontrollable anguish. As if he had read her mind, he looked out over the horizon as if he was looking for someone.

Sneering with a deranged grin, he turned his attention back to her.
Her gut wrenched with the reality. Nobody would be coming for her. How had he known that? In one swoop, he'd snatched her cell, throwing it in the ocean, and seized hold of her.

There had been no stopping him. Schlepping onward, he held on to her by the hair. Her skirt ripped from her waist, her blood gushed everywhere as he dragged her heartlessly. He was unbothered by her nerve curdling screams.

"Shut your wailing, Mo," he muttered. He had called her Mo on several occasions since they'd landed.

Mo? Finally, he'd reached his destination. Her mind slid into a world of unconsciousness as they gazed upon her doom, the black cave.

Tyro startled Moriah as he wrapped his arms around her. He had been shaking her and calling her name for several moments now.

Shards of images floated through her mind as she fought them off. Her eyes swelled with tears as she remembered the deplorable cot Fletcher had kept her tied to... the darkness and stench of the cave... his helicopter going up in flames. She had been stranded, left alone on a deserted island to die.

Chapter 37

Her mind stumbled back to her current dilemma. Her eyes skimmed past Tyro. She avoided his intense stare. She thought of her regret of getting involved with the case. Why had she agreed to work with the detectives?

They'd told her she only had to get him to talk about his last assignment and report what she'd learned back to them. They said the information could help her get Amelia back. They lied. And they hadn't told her everything; but she suspected that Parker and Petra were being investigated as well.

Didn't they know the man was crazy? Why had they set her up—put her life in danger? She knew he had recently piloted for a rich family and that something went awry. She had thought the authorities had wanted him because he had stolen something. She hadn't discovered he was actually being investigated for murder until that day when she'd been thousands of feet in the air. *He's wanted for murder...* was the last text that had flashed before the signal on her cell died. By then it was too late.

Her lips quivered as she subconsciously rubbed the long scar that ran down her inner thigh.

"What happened?" Tyro lifted and placed her leg in his lap. Slowly, he ran his hand along the thick and lumpy wound protruding through the material. Her stare was afar off as she methodically slid a portion of her pant leg up to expose her disfigurement.

"What is it you're not telling me?" Tyro sat silently, waiting as he studied her face.

"It was an accident." Her lips quivered as she tried to squeeze out a smile. She moved away from him, placing her leg back on the floor. She assured the material covered it completely. He was right. She couldn't tell him, how could she? She didn't trust him.

As Sable descended the helicopter, Moriah spotted the gruesome opening of the black cave. The memories of the horrible things Fletcher had done to her gripped her soul. She couldn't control the quivering in her throat. Fear shot from her eyes. She shook uncontrollably.

"Moriah. What's wrong?" Tyro reached for her. She snatched away.

"How dare you." Her eyes closed as she spoke the words through gritted teeth. "You selfish pig. Don't you pretend to care anything about me." She groped her face and let out a desperate cry, the swell of tears she'd been holding back flooded her cheeks. "We should head back now," she demanded.

Tyro pulled her close. "Talk to me," he whispered in her ear. He rubbed her back as he tried to comfort her. She stiffened at his touch. Shutting her eyes, she refused to look at what lay below her for another second. She felt trapped with nowhere to turn, no one to trust, not even the man she loved. He was using her, just like the detectives. She wanted to blot everything out—including Tyro.

Bringing her there was a big mistake. Or, had he planned for it to happen this way? *Why?* She felt the large gash reopen in the middle of her chest. Tyro had ruthlessly ripped the stitches out for his own selfishness, regardless of the consequences.

He didn't care about her, her pain, or how it would affect their relationship. He hadn't cared at all. But he'd promised.

She'd thought she would die in that place. And now the man who, just last night, vowed his honesty to her had brought her back there to relive the hellish nightmare all over again. Why?

Agony seized her as the helicopter lowered closer to land. Flashes of the horrible memories coursed through her mind. Unable to hold back her meltdown, her chest heaved deeply for air. There'd be

238

no stopping it now. "You lied," she bellowed. Her eyes burned through him as she braved to look into his gaze.

"Take me back... turn around!" Her anguish echoed through the cabin as she screamed. She groped wildly at the air. Scratching, striking, and kicking uncontrollably at Tyro, the pilot, and anywhere her fingers and feet could reach.

"Whoa, whoa, Moriah." Tyro held her firmly by the wrists to restrain her until she tired herself out. She had never wanted to see that place again, under any circumstances.

"Moriah... Moriah." Tyro called her name several times as he pulled her into his warm embrace. Her eyes fluttered as they rolled into the back of her head. She fell limp in his arms. He held her by the shoulders and patted her face as he tried to revive her back to consciousness.

A few moments later, she aroused. "Please... I can't go back there... I'll die... please, take me back." She panted for air. "Take me away from here. I can't go back there... Ever again."

"Let me go," she pleaded through shallow breathing. She sank to the floor. Her glazed eyes stared into nothingness.

As Sable steered the helicopter back to the Simmonds Island Estate, Tyro stole a glance up at his pilot. Her eyes glimpsed back at him as she tilted her head in a series of slow, calculated nods. Tyro felt numb. Their suspicions had been confirmed.

Chapter 38

Moriah insisted on remaining crouched on the floor as they flew back. She trembled as she kept her knees pressed to her chest. Her head was buried beneath her arms. When they reached the Simmonds Island Estate, Tyro snapped from his train of thoughts. Sable touched the helicopter down with a sense of progress. Another piece of the puzzle fit into place.

He had convinced Moriah to return to his home instead of taking her back to hers. She refused to allow their family doctor to examine her.

He had his staff transport her from the helicopter to his house. They helped her to get settled comfortably back in her guest suite; still, she was unable to rest.

The surmounting allegations of the media, pending criminal charges, and seeing that island again caused her world to cave. She felt discombobulated, ashamed, lost, and betrayed all at once. She flung the covers back, leapt out of bed, threw on the clothes she'd worn when she first arrived, and stuffed her remaining belongings into her small carrying bag.

Marching out of the bedroom, her bag thrown over her shoulder, she'd determined to settle for nothing less than for him to take her home. Now. She paraded into the kitchen in search of Tyro only to find him watching another episode of *I Love Lucy*. She stopped short as she stood behind him watching as he guffawed at the redhead's silly antics.

She stood and studied him for a long time. His shoulders jerked repeatedly as he laughed. He used the back of his hand to wipe moisture from his eyes as he shook his head in amusement.

But as soon as the show ended, his shoulders tensed. He reached for his device to search through other episodes. Moriah could tell he was only masking his pain. It was a place she'd been many times. Thick bile rose in her throat.

Mindlessly, he stopped at another video. He stared at the stilled program for a long time. It was as if a million thoughts were running through his mind. She wondered if he was thinking about her. Her behavior? Was he ashamed of her? Was he tired of her outbreaks, her senseless anxiety attacks, and her elusiveness?

But, what about him… what he had done to her? He hadn't been honest himself. He used her.

Still, she was torn. She admitted that she loved him. She wanted nothing more than to tell him the truth, the whole story. But, how could she after what he'd just done to her? She closed her eyes and breathed deeply. There was a risk in her holding back, and a risk in telling him everything, each having its own repercussions.

And what if she was wrong about her suspicions of him? Would they needlessly lose any chance of having a friendship… a relationship? What would he think of her after he found out what had happened to her? Her scar… the emotional baggage and fear…? The lie. She'd known about Mrs. Simmonds' death before meeting Tyro. But she hadn't known she was his mother. It wasn't until she'd met Quincy the other night that she was able to put it all together.

Her heart waned back and forth as she watched him sit there in agony. She could feel her own anxiety creeping up her spine. *Oh God, what if I lose him?* As if he could sense her presence, he jerked his head around.

Immediately, he leapt from his seat and bounded toward her. His eyes searched her face. "Are you okay?" He pulled her into his arms. "I hope you're feeling—"

"I... I'm okay." She kept her eyes on her feet. He lifted her chin. His eyes searched in expectation.

"I will not let anyone hurt you again, Moriah." His eyes pierced into her soul as she melted in his arms.

She told him what she knew about Fletcher, which wasn't much.

"Whenever you're ready," Tyro said, knowing she understood what he meant. When she was ready to talk about the rest of it. He knew there was more. She forced a smile and let out a slow breath.

They held each other in silence for a long time. No more questions asked. No explanations demanded.

"Let's go down to the beach," he suggested, breaking the silence in an upbeat tone. "I could use a good swim." Moriah really didn't feel like going to the beach. She preferred to be taken home so she could collect her thoughts. She couldn't dismiss the fact he'd taken her to that same location, to that same place.

Was it a coincidence? Did he know or suspect something? She sighed. Not wanting to ruin the rest of their time together, to the beach they went. He would take her home later on that day. That she was sure of.

Chapter 39

Moriah lay quietly on the queen size lounge under a huge cabana. Situated in a secluded area at the end of the beach by his house provided the privacy for a perfect getaway.

She felt much better. He didn't pressure her to talk about it, or throw any subtle hints, which helped her to put today's incident behind her.

Tyro was trekking out of the water after his ten minute, power swim. His hair, curled from the salty water, sagged sexily over his head. She lowered her shades and soaked in every muscle as he came closer toward her.

She looked at the water dripping off of his fresh tan from the short time he'd spent in the water. Just for this one time, she allowed herself to wonder what it would be like making love to him. She hurriedly pushed the thought out of her mind.

He bent to pick up his towel and brushed his mouth against her lips. She didn't move away. He leaned back in again. Their eyes locked. Oh yeah, she knew if she didn't pull away, she would be in trouble. His kisses, his touch, his scent were breaking down her resistance.

"I found something on the beach yesterday." She reached to retrieve the necklace from her pocket. Holding her wrist gently, he prevented her from removing it.

"It can wait until later." He leaned in and brushed his lips against hers again. "In fact, whatever it is that you found, keep it. It's yours." She hadn't wanted to, but she moved away. His lips were tantalizingly seductive. Although she'd liked the sensation that ran through her body, watching him as he towered over her, she took the opportunity to move away as he leaned toward her again.

She resisted the urge to run her fingers over his well-sculptured chest. She wondered what it would be like to kiss him, to really kiss him without holding back, giving it her all. Everything.

"No, it was on your property—well, your dad's property—I think you should have it." She leaned her shoulder back and squinted up at him.

"Okay, if you say so, but it will have to wait until later." He stood next to her and dried himself off.

"Hey!" Moriah quipped. "You're dripping water on me."

"Oh, I am, am I? Well, guess I'll just have to dab it off of you." He reached the towel toward her belly. "Oh no you don't!" She playfully pushed his hand away.

"Well, then you leave me no choice!" he teased as he swooped her up in his arms. He carried her toward the water. They swam around in the warm turquoise water for the longest time as they determined to set their differences aside. They would enjoy their time together.

"Tyro, you need some sunscreen. Your shoulders are starting to look like a lobster." As they raced back to the cabana, he tugged on her waist, pulling her back slightly so that he would reach it first.

She squealed in delight as he tickled her. She curled her legs, kicking and laughing until she confessed she'd had enough. He handed her the bottle of sunscreen. After he dried off, she massaged the white substance on his shoulders, back, neck, and arms.

She handed him the lotion for him to take care of his legs and stomach area. "What, you're not finished. That's only half a job, my dear," he said as he took the liberty to lean in for a kiss.

"Um mm," she responded as she kept the towel wrapped around her waist and turned over for him to lotion her back. "Oh, I see how you are," he teased.

She turned to face him as he finished rubbing the creamy potion in thoroughly. The smile on his face was priceless. "And just how do you see me, Mr. Simmonds?"

"Let's see. I already told you how sexy... gorgeous you are. I'd also say that you are afraid and very secretive. And lonely."

"Lonely? I'm not lonely. I am only as careful as I—"
He pulled her into his arms, interrupting her as his lips pressed against hers. Passionately. He beheld her expression as he pulled away.

But he knew she wasn't ready for that kind of affection. No way could he get in between her relationship with God. His mother had raised him better than that.

Besides, he doubted Moriah would go for it. He couldn't allow himself to be careless in his assumption of her feelings toward him. And then, there was the undeniable fact that not only was she hiding something. She was deathly terrified of whatever it was. He wondered if the scar on her leg she kept covered up had anything to do with it. He strongly suspected that it did.

He caressed the tears trickling from her eyes. "What is it, my love?" he said, kissing her cheeks as he spoke. "Trust me. Let me help you through whatever it is you're going through."

Moriah knew she was in trouble being there with him in such a way. She shouldn't have let things go this far. *Lord, please... help me get out of this before I... I...* Her head was screaming for her to get her behind out of there, *now*! But, her body begged for her to stay.

"Tyro," her voice was shallow and quivered. "There's something I need to tell you," she said as his lips brushed a second time against her neck. She peered into his eyes. His touch was gentle, slow. Feelings she'd never known existed pulsated through her entire being. Succumbing to the promise of safety that she'd yearned to know, hoped for when he was near, she wrapped her arms around his neck. Her better senses flew away like the squawking gulls they'd shooed away earlier from their picnic basket.

"I... I..." Moriah was sinking into the passionate desires throbbing inside of her. Her resistance faded with each tender kiss of promise of what could be. She gazed into his eyes. She felt him searching her inner most being. The lines around his eyes curled. His eyes twinkled. The pull into his world was steadfast, as the presence of his sadness, his darkness melted away. Their eyes remained locked. She wanted to look away, but she couldn't. She dared not as their worlds melded. His heart pounded equally as fast, in rhythm with hers.

No words were spoken, yet, she knew. Letting him touch her soul like that, she was like a lamb being led away to greener pastures, or to the slaughter. Her mind became hazy. But the pull was undeniable. He wanted her beyond the physical. He needed her to trust him. But was she safe? Would he break her heart? Would he only be using her to get to what he wanted? Needed?

Did he see her only as the means to an end and that end being his closure? Still, she couldn't resist. She didn't want to. She questioned letting her guard down. *Is this what You meant, God? Is Tyro my saving grace?* She allowed her lips to draw closer. She'd not hold back now. She would kiss him with everything she had in her. And she'd receive all the passion he had to pour into her. There was no space, no air between them. She lifted her head as she surrendered to his demand. *Yes, this feels so...right.*

"Eh em," the familiar feminine, gruff voice called.

"What is it?" Tyro's words were forced through gritted teeth. His gaze remained on Moriah. He knew if he looked away, she would retreat. He'd lose the momentum.

"Um, I hate to interrupt..."

Tyro sighed. He leaned back and tapped Moriah on the nose playfully with his index finger. "Stay right here."

Moriah was embarrassed to say the least. She pulled the towel lying at the foot of where she was lounging over her. She willed herself to turn her head to see where he was heading. She watched as Sable, still wearing her flight gear, pulled him a distance away. Whatever it was that she was saying, slowly beguiled him.

Tyro crossed his arms as he stood listening to his pilot. Moriah couldn't bear to watch as his disposition changed. His body tensed as he raised his shoulders. Attentively, his ears perked up toward his pilot's words. Suddenly, he snapped his head toward Moriah.

His hands dropped to his side; his fingers curled into tight balls. His eyes blazed with utter disbelief as he shot her a fast look that made her cringe.

Without saying a word, giving her a smile, or even a hand gesture of some sort, Tyro turned his back and stormed away. Moriah stumbled to her feet. She watched as his feet pounded furiously into the silky white sand, dragging her heart, her hopes, and her dreams right along with him. It was as if nothing they'd shared just moments ago had mattered.

And then the words he had said yesterday while they were in the garden gushed over her like a tidal wave. *He knows... He knows the truth that I'm not as innocent as I led him to believe.* The look he just gave her told her of his disgust and distain for her. It worried her. He was ashamed of her and wanted nothing more to do with her.

It was at that moment Moriah knew that Tyro would not be coming back to get her. She removed the sapphire necklace from her pocket and fidgeted with it between her fingers. She buried her face in her hands, no longer able to fight back the tears. The necklace slipped between her fingers just as her world went blank.

Part Three

When you passeth through the waters, I will be with thee; and
through the rivers, they shall not overflow thee:
when though walkest through the fire, thou shalt not be burnt;
neither shall the flame kindle upon thee.

Isaiah 43:2 KJV

Prologue

Three times it had happened so…

Tyro sat straight up drenched in sweat. He'd had the dream again. This was the third time and each time he'd failed to save them. He failed to save his mother. He failed to save the woman he loved. He failed to save his Shepherd. He'd awakened just as the situation called for him to choose which to save first. He couldn't remember his choice.

He shuddered as he thought of his relentless struggle. He'd been unsuccessful in getting there in time to save them. He saw them drowning in a sea of water… or were they in the midst of flames… or were they falling from a high cliff? Confusion clogged his memory.

Had he chosen to save his mother first, or the mysterious woman who kept appearing in these dreams? Or Sheba? Or was it the other way around? He remembered trying to grab hold of one of them, which one, he didn't know now. All he knew was that they sank farther out of his reach. He'd whirled around in a panic, looking for something to throw out to them. He found nothing. He turned back to the cries and whining for help. His mother was gone, out of sight. His fear that he wouldn't get to the others in time was a heavy rope choking him, holding him back. He was swimming in place.

He sat on the side of his bed and wiped perspiration on his sleeve. The vision of his nightmare slowly slipping into his subconscious like it had in the past. He knew if it had been a real situation, he would have lost all of them.

Chapter 1

Tyro insisted on going in first. Searching his surroundings, his eyes strained to see through the darkness. The flashlight on his smart watch provided the only light inside the deserted cave. He suspected that it was the same cave where Moriah had been held captive just three months ago.

The light bending around the narrow cavernous opening barely lit the place. It was instantly swallowed up by the darkness. What he was able to see made his heart stop.

He focused his light on a rusty military bunk hidden in the back right corner. A rope looped from the deteriorating headboard captured his attention. His eyes trailed behind the dim light down the deplorable mattress. Another rope hung from the foot rail.

Even from where he stood, he could tell the ropes weren't old or moldy. It was possible that someone had recently been tied up in them. He closed his eyes for a brief moment to clear his mind. He couldn't imagine the terror of anyone being restrained in such a place.

He twisted slightly and shined his light towards the footsteps racing toward him from behind. Quincy bounded in with a flood of light not realizing it had temporarily blinded his son. Mario followed with a high powered battery-operated lantern giving full vision to their worst fears.

Their eyes shifted from one corner to the other. Within a quick swoop in a panoramic view, deplorable took on a whole new meaning. Old cans and packages from food rations, trash along with other unidentifiable debris cluttered the floor. The stench of rodent and possible human waste caused Quincy to gag. The three of them covered their mouths as they hurried outside. They had seen enough.

Sable walked over to them as they huddled together. "How ya holding up?" she asked, training her eyes on each of them. The blank expressions and head shaking and shrugging of the shoulders, told her they were barely holding on.

They wanted closure. They needed answers. They wouldn't be able to rest or go on with their lives until they found out who had killed Laino—the woman they all loved—and why she had been killed.

And what exactly did Sable think she'd prove by flying them off to this deserted island? What did seeing the cave and seeing the horrible condition it was in have to do with anything? After seeing Moriah's reaction that morning when they'd taken her there earlier, Tyro had to come back. His father and uncle insisted on coming along. If this was Laino's fate, they wanted to see what she had been up against.

Tyro shifted so he could no longer see the tall black rock. The one that had caused Moriah's meltdown the moment she caught sight of it. He needed to keep his head clear. How had she gotten tangled up in this?

Sable held a brown paper bag out between her two fingers for their inspection. His eyes noticed her gloved hand.

She placed the bag on the ground with meticulous care. Slowly, she removed a long blue item splashed with colorful flowers. She held it before them to inspect it. Now her attention was mainly focused on Quincy. "Recognize this?" she asked.

Watching Quincy's face contort in sudden anguish confirmed that the garment had belonged to his wife. He recognized it right away. It was her favorite sundress. She had worn it on the last Sunday they had gone to their chapel. Falling to his knees, he buried his head in the material sobbing silently. The garment dangled between his hands as he desperately tried to savor any remains of her scent, her perfume.

251

"Eh, what about this?" Sable said, snapping her fingers at one of the detectives. He trotted over and handed Quincy a matching sweater with the same exotic floral print.

Mario leaned over and helped Quincy up from his knees. Quincy's hand trembled as he reached for the item. "It's her sweater. How... where... why was it not with the dress? Where did you find it?" His eyes narrowed. "She never wore the dress without it."

"We'll go over all that tomorrow when we ask *our* little girly friend." Her response was laced with accusation.

"I want you to answer my question now!" Quincy demanded. "I hired you! You are to answer to me, Detective Lofthouse. To me! Is that clear?"

"What?" Tyro and Mario said simultaneously. "What is going on?

"You mean to tell me that Sable is a detective?" Shocked, Tyro faced his dad. "What's this all about? And don't tell me I can't handle it." His eyes locked with Quincy's.

"FBI," she stated matter-of-factly. "And you didn't hire me." Her shoulders pushed back as she addressed Quincy; his face turned as white as his hair. "You just happened to *conveniently* find me."

She turned to Tyro and popped a piece of gum in her mouth. "It seems your Miss Styles has some explaining to do." Her Brit accent was more apparent now than before. "She was wearing this same sweater when we rescued her off of this island"—she leaned in, directing her authoritative tone toward Tyro—"three months ago." She paused. "How long did you say you've known her?"

"FBI...? Wait... What did you say?" Tyro asked.

She ignored his question as she turned to give credence to one of the investigators vying for her attention. A new piece of evidence spilled over in his hands as he hurried out of the cave.

Unable to swallow what he'd just heard, Tyro, without thought, took hold of her as she turned to walk away. Sable glared down at his hand gripped around her arm. "If you don't mind," she said politely, but in a stern manner. She removed her arm from his grasp. "I know this is upsetting, and you've been kept in the dark. But what I have to say or conclude about this whole ordeal will have to wait until I question her tomorrow." She raised her hand to shield her face from the sun as it began to set over the horizon.

"Have Mr. Simmonds," she nodded her head towards Quincy, "fill you in on what he knows." After walking a few feet away, she turned and spoke. "I assume she's still at your place. I'll meet you back there as soon as we wrap up our final investigation here."

Tyro's mind swirled. He'd second-guessed himself. Sable hadn't told him the whole truth when he'd stormed away and abandoned Moriah on his island. He had no idea Sable was FBI. She'd misconstrued her words and he believed her. He wondered what else he might have overlooked. His mind raced back over the phone calls and texts he'd received from her and his father.

He suspected that his dad was being misled as well. What she'd led him to believe, causing him to abandon Moriah at the beach caused his heart to race. *What have I done?*

An overwhelming feeling that he needed to get back to Moriah as quickly as possible, rushed over him. He turned to get his Uncle Mario's attention. Sheba bounded out from the tall brush several yards from where his uncle stood. She was carrying something in her mouth. He moved quickly toward her and commanded her to go back with a point of his finger. He glanced over to ensure the investigators hadn't noticed her, especially Sable.

He walked Sheba farther back into the brush out of view.

"Good girl," he said, rubbing her head. He carefully removed the strange object from her mouth.

Sheba sniffed it and whined when he laid it on the ground. It was the remains of a garment of some kind, a pair of pants, or a long skirt. He couldn't tell.

The long piece of material had been ripped badly in numerous places and was stained with blood.

Sheba repeatedly pawed at the cloth; sniffing over it, she whined. She looked up at her master and let out a quick bark. "What is it, Girly—?" He paused, recognizing he was about to use Moriah's nickname for Sheba. There was something about the way Sheba acted. Did this garment belong to *Moriah*?

But, how, why was it here. He remembered Sable saying that she had been wearing the sweater that matched his mother's dress when they'd rescued her from this place. What was she doing here in the first place?

He walked back with the garment concealed beneath his jacket. He wasn't about to turn it in until he figured out why Moriah had been there and what happened.

Chapter 2

As the helicopter pulled away from the Simmonds' private island estate, Moriah stared out the window in disbelief. She couldn't believe Tyro had blatantly left her hanging at the cabana. Alone. Stranded. When he'd stormed away without saying anything to her, she suspected whatever Sable had told him had everything to do with her.

Feeling disconcerted, she watched the objects below evaporate into nothingness, just like her relationship with the man she'd fallen in love with. She closed her eyes and swallowed the hard reality. Whatever relationship they may have had was over.

She twirled locks of her hair mindlessly around her fingers. She determined to shut the world out until she got home where she could sort through... make some kind of sense of everything. She breathed deeply as she focused to clear her mind. It wasn't working.

She stared at the back of the new pilot's head—Nelson, whom she'd never met—and wondered what he knew about all of this. But she was too drained to worry about it. Mickey had surprised her when she'd hopped in and sat next to her. Moriah looked perplexed.

"I was asked to escort you. Mr. Simmonds asked that I ensure that you arrive safely to your destination," Mickey informed her.

"Destination?" Moriah's brows rose. "Tyro told you to do that?"

"The order came from Mr. Quincy," Tempa, the red headed one candidly stated. She had bounded up into the craft practically without any assistance and had sat up front with the pilot Moriah wasn't familiar with.

"Nelson can fly us wherever we need to go just as good as anyone else." She batted her eyes as he began working the controls. Moriah cut her eyes over at Mickey. Mickey quickly lowered her head as Moriah continued to stare at her.

As they flew over the Chesapeake, the events of the past weekend flashed through Moriah's mind. She took a deep breath and breathed out slowly as she tried to keep herself calm. Sweat beaded on her forehead. Her hands began to tremble. *It was not supposed to end like this.*

She thought of Tyro. Shame flooded her consciousness. What had Sable told him? She held back the tears threatening to stream down her face. *What did I do to make him look at me that way? What if they found the journal I buried on the island? What if he reads it... Oh God, does he already know?*

Moriah regretted burying and leaving the journal behind. All the things that had happened to her, the unfathomable things she had to do on that island to survive. Shame seized her. She had to go along with Fletcher's multiple personalities. At times, she had to pretend to be one of his war buddies. Other times she had to play along that she was his mother... his child. As his mind deteriorated, fading in and out with multiple personalities, there were times when he'd thought that he was her hero. In his mind, he was keeping her safe, not mindful that it was he who'd placed her in danger in the first place.

It was all she knew to do to keep his dominant personality from surfacing, the one who wanted to kill her, or she would have died.

She used the time while he was asleep to write in a journal she kept hidden in the dark corner of the cave. He would only sleep a few hours at a time and she never knew what state of mind he would be in when he awakened. It had been days since he'd had his medications and the state of his mind had become irrational. Demonized.

She felt if she just buried the book and left it there on that island where no one ever came, she could leave all the horrible things she endured behind.

Her mind tossed between the need to sleep and the mental anguish swarming around inside her head. As Nelson lowered the helicopter, her mind snapped out of its deep thoughts. She hadn't realized they had already flown over the Delaware River. The cabin inside of the helicopter was quiet and void of any conversation. She leaned forward and noticed they were not landing at the Wilmington Airport, or at Tyro's office complex.

She turned toward Mickey who had kept her head turned away from her for most of the flight. She knew she was trying to avoid being asked any questions.

Concerned, Moriah sat forward and noticed they had landed on top of a high-rise building that sat off of a major highway. She could tell they were in New Castle, Delaware. She recognized the overhead sign for the Delaware Memorial Bridge.

A short and stout man, who apparently hadn't shaved for several days, opened her side of the door of the helicopter. Without any formal introduction or explanation, he grabbed hold of her arm and attempted to whisk her out of the helicopter.

"Let go of me!" Moriah demanded as she snatched her arm from his grip.

"Sorry, Ms. Styles. If you want to live, you best come with me. Now."

"What are you talking about?"

He reached in again; this time he managed to secure her and move her out of the craft. Whisking her away as if it was about to downpour, a door swung open when they were closer to the entrance to the building. Rushing her inside, they disappeared from the outside world like mice scurrying into a hole. It took a few moments for her eyes to adjust to the stale darkness.

"I'm sorry, I couldn't warn you," Mickey said as she scuttled alongside her, heading toward the penthouse suite.

"It's best this way. At least now you're safe. I'll be right—"

"Safe?" Moriah gave her an incredulous glare as she interrupted her.

She wondered if this whole ordeal had something to do with the runaway fairy tale saga. She realized she hadn't watched the news since Saturday evening and she had no idea what was going on with it. Were there new developments that would cause her or Tyro to be in danger? *Is that why he left in such a hurry?*

Moriah knew that couldn't have been it. He had been too protective of her and he would have never left her like that if he thought she was in danger. *Would he?*

She looked up into the face of the man who had just whisked her into an elevator. It was dingy and smelled of mold. She wondered if it was indicative of where they were heading.

Although she wanted to, she resisted asking him if this was about her leaving the accident.

She didn't know what he or Mickey knew about her *little* incident.

And neither would she have the chance to find out. As soon as he opened the keyless door, he rushed her inside.

Before she could turn to protest, the man left immediately, pulling Mickey out the door with him.

She heard the chamber turn from the other side. She was locked in. She wanted to bang on the door and demand that he let her out. But she knew it would be useless. Even though she was exhausted, she knew it would be better to save her energy and think her way out of this situation.

Chapter 3

Tyro pushed his private jet across the Chesapeake as swiftly as it could fly. He was furious to find that Moriah had been taken away without his knowledge. Quincy had gone too far.

When Quincy realized that Sable had duped him, he disclosed where Moriah would be. He had instructed the pilot to take her to the Simmonds' Riverfront penthouse suites. In fact, he had told his son everything he knew about his suspicions. The situation had gotten out of hand and beyond his control.

After reading the headlines from the Daily eNews, Tyro knew she was in danger. He didn't put it past Detective Sable to use her as bait to catch this Mr. Casillas, or Fletcher… or whatever his real name was.

He'd try to console Mario, letting him know that just because he was his former Navy Seals buddy and that he'd hired him at one time to work for the family's business, didn't make any of this his fault.

Tyro appreciated that he'd jumped right in to help ensure Moriah's wellbeing. He was following behind, although at a slower rate, in a helicopter. Quincy and Sheba were riding with him.

He glanced over at the headline of the news article he'd placed on the seat next to him. He expelled his breath after he read the caption again. He couldn't get the thought out of his head…the fear out of his heart. The man suspected of killing his mother had slipped right through the FBI's fingers months ago.

If the authorities had done their job, his mother's murder could have been avoided. He couldn't believe it. How could a government agency be so careless and stupid? Incompetent.

The FBI had known all along who his mother's suspected killer was and they'd let him get away. He suspected that he'd been the same guy Moriah had told him about who had abducted her. He couldn't put all the pieces together. There were too many unanswered questions. He thought about the clothing Sheba had found behind the cave.

But one thing he knew, Moriah had nothing to do with his mother's murder as they'd led his dad to believe. And now the maniac was on the run and Moriah was in danger again.

Tyro was ten minutes away from landing. He was amazed how Moriah's life and safety had taken precedence over his own need for closure. He loved her. He needed her. She had become his everything and he wasn't going to let her get away from him again.

He squashed the feeling that he'd been foolish for not trusting her... for using her. Guilt crawled up his back. But he'd have to deal with it later. The sooner he could get to her and ensure her safety, the sooner he could get the answers he needed to prove her innocence.

His heart pounded as he thought about the findings from the deserted island. Although it was never delivered, a ransom note had been pieced together with large letters clipped from magazine ads. It demanded money, or else he would never see his darling sister again. He remembered how Mario had stumbled backwards after the investigators had shown it to him just hours ago on the island. The note indicated the killer's whole beef had been with his Uncle Mario.

Tyro's mother had possibly been killed over a kidnapping attempt that had gone wrong. He could understand why his Uncle Mario felt responsible for her death. And now, somehow Moriah was caught up in the midst of it.

He received permission to land his plane at the Wilmington Airport where his Range Rover waited for him. He sped off, having no time to wait for Mario or Quincy to get there in the helicopter. He headed directly to their Riverfront high-rise condos. He reached his unit to no avail; Moriah wasn't at his penthouse suite where Quincy assured him she'd be.

***

Meanwhile, Moriah wondered if Tyro knew where she was. Her current dilemma surely had the footprint of Quincy all over it. She didn't trust him any more than she cared for him. But still, she couldn't be sure what part Tyro had played in it either. Not with the way he'd been acting since the phone calls started yesterday afternoon.

She pulled her phone out to look up Mario's restaurant. She was sure he had no idea she had been kidnapped. For some reason, she trusted him.

But if she was being held against her will she highly doubted Mickey would be in on such a criminal offense as this. Something wasn't adding up. Her heart rose in her throat. But she knew she would have to keep it together in order to figure out what was going on. Now was not the time to lose control.

There had to be a logical reason for what was going on. *Think, Moriah... think... Why do they feel I'm in danger? If I have to 'fess up and face the consequences of leaving the scene of the accident... near accident, so be it!* she reasoned within herself, trying to reduce the severity of her actions—at least as far as she was concerned.

After exploring all the possibilities, unfortunately, she was still in the dark.

She looked around at her surroundings. The penthouse wasn't as plush as she imagined a wealthy person like Quincy would have. A three-star rating, maybe, but it definitely lacked the elegance and glamour one would expect of a billionaire.

The Sunday WilmingTone Daily lying neatly on the coffee table caught her attention. Her eyes zeroed in on the headlines. Her fingers trembled as she reached for it. She froze in disbelief.

She pulled the paper closer. Her eyes weren't deceiving her as they swept over the bold, large print for the second time. Her heart fluttered and her breath caught in her throat.

FBI CONFIRMS SUSPECTED MURDERER OF LOCAL BILLIONAIRE'S WIFE IS ALIVE.

Chapter 4

"He's... he's alive...?" she stammered. The revelation of what she read penetrated her understanding. Her eyes watered as they raced across the page pulling in key words:

KILLER IS NOT DEAD... the leading caption read. *Casillas Leroy Fletcher was believed to have died when the helicopter he flew for the Thomlin-Smythe Marketing Agency, known as TSMA, was dragged from the waters just off the coast of No Man's Island several months ago.*

Moriah clasped her throat as she fell backwards on the sofa. She held tight to the paper and as her eyes flew across the words, she swiped away the tears obstructing her vision.

Once considered dead, as the helicopter for the TMSA was pulled from the ocean just off of the Chesapeake, no body had been found. Authorities initially stated that his body had been swept out to sea. They released a report earlier today that they have new evidence that Fletcher has been in hiding.

Traces of Mrs. Simmonds' blood, along with other unidentified blood has been found in a dilapidated shack outside of Milford.

Mrs. Simmonds' picture was plastered in the midst of the article.

The names of the other victims will not be released pending further investigation.

She bolted from her seat. Visions of the envelope... the rat... Fletcher... raced through her mind. *He's alive?* She struggled to steady herself but couldn't stop her legs from giving out on her. She fell to her knees. "Oh God!" she cried.

Moriah turned the pages to finish scanning the article when a note fell from between the pages. Reading it, her hands clasped over her mouth.

For your safety, Miss Styles, we urge you to stay within the bounds of our protection. We will explain more later. Please take this opportunity to rest. We discontinued the Internet and phone service for your protection. This includes Wi-Fi. We hope you understand when we explain the escalated situation more thoroughly. Until tomorrow, please enjoy the comforts of the arrangements. Det. Mark Smith.

"Who is Detective Mark Smith?" she mouthed. She wondered if the article was a valid reason for her to be confined in this manner. *Is this legal?* If what the article said was true, she could very well be in grave danger. Or, was this Quincy's doing? She stewed on that thought, not liking the possibility one bit.

And the abrupt manner in which Tyro had left didn't make her feel warm and cozy either, much less any safer. The whole ordeal was too overwhelming for her to think clearly.

A knock at the door jolted her.

"Who... who is it?"

"Room service, ma'am," a strange and contrived voice answered, overpowering Mickey's attempt to speak.

"It's okay, Miss Moriah... I'm coming in too," she managed to say after having to over speak him. Moriah let out the breath of air after she'd looked through the peephole. An elderly gentleman held a tray over his right shoulder. Mickey stood beside him holding an armful of clothing.

She opened the door slowly and allowed Mickey to enter first. The officer who followed the older gentleman carrying the tray watched carefully. The server described each course of her meal. He lifted the lids and waited for her approval.

She picked through her meal. It was now around five-thirty. Reading the note from Detective Smith for the third time, she became more agitated.

"Well that explains it." She was referring to the *not so elaborate penthouse suite*. His business card sat on one of the end tables. Moriah wondered what *situation* he was talking about. Was he referring to her leaving the scene of an accident? Had someone threatened her, or Tyro? Or did any of this have to do with the reason Tyro had fled so suddenly?

She thought about him and wondered what he was doing. Would she see him again? Did he want to see her again? Was he in some kind of trouble? How much trouble was she in? There were just too many questions and no sign of any of the answers in sight.

Moriah looked at her cell and plopped it back on the sofa next to her. There was no use in trying to call Mario or Nettie. All of her outgoing calls had also been blocked. If this was truly all about the killer, why was she restricted from making any calls?

Moriah used the elaborate toiletries Mickey provided and took a long, hot bath. She grew tired of surfing through the few TV channels that were unrestricted. For some reason, she was even prohibited from seeing the news or making any contact outside of the confines of her eight walls. Twelve if you counted the bathroom.

One thing was for sure, Moriah hadn't learned to survive by being pent up in some makeshift run down wannabe penthouse. Neither would she care how luxurious it was, or wasn't. She needed answers. She needed to get back to her life. She had clients waiting and a business to build.

Tomorrow she'd do some investigating on her own to find out what was going on. She packed her few belongings and stowed her carrying bag by the door.

A light tap on the door roused Moriah from her thoughts. She sighed with relief as Mickey closed the door behind her. She had come to attend to the clothing and items she'd brought earlier.

After Mickey helped her get settled in, she looked down when Moriah approached her. Knowing that they couldn't talk earlier, she'd hoped that Mickey would be able to tell her something to help her sort out this mess.

"I'm sorry, but I was forced to betray you." Mickey said as Moriah held her gently by the arms.

"You don't work for me, remember?" She pulled her in for a quick embrace. "Do you know what's going on?" she asked, treading lightly. She did not know how much Mickey knew, or if she knew anything at all.

"I don't know much; I just know it has something to do with *the* Misses' killer. Mr. Simmonds insisted I stay with you, until..." her voice trailed off.

"Until what?"

"I'm... I'm not sure. But I think that it has something to do with the person who killed his wife. All I know is that they think you're in danger too."

"They... they who? Mickey, please tell me, don't hold out on me. I can't stand being held here like a prisoner."

"Oh no! You're no prisoner. They just want to keep you safe. That's all I know; that's all I heard, except that..." she turned her head toward the door as if she could tell someone might be listening from the other side. "They suspect you," she whispered.

"Me!" Moriah leaned her shoulders back. Her brows pulled closely together. "For what?" She pulled Mickey over by the window to avoid being overheard.

The servant shrugged her shoulders. "None of this makes any sense. They can't think you're out for his money..."

In her anxiousness, she had taken hold of Mickey's arms harder than she realized. "What is it you're afraid to tell me?" She

266

removed her hands immediately as she felt Mickey's sudden rigidness within her grasp.

"I don't know. But there is something I should tell you." She kept her gaze on her shoes.

"What is it? Please… I promise, I won't repeat it."

"I wasn't completely honest about the necklace… well, sort of not." She met Moriah's gaze before shifting her eyes back to the floor.

"What necklace, what are you talking about?" Moriah asked.

"Oh Ms. Moriah," the servant bubbled over with excitement as if a sudden revelation rained down on her. "It's perfect for you. The necklace should belong to you. You're much better for him than her…" She looked away as her regret for opening her mouth spilled from her eyes. "She only wanted him for his money and status," Mickey finally said.

"Who wanted who…? What money?" Moriah asked as she tried to make sense out of the servant's babbling. "What does this have to do with me being here?"

"Mr. Simmonds, he's very wealthy man."

"I know. And it's a shame that he's not half as polite as the money he has."

"Oh no, I'm not talking about the Mr., mister. I mean his son, Mr. Tyro." She smiled brightly finding the confidence to go on. "Mr. Tyro has his own money. In fact, from what I understand, he has much more of it than his dad.

"What?" Moriah said as she spun around.

"You're the only woman he's ever brought to his home, except for *her*." She decided to spit it all out.

"The necklace I suggested you wear last night belongs to Tyro." She lowered her head. "His mother had given it to him for his bride. I thought that if he were to see you wearing it, he would see how perfect you are for him."

Moriah walked over and lifted her face. "That's not for you or anyone to decide but him." She folded her arms but immediately dropped them. She'd seen the hurt in Mickey's eyes as surely as if she'd just scolded her like a child. "Would you do a favor for me?" Mickey's head bobbed in nervousness. "Please give the necklace back to him for me. I left it on the dresser. And no more matchmaking—okay?"

Mickey nodded and smiled.

"You have nothing to be ashamed of. You are a beautiful person with a heart of gold. Always hold your head high, you got that?"

"Yes. I do." Unable to control her relief, she fell into Moriah's arms like a good friend. Moriah returned her affection.

She stared afar off as her mind pondered on what Mickey had just told her.

Mickey sensed her bewilderment. "I know you don't want him for his money. I knew that the moment I saw you the other night when I... we helped you into your night clothes." Mickey's eyes gleamed in assurance.

Moriah barely hearing what she'd said placed her hands on her hip. "So that's it," she said. "They think I want him for his money? Is that what this is all about?"

Mickey, already feeling she'd said too much, hurried to the door. She turned before opening it to leave. "I don't know what happened back there on the beach, but he really cares about you. I know he loves you. I just know he does." She opened the door and slipped out.

As the sun conceded for the day, Moriah's eyes drooped from the weariness. It was only six-thirty when she'd fallen asleep. She'd spent that last ten minutes gazing at her mysterious prince's photo on her cell.

Unwilling to sleep in the bed, she drifted down lazily onto the sofa. She wondered if she had understood Mickey correctly but she had been mindful not to pry anything out of her that didn't concern herself. After all, she was talking to the family's hired employee. Still she wondered. Did she say that Tyro was wealthy? If he wasn't living off of his dad's money, why did he put up with him?

If he thought he could treat her any kind of way because he had money... She realized she knew even less about the man she'd fallen in love with. Her cell slipped from her fingers. Her mind weaved through a tangled web until finally, she sputtered into sleep.

Chapter 5

Monday morning, Moriah's eyes fluttered open to a strange man's face staring down into hers. *"Tyro?"* she muttered as her eyes pulled the sandy hair into focus.

"Ms. Styles," the voice called to announce his presence, again. Bolting upward, she gasped in confusion of her surroundings. She blinked several times. A huge nose, crooked in a few places, came into view as her eyes cleared from the fuzziness of being awakened suddenly.

"Sorry, I didn't mean to startle you." He shifted his eyes toward the door. "We knocked several times and got concerned when you didn't answer."

"Were you planning on going somewhere?" the roguish looking man asked. His eyes trailed back to her from her bag. *We?* She tried to peek around the burly man blocking her view. There were at least two others standing behind him.

"I'm Detective Smith. Is this yours?" He handed her a small black object and jumped right into his point. Moriah looked at it. She shifted her eyes from the object he held out to her to his expressionless face.

"Take it," he urged.

She placed her feet on the floor and removed it from his hand. "It's my cell. My old one... I lost it a while ago."

"Do you remember where?"

Her mind trailed off to the last text she'd received on it. Fletcher was to have flown her back to Delaware in her company's helicopter. Instead, he had taken a detour and had kept circling around a mountain. A text from a familiar source had sputtered in and out on her cell. The texts always appeared from Unknown Caller, known to be from the covert name, OBR for *Operation Black Rose*. The detective was the same one who had vowed her safety. She remembered it clearly.

Unknown Caller: where are you?
Moriah: dunno… it's dark… flying in circles…
Unknown Caller: use compass on ur cell
Moriah: calibrating now… he's crazy… you didn't tell me… I'm scared…
Unknown Caller: what compass read?

The coordinates on the compass on her cell had rolled slowly into view. She had taken a quick glance up at Fletcher. He was struggling to maneuver the cyclic stick to steady the helicopter. Something was wrong with the controls.

Moriah remember her last text entry: compass kps rolling… 9lo SE… SW??? I dunno!!! HELP ME… U PROMISED I BE SAFE…

It was at that moment that the helicopter took a sudden deep dive. Moriah screamed. When the craft recovered its longitude, her cell had lost signal. She panicked as she stared in disbelief down at the dark black screen.

"Ms. Styles." Mark Smith's firm, but gentle voice broke through her thoughts. "Are you all right?" She hadn't realized she was trembling. The evidence of sweat bled through the front end of the satiny robe she'd been hugging tightly to her chest.

"Look, first you come in here, scaring me half to death. Then you start pounding me with questions. I don't know who you are—"

"You were about to tell us how you lost your cell phone," Detective Smith reminded her.

She looked away. She didn't have to answer to them. She jumped when a familiar figure suddenly burst through the door.

"What is going on here?" Tyro demanded, pushing his way to Moriah's side. Her eyes shot up to meet his. Her lips trembled as she tried to restrain her relief from spilling out over her face. But only for a moment. He'd come for her. Her heart raced, but her feet moved faster. She leapt into his arms. She buried her head in his chest as he enveloped her into his protection.

His cell rang. He hesitated to break their embrace to retrieve it from his jacket. "That's not going to happen," he barked into the phone. Moriah, surprised at his tone and defiance, shuddered from the outburst.

"He's standing right here. You'll need to call him for yourself. Ms. Styles is coming with me."

Moriah stood staring at the floor. She swiped a loose hair behind her ear as she tried to hear what was being said on the other end of the phone. She could tell from the British accent blaring from the other end, he was speaking to Sable.

"She's not under arrest. She's not being charged with any crimes, and as far as the law's concerned, you're illegally holding her against her will." He pulled her closer. "That's kidnapping."

He lowered the phone away from his mouth. "Get dressed," he commanded as he placed a kiss on her forehead. "You're coming with me." He encouraged her to get moving with a nudge of his hand.

Moriah hurried into the bedroom, changed into a leisure set Mickey had packed for her back on the island. She grabbed the few items she'd left out that she had planned to use in her attempt to get away from there.

Tyro knocked on the bedroom door. He'd come to see what was taking her so long. His eyes scrolled over her. He took note of her tiredness and the weariness that weighed her down. He surmised it had been from the lack of sleep. He hadn't been able to sleep either.

He was glad he was able to find her. Safe. Alive. He didn't know what he expected but he knew his imagination had run away with him with her attacker on the loose.

He had no idea his father had so many connections with downtown. He'd have to find out about that later. He only wanted to get her out of there so he could protect her on his own turf.

He took her hand and with one motion, he swooped her into his embraced. His lips brushed past her face as he whispered in her ear. "Sorry about leaving you. Right now, I need you to trust me. I'll explain later. Okay?"

She nodded although he hadn't waited for her reply. He'd taken hold of her hand and led her out of the room.

"What do you think you're doing?" Detective Smith demanded.

"We're out of here." Tyro guided Moriah past him, stopping briefly to grab hold of her overnight bag. The detective whipped out his phone and began feverishly punching numbers. By the time someone answered on the other end, Tyro had helped Moriah into the helicopter. He sat next to her and gave Mario the go ahead to lift off.

Mickey turned around and smiled at her from the front seat. She had called him. Moriah smiled back at her as best she could. She was relieved as their helicopter ascended quickly, leaving the helicopter she'd been flown over in behind.

Tyro, feeling her tension, rested her head on his shoulder. He fingered through her hair in slow, comforting strokes. Whispering softly, he told her she was safe now. She was with him. When she lifted her head, he coaxed her head back on his shoulder, encouraging her to rest. He would wait until they were alone to get the answers he needed. This time, in a way, she'd feel comfortable talking about it. The fear of losing her had caused him to change his approach.

Chapter 6

Moriah had fallen asleep by the time Mario landed the helicopter. She awakened slowly to Tyro's gentle nudge. Her eyes slid open and began drinking in her surroundings. Alarmed, she bolted her head off of his shoulder. She blinked rapidly.

"You okay?" he asked. He waited beside her for the few moments it took to pull herself together. "We're here." Her anxiety melted when she glimpsed his warm smile. "I'm glad you were able to rest."

"A little," she responded and accepted his hand to escort her out of the copter. While they were in flight, he'd told her he was taking her to his condo at the Riverfront.

So, here we are. Now what? she wondered.

"Hungry?" Tyro asked after she'd firmly planted her feet on the ground. She glanced around at her surroundings from the top of the extremely high, high-rise building where she stood.

"Starving," she replied between gaping yawns.

"Come on," he said, guiding her by the arm. "I know just the place to take care of your hunger." He winked. "Mickey will take care of your belongings." He handed Moriah's bag to his staff who stood patiently by.

"Sure will!" Mickey said in a bubbly tone as she removed the items from his hand and beamed over at Moriah.

He guided her to the rooftop garage. She sat in the passenger seat of his Range Rover. Amused by the panoramic views, they descended inside the glass elevator while seated in his car.

The elevator opened automatically once they reached the bottom. He finessed his vehicle toward I-95 North heading for Philadelphia to attend an exclusive country club.

"I can't go there dressed like this," she protested once she found out where they were headed.

"You'll be just fine." He took her hand and kissed it tenderly. She wanted to withdraw it from his grasp. He had a lot of explaining to do, deserting her like he did yesterday. But instead, she held tightly to his hand. She had been left all alone in that dumpy hotel and she had longed all night to feel his tender touch. The talk could come later.

As he drove along, he considered how she might feel if all eyes were to stare at her attire. She was right. Taking her to the exclusive, predominantly-white-attended social club, one which he rarely frequented, made no sense. It was his dad's thing, not particularly his. He hadn't considered the fact that she may not be treated with the highest respect because of her perceived status. He had only considered the exquisite brunch they served.

Detouring farther north, he headed toward an upscale country-style restaurant in Philadelphia. Its old city charm with floor to ceiling windows reminded her of the chapel. She enjoyed the country brunch cuisine, especially the red velvet pancakes. They were to die for.

Moriah settled into Tyro's dual suite penthouse condo comfortably. She had her own wing. He'd also advised her he could stay in the unit down the hall if she felt uncomfortable with him being there. She conceded there was no need for him to do so. He had been the perfect gentleman and she was fine being in the same space with him. Besides, she had the entire guest suite to herself, except for Sheba who liked sharing the space with her.

She pondered about their ride back to his condo. It had been quiet as if they both were in anticipation of their next conversation, same as it had been at the restaurant. He'd change topics whenever she broached the subject of why he'd left her so suddenly yesterday. It annoyed her when he tried to coerce her into talking about the whole *Fletcher* ordeal, as he called it. Yet he wouldn't talk to her about why he'd left her. He at least owed her that much.

She didn't push the issue. With that maniac still on the loose, she needed to think through what her next move would be. For now at least she was safe.

Her immediate concern: she had a business to run. She couldn't just stay cooped up in some apartment, no matter how elaborately furnished and equipped with the latest state of the art technology it was. She had bills to pay, a life to live, and clients waiting. She was desperate to move out of the dilapidated motel she and her best friend Nettie shared. There was no way she was going to make it all happen hiding like a chick under her mother's plumage.

Sifting through her choice of wardrobe, she laid the casual business attire on the bed, not noticing Tyro leaning against the doorframe. He watched her closely as she hurriedly packed the remainder of her things.

Unaware he was there she spun around startled when his cell rang. Her eyes narrowed. *Not again!* She stood and pulled the afghan she was folding to her chest. She let out a long breath. This time it really was business related. He needed to go to the office. She could only decipher that a fight or something happened at the yard.

"Is everything okay?" she asked as she continued to roll and place the last of her clothing in her carrying bag.

"I was thinking." He quickly stepped back as soon as he realized he'd stepped into the room. "Why don't you come with me to the office? You could work from there. We could stop at your place on the way and you could pick up your laptop and clothing, and anything else you'll need for several days." He observed her demeanor. "I'm sure you'd feel better having your own clothes."

"Why do you do that?"

"Do what?"

"You avoid answering my questions. It's as if what you have to say is more important."

"I don't mean it to be that way." He stood straight and dropped his hands to his side. "May I?" He pointed at the space between them.

"Sure, why not. You can come in if you want to. It's your place."

"I just want to make sure you're comfortable."

"Well why don't you answer my questions since you care so much about how I feel?" She stared at him as he stepped closer.

"You said I could come in."

"That's not it and you know it, Tyro. You deceived me... No, you downright lied to me—taking me back to that place and then you had the nerve to leave me on your beach like I was a cheap date." She snatched the zipper closed on her bag. Her hands balled into fists, then she folded her arms across her chest. There'd be no holding her thoughts back now.

"You were the one who convinced me to stay. 'Come to the beach with me, relax', " she said mockingly. "And all along you were waiting for Sable to come back, weren't you?" She jabbed her finger in his face.

He gently took hold of her hand and pulled her into his embrace. Her body remained rigid. "I was wrong, Moriah. I should have never doubted you."

"Doubted me?" She pulled away. "Doubted me for what?"

"I'll tell you more as we're on our way. If we're going to stop at your place, we better get going."

Moriah seethed inside that he again avoided answering her question, but complied. She thought of her place.

Although she and Nettie kept the place neat and tidy, she was apprehensive about him seeing where she lived. She also wasn't too sure how she felt about going to the office where his mother had been slain. Her nerves stood on edge just thinking about it. What if some of the evidence was still there? She'd have to work hard to get past it.

Chapter 7

Going back to her motel apartment wasn't as bad as she had anticipated. The musty smell from being closed up was embarrassing, although he made light of it. But he had been the one to insist on coming in with her. He'd said there was no way he was going to allow her to go in there by herself. Not with her attacker still on the loose.

Moriah gathered enough clothing for more than a week. She briefly spoke with Nettie on her cell and was relieved to know that she'd be staying with her brother until further notice.

On the way to the office, Tyro told her what he'd learned about Fletcher and that the FBI was convinced they had the right guy. That's when he let it slip that Sable was really an undercover agent for the federal bureau.

"I *knew* it," Moriah blurted.

He was relieved that everything he knew was out in the open, except for the piece of clothing Sheba had found on the island. He was sure it belonged to her and thought it would be best to wait for a better time to bring it up.

He also had hoped she'd talk about what had really happened to her, but he knew that would take time. He knew he'd have to work at regaining her trust. For that he was determined to be patient and understanding.

Tyro settled Moriah in one of the empty offices. He insured she had everything she needed before leaving her alone to get some work done. He went to check up on the incident that happened in the yard.

She browsed through her emails and returned voicemails clients had left for her over the past few days. Nothing urgent had come up. She was elated by the numerous requests from her soon-to-be new clients. Actually, they'd been former clients of hers while at TSMA. But since they were the ones reaching out to her, she had every right to take them on as new clients to her newly formed company, M&A Marketing.

They were large accounts. Acquiring them would have her on her feet sooner than she'd anticipated. She suspected something had gone awry with them at TSMA. Maybe it was because she'd pampered them so and they appreciated her way of handling their business. She knew the Smythes didn't have anyone of her caliber to have replaced her so quickly.

She had hoped that it would be only a matter of time before some of her former clients pursued her business. Like she had told Nettie, she wouldn't go after their clients. But she wouldn't turn them away if they sought her out either.

Several hours had passed. Within that time she'd scheduled appointments, sent out invoices, and sketched out the marketing displays to be completed within the next thirty days. After she'd estimated the net proceeds from the four jobs she just acquired, she leapt from her desk and did a happy dance. If everything went well, she'd have enough to move to a decent apartment and living expenses for the next three months. She'd even be able to afford a down payment to lease a decent truck.

When she thought about the infamous Shrek mobile, she sighed. Tyro never told her where he was hiding it. She determined that she'd take a snoop around the yard for it when she got a chance to. But for now the truck didn't matter.

She reasoned that she would use the proceeds from the jobs that followed to put down a retainer fee to start her appeal on the custody battle. The rest she'd invest back into her company. The way things were picking up, she would need to hire an assistant soon. And she knew the very one she'd hire.

Caught up in the moment of seeing light at the end of the tunnel, she was overjoyed. She waved her arms in the air and wiggled her fingers as she did a side-to-side, back and forth two-step move.

"Somebody's happy," Tyro said as he knocked on the partially opened door. Sheba squeezed through and trotted over to her. Her tail wagged rapidly and made a series of thumping sounds as it hit the side of the desk. She raised her head and barked. Moriah stooped down and rubbed her behind her ears. "That's right, Girly Girl, I'm gonna buy your little pups some pretty little ribbons and bows. They're gonna look so cute!"

Moriah looked up when Tyro chuckled. "What?" she asked after she stood. She leaned her shoulders back. "You've never seen dogs with bows on their heads?"

"Maybe on lap dogs or those little, cutesy doggies you ladies like to carry around in your purses," he emphasized *cutesy* with his two fingers. "But not for any dog of mine."

He ducked as Moriah threw a paper clip at him. "Oh, so you're getting violent on me, are you?"

"Nope. That was just a warning, wasn't it, girl?" Sheba barked once as she joined in the playful atmosphere.

Tyro snapped his finger and pointed to his side. Sheba complied with his command and immediately sat at his feet.

"What's gotten into you, Mr. Party Pooper? No need to get all riled up over some head bows." His face fell solemn. "Tyro, is something the matter?" She walked over and stood in front of him.

"I'm concerned about her. That's all."

"You said she's had pups before. Is there something going on with her this time around?"

"I'm not sure. I've been right there through all her deliveries. I know how she carries. I think she's in the early stages of pre-mature labor."

"Tyro, it's too soon." Moriah clasped her chest.

"I know…" He nodded.

Grabbing her cell, she punched in numbers at rapid speed. "I'm calling Nettie. She'll know what to do. She's finishing up her internship at the finest veterinary clinic in the area."

"I don't know about that. I've always—" Tyro stopped abruptly as Moriah lunged to put her cell up to his ear. After he explained Sheba's condition, Nettie convinced him of the potential seriousness of his Shepherd's condition. Hearing the urgency, he agreed to have her at the clinic within the hour.

Chapter 8

"Thanks for coming with me," Tyro said. He helped Sheba into the back seat. Moriah insisted on sitting back there with her as she did on the way over.

"You're gonna be all right, Girly," Moriah told her as she stroked her head. Sheba laid her head in her lap. Her big eyes beamed up at her.

"I know you've got to be starving," Tyro said. Sheba lifted her head and barked.

"So you're hungry too?" He was relieved that he could take his Shepherd home. For a while there, it was rough sailing. If his dog would have had to stay overnight, there was no doubt that the both of them would have insisted on being right there with her.

Despite the lead vet agreeing with Nettie's recommendation that this would be her last litter, everything else was fine. He said she would need a little more exercise to build up her strength. Tyro knew of his neglect. With everything that had been going on, he hadn't been walking her as much as he should.

After they settled back in his condo, he made a quick call to his uncle Mario. He confirmed that everything had settled down in the company's yard. The friction between the union and non-union worker had escalated more than he wanted to deal with at the time.

He was glad that Mario had stepped in and had gotten everything under control. It's not that he wouldn't have been able to sooner or later, but Mario's former military conflict-resolution skills resolved the issue much quicker. He was grateful that it had allowed him to get back to see what Moriah was up to sooner than he'd anticipated.

Now that Sheba had had her meal and was resting comfortably, the altercation at the yard from earlier that day weighed heavily on his mind.

Tomorrow he would have to suspend both of the parties involved while the situation was under investigation. From what Mario filled him in on, only one of the men's actions warranted termination.

It was the union employee. He'd been a troublemaker since the day he was hired. But if he only fired the one, and not the other, he'd have a long, drawn out legal issue incited by the Union on his hands.

Tyro felt bad about having to fire Orlando to curtail the issue. Not only was Orlando one of his best workers who'd never given him one moment of trouble, he had a wife and three kids, and his twins were due to be born this Christmas. Still, he was committed to do right by him at any cost.

A hard knock at the door jolted him from his thoughts. He hurried to the door. It could only be one person knocking like that. His father. He was glad Moriah had finished eating her dinner and had decided to take a relaxing bath.

"You gonna eat that?" Quincy pointed to Tyro's untouched meal.

"Help yourself." Tyro sat back on the couch and petted Sheba along her back.

"Well?" Quincy snapped just before stuffing his mouth with a hearty bite of duck tacos.

"This is going to be her last litter," Tyro said mid stroke as he looked up at Quincy.

"I could have told you that. In fact, I told you the last time."

"Dad. Please."

"What's wrong with you? Is it that girl or your boys in the yard that's got you on edge?"

283

Moriah, wrapped tightly in a luxurious but oversized bathrobe, walked into the room while blotting her hair dry with a towel. She stopped abruptly the moment she saw Quincy.

"Hello, Mr. Simmonds. Sorry. Didn't know you had company," she said looking directly at Tyro. She pivoted and headed back in the direction she'd come.

Quincy mumbled something. No longer willing to restrain himself, he came out with it, loud and clear. "She has gotten mighty comfortable around here now, hasn't she?" he asked in an insinuating tone. He jutted his head toward where she'd just gone. "You let her finagle herself into moving in here?" he asked incredulously.

"I'm sure you're not here to discuss what's going on in my life." He stood to guide Quincy toward the door.

"Now you wait just a minute!" Quincy yanked his arm free. "You going to choose that *nutcase* over me? Think about what you're doing, son. You really do not know what you are getting yourself into."

"And I suppose you do?" Tyro folded his arms over his chest. "So why don't you tell me?"

"I have already told you everything I know." Quincy's white brows furrowed together.

"That's what I thought. You know nothing about her. You let that detective use you. I should have known something was up when you insisted I go along with your nonsense. You didn't even know Sable was with the FBI." He held the door open for Quincy to leave. "Both of you are wrong about Moriah."

"She knows something. I am telling you. That girl is lying to you," Quincy said, stopping short of leaving.

"You ever think that maybe she was a victim too? Didn't Sable say that Moriah was in danger?"

"Oh, hockey-crap! You do not believe that yourself. Think about it, son before you get hurt. Your mother's killer is out there somewhere. She may just be leading him to us."

"For what?" Tyro sassed.

"To finish what he started."

"What?"

"Didn't you learn anything, son? This Fletcher guy had intended to kidnap my wife... your mother, need I remind you. That girl was in on it."

"Now you've taken things too far. Good night." Tyro shut the door much harder than he intended.

He turned to see Moriah standing there with her arms folded across her chest. She spun on her heel and tightly closed her door. Tyro heard the chamber lock immediately afterwards. He didn't bother to knock. He felt it was best that they have some time and space between them. Besides, he had an immediate pressing issue he needed to deal with. His Dad. It was long overdue.

Chapter 9

Tyro heard Moriah unlock her door moments after she'd closed it. He figured she'd had a change of heart. Still he didn't disturb her.

A half hour later, before he left out of his condo, he peeked in on her. He found her curled with a bed pillow tucked under her. She was kneeling on the floor in a praying position. She was sound asleep. A light whispery snore escaped from her.

He smiled in amazement at how she could sleep so peacefully almost anywhere. He pulled back the plush bedspread and top sheet and placed her delicately in the bed.

She roused for a few seconds. Shushing her, he lulled her back to sleep. *"I love you too,"* she mumbled as she turned on her side into a fetal position.

Tyro kissed her on the forehead. "Somebody's having a good dream," he whispered. Stroking her hair a few times, he pushed a curly lock that had fallen out of her wild ponytail from her face. He chuckled at the scarf wrapped around her head. It was cocked crookedly and high on one side. He wondered what had been the point of wrapping her hair seeing how it wasn't doing it any good.

He pulled the comforter up to her chin. Standing over her for a few seconds longer, he gazed tenderly at her. His heart stood still. How had he come to love her so much, so fast? He stroked her face. Her arms. His body longed for her. Not like it had for the other women who'd thrown themselves at him. His need, desire for her was different.

His heart fluttered. Being with her felt so right. He knew she was the one. In his mind, he could justify climbing in bed with her even if it was only to hold her—although he knew he would want more. Much more. He turned his head away. He would respect her wishes. Besides, the last thing he needed was for her to wake up to find him lying next to her. He imagined her going ballistic on him like she did yesterday on their morning excursion.

She seemed so innocent lying there. Still, he couldn't ignore the questions he had regarding what happened on that island. He truly doubted she had anything to do with Fletcher's scheme to kidnap his mother. He knew there was a lot his father wasn't telling him. Something about the whole situation gnawed at him.

He gently closed the bedroom door and grabbed the remainder of his food. He slipped down the hall. Sheba stood beside him as he knocked on the condo door at the opposite end. He knew his dad would be there. The weather had gotten too risky to fly back to the island.

Having a second home inland close to their establishment was another one of Laino's brilliant ideas. They'd purchased the entire top floor of the Riverfront Towers and turned them into elaborate penthouse suites. Tyro had combined two of them for his private domain.

Their condos were conveniently located just minutes away from their multi-billion-dollar trucking enterprise. Laino had strategically thought through every detail. During the week, they lived on the riverfront and flew home early Friday afternoon for the weekend, weather permitting.

After attending service on Sunday, they'd often have a brief meeting to cover any pressing or urgent issues before Monday morning staff meetings. And then it was strictly friends and family time—food, fun, and games. They were a team, a perfect model for any family. Together they'd worked, played, and loved hard until tragedy had struck the Hernandez-Simmonds family conglomerate. Losing Laino meant losing their heart, soul, and the glue that held

287

them all together. Not only for their business, but also—most importantly—their family. Grief and listlessness continued to rip them apart at the seams.

Tyro was surprised to see the door to his father's condo ajar. He peeked in cautiously with Sheba by his side. He heard a big crash. It had come from the kitchen area. Sheba barked and lunged forward, reaching the commotion first.

Quincy had just finished knocking down a whole wall of cabinets. He sat in the only chair that remained in the unit. His head lay on the backs of his hands as he leaned on top of the sledgehammer propped between his feet. He was breathing heavily. He turned his head to see his son standing there glaring at him as he caught his breath.

"Dad, what are you doing?" Tyro turned in several directions looking for a place to set the bag of food. The unit had been completely gutted. All that remained was the counter portion of the sink and a few kitchen cabinets. He set the bag on the counter and removed the weapon of destruction from his dad's possession.

Moments later, he guided his grief stricken dad to the balcony, taking the bag of food with him. Quincy swiped a tear away and wasted no time finishing off the crispy duck tacos drenched in Asian mango salsa he'd started on earlier.

They sat at the table on the balcony and ate in silence. Afterwards, they took in the scenery surrounding them. From one angle they could see parts of downtown Wilmington. Unlike New York, the city was asleep except for a few workers bustling to and from their shifts. The Delaware Memorial Bridge was gorgeously lit. The lights on the cars as they traveled over it made them look like tiny ants climbing over a hill. The views were captivating. Serene. Calming.

"Your mother loved this place, you know," Quincy said, breaking the half hour of complete silence.

"Is that what this is all about?" He turned and looked over the pile of debris from Quincy's demolition. "You could have gotten the boys from the yard to do it for you, you know."

His dad wiped a tear trickling down his face. He removed a handkerchief from his back pocket and wiped his nose.

"I know, Dad." He reached over to lightly shake his dad's arm. "I know it's difficult—" He stopped abruptly, not knowing exactly what to say. He turned again from viewing the chaos inside his father's unit. He wasn't sure if it was spurred from grief, or his guilt from the way he'd carried on with his mother before she died.

"She reminds me a lot of your mother," Quincy blurted as if his thoughts had escaped him. "I still do not approve of her... not for you, son."

Tyro sat up straight. "What exactly is it that you think you know, Dad?" He faced him square in the eyes. "Come out with it. Let's get this out in the open, now!"

Quincy balled up the messy wax paper from his meal and tossed it back in the bag. "I already told you what I know."

"Oh come on, there's got to be more to it."

"What more evidence do you need? She was wearing your mother's clothing for God's sake."

"She was stranded, Dad. It's apparent to me as well to everyone else that this Fletcher... maniac... had every intention of kidnapping Mom. He somehow had access to some of her belongings. He had been her pilot for a short while, remember?"

"Since you seem to have all the answers, then how did *she* get them?"

"That, I don't know. I'm sure there is a logical explanation." His irritation swelled. "How come everyone else can see she had nothing to do with... with...Mom's death, but you?"

Quincy glared at his son. "I'm not buying it, son. She's hiding something and I have every intension of finding out." He rose from his seat. "Now are you with me or not?"

Tyro trailed back inside behind his father. "Oh, no. I'm not going along with any more of your shenanigans. And if you really want to get to the bottom of it, let me handle it."

Quincy heaved the empty food containers and bag onto the pile of debris in one toss. He grabbed the sledgehammer and headed toward the master bathroom.

He followed Quincy toward the left wing. "I let you handle the situation your way. You see how that turned out." He grabbed the hammer from his father, marched past him and within five minutes, he'd finished demolishing the remainder of the kitchen. He headed back toward the master bathroom.

His frustration consumed him. His father just couldn't seem to help himself. Or either he didn't want to. He swung the sledgehammer several times. The vanity came crashing down. He swung hard into the toilet. Water spewed everywhere. He'd forgotten to turn off the water. After he cleaned up the spill, he ripped out the marble in the shower. Why did his father have to go there and ruin a perfect moment between them? But the truth of the matter kept creeping up his spine. He was just as frustrated with Moriah.

She hadn't given him much to go on. He didn't like having to fight in the dark. Who was this Fletcher character to her? How did she get mixed up with him? If she had been held captive on that island, how... why? There were just too many unanswered questions. He didn't appreciate having to build a relationship with her in blind faith. How was he to keep her safe if he didn't know exactly what or whom he was up against?

An hour later, Tyro hurried to clean up to leave before he'd say something that would damage their relationship beyond repair. His father had crossed the line again and he wasn't going to put up with it much longer.

It was almost 11p.m. He was far from being tired even after he finished demolishing his father's kitchen and master bath. He appreciated their time on the balcony; it had been good father-son quality time. He enjoyed every bit of it. He felt his father had too. It had been a long time since they'd been together like that. He couldn't understand why his dad had to ruin it.

Still he'd worked off enough steam and got past his agitation. In fact, tearing down the bathroom caused his mind to burst with creativity about his own little project he was working on. In his excitement, he'd shared his idea with his dad and requested he come see it tomorrow.

"Fine," his father gritted. "Guess I have no choice but to wait to see it tomorrow." He sneered and snatched open his front door to let his son out. Tyro had reached his unit when he heard his father complain loud enough for the whole building to hear. "Far be it from me to wake your houseguest," he said in obvious irritation.

Chapter 10

Tyro stepped into his condo and eased his door closed. To his surprise Moriah was sitting in the great room. He was glad to see she was enjoying the fire he started earlier. Sheba startled her when she trotted over to her.

"Deep in thought?" Tyro asked as he sat on the sofa next to her.

"I couldn't sleep."

He reached to massage her neck. She rolled her head slowly and moaned in relief.

She arched her back, pulling slightly away from his touch. "What if she's right?"

"She? Right about what?" He resumed the task of massaging her head. She sank down onto the floor and placed a pillow on his knees where she leaned her head back to rest.

"What if it's not safe for me to go back to my normal life right now?" She'd overheard Sable through the phone earlier. She felt like Detective Smith would stop at nothing to get the information he wanted from her, even if he had to squeeze her like a tube of toothpaste. She was sure of it. She thought about when Tyro had come for her. It had been in perfect timing.

"You can stay here as long as you need to. I think the investigation is going to be closed soon."

"But what if it's really not over? What if —"

"If what?" Tyro slid down on the floor next to her. He pulled her into his arms. "I know seeing that island the other day was hard for you. I couldn't imagine…" He paused to choose his words wisely. He pulled her closer into his arms. "When I left you Sunday, that's where we went." She pulled from his embrace.

"You what? Why?" She turned and stared at him in disbelief. Stiffness shot through her like a rocket.

He blew out a deep breath. "We think her killer was planning to kidnap my mother and hold her hostage for ransom." His voice quivered. "It was an accident… her death was a senseless accident." He lowered his head into his hands. "It doesn't make it any less painful," he blurted out mindlessly.

Quickly, he changed the subject. "You know, my dad and I actually enjoyed each other's company tonight." Not wanting to raise needless concern, he didn't mention the tiff that had emerged between them.

"I wondered where you were."

"It seems like he's found a little strength to move on."

"Oh, what makes you say that?"

"He demolished his entire unit by himself today since coming back from that place."

Her head popped up. Her eyes squinted in curiosity.

"I think having a better understanding of what happened is helping him. I saw the blueprints. He's planning to remodel it. Although I think he's going to continue to live in another suite." He looked afar off, "No amount of remodeling could erase the painful memories."

"What about you? Is it helping you too?"

"Knowing why she died doesn't make it any easier and it won't bring her back. It just adds another piece to the puzzle."

"I'm really sorry about your mother, Tyro."

He kissed her forehead and hugged her tighter. "We found his dog tags in the cave. We're pretty sure we've got the right guy even though there are still a lot of unanswered questions."

Not willing to go there just yet, she redirected the conversation. "Your father has a lot of anger pent up in him. Negative energy will eat you up inside. The moment it has a hole even as tiny as a pinhead, it'd be like the Hoover dam breaking loose." Not wanting to skirt around her concern, she turned and faced him. "You and Mario seem to have the same issues."

He looked away. "I know." The room fell quiet. Tender. He toyed with the pillow between his fingers before tossing it backwards over his head. It landed perfectly on the couch. "What about you? How are you holding up?" He wrapped his arm around her shoulder. "It had to be pretty traumatic being in that horrible... in a situation like that."

She closed her eyes and took in a deep breath.

"Moriah, you can talk to me." He turned her shoulders so she faced him. "No matter how painful it may be, I'll be right here with you."

They gazed into each other's eyes. "I'm sorry I violated your trust. There is no excuse for what I've done." He refocused her attention his way. "I know it will take time to regain your confidence in me. And I know there may be a lot you can tell us that could clear up some of the unanswered questions, but only as you're ready to talk about it." He gave her a few moments to take it all in. He wanted her to understand. He was sincere and meant every word he said. "I give you my word, I will never mislead you again."

The warmth in his eyes she so craved melted her heart away. She was pleased to see that the darkness wasn't there as he spoke of his mother. She'd searched carefully to see if it loomed in hiding somewhere. His demeanor was void of it. His eyes shined in their normal gorgeous steel grays.

"Whenever it's too much for you, stop. But you need to get it out. It's not good for you to hold it in. Trust me, I know." He pulled her back into his arms and held her gently. "You're not alone."

She fiddled with her hands. It was time. She began telling him her story. As she spoke, Tyro held her, comforting her as she cried. When she froze and was stuck in getting through the turmoil and when she'd lost her way, struggling to find the words she'd buried deep inside, he remained quiet.

And on occasion, more than a few, he'd gently rocked her, cradled in his arms. She paced the floor when she couldn't keep still. He gave her the space. Not judging her. Not rushing her. He didn't pressure her. Hours had passed. He'd been listening tentatively. He did everything he could to circumvent his outrage. What she'd gone through made him seethe inside. And still he surmised she could only get through half of it.

Listening to her he grew angry, although he tried not to let on. The thought of her having been tied up, tortured, and left fighting for her life punched him deep in his gut. *Had he raped her?* He felt the horror ravaging inside of her as she spoke as if it were his own. He knew it was not his place to ask her, even though the thought of it caused his hatred for the guy to increase even more.

He thought of his poor mother. She'd died fighting for her life. And now all of it lumped together birthed an overwhelming need for revenge to churn in his innermost being. His fury boiled deep like a seething volcano ready to blow. His fists were clenched tightly. He lurched to his feet, trembling.

Like a flaming torch, his mind billowed back and forth with images of his mother, Moriah and his imaginary images of Fletcher. He tried to shake the thoughts out of his mind.

Moriah rose and reached for him. "Are you all right?" Hearing her voice slowly cajoled him back to the present. She spoke again. The pain in her eyes met the shame in his for losing it.

"I'm sorry, Moriah. I lost it for a moment."

She fell on his neck and wept. "I'm sorry if this is too much—"

"Shhh." He kissed her forehead. "It's not your fault." He lifted her face between his hands. Gingerly, his thumbs stroked away her tears. "You didn't deserve what happened to you. Nobody does." They fell into an embrace and held on to each other for a long time.

He guided Moriah to the couch. She lay quietly in his arms. He felt her relax. Taking in all that she said, he concluded that both she and his mother had done the one thing that assured that their assailant wouldn't get away. The evidence that had been removed from under his mother's nails and from the scene of the crime and the cave would be enough to identify their perpetrator. Everyone was convinced it was the same person.

Tyro could only hope that the DNA was a positive match for the suspect at large and that justice would prevail soon. It was a struggle, but he was able to rein his mind in and back to a safe place. He considered his need for revenge but was determined to focus on what she needed. He'd put his own needs aside until later.

Chapter 11

A few days had gone by and Moriah seemed to be weathering her temporary environment in his abode well. No doubt keeping a watchful eye on Sheba helped to refocus her attention. One morning as he drove them to the office, out of the blue she'd asked if Quincy had come to terms with his suspicion that his mother had been cheating on him. From what she'd learned about her, she couldn't imagine her doing something like that. She seemed to have loved her family. She had to know the turmoil it would bring and disrupt the course of her family. And business.

"I've been thinking," she said as he turned into the yard. He walked around and opened her door as he did every time. She appreciated his care towards her. She was convinced it was his way, whether he was in protective mode or not.

"Uh, should I brace myself?" he teased. He held her by the hand as she got out of the car. "Looks like Sheba may need more assistance than I do." She nodded toward the back seat. His Shepherd's stomach bulged like she had swallowed a cow. The dog waited patiently. Tyro pushed a button on the back door where the child safety lock used to be. A mechanical sounding high pitched beep sounded as a set of stairs began to descend from under the bottom rim of the car.

"Huh! Ain't that something. When did you put that in?" She watched in amusement as the bottom grid settled flat on the ground.

"I installed it this morning. I started working on the plans the evening after we returned from the vet."

"Well, go head on, Girly Girl. Live like you're the Queen of Sheba!" She chuckled. "May I?" she asked, pointing her finger toward the button after Sheba had cleared the steps.

He chuckled. "Help yourself. It also can act as a lift. You want to—" He contained his enthusiasm and relished seeing Moriah's astonishment. The stairs retracted with ease when she pushed the button.

They headed toward the office. "Now what's going on in that pretty head of yours?" He eyed her from the side when they walked into the office. Quincy had just poured himself a mug of coffee. She was relieved that there wasn't any evidence of liquor mixed in with his brew. "Good morning, Mr. Simmonds." She smiled, not waiting for his reply. He did manage to mumble his usual response.

She placed her purse on the shelf in the closet inside her office. It was a very nice office with a great view of the pond and back woods. If she stretched her neck, she could see the helipad to the far left. She liked the idea of being able to tell when Tyro landed from his frequent trips back and forth to the island. He rarely took Sheba along because of the recent diagnosis of a high-risk pregnancy. She was in good hands though.

Quincy kept a careful watch on the Shepherd, which proved to be an inconvenience to her, since Sheba liked hanging out in her office. This gave Quincy plenty of opportunity to pop in unannounced. She determined not to make a big deal of it. After all, Mario and he had voted unanimously for her to lease the office at an extremely discounted price. His vote had to count for something in her eyes.

Orlando, who was on suspension and also one of Tyro's top employees, stopped in frequently to check up on Sheba as well. He took a special interest in her. Although Tyro had promised him one of her pups for his children, she was convinced he would've come just the same. She gathered that he was just that kind of person. She sighed as she thought of his potential plight. Surely there was something Tyro could do to save his job.

"Well…" Tyro planted his hands in his front jeans pockets. He removed one of them to gesture for her to come out with it. She had something on her mind. He was eager to find out what was brewing in that head of hers.

***

Tyro stepped into the dark room. He was disappointed when the lights didn't come on with the flip of the switch. He'd forgotten that quickly. The landlord told him the utilities were off when he had handed him the keys.

He'd followed Moriah's suggestion and contacted his mother's former chauffeur, Barreo. And now here he was, standing in the midst of the place at the address he'd given him. He switched on the flashlight to his smart watch. His face contorted. He was completely clueless as to what he was looking for. He felt just as much in the dark as the room he stood in.

He searched around the dimly lit room. Maybe he should have had Moriah to come. After all, she had offered.

The apartment, or studio—which it was he hadn't determined yet— was located on the top floor of an old store on 9th Street in downtown Wilmington. For the life of him, he couldn't think of any reason why his mother had been coming there. *Had she been seeing… or had she fallen in love with some irresponsible fly-by-night artist?* Tyro shook that notion from his head. He remembered the landlord telling him the place had been rented to an African American woman.

Glancing at the slip of paper, he rechecked the address Barreo had given him to assure himself that he'd written it down correctly. At the time when he'd told him, Tyro had questioned him about the location. The former chauffeur repeatedly assured him through his thick accent it's where he had taken his mother several times a week for months, up until the time she'd passed. But said he had no idea what she had been doing there. "Of course," Tyro had responded, knowing it was a moot point for him to have asked—he had only been the employee.

It didn't make any sense. *Why would she come here?* He mused within himself. He continued to look around the vacated premises. He had to get to the bottom of where his mother had been going. If he could prove what she had been doing, it would put an end to his father's nonsense and accusations. Neither had mentioned the alleged affair since the time they'd argued about it. Their relationship was only held together by a frayed thread.

Mom, what were you doing here? he cried out, only to hear his voice echo back to him with no answers.

Did Fletcher have anything…. He wiped that thought out of his mind.

A mouse scurrying across the dusty wooden floor caught his attention. He watched as the mouse squeezed itself into a tiny crevice. It was then that he noticed the corner of a card of some kind sticking out between the floor and baseboard.

He turned to leave, but the white object gnawed at his mind to retrieve it. After all, he'd just spent the last twenty minutes looking through the debris of papers and other art supplies that had been scattered around the room. He was looking for any clue that might lead him to understand why his mother had cause to have come as often as she had.

Was she taking art classes? Was she learning to paint, sculpt... what? And why would she have kept it a secret?

When the landlord had come to check on him, he'd asked questions about the tenant. Ironically, he hadn't been able to give him any clues as to why his mother may have been coming there. All he could tell him was that the former tenant created several forms of art in the place. They were mainly commissioned pieces of work for high paying clients. The artisan hadn't sold her items on the open market that he'd been aware of, like most artisans who'd rented the studio in the past.

She'd paid her rent on time, in cash. That's all that seemed to matter to him. He didn't have a valid lease. She'd been a month-to-month *tenant*. He didn't recognize Tyro's mother from the photos he'd shown him on his cell. He insisted on having him look at several pictures of her. The owner grew weary of his questions. Tyro valued his time and slipped him a hundred-dollar bill before he took a chance showing him the final photo. He was relieved when the guy shook his head indicating that he didn't recognize Moriah either.

The money Tyro had slipped the owner had only afforded him a little more information than he'd been willing to give beforehand. Not that it helped any. He'd said that all he knew was that his former tenant had gotten married suddenly and moved her studio to her new home. He had no idea where she lived. He'd quickly offered that bit before Tyro could ask.

Tyro asked for a few more minutes and he'd return the keys back to him. Just as he was about to close the door, again his eyes shifted over to the glossy piece of paper sticking out of the crevice. He sighed as he succumbed. What could it hurt by seeing what it was?

He walked over to the wall. Meticulously, he worked the object that had been tightly wedged in between the crevice to keep it from tearing.

When he finally retrieved it, he wiped sweat from his brow. He took it into the tiny bathroom by the only window that hadn't been obstructed with plywood. His heart skipped a beat as his eyes pulled the object in view. Clenching the item tighter, as if it would fly away, his eyes washed over the beautiful woman dressed in a sky blue full-length gown. The shoulders were puffed and ruffles curved around the collar. A series of small brown velvet buttons were fashioned from the neck down to the waist. The dress was a replica of a nineteenth century Victorian.

He recognized her right away. She was his mother. She was dressed in the gown his father had bought her for their last wedding anniversary. His father loved her in that dress. She was laid to rest in it.

And now, here she was wearing it in a print on a greeting card. He could tell it had been duplicated from a portrait painted by DeBorah's Studios. The item he held in his hand was a mockup for Christmas cards.

His eyes raced over to the address of the studio where it had been made as stated in fine print on the back of the card. He sighed deeply as he realized he was standing in the very address it noted.

Chapter 12

Quincy stumbled backward and collapsed on Tyro's sofa. His eyes remained fixed on the face of the woman on the card. She had been his everything.

"It made perfect sense for you to have gone there," Mario said in Tyro's direction.

"Moriah was the one to suggest that I find out where Mom's driver had been taking her. I never thought to locate her former chauffeur since he'd resigned and moved back to Brazil soon after she passed," Tyro offered proudly.

"You're a smart lady," Mario commended and gave her an approving smile.

"Glad I could help." Moriah nodded slightly. "There's something else to consider." Quincy's head shot up, giving his undivided attention. "Have you looked through your bank statements to see who she made payments to?"

"I checked and I had my accountant check the records numerous times. Apparently, she paid in cash."

"Or she didn't pay at all," Moriah chimed in. "Perhaps Mrs. Simmonds was getting the painting made for a charity or fund raiser. It's not uncommon. A lot of artisans are commissioned for charity causes."

"Good point. Quincy, did Laino mention any events for the auxiliaries she was working with?" Mario asked with a sudden rise in interest.

Quincy shook his head. Pulling his eyes away from the photo, he remembered how he had acted when she told him she needed to get the gown cleaned. That's when he began to verbalize his suspicions of her affair. He had forgotten all about the gown until the cleaners called to advise it was ready to be delivered. His last memory of the dress was of his wife's burial cloth being pulled over it... over her.

"Dad... Dad!" Quincy's mind emerged back to the conversation after Tyro shook his shoulder several times.

"Huh... what?"

"What was the event Mom had been so adamant about all of us attending?"

"I don't remember. You know I hardly paid attention to any of that stuff," he mumbled. "I just went along with whatever she wanted to do since it made her so happy." He twirled his hand around in the air to allude to his absentmindedness.

Tyro closed his mouth after he noticed Mario giving him a slight shake with his head. He knew exactly what his uncle meant. Now was not the time to hone in on his father's lack of attention to details. Anyone that knew him knew that it was one of his major shortcomings.

"Mr. Simmonds, may I ask what Mrs. Simmonds had asked you to wear for the event?"

His brows folded as if to ask what that had to do with anything. "I don't know, she never told me since I wouldn't have remembered anyway. She'd have one of the girls to lay my clothing out for me the day of the event," he said quickly, cutting her off.

Mario nodded at Moriah. She nodded back. She would look into the matter later to see if Tempa had been told what he was to have worn.

She'd look for additional clues that may lead them to the artisan in hopes of obtaining the painting. Even still, thanks to Moriah, the mystery of where Laino had been going had been solved.

She looked at Quincy. She could tell a heavy burden had lifted from his shoulders. She understood the relief he must have felt to know that his deceased wife had not been having an affair. Tyro expressed his gratitude to her. He was glad that he'd decided to confide in her when he had regarding his dad's accusations.

After Tyro read a text he'd just received, he leapt up from his seat. "Remember I told you I have a surprise for you?" He excused himself, guiding her toward the door along with him.

He escorted her into his car and whisked her away toward the company's yard.

"Tyro, what are you up to?" Moriah crooned. She eyed him, then turned her head to peer out the window. "I know, I know, don't be ruining your surprise."

"I really like the picture frames you got me," he said. He was reminded of them after she mentioned to him not to spoil his surprise. It was the same thing she'd told him when she'd purchased them. And it was only a few days ago that he remembered he had them. He had decided to bring them to the condo since he'd be spending a lot of his time there. "They really look great in the condo; don't you think?" He studied her reaction for a few seconds while stopped at a traffic light. "Does it bother you that I keep them here? I'll be spending most of my time inland until after Sheba has her pups."

"Nope. I think they're perfect just where you have them. I do have good taste, don't I?" she teased and nudged his arm just as he guided his Rover into their destination.

Chapter 13

"Close your eyes and no peeking," Tyro told Moriah.

"How can I see anything with your hands plastered over my eyes?" she teased.

"Watch your step." He guided her around the side of his office building to the garage in the back. "Now you may open them."

"Ooo-la-la. A garage door! How nice." She smirked.

"But wait, there's more," he said as if he were announcing an infomercial. He pressed the remote. The double bay garage door lifted slowly, too slow for her liking.

"Tyro, you're killing me here," she squealed.

"And just what is this?" She leaned her shoulders back and squinted her eyes.

"Your new truck!" Tyro said with more excitement than he could contain.

"Are you kidding me? It's beautiful," Moriah said after she walked around the brand new commercial truck and stared up at the bucket lift on the back. Her eyes welled with tears. "How much is this going to cost me?" She paused. "Tyro, I can't accept this."

"Somehow I knew you were going to say that." He gently took her hand. "Come with me. I have the lease papers all drawn up. Once you review them and sign them, she'll be all yours."

"Five hundred for one month? Is that all? You're going to lease this truck to me for only that amount?" She pointed to the terms while holding the contract out for him to see to ensure there wasn't a mistake. "$500.00 for one month and then it'll be paid off... I'll own it free and clear?"

"Yup! Or would you prefer to pay $1.00 for five hundred months? I could have the terms on the lease changed," he teased.

"That's not enough! I can't—"

Tyro put his finger up to her lips for her to quiet down. She closed her eyes and breathed deeply before one of her eyes popped opened. "Okay, what's the deal here?"

"It's my gift. I owe you... the green monster, remember?" He guided her to sit at his desk. "I knew you wouldn't accept it flat out; so, I figured the $500.00 would be a good compromise. That's what you said you paid for that old Shrek Mobile, right?"

"Yes, but still—"

"I want nothing in return. I only want you to be happy. You can't keep delaying your jobs because you don't have the right kind of utility truck. And you are losing money, because you won't let me lend you any of ours." He gleamed with hope that he'd found the perfect solution. He thought of Moriah as a wise businesswoman, only she'd been letting her pride get in her way.

"I tell you what." Moriah swiveled her chair from looking out of the window. "You keep the new truck for your business and I'll lease one of your older models, same terms and conditions. Deal?"

Tyro sat in one of the chairs in front of his desk and propped his feet up. "I don't know about that. You see, my trucks have been well broken in. It's gonna cost you a little more for one of them."

"Oh? So tell me, Mr. Used Car Salesman, what's your price?" She crossed her arms but couldn't resist chuckling.

"Uh, I don't know... let's see...," he teased. He snapped his fingers. "You must park the vehicle here at Laino Enterprises' garage and get it fueled for free for the next six months. No, make it thirty-six months." He eyed her from the side of his face. "That's my best and final offer."

"Tyro. I don't want your charity." She rose from her seat. "But I'll go along with it only... and I mean *only* under one condition." She crossed her arms and stared back out of the window.

"Is that so?" He stood beside her as they both gazed out to the yard. Orlando was in the distance tinkering underneath the hood of another truck.

"Is that truck right there for sale?" She nodded her head toward the lime green utility bucket truck. It was a much older model but it had its appeal.

"What is it with you and big green trucks?

"I'm not finished stating my terms here, if you don't mind." She nudged his arm with her shoulder.

"In addition to selling me… leasing me the green truck, you must let me hire Orlando."

"Ah, trying to steal our crew from us, huh?"

"Well, the way I see it, it would be a win-win situation for the both of us." She turned to face him. "Didn't Mario say that he found the other man to be at fault for starting the fight, but both had broken company rules for fighting?

"Well…" she continued before he could get a word in, "you could release them both to be fair, and then I'd get to hire Orlando." She looked back at the man who was gunning the engine to the truck he was working on. She had her eyes on the truck and the perfect employee to go with it. "Seems fair to me," she added with a cunning smile.

"If you were to release him, you wouldn't have to deal with the legal headaches the Union would raise for firing only their constituent."

"Aren't you the clever one? He loves that truck, you know."

"I could tell it's his baby."

"It only runs well for him. He's the only one that could get that baby up and running," he said thoughtfully. "There's really nothing wrong with it or I wouldn't sell it to you—"

"I'll take it, and the driver-mechanic too!" Moriah said before he could talk himself out of it. "Do we have a deal?"

Chapter 14

Moriah was pleased that things were going well between her and Tyro even with them working so closely to each other. When at work, she and Tyro kept business as business.

They recently signed off on the acceptable terms to extend her temporary lease. She'd continue to rent office and garage space at Laino Enterprises for an additional six months. She assured that Quincy and Mario also agreed to the terms and arrangement.

When they were home, he mostly slept in his dad's unit while she stayed in his. Occasionally, they shared lunch out on the back patio. The office staff also migrated there. Quincy tried to join in but found it full of memories, making it too grievous for him to enjoy the space. Whenever he'd look at Laino's favorite rocking chair, his face fell solemn. Although it had never been a spoken rule, no one had sat in it since she'd passed. Moriah honored the sentiment and avoided sitting in the seat as well.

Her eyes took in the serenity of her surroundings. The swans didn't seem to mind sharing their luxurious pond with the flocks of geese and other wildlife. Gazing over the still waters the tranquil sound of the gorgeous water fountains in the elaborately constructed pond pulled her mind from the world. She closed her eyes and took in the earthen smells of nature. Fragrances of lilies and wildflowers bloomed in the air as the water majestically plummeted back into the pond.

She and Nettie were scheduled to move into their own townhouse in a few weeks. She felt at peace. Things were turning around in her favor. Tyro was the perfect gentleman. He gave her the space and privacy she needed.

If she and Tyro didn't have an outing planned, he kept busy and practically stayed out of her way. He remained inland mostly, due to Sheba's due date, which was only a few weeks away. He didn't want to risk having to fly her across the Chesapeake, especially if there was bad weather.

He trusted only Nettie and Dr. Croix to handle the birth of Sheba's puppies.

Mickey was the perfect office assistant. Moriah paid her a decent salary and she was able to leave most matters in her capable hands whenever she was out of the office. She was grateful that Quincy had recommended that she hire her. She would have never asked. Although no one told her directly, she knew he was the one behind the whole idea.

She let him know how much she appreciated it when she whispered a soft thank you in his ear at her office inauguration party.

Tyro had moved Moriah's small work crew to the east side bay to avoid any conflict between Laino Enterprises' crew and Moriah's, mainly Orlando.

He stood looking out the window on the far end of the office complex. It was his mother's former office. Since she died, no one ever went in there. He stared at the fall-like colors lining the trees along the wooded area behind the building.

"No wonder she loved this office," he mused out loud as he took a small break. He'd just spent all morning working on an issue. It was the first of his investigations into his findings the week he'd worked undercover. He'd discovered the fixed logs when he located Moriah's infamous Green Monster. One of his drivers had carelessly left it in the truck. Needless to say, he no longer worked for Laino Enterprises.

Instead of making deliveries, some of his drivers were fudging time on their delivery reports. At first he thought that their entries were simple mistakes. But when he read through the report of the private detective he'd hired to work undercover, it confirmed his mother's suspicions.

He also discovered the garage full of undelivered packages in Larry's garage. *Why didn't I see them when I was there?*

The packages had not been delivered to the corporations. Some of them had been stamped as far back as last Christmas. No wonder he'd recently lost 3 major corporate contracts. It was easy to pinpoint the time the dishonesty started.

Some of his drivers had been taking advantage of him while he was out of the office grieving the death of his mother. Even though his division was still profitable, his foreman was aware of the late and un-delivered packages. He should have advised Tyro and for that, he'd have to let him go.

Still, Tyro blamed himself. He looked at the checks and balances sheets over the past six months. They had not been utilized at all. The last form completed was dated over six months ago, the same day his mother died. *So this was what she wanted to meet with us about.* She'd been asking them to work undercover since the last Christmas holiday. That's when her suspicions arose.

He removed the remaining papers from her desk and closed the door behind him.

His mother was right. There had been some undermining going on in his division. No doubt, the same had been going on in his father's as well as his uncle Mario's divisions.

After having an emergency meeting with his father and uncle he found himself tapping lightly on Moriah's office door. It was open, but he still gave her the respect not to intrude. "You've been in here for hours." She kept her eyes fixed on the computer screen as she waved for him to come in.

"Everything okay?" He stood in front of her desk with his hands stowed in his front pockets. He was determined to take his mind off of his own troubles. From the looks of it, she could use a little break herself. "Hello... is anybody home?" he teased as he knocked lightly on the desk.

Moriah's head snapped up. She glanced back at her computer, leaned back in her chair, and sighed.

"I know that look," he said. "What gives?"

"I just got another email from my attorney."

"And?"

"He wants another $10,000.00."

"For what?"

"In order to work on the next steps for my case. He said we were granted an appeal and that I have a good chance of being handsomely rewarded for the Smythe's wrongful termination." She pumped quotation marks sarcastically in the air. "And... he wants 40% from whatever restitution I gain."

"Is it all worth it? I mean, your time and the stress of it all. You've already cleared your name of the malicious accusations. And soon, you'll be compensated for the pain and suffering they caused—although I know no amount of money could ever repay for you being defamed." He put his hands up in defense. "Don't get me wrong, but the appeal could take years and you have to consider the stress. Is it worth it?"

"It's not about the money, Tyro. You were an attorney once and a very good one from what I hear. So you should understand."

"I do understand. I've also seen the wear and tear it has a person's life, family, career, as well as their emotional state of being. There were many times I had to hold my tongue because I was their legal counsel. I only did what they hired me to do.

Right now, your business is doing very well and you're about to purchase a condo, not too far from mine, might I add." The grin on his face didn't last for too long.

"So, you think I should just count my blessings and move on?"

"Yes I do, to be honest with you." He took her hands into his. "I wish I could have been this blunt on numerous occasions with my former clients.

"Look." She removed her hands from his and stood up from her desk. "I really appreciate your help with clearing my name. But this goes far beyond the money." She blew out a heavy breath and brushed her hair back with her hand.

"Then what is it?" Tyro couldn't shake the uneasy feeling that there was still something she wasn't telling him. That, he didn't like one bit. He'd laid all his cards on the table. Told her everything. Apologized for the way he had acted toward her back on the island. He'd done everything he could think of, including giving her time and distance to forgive him. Whatever she was keeping from him bothered him; although he refused to hire a PI to look into her whereabouts. He wondered where she would go when she'd leave the office suddenly. Or the times she insisted on riding separately and she'd come into the office several hours later.

Sometimes she'd tell him she had to see her lawyer, or check on the status of her condo, or it was a business appointment. And not that he didn't believe her; he did most of the time, except for the times she'd come back to the office all frazzled about something.

She stood looking out of the window. He walked over to her and gently turned her around. He lifted her chin with his finger. "When, Moriah? When are you going to tell me what's really going on with you?"

She turned her head so that she didn't have to face him. He wiped the tear trickling down her cheek. "Come on," he said and closed her laptop. "I know just what you need."

Chapter 15

Moriah held Tyro's hand as they strolled along the Riverfront.

They'd just finished eating their lunch on the deck of the new restaurant Mario opened a few days ago. Although a risky move, being that he'd just opened his first one up on Main Street several weeks ago, she wished him well and she could tell Tyro was proud of him.

"Great job," Tyro said, turning to look back at the sign Moriah had created for the restaurant. "No one expected you to do it for free, you know. You're running a business and—"

"I wanted to do it. After all you all have done for me... it's the least I could do. I wanted to show my gratitude. That's all."

"Appreciation duly noted. Besides, I think it was an excellent idea, having my father help out at the restaurant in the evenings."

"Mmm hmm. But he sure has a way of turning off the ladies," Moriah teased.

"Well, if you hadn't ruined everything..." He smirked, entwining her arm with his.

"Oh, whatever do you mean?"

"He didn't appreciate you playing matchmaker. He didn't hit it off with Dango from the Art Shoppe. Remember?"

"I know." She held up her hand as if to pledge. "I won't be doing that again."

"My father is more laid back now. I guess working there must take his mind off of things," he said, taking her arm back into his after landing a kiss on the back of her hand.

"I'm glad he's staying——" Moriah stopped short of what she wanted to say. Quincy had been up to some of his old tricks. For a while, he'd keep to himself. The next day he'd be meddling in not only Mario's and Tyro's divisions of their business, but she also learned that he tried to stick his nose three times into hers as well.

It'd been a while since she had to kindly ask him to tend to his own business when she caught him questioning Mickey about her business financials.

A thought crossed her mind that caused her to cringe.

"And how are you doing, Tyro?" He stopped mid stroll when she tugged his arm.

"How am I doing? I'm fine," he said after removing a puzzled look from his face. "Where did that come from?" he asked.

"I care about you; that's why I asked."

"I could say the same about you. Family's important, you know."

Moriah knew exactly what he meant. She wasn't sure why she couldn't tell him about Amelia or her parents, even though he'd asked about her family on numerous occasions. As far as the lawsuit was concerned, if she were to drop the appeal it would mean that she would lose her leverage to regain legal custody of Amelia.

He finally stopped asking her about them a while ago after she'd told him she wasn't ready to talk about it.

She tried to assure him that she would discuss it when the time was right. But she could tell he was sorely disappointed that she was keeping something as important as her family off limits to him.

Not that she thought it was fair. But for now, it was in her best interest not to.

A fall-ish wind caused numerous leaves to scuttle across the paved walkway. She watched them skip and tumble along in the breeze as if they hadn't a care in the world. How she longed for the former days when things weren't so complicated.

A tinge of remorse caused her heart to flutter. She squeezed his arm unaware that she was doing so. "Are you okay?" He stopped and pulled her to face him.

She lowered her face and her countenance fell. He lifted her chin.

"Is it something I've said... or done?"

She shook her head.

"What is it?" He held her at arm's length and studied her.

She turned her attention to the leaves that had innocently settled at the feet of a homeless man sitting a few feet away. She recognized the shoes. They used to be Tyro's. They were the same ones he'd worn the night he rescued her. The night she could have been killed. Devastating events, the ones that altered... damaged her life washed over her mind.

She pushed them aside as anxiety clawed at her. She knew she had a few more hurdles to get over. What would he think of her once he found out about her parents' mental illnesses, her sister's suicide, and even Amelia's father's sudden demise? Would he still want to be with her knowing all these issues were a part of her everyday battles?

Moriah focused on the shoes before she noticed the man's face. "Mr. Willie?" she stated in surprise to find it was him who was wearing the shoes. She looked from him to Tyro, who pretended not to notice.

"You're looking good, Mr. Willie. That's sure a nice suit you're wearing," she said, taking note of the new stubble growing over his recently shaved face.

She'd never seen him look so good. He seemed at peace.

"Is there something you're not telling me?" She leaned back and angled her head to the side while looking at him with suspicion.

He grinned from ear-to-ear. "I got nothing to hide. This man right here and his sweet dog *saved my life*."

Tyro tried to pull Moriah along, but she dug her heels in and refused to be drawn away. If there was something that had happened to him, she wanted to know about it.

"Yes, indeedy," Willie continued, "I was lying right here one night... right here on this bench, minding my own business." He looked up at her and pointed to where he was sitting for emphasis. "It was a full moon you know. Some up to no good kids started making trouble, pushing and shoving me around.

"They knocked me to the ground and tried to make a soccer ball out of me." He looked in Tyro's direction with appreciation. He had just stepped aside to answer his cell.

"I would have ended up in the river." He turned and looked over his shoulder. A sparkle of gratitude twinkled in his eyes. He turned back and looked up at Moriah. "If he hadn't come along when he did—"

"I told you it's too dangerous for you to be out here like this," she scolded him as if she were about to drag him to a place of safety. "Here's $100.00; no, take $200.00. Go get yourself checked into the YMCA for a week or two. I'll keep up the payments for your room. I told you this before."

"I don't want your money, Ms. Riah. I got my own place now. And a job too."

"Oh, you do, do you?" she stated, pleased but somewhat perplexed. Her eyes looked in the same direction to where his eyes trailed off. Tyro was heading back toward them.

"You ought to just tell him before it's too late. He's going to find out sooner or later." Willie whispered after getting up off the bench. He tipped his invisible hat and shuffled away. Tyro was only a few feet from where she stood.

Moriah watched Willie stroll along as if he hadn't a care in the world. Her face puzzled. How did he know what was going on inside her head? How did he know that she hadn't told him? What exactly was he referring to, Amelia...her parents... her family's mental challenges... or something else?

"You take care of yourself," she called after him. The way he waved his hand caused her to smile. It was as if he was saying that all was right with the world. At least it was so in his world.

She turned and narrowed her eyes at Tyro in suspicion. No doubt he had something to do with her old friend's change in status. She melted on the inside just thinking of Tyro's big heart. It was then that she remembered that Willie wasn't wearing the old beat-up jacket she was used to seeing him in, but a newer, sportier one. She suspected he'd had something to do with that too.

She turned her attention back to Tyro. He seemed lost in thought. When she noticed the perplexed look on his face, she decided she'd let the matter go... for now. "Is everything all right?" she asked as soon as he was within earshot.

"Can you get away for a few days?" he asked in a serious manner. "There is something I think you should know."

Chapter 16

Tyro jogged along the Riverfront with Sheba. His mind raced ahead of him. It'd been a few days since he and Moriah had returned from their urgent trip to Florida. The man the authorities had in possession was not Fletcher. Moriah had confirmed it for them. She was absolutely sure of it. Neither did the DNA match. Since Tyro's doubt and suspicion in the past had caused him to make rash decisions, he'd been totally honest and open with her about the findings in his mother's death.

Most importantly, he wanted to make sure that she was safe. Needless to say, the authorities still hadn't captured him.

He was pleased that they'd been spending a lot of time together. And it relieved him that she was more relaxed with him, although it was evident she was still hiding something. He wanted to move their relationship along. Make a commitment. But he hadn't pursued it, because her lack of confidence in him ate at him. Besides, she wasn't ready. He knew where she stood as far as her boundaries and he had accepted that. But kissing… he saw nothing wrong with a little kiss here and there. And since their conversation the other night, he wasn't going to press the *kissing* issue either.

Their relationship was mainly on her terms, giving her time to heal. It made him the better for it. He thought about his former engagement with Glorieta. Looking back, he was glad he hadn't married her, or anyone for that matter. He felt complete, content with Moriah and would have never gotten to know her like he had, if he'd been married to someone else.

His mind wandered on about God. He still hadn't come to terms with why such a tragedy had to happen to his mother, Moriah, or anyone for that matter. His restlessness regarding the matter made him appreciate his conversations with Willie. They'd been very insightful.

He cleared his head and continued on with his evening exercise with Sheba, just as the vet had ordered.

"Hey there, Mr. T," Willie chimed, seeing Tyro and Sheba jogging his way.

"Willie." Tyro greeted him and sat next to him on the bench. Sheba lowered herself down gracefully onto the ground and panted. Tyro slid the lid off of the portable water container he'd made just for her. She lapped the water and rested on her side.

Willie leaned forward to look at her bulging abdomen. "She's gon' have her pups soon."

"Yep, about a week or so," Tyro said proudly.

"How many you thinkin'?"

"Oh, eight… nine, maybe. Her other litters have been around that."

Willie blew out a long-winded whistle. "That's a lot of pups."

"Mmm huh," Tyro responded, looking off into the distance.

Willie nudged him. "Something on your mind?"

"That obvious, huh?"

"Yep!"

Tyro blew out a long breath. "I don't get it." He paused. "You said that you used to be a pastor, right?"

Willie gazed far off in the same distance that Tyro was staring. "I was. Gave it up though."

Tyro turned for him to say more. "What happened?" he asked when he offered nothing more.

"Oh, let's just say others thought they could do my job better."

He puzzled his brows hoping that Willie would go on without him having to ask. "People do that… to pastors?" He mused. "So

320

what did you do?" He skipped a few stones he'd picked up by his feet, one after the other into the water.

Willie gazed into the darkening sky. "I walked. Left it all. Been living out here under God's great creation ever since."

Tyro wanted to ask about his family. He suspected he had a wife and daughter. He returned the photo of the three of them he'd found in Willie's old jacket the day he'd gotten him a new one.

"Sometimes I can hear my wife praying for me. It's like her voice brushes past me as the angels carry her prayers up to heaven." With that said, he stood to his feet. He reached for Tyro's hand. "Thank you for everything, my man. I think it's time for me to go home now."

Tyro had no idea what Willie meant when he said it was time for him to go home. Did he mean to the apartment he'd rented for him? Did he mean back to his wife and kid? Or did he mean... A perplexed look spread across his face. He shook his head. He thought about all of their past conversations. The man was so full of wisdom and he enjoyed talking to him. He was able to answer some questions Tyro had about God and relationships.

After considering it further, he didn't think the guy would cause any harm to himself. He shook off the notion that he would do anything foolish and headed to his condo. He was eager to see what Moriah was trying her hand at cooking tonight.

"I hope you're extra hungry," he teased Sheba, knowing she could eat anything at the drop of a hat. She whined. They jogged toward his building. "I know, girl, at least she's trying!"

Chapter 17

Today was an exceptionally warm Saturday morning for it to have been early October. With Sheba's due date being so close, Tyro and Moriah decided to take day trips, instead of weekend getaways. He'd told her to meet him outside his condo in five minutes. But she didn't have any idea he'd show up on a motorcycle.

"You ride?" she said, amused. She looked from the bike to what she was wearing. "I can't get on that thing in this. I'll be right back." Ten minutes later, she returned in a comfortable pair of stretch jean leggings, a pair of riding boots, and a gray leather jacket.

"Ah, aren't you the brave one? Don't you remember what happened the last couple of times you wore that jacket?"

"If I can take being pinned up against a grocery store freezer and being slung from a truck, I'm sure I can handle anything at this point." She took the helmet he handed her and placed it on her head.

"Here, let me help you." He removed the black cases she carried from over her arm and around her neck. He stowed the smaller one inside the compartment in his seat and clamped the other one to the seat railing on the back. He held her by the arm as she climbed onto the motorcycle and sat behind him.

Heading up Route 1 West, he knew she would appreciate today's outing. It was his turn to choose, surprise her. The only hint he gave her was for her to bring her camera. She felt comfortable riding with him. He wasn't popping wheelies and doing cycle stunts like other bikers that had passed them. Neither had he revved his engine or acted as if he was tempted to race when other motorcycles pulled alongside them.

"I love this place," she squealed when he turned into the entrance to Longwood Gardens. The gardens were breathtaking this time of year. The leaves lining the driveway into the gardens were a mixture of glorious golden and orange hues.

She was pleased with his thoughtful choice. She'd been mesmerized by the gardens on his island. She felt a little sad that she wouldn't have the opportunity to go back until after the puppies were born and weaned.

Immediately, Moriah pulled out her camera and began snapping pictures. She was glad that he had her to bring it.

She loved taking pictures of the scenery, of him, and of families with babies. She wondered for a moment if he ever wanted to get married. Did he want any kids? She thought he would make a wonderful father.

She asked another couple if she could take a picture of them. It was something about the joy of being with each other that shined through on their faces. Newlyweds. They agreed to let her take a series of photos and she emailed them to them right from her phone.

They were just as happy to oblige her and took shots of her and Tyro. When she wanted to catch a panoramic video of them with the scenery behind them, she set the timer on the camera and set it up on her portable tripod.

She was amazed at how they came out. How good she and Tyro looked together. For a moment, when they drew an audience—unsolicited—she thought she heard people whispering that they looked like the mystery couple on TV. At first she thought it was only her imagination until she heard someone speak up and say "It was all made up." "The news didn't have anything better to report." "Everybody knows that fairy tales aren't real." She sighed silently in relief that that was the end of that conversation.

After several hours of touring the various exhibits and museums along the gardens, they rested lazily on the grass. The sun beamed as if smiling on them. She admired the gorgeous sky. The fluffy white clouds formed in very interesting shapes and formations trailing along. She turned her attention to him. He scooted closer. Their eyes locked. He leaned in. He was going to kiss her! Her heart pounded.

She remembered their time on his beach. Guilt nipped at her from when she'd let her vulnerability creep up between them. Kissing him like that... As far as she was concerned, things had gone too far. She vowed she'd never allow herself to get into a compromising situation like that again.

"You know we're supposed to kiss now." His coyness interrupted her thoughts.

"You sure do know a lot these days." She folded her arms. "What rule book are you reading?" She stared at him.

"It says it right here." He pointed slowly from his heart to hers.

"Then, let's keep it right where it is." She pointed from her heart to his. "Until it's the right thing for us." She had her standards. She'd determined to never push past them again. She shook away the thought of where things could have gone. He would have to accept it as just that. Tyro gestured with a boyish pout. He may not have been happy with it, but it was her decision. It's not like they hadn't had this conversation before. She hoped this would be the last time she'd have to tell him.

She threw a twig at him and chuckled. He lifted his hands in surrender. Her shoulders relaxed. She still had her times of dealing with the guilt and shame of having had her innocence stolen from her several months ago. God was working to restore her heart. In His eyes she was pure. *It's a matter of the heart, My heart,* God had once whispered to her. Several moments of silence passed between them. He picked up her camera. "I didn't know you were so good at taking photographs," he said, looking through her camera roll.

"It's one of the things I love to do in my spare time."

"Well from the looks of these, you should do it more often. Have you thought of publishing your work?" he asked, clicking through various pictures.

He'd run across several pictures of a little girl. "Who's this cutie?" One picture in particular had caught his undivided attention. Her brownish blonde curls were blowing in the wind and she was licking a multicolored lollypop that was almost as big as she was. But that wasn't what caught his eye. Her resemblance was strikingly familiar.

Moriah having already risen from the ground, looked over his shoulder. "You think that's amazing, look at this." She grabbed the camera out of his hand and began snapping shots of him after gently pushing him over by his shoulder. Tyro saw it for what it was but decided to let it go. Still, in the back of his mind he wondered who that little girl was. Was she her daughter? He froze with the consideration that that was what she'd been hiding from him. Moriah has a child?

Chapter 18

Sunday morning a sudden downpour caused Moriah and Tyro to hurry back to his condo. Their plans for another day of their well-deserved break from running their businesses would have to wait. They'd have to ride to Philadelphia another day, although she was eager for him to taste one of Philly's famous cheesesteaks. A tinge of guilt rolled down her spine. She hadn't been to church since her time in the chapel. Well, really since she'd been offended by her former pastor. She'd promised God, she'd work through it. She made a mental note to set up a meeting with him.

As they entered his condo, Tyro disappeared to gather two towels for them to dry off.

She was glad they hadn't followed his original plan. Sailing off of the coast of Mexico would have been too much of an adventure getting there and back in one day.

She bustled into the living area and was surprised to see Quincy sitting by the fireplace. Quiet. A glass of fruit juice rested on the table next to him. Sheba was sleeping by his feet.

Lately Quincy had been staying to himself. He'd been somewhat subdued, humbled really, after realizing that Laino had not been having an affair.

Tyro said his dad had been occupied trying to find out the mystery behind the greeting card. He told her that none of them had seen that particular painting of her before. Tyro also concluded that his dad was content to believe that that's where she'd been spending her time when he thought she had been going elsewhere.

Quincy told him he was sure she was getting her portrait painted as a surprise for him, for their anniversary. If he weren't so relieved in knowing the truth, he would have felt more like a fool for doubting her love and loyalty.

"Well, hello there," Moriah greeted him with apprehension. She wasn't able to determine what kind of mood he was in. He seemed somewhat mellowed out. Still she wasn't going to cause a sleeping volcano to erupt.

Nonetheless, he politely excused himself and left the condo.

Tyro returned and gently wrapped a towel around her shoulders. She carefully blotted her hair dry with the end of it.

A firm knock on the door startled her. She assumed it was Quincy again. Perhaps he'd left something.

"I need to get some work done. I'll work from my room, if you don't mind." Without waiting for his reply. She turned to head to her room. Tyro reached for her arm and gently guided her to relax. He suspected she was uncomfortable that it might be his dad again at the door. He promised to make her a cup of tea as he swiftly turned the fireplace up higher. She conceded and melted into the plush sofa. She kicked off her tennis shoes and watched him traipse to the door.

Someone was pounding harder by the time he'd answered it. He was certain there was only one person who would be knocking like that. Since his family and staff were the only ones who had access to the top floor suites, he was certain it was his dad. He flung the door open.

Sable waltzed in like she owned the place. *What does she want now?* The knot in Moriah's stomach tightened. She studied the manner in which the detective... FBI... whatever she was, had walked into the room.

"Miss Styles." Sable's greeting was short, contrived. She wasn't the least bit surprised that Moriah was there.

She knew the woman definitely hadn't stopped by to chitchat. The last time she'd barged in on them like that was while they were away on his island and Tyro had abruptly abandoned her. *What gives with her following him around like a watchdog?* Moriah wondered. Detective Sable Lofthouse wasted no time with further preliminaries or pleasantries.

"You know," Sable began when Tyro excused himself to answer a call, "you may think your little girl is safe, but I'm not so sure about that." She propped her hand on her chin and watched Moriah suspiciously.

"Just what are you getting at?" Moriah narrowed her eyes and stood to her feet.

"I take it that he doesn't know, does he? Now just why is that, Ms. Styles?" she asked as she walked over to the window. She placed the large envelope she carried under her arm and slid it slowly enough toward her to make sure Moriah saw it. She slid her hand in her side pant pocket and jiggled her keys. "Sure is coming down like cats and dogs out there." She shifted to gaze at Moriah.

"Guess that's how it's going to be when he finds out your little secret." Moriah opened her mouth to respond, but hesitated when Tyro returned with a bottle of water. He handed it to the *good* detective. Keeping the package leveraged next to her, she twisted the cap off and guzzled the water down like she'd just run a 10k marathon.

His cell rang again and he excused himself and left the room. Moriah was glad for the distraction.

"What do you know about Casillas?" Sable's question felt more like an accusation. Moriah sat up straight. She shrugged. The name meant nothing to her. Besides, she was reserved about sharing anything. She didn't trust her. She vaguely remembered the name but couldn't remember where she'd heard it.

Sable walked toward Moriah, leaned down, and spoke in her ear. "One way or another, you're going to give me what I want. The simple way, or my way."

Tyro caught the end of Sable's threatening antics when he came back into the room. He stepped between them. She put up her hands in mock surrender and strutted toward the door. She turned to speak directly to Moriah. "You got my number, Ms. Styles. I suggest you—"

"That's enough!" Tyro blocked her view of Moriah and escorted her out the door.

He walked over to Moriah who had plopped down on the couch. "That woman has some nerve to come up—"

"What does she want from you, Moriah?"

"What makes you think that?"

"I can't protect you if you keep hiding things from me."

Moriah didn't think anyone could protect her. How could they? She'd been the one who had the only thing that would keep her alive when Fletcher caught up with her. And now that she knew he was alive and that she had the one piece of evidence that would convict him; she trusted her life and Amelia's with no one.

Moriah stammered. "I... I'm sorry. I want to tell—"

"What's it going to take, Moriah?" His tone now clipped and laced with disappointment.

"For what?" Her face puzzled in question.

He marched out of the room and came back a few seconds later.

"For you to trust me." Tyro held out the blue dress they removed from the cave to catch her attention. "What do you know about this?"

She recognized it right away. It was a dress she'd worn… *Fletcher… he'd made me wear it.* Her mind trailed back to the incident. *"See, I came back for you,"* the deranged personality had said, caressing her face with the back of his hand.

Tyro's words snapped her out of it. She heard his voice, but she couldn't believe what he'd just said. Her head flung upward. "What?" she responded incredulously. "Your mother's?" Her back moved off of the couch. "This belonged to your mother…? Oh my God!" Moriah cried. Tears poured down her face. She buried her head in her hands. "I didn't know…I didn't know whose —"

Tyro pulled her into his arms. "Please trust me, Moriah. I know I could never erase away what happened to you." He tenderly held her by the shoulders. I will do all I can to protect you. With him still being on the loose I need to know what we're up against. What does he have on you that keeps you in fear of telling me? What does Sable think you know?"

She thought about Amelia and pulled away from him. "I don't know why they think I had something to do with your mother's death," she stuttered. "I didn't even know your mother... I've never met her." Her eyes bore into his. Pleading. Begging him to believe her. "I didn't even know who you were several weeks ago."

He sighed heavily. "Despite what others may seem to believe, I know you're innocent. But there is something you're not telling me. And that's what makes it so hard for me to trust you." He kept his eyes fixed on her.

She lowered her eyes and kneaded her fingers into each other. She avoided his gaze.

Several minutes later, his door chimed. "The food's here."

"I'm not hungry."

"You were starving ten minutes ago," he said just before opening the door.

"Lost my appetite." She felt too consumed with worry to eat. Her mind wandered back to her niece. Her heart palpitated. Was Amelia safe? Do the Smythes know he's alive? Do they know they need to keep her guarded? What if he kidnapped her? Moriah didn't know why the government wanted what she had so badly. All she knew was keeping it hidden was the only leverage she'd have to get Amelia back from that monster, if it ever came to that.

"Mario!" he said, pleasantly surprised that he'd brought the food over instead of sending it by courier.

"Good to see you too." Mario quipped and embraced his nephew after setting the food on the dining table.

"What's up?" Tyro asked, giving him his full attention.

Mario turned his attention toward Moriah. "How're you? Is my nephew treating you okay? Because if he's not, you just let me know and I'll take care of him right here, right now for you!"

"I'm sure you haven't come all this way to threaten me," Tyro said jokingly. He crossed his arms and focused on Mario.

"Is everything all right?" Moriah was alarmed. She rose from the couch to face him.

"Look, I'm going to be straight with you, Miss Styles." He turned his attention directly to her. "The helicopter that Casillas... Fletcher flew you to that island in has been searched thoroughly. Please, let's sit." He gestured with his hand toward the table that now held the food he'd brought.

She sat quietly at the rounded table. "What's that got to do with me?" Her eyes held his intense and searching gaze.

Chapter 19

"Look," Mario began, "Far be it from me to accuse you of any wrongdoing. I think it's commendable that you've come away from that situation. Alive," he added for emphasis.

She was about sick of people telling her how lucky she was to have survived. No one knew the devastation she lived with in its aftermath every day. Including Mario and his family. But because of her own pain, she could identify with what they must be going through. She bit her tongue.

"The Feds think differently of your story," he said gently.

"I don't care what they think of her," Tyro said, rising instantly from the chair he had just sat in.

Mario held out his hand. "Let me finish. They wouldn't tell me exactly what they're looking for, but I have my ways, sources of finding out." He looked from her to Tyro. "All I know is that they believe you have something, some piece of crucial evidence from the crime scene in your possession." He walked closer. With the concerned look of a friend, he admonished her. "And technically, if you do, Ms. Styles, it's a federal crime to withhold any items from a federal investigation." He studied her face.

Tyro stood behind her chair. "She has told them everything they need to know."

"Tyro, the best way to help protect her is for us to stay level headed. None of us can afford to get defensive. Doing so will further confirm their suspicions."

Taking her seat, she asked, "Let's say a person does interfere with this kind of investigation. What could happen? After all, he committed crimes against me. No one has asked me if I want to press charges against him." She twisted her lips and struggled to forbid the menacing thoughts, fear from pulling her under. She had to remain strong. "Have they captured him yet?"

Mario looked at Tyro who discreetly shook his head. "She doesn't know? You haven't told her?" he asked incredulously.

Tyro sighed. "You've been released into my care."

"I'm what?" Her head snapped up. Her eyes shifted from Tyro to Mario and back to Tyro. She bolted from her chair. "So all this time, all along, you were my watchdog?" She thought on the matter further. "You mean to tell me that you and your PIs have been following and spying on me, following us... watching my every move?" Appalled, she stumbled over her words.

"It was for your safety." Tyro stepped toward her.

She snatched herself away from his touch. "And just why didn't you tell me if you wanted me to be *so* safe. Shouldn't I have had the right to know that my life was in danger... that people, including you, were following me? Is my cell... am I bugged too?"

A hard knock at the door startled her.

"With all that you've been through—"

Her clipped response cut him off. What could he say to justify his actions? "Oh don't think that gives you the right to... to what—lie to me? Deceive me? Babysit me?" Their activities over the past several weeks turned over in her mind. "You knew all along that we were being followed, watched, spied on. What about my privacy, Tyro? What about honesty? I don't believe you. I'll never trust you again. Never!" she screamed and stomped out of the room. But she ran right smack into Sable. Mario had just let her in. "Oh great. More concerned citizens on my behalf, I suppose." She tried to push around her, only to find Detective Smith standing behind her. His massive frame blocked her escape.

"Actually, Ms. Styles we're more than just citizens. We're agents of the United States government sworn to protect the people and security and integrity of this country," Sable offered sternly although she tried to be polite about it.

Moriah noticed she was still holding the same envelope she had when she was first there that morning.

"Please, have a seat, enjoy your lunch," Sable said interrupting her thoughts. She pointed toward the table and tried to direct her to take a seat.

"I'm fine right where I am. In fact, I'm not playing this game with you, or you, Detective Smith." She looked at the package Sable swiftly stowed under her arm. Her eyes narrowed. "Am I under arrest? If not, I don't want to be part of this... this... whatever it is that you have going on here."

Mario's back was facing her. She saw him lean over and whisper in Tyro's ear. Her mind raced back to the night she'd run into him at Tyro's on his island. "Unbelievable!" she yelled. Lifting her head, she rolled her eyes across the ceiling.

She assessed the situation. She wasn't under arrest and she wasn't being detained, or was she? She crossed her arms and narrowed her eyes. She glanced suspiciously around the room.

She wanted answers. She doubted she'd get them from Tyro or Mario despite his so called, *sources*.

"Don't fool yourself, Ms. Styles," Detective Smith bellowed. "He'll be back to get it. He wants the same thing we want, only he'll want to finish what he—"

She spun around. Her tone was snappy. Authoritative. "And just how do you know what he wants?"

The petite pilot stepped forward. "I think it's best we start over." She held her right hand out to Moriah. "Let me formally introduce myself." A no nonsense smile grazed her face. "I'm Federal Agent Sable Lofthouse. I'm with the Federal Air Marshal Service."

Moriah cocked her head as the familiar name silently rolled off her tongue. "*Lofthouse.*"

Her mind grasped at memories from pieces of conversations... texts from the *unknown* name... confidential conversations. Sable's voice sounding more familiar now. That's when everything fluttered into place. The last text, *"we're coming to get you,"* had come from *"OPERATION BLACK ROSE."* All along, Sable had been the person behind the unknown name.

Chapter 20

Sable watched Moriah stumble and collapse into Tyro's arms. Pushing the food containers to the far end of the table, she wanted answers and she wanted them now. Time was running out. Her face was set as stone. They may think it's all fun and games, time for lovey-dovey, but Sable was trying to save her life. And she was determined to get what she wanted from Moriah to do it, no matter the cost.

PLOP!

A picture taken of Tyro and Moriah at the Gardens landed on the table. She pointed to the photo. "Seems like we're not the only ones following you. See that figure right there?" Sable asked.

Moriah, Tyro, and Mario looked closer. Someone was definitely in the bushes, watching them. Moriah made out the camouflage jacket. The right sleeve had been ripped completely off. It was him. She was sure of it. She remembered when he'd torn his jacket. He'd used it to stop the bleeding on her leg.

Moriah's eyes widened in alarm. *He knows where I am? Oh God, I hope that he doesn't... No! Please God. Please don't let it be me who led him to her.* She feared for Amelia.

"Believe it or not, we care about your safety," Sable's heavy accent plowed through Moriah's thoughts. "As well as yours, Mr. Simmonds." She swiveled to face him. "By the time we got to him"— she pointed to the figure in the picture standing in the shadows—"He was gone."

Seconds later, she slapped another picture on the table as if she were playing Spades. The photo of Fletcher kissing her in the helicopter stared back at her. Moriah's eyes shifted from the photo to Tyro and then to Sable. "I've seen it before. Nothing new." She held her gaze and refused to buckle under the detective's intimidation. Sure, the aftermath of that kiss came back to haunt her. Because of it, she'd lost custody of her niece, her job, and her peace. And she probably would now lose Tyro.

She didn't expect him to want anything more to do with her. Why would he? From the way the picture looked, she'd been kissing the man suspected of killing his mother. The evidence was right there for everyone to see. Even Mario seemed taken aback by it.

No, she hadn't told Tyro fully about her and Fletcher. What was there to tell? When she'd first met him—before it was evident that he was schizophrenic—she had kind of liked the guy. Sure, she had been attracted to him, but nothing more.

Sable slid the last photo down with ease, more compassion. Moriah turned her face away from the horrible display of a woman lying in her own pool of blood. The woman's eyes were staring in the distance, her hand reaching forward. Her mouth was poised as if she were saying something... as if she'd been pleading for her last words to be heard.

She lowered her eyes. She'd seen enough. *What is she trying to prove?* She considered Sable's motive. Whatever it was, she was determined that it wasn't going to work. Her tactics were not going to drive a wedge between her and Tyro. He'd been a source of strength.

No, he hadn't been completely honest with her. But she needed him. If she was going to keep a step ahead of Fletcher, having the undercover agents watching over her as well as Amelia, she was sure of it, was really to her advantage. She'd deal with Tyro's dishonesty when the time was right.

Tyro's eyes shifted away from the picture of his mother. He picked up the one in particular of the man kissing Moriah. His brows rose. Moriah's face was prevalent. Although it had only captured the back of the man's head, his hand was definitely on her chest.

He could tell by the way his arm was positioned he had taken a selfie. He turned to Sable. "I assume you pulled this from his camera load from the cloud." He lifted the photo toward the agent before allowing it to cascade back to the table. "Is that correct?"

"Sure did." She kept her eyes trained on Moriah.

"Did you have this particular shot pulled?"

"What?" Her eyes narrowed at him.

"Wasn't this picture taken with an iPhone?" he asked, recognizing the quality of the photo. "There's a feature on it that would have captured several seconds before the photo was snapped." He tapped his lips with his index finger in contemplation. He pointed back to the picture. "It would show any movements before the actual shot was taken." He walked over and placed his arm around Moriah's shoulder.

I'm impressed. Now he's acting like we're a team. I'm sure there will eventually be some fallout about the kiss and the touch, but for now, we are a united front.

"We haven't been able to locate his cell or the video camera that was in the cabin." Sable glanced at Moriah, giving her time to respond. "The cell very well could have been lost at sea," Sable said after giving her ample time to speak up. "But the video camera was removed.

"Why not pull his iCloud account. Let's cross our fingers that that's where he stored his photos."

"All right. I'll do that. And when I come back with the proof that she's withholding evidence in a federal investigation, she'll be coming downtown with me."

Chapter 21

Moriah woke up with a feeling of heaviness. She didn't know what part yesterday's events played in her somber mood. She closed her eyes and let out a hard breath. There was no use fooling herself, she felt down because of Tyro. She'd seen his disappointment when he saw the photo of Fletcher kissing her. There was no denying it. For a moment he looked as though he'd been slapped in the face. His countenance fell. But she was pleased watching as he pushed his feelings aside and went to bat for her. It made her feel good. It was then she knew he really did have her best interest at heart. She smiled now, but only for a moment just thinking of it.

She hoped the agency would be able to pull the shot. The truth of what really happened surrounding the kiss and him touching her inappropriately would come out in the wash. Doing so would paint a better picture of her and help bring the truth to light. She was not the kind of person the agency thought she was: conniving and deceitful. Nor was she Fletcher's accomplice.

No doubt it was now Tyro's immediate point of focus to get to the bottom of it. As Mario was leaving, she overheard him tell his uncle that he wasn't going to leave chance into the FBI's hands. She gathered that he didn't trust the FBI's motives any more than she did.

After everyone had gone, she and Tyro talked. She told him about the kiss. Not that she felt compelled to, or that she owed him an explanation; she wanted to.

"Seems like we're going to have to work at not keeping things from each other," he'd said. He didn't mention anything further about the undercover agents. Neither did she ask. It was a given, they'd be around. She wasn't able to ask if they were also watching to protect Amelia. She still hadn't told him about her.

She would have to find that out some other way.

The reality of her dire situation was caving in on her. She felt with Fletcher on the loose, things really had spiraled too far out of her control. How did she think she could do this alone?

She grabbed the bible from the nightstand and referenced several scriptures on God's protection. She turned to the second book of Samuel. Flipping through the pages, she located the twenty-second chapter and read the third verse.

The God of my rock; in him will I trust; he is my shield, and the horn of my salvation, my high tower, and my refuge, my savior; thou savest me from violence.

Moriah paused and pondered. Her mind twined back to when she'd been abducted. She remembered calling upon God. She remembered the various times she felt His assurance covering her. It had given her the strength to keep her head straight, to hear His way of escape.

She whispered from a heart of thankfulness and continued on to the fourth verse.

I call on the Lord, Who is worthy to be praised, and I am saved from my enemies.

She felt His presence tugging at her heart. He'd come for her to lay her burden at His feet. She struggled within herself.

Did this mean she should tell Tyro that she had the videodisc? What if he asked for it? What if he watched it? And what if he turned it in? Then what?

She'd have nothing to negotiate with, no bargaining advantage to keep Amelia safe, or for him to keep her alive. With the evidence presented yesterday, she was sure he was after her and that he'd stop at nothing until he got a hold of her. *He wants the disc,* she reasoned within herself. *Once he has it, or finds out I no longer have it, I'll be as good as dead.*

A bird landed gracefully on the railing to her balcony. Her French doors were open. She lifted slowly from the bed, slipped her feet into her slippers, and walked quietly outside. The bird kept its eyes on her. Tilting its neck in several directions, it studied her, ready to take flight at the slightest sign of danger.

She stood still and observed it. She thought how trusting, how brave for it to have flown so high and for allowing her to come so close.

Did God have it fly there? Was He using it to teach her something like He'd used various parables to teach his disciples?

What was He telling her? She watched the bird take off in a sudden moment. Without thought she'd moved her arms. To her, it was an innocent gesture. She'd felt the need to hug herself. The bird had perceived it as danger. He'd used what God had given him to protect himself, to get out of harm's way.

Within an instant, he flew away as if he hadn't a care in the world. What great faith the bird had that at the moment of trouble, his wings would carry—she stopped abruptly. *That's it. The bird had both faith and courage.*

She hurried back inside and turned to the second book of Thessalonians. Reading the third chapter, she stopped at verse three.

Yet the Lord is faithful, and He will strengthen you and set you on a firm foundation and guard you from the evil one.

It was God's faithfulness that gave the bird the ability to fly there in the first place. Faith had guided him; courage had strengthened him. Faith and Courage were the wind beneath its wings.

She had to have faith to believe that God would protect her. Yet, she needed courage to carry on with what she was to do.

She looked up expecting to see her little friend had flown back. He hadn't.

She felt a tinge of fear waving at her mind. She recited the powerful verse that had gotten her through many a tough time.

God has not given me a spirit of fear. But He has given me a spirit of power. And He has given me a spirit of love and of a calm and well-balanced mind, discipline and self-control. Amen.

Moriah realized she'd been feeling sorry for herself, her situation. Not that she didn't take seriously the threat of a maniac who was after her and was still on the loose. But for her to get through this and have it work out for her good, she'd need to stay in faith. Keep her head clear, her mind sharp. A quiet assurance washed over her. She lifted her eyes and spread her allegorical wings. She was ready to handle her day and anything that might come her way.

Chapter 22

Bounding out of the bedroom, Moriah headed to the kitchen. She felt new. Refreshed. Assured, until she landed right smack into Quincy's arms, by accident of course. He reached out to steady her balance when she'd stumbled backwards. "Sorry," she offered. They observed each other face-to-face, eye-to-eye. She could see he despised her.

Not willing to engage in confrontation, she lowered her eyes.

Just as she was about to step around him, he spoke.

"Coffee?" he offered. He turned and headed back into the kitchen. As if something reminded him, he looked up. "You are not much of a coffee drinker, are you?"

She tightly smiled and shook her head.

"Tea. Right? What about some tea?" Before she could respond, "You like Chai," he blurted as if he'd just received a revelation.

She could hardly believe her ears. He remembered. It took a minute for him to get there, but he remembered. She watched in amazement. He muddled through his awkwardness filling the teapot with water and finally setting the kettle on the stove to boil. The man was hopeless in the kitchen, but at least he tried.

"Here, let me get that for you," she said after a few seconds of watching him fumble through getting the leaves into the infuser. She could tell he wasn't sure if the ball went in the pot or cup.

He stood with a confused look on his face. The metal tea ball dangled from his hand. She couldn't help it. She had to chuckle watching him repeatedly pivoting from the whistling teapot to the teacup on the counter.

"Join me?" He pointed his mug to the open balcony when her tea was ready. It was a gorgeous day. She thought of the little bird she'd seen earlier. She sat at one end of the oval bistro. She shifted in her seat when he came and stood next to her.

She caught him eyeing her from the side. *Okay, come on out with it,* she thought. She turned and glanced over her other shoulder to peek back inside. She hadn't seen or heard signs of Tyro. She knew he was an early riser and ruled out the possibility that he would still be sleeping.

She sipped her tea. "Have you seen Tyro?"

He slid out the chair that sat directly next to her and joined her.

"This is delicious, by the way." She tipped her cup his way. She didn't know why she felt a bit nervous. But he had taken his time answering her question, if he was going to answer it at all.

"Gorgeous view." She commented, more so to herself. She wasn't sure why he bothered to sit out there with her if he wasn't going to say anything. It wasn't like they had anything to talk about, unless he'd planned to grill her about yesterday. *But that ain't gonna happen*, she argued within herself. She was not going to go there with him. Not today.

"He took Sheba for a walk," Quincy finally said. He swirled the remains of the black liquid in his cup and stared down into it as if he were reading tea leaves. "You did well holding your own yesterday."

Oh, here we go, was what she really wanted to say, but held her tongue instead. Perhaps God was putting some wind beneath both of their wings. Putting their differences aside. "Yeah? I don't know about that," she humbly responded.

She'd caught a glimpse of him staring at her from the side. His eyes were narrowed. "What's on your mind?" She faced him dead on. It was as if a gust of wind propelled her along. She might not like what he'd have to say, but at least it would be out in the open.

Keeping his eyes fixed on her, he lifted his brew to salute her. "Things have been falling into place around here because of you." He tilted his cup and drained it.

Moriah was stunned. Quincy Simmonds had just given her a compliment. Or had he?

She wondered what exactly he was referring to. Was it because she'd suggested Tyro find out where his mother had been going? She could understand Quincy feeling relieved after learning her whereabouts. Maybe because she suggested he help Mario in his new restaurant and appreciated the little nudge to help him to get on with life. Or maybe, just maybe, he could see the difference in his son.

She thought further about that. Tyro no longer succumbed to long days of depression, shutting himself in, inside his own world. He'd shared with her that he'd talked it over with his doctor. He recognized that instead of dealing with his dad's disposition, he was using his own despondency to avoid him.

She looked at the white haired man. His hair flailed this way and that in the sudden gust of wind in the midst of his own storm.

"But?" There, she'd said it for him. The hesitation was getting to her. It felt like the famous cliché to the infomercials, "But wait… there's more!" was about to sound off.

As if he'd read her mind, he continued. "However, Miss Styles, I don't think you are good for him."

"Who said it was up to you to decide whether or not I am?" Her words shot out like a speeding bullet. She felt as if the wind had been deflated out of her sail. And here she'd thought that maybe, just maybe there was hope he had accepted her.

Looking down into his empty mug, he stood from his chair. He pointed it toward her. But before he could speak, she interrupted him.

"I know, don't take this personal, right?" She leaned her shoulders back. "So in your opinion, what comes next?" She rose to face him. The wind had picked up. Her hair was blowing this way and that. A storm was surely coming.

"Look," she said. She held her hand out as he attempted to talk. "Just hear me out. I like *your son*," she said with emphasis, "a whole lot. And I know that you're very protective of him. I get that. *And...*" Her words clipped, boiling with indignation over the man's self-righteous arrogance raising her voice more than she'd intended. "You're also worried that all I want is what I can get from him." Narrowing her eyes, she folded her arms and let the rest of what was on her mind rip.

"But you are wrong. I don't need his money, your money or anybody else's... donations!" she said for lack of a better word. She hadn't realized she'd been jabbing the air with her finger.

She dropped her hands to her sides and softened her tone. Still her voice trembled. "If anything, I'm grateful that I met your son. If I hadn't, I would have never gotten to know about the kind, loving soul his mother was. Everybody that speaks of her does so with great admiration and respect."

She eyed him praying that she'd be able to hold her tongue from what was really on her mind to say although he knew he wasn't Laino. Still, it wouldn't hurt for him to be kind.

She turned back just as she stepped over the threshold leading from the terrace. Her tone was softer and sincere. "I regret that I never got a chance to know a woman like her. But she's not here. I'm not expecting you, or your son, or Mario to be a replica of Mrs. Simmonds. But who she was and the love she stood for should at least have a little residue, a resemblance of her. If anybody, it should be with you."

"Are you finished, Ms. Styles?" A slight smile peeked through his mustache.

She gripped her lips together. She had said enough.

346

"What I wanted to say, if you had given me a chance to talk, was that you are perfect for him."

The words tumbled around in her chamber. Moriah's mouth gaped open. She thought to ask him to repeat himself just to make sure, but clearly she'd heard what he'd said. *I'm perfect for him?* Quincy maneuvered himself to step around her over the threshold. He placed his mug in the sink. He mumbled something about her having a fiery spirit like his wife and closed the door behind him.

Chapter 23

A few minutes after Sheba and Tyro returned from their outing, Tyro tapped lightly on Moriah's door. Not wanting to surrender her sanctuary of peace and serenity, she remained undisturbed on the balcony and continued her time with the Lord.

Several hours later, she returned her bible back to its place, and stowed her journal in her computer bag. Quincy's words had weaved through her mind on numerous occasions. She had to admit, what he'd said about her being *perfect* for Tyro had caught her off guard.

She was so delighted that he had accepted her, although afterwards, she'd felt foolish about her outburst. Still, she'd let no guilt of her "fiery spirit," as he'd put it, take root in her mind. Of course she'd apologize when the time was right. She was no fool. He may have felt she was right for his son, but she knew firsthand that in itself came with its own challenges. Quincy would still be his normal tyrannical self.

Sheba scratched at her door. Eagerly, she let her beloved companion in, the bulge in her stomach having gotten larger, seemingly overnight. "Girly Girl, it won't be long now before you're gonna be a momma again soon!" Sheba looked at her and whined.

Moriah learned earlier that this would be her sixth litter. She normally had up to nine pups. "I guess you like being a momma, huh?" she said, not really expecting an answer. But Sheba barked lightly once. Whining, she pranced over to the set of bed steps stowed by the French doors and pranced back over to the bed.

Moriah pulled the steps close to the bed. "Here you go." She watched Sheba labor gingerly up the few steps and lay on the bed. She rubbed her behind the ears. Sheba groaned as she rolled on her back. Her paws were posed as if she were waiting for them to be manicured. It was the cutest thing watching her fall asleep like she was the Fresh Princess of Bel-Air.

When Moriah laughed out loud, Sheba jerked her head up. When she saw there was nothing to be concerned about, she grunted and rested her head back on the bed. "Sorry," Moriah said thoughtfully, not minding the fact that she was talking to a dog, nonetheless.

She thought about all the love and care Sheba would need. There's a lot that goes into taking care of a dog, and breeding her too. It made Moriah consider her own life. How complicated it had become.

She still hadn't decided when she'd tell Tyro about her niece and her parents. Amelia. Her heart ached for her. She and Nettie would be moving in a few weeks to their own townhouse. She was excited, but kept her excitement in reserve. Amelia would not be moving with her. And until after she'd won her appeal, neither would she be allowed to visit.

She quietly slipped off of the bed. She walked into the closet and removed an elaborate keepsake box from the shelf. It was one of the items she'd brought with her from the motel where she'd been staying.

In deep thought, she walked over to the bed and placed it there. Heaviness tugged at her heart. Opening the box, she smiled as tears formed in her eyes. She lifted the picture of her sister and Kenny holding their eight-month-old Amelia between them. Their smiles were so bright. Their future so promising. Moriah couldn't help but wonder how everything could have gone so wrong so quickly. The photo had been taken days before Anaya took her own life. Within a month's time, Kenny had ended his.

She plundered through the box looking at various artifacts. The memories of things and the way they used to be. Oh how she wished for them to still be the way they were.

She spread across the bed several of the pictures Amelia had drawn for her. She ran her fingers over the indentations and various colors. She tried to imagine what was going through her niece's mind as she drew them. She drew of things in her world. The way she saw them. What she knew. But every one of them had included Moriah. And several of them included Spiky, the puppy her grandfather, Parker, had promised to get her for her fifth birthday.

She sighed. Amelia would be five in December on Christmas Eve. Her hand rose to her chest as she picked up a card Amelia had made for her at her pre-school. It was from last Mother's Day.

She covered her mouth to keep from crying out as she read the words her niece had written inside. In words that only a four-year-old could convey so well, she'd written: Dear Auntie, you are the best mommy. I love you. It had been signed with big, uneven letters by the four-year-old she'd grown to love as her own.

Moriah gazed at the card. She had found it in Amelia's book bag. Her niece never had the chance to give it to her. On the day the court had granted Petra and Parker complete custody, Petra was so quick to remove her from her school that she'd left her belongings behind.

She thought it was totally insensitive for her to have removed her so suddenly. It was the only day care Amelia had known. She loved her school. Moriah was sure she missed her friends and the teachers she'd grown to love and adore as well. Nevertheless, Moriah was thankful that the school had called her, and not Petra, to pick them up. She was sure that she would have never received the card.

She placed the things neatly back into the box and set it back on the shelf. She slid to the floor and let out the cry she'd been holding back. It was then that she decided to do what must be done.

Realizing she'd let things go on like they had for too long, she dried her eyes. Rising from the floor, she wrote a note for Tyro and left it on the dresser.

Her life had been spiraling too far out of her control. She was determined she was going to get her life back on track. She'd had enough of hiding.

Her mind fell back on how Tyro had used her. Manipulated her when she was on his island. She thought she'd be able to move past it even though she had forgiven him. But she just couldn't ignore the fact that it had happened. And if she were to be honest, she didn't appreciate that he didn't tell her she was being followed. Watched. After all, it involved her. Her life. Her safety. And what did he mean she had been released into his care?

Her mind was made up. With all that had happened to her, the walls around her heart had to remain.

She reached into her purse. She wrapped her fingers around the key to the safe deposit box she'd placed in her mother's name. She placed several articles of her clothing and toiletries in an overnight bag and threw it over her shoulder. She'd send for the remainder of her belongings later.

There was one order of business she needed to take care of first. And then she was going to see Amelia.

Chapter 24

The middle-aged couple smiled sweetly as they said prayers with their precious granddaughter. "Poppy," four-year-old Amelia began with eyes too bright for sleep, "is Auntie dead too?"

The couple exchanged a quick glance with each other. "Nooo," her grandfather crooned. "Why do ask such a thing, Rosey?" He called her by the nickname he and his wife had given her the day they buried their son. The sweetness of having her in their lives was like the rose that had sprung from his grave.

"Amelia Rose," Her grandmother interrupted. "You stop asking such silly questions. "We told you—"

"We know you miss her." Parker said as he patted the air for his wife to cool down.

"Can you read me a story?" Amelia asked keeping her eyes only on her Poppy.

"If you promise you'll go right to sleep when the story's over." His eyes twinkled. He would have read to her even without her promise. "Deal?" he asked, picking her up for one last hug and kiss. "I see you're far from sleep, so, just one more story, then it's lights out for you, young lady."

"Okay," she agreed, wiggling her toes under the covers as he tucked her beneath the pretty princess comforter.

"Parker, it's after 7:30. She should be sleep by now. You know the child has to get up early in the morning."

"Oh Petra, one more story isn't going to hurt, now is it?" he said, escorting her to the door. "I'll only be just a few minutes."

Petra looked back over at her granddaughter and sighed. "You're right. As usual, you're always right when it comes to her." She walked back over to the bed, tucked the covers around her, and patted her on the cheek. "You go right to sleep when your grandfather's done, you hear?"

The little girl nodded. "Gammy... grandmother, I didn't mean to make you sad."

"Oh nonsense, child. I know it's hard for you not being able to see your auntie," her tone softer now.

"Can I go see her tomorrow, please?" she whined.

"Soon," her Poppy promised. "You will see your Auntie Moriah soon. Now, we better look and see what Eloise the Purple Elephant is doing before she runs away!" He slid from behind him the book with the giant elephant smiling widely on the cover. His eyes sparkled as he read. Amelia's eyes gleamed at the majestic sound of his voice.

Ten minutes later, Parker walked into the kitchen. Petra had made him a cup of coffee and had set it on the island. He gazed over at her and noticed her far away stare as she held their son's picture in her hand. Parker wiped the tears that trickled down her face. He pulled her into his arms. Silence enveloped them. There were no words to say. They knew the pain each felt. This had become an unspoken rule. Only if one of them needed to talk, could they say his name, other than that, they'd endure their pain in silence.

But this time, it was different. "Just say it, Parker, just say it!" Petra pulled from his embrace.

"What is it you want me to say?" His eyes too telling of his sorrow and pain.

"Get it over with. You blame me for Kenny's death. Go ahead. Say it!" Her voice rose in anguish.

"Please, Petra, let's not go through this again. For the last time, I don't blame you."

"Who, then? Who's going to pay for taking my baby away from me? Who?" She lifted the cup her husband left untouched and dumped the tepid substance down the drain.

"What about that irresponsible excuse of a woman… conniving wench!" she spewed with great disdain.

"Oh come now, sweetheart. You loved her like a daughter. Moriah's not to blame for Kenny's death. No one's to blame. We both missed the signs. How were we to know——"

"Don't you dare speak his name in the same sentence as hers! I told you something wasn't right, that he wasn't well. And then you let him grant custody to… to her? Why shouldn't I be upset about the whole thing? I lost my son and I lost my granddaughter in the same day until I took matters into my own hands.

"And you see what trouble that has gotten us into. Setting that girl up like that was conniving if you ask me."

"Well, I didn't ask you. I did what I had to do. If I hadn't, Amelia would still be in the custody of that crazy woman. And she had the nerve to take my Rosey over to see those crazy parents of hers. So yes, I took matters into my own hands because you didn't have enough spine to do it."

"But look what it got us into. You tampered with evidence, Petra. Did you ever stop and think about what that could do to us as a family? Our company? For Pete's sake, Petra, I wish you'd stop and think sometimes."

"Moriah is not our enemy. Didn't she allow us to have Amelia… our Rosey, anytime we wanted? She loves her as if she were her own." Parker reasoned.

"Yeah, and you're too shallow to see what really happened. When her sister died, it was the perfect opportunity for her to have Amelia and Kenny, an instant family. Can't you see that?"

"That's nonsense. You don't even believe that yourself." His voice rose louder. He took a deep breath.

"Look, sweetheart. Look at me." He held her tenderly by the shoulders. We've been through too much together to let anything come between us now."

"I just don't want to lose her too."

"Then I think we should come to terms and all work together on raising our son's child."

"But, she's all we have left of Kenny." She narrowed her eyes as she glared up into his. "I can't do that. I just can't and I won't!"

Chapter 25

After Sheba had abandoned Tyro to visit Moriah's wing of his condo, he finished the room he'd been working on. It was Sheba's newfangled bathroom. He jolted when he noticed Moriah standing at the door. She'd been gazing around with a puzzled and somewhat amazed expression on her face. He hadn't seen her suitcase.

"Well hey there!" he said, standing up from where he had been kneeling. "Pretty neat huh?"

"You do all this yourself?" she said after looking around for a few moments.

"Yep. All by myself!"

"Is this a bathroom for Sheba?" Her eyes widened in wonder. I've never seen anything like it!" She looked at her watch and shifted to rest on her other foot.

"You okay?" he said immediately, reaching to assist her.

Moriah didn't have a lot of time to dilly-dally around. "No... yes...

"Look," she sighed as she forced a smile. "I really, really need to get going. Something urgent came up."

Following her to the door, he wiped his hands on the cloth he was holding. He reached to remove his keys from the drawer of the table in the foyer. "Okay, no problem," he said with disappointment. He was eager to show off his handiwork in action to her.

"I don't need you to drive me. I have a car now, remember?" Her face crinkled into a weary smile. She touched his arm. "Thanks for everything. You've been a good friend."

"Moriah—"

"Don't. Please." She held her palm out at him. "I don't have time to explain." She held his gaze. She knew he was waiting for an explanation. "You wouldn't understand."

"Try me." His eyes fell on the suitcase stowed by the door. "Did you just put this here?" He pointed. "Did I do something, or say something that upset you?"

She lowered her head. "Tyro, please. Why does everything have to be about you?"

"About me? Me?" he asked mindlessly repeating himself. Folding his arms over his chest. He tilted his head as he gazed from her bag to her eyes. "I don't know what to say, Moriah. I've—"

"Then don't say anything. I need to do this for me. For us."

"Us? Us who? What are you talking about?"

Moriah opened the door and carried her bag with her. "I'm sorry, Tyro. I have to go. Thank you for every—"

"Save it." His words were sharp and final. He quickly pivoted and headed back to his project.

Moriah held back the tears as she closed the door behind her. She took a deep breath and let it out slowly and waited for the elevator to reach her floor.

Tyro placed his cell back in his pocket and screwed in the last wing nut to the apparatus he had invented on the wall. Thinking it was Moriah coming back in, he never lifted his head when the condo door opened and closed a few moments later.

"Ha!" Will you look at that?" Quincy raved as he gave his son a congratulatory slap on the back.

"Pretty impressive huh?" Tyro said. He tried to hide his disappointment that it wasn't Moriah standing there. He felt betrayed that she would let her secret come between them. He'd determined until she was ready and realized that he cared for her, he couldn't keep her against her will. He was worried about her. He cared about her safety.

"I would say so," he responded to his son's remarks. "Sheba, what do you say?" Quincy said as they chuckled at the way Sheba just stood between the multi-directional body blower. Her eyes curled shut in delight as the jets blew warmly over her fur. The way Sheba stood there under the eight powerful jets, her fur blowing in the wind with her tongue hanging out reminded him of the commercials he had seen of dogs standing on surfboards riding the waves.

They both were convinced that Sheba was smiling. Tyro taught her what buttons to push for the shower, the doggie soap, and the hair dryers, and even how to flush her waste to go down into a special depository tank.

It had only taken Tyro two days, four hours, and twenty-six minutes to turn a former powder room into Sheba's own fully functional bathroom. "Just in time, too." He looked at her from the corner of his eye. "Tomorrow you're going to the vet."

Sheba whined at his announcement. "There's no getting around it. You're appointment is at noon. And you're going to be smelling good too," he said as he inspected his Shepherd to ensure she was completely dried off. Sheba turned and repeatedly licked Tyro's hand. "You're welcome. You're welcome, girl." Tyro watched Sheba strut happily out of her new bathroom. But his excitement over his latest invention went out the door when Moriah had left earlier.

Chapter 26

Tyro had just come from taking Sheba to the vet. He was pleased with her progress and she was due in a few short weeks. He hadn't heard from Moriah since she'd left yesterday. Neither had he slept well.

He'd tossed all night wondering what could it be that she was so afraid to tell him. Why couldn't she just trust him?

The knot in his stomach tightened. He felt uneasy thinking of her out there on her own with her perpetrator still on the loose.

He kept abreast of the texts and calls he received from his private investigators. The moment she left, he'd texted them to keep an eye on her. He never asked where she was or what she was doing. He just wanted to make sure she was safe.

He couldn't help the thought from churning over and over again in his mind, of what made her run off like that. Or was she afraid he was getting too close to finding out what she was hiding. He'd decided that he'd keep his distance. He was not going to go chasing after her. As soon as he confirmed that this Casillas, Fletcher guy or whatever his real name was, was locked up behind bars for good, he'd call off his PIs.

Still, he couldn't help but wonder if she'd regretted telling him what had happened. She hadn't returned to the office either.

Heading towards the Brandywine River, he turned onto Seventeenth Street and drove down Monkey Hill. "'More exercise,' huh?" he said, repeating Nettie's words about Sheba as he removed her leash. Her puppies would be here soon. He agreed. She could use the exercise.

He was pleased with her care and attention to his Shepherd. He had no idea that the new intern working at Dr. Croix's practice was Moriah's roommate. He had recognized her from somewhere when he met her briefly outside of Mario's. She'd also looked at him with familiarity. It wasn't until Moriah had contacted Nettie when they thought Sheba was in trouble and she'd come to the vet's office with him that it registered. Their previous encounters if at all, had been brief since she'd been finishing up her clinicals at the animal hospital. *What a coincidence in the timing,* he thought to himself.

Sheba looked up into his face, barked once as she anxiously waited for the command. "Go ahead, girl," he said as Sheba took off running like a rocket, although a little sluggishly. A good run was all she needed.

The vet had given the okay for her to have more rigorous activities. When he told Tyro she needed more exercise, he knew it was true. He hadn't been taking her on the long walks or runs like she needed. Not since he lost his mother. Anguish tried to grip him, wrap itself around his heart to take up where it had left off.

He thought of Moriah. Her smile. She had become like a breath of fresh air. He felt anxious about his decision to let her go. She couldn't be trusted. The knot had moved to his throat. He became agitated that he'd let himself care so deeply about her. He doubled back on his decision; should he insist that she let him into her world? What could he do? He couldn't make her trust him. But maybe he could be more persistent.

He swallowed hard. He decided he'd let the matter work itself out. She was the one who'd left him. If she'd wanted him in her life, she would have said so by now.

His cell rang. He nabbed it from his pocket and answered it in one quick swoop. "Hey. Dad." His enthusiasm lowered. "No, just watching Sheba swim in the river," he offered. "You'd think she never got out." He chuckled, masking the disappointment that it wasn't Moriah. "Yeah, I know… I know she needs to get out more."

"Everything okay?" he asked Quincy sharply to get to the point of his call. He wanted to avoid prolonging the interruption.

He loved his dad, but if there was anyone that could sour his mood or drag him further into his despair that person was currently on the other end of the line. Tyro understood perfectly. He had lost her too. His father had lost his wife and life-long partner. "Dad, I think I better get Sheba out of the water. The current is a little too rough... not tonight. Maybe I'll come by Mario's for dinner tomorrow." He sighed. The last thing he wanted was to be sitting around with Mario and his dad drinking a bottle of Domaine de la Romanée-Conti, aka DRC as Quincy properly called it, wallowing in their sorrows over something none of them could change. Tyro had gotten to the place where he was ready to move on.

He thought he saw Moriah's new car turn the corner on the same hill he drove down earlier. He whistled for Sheba and jammed his cell into his pocket. He removed the towel from around his neck and waited for Sheba to reach the shore.

After he'd dried her off, he headed toward the narrow street and turned in the same direction that he'd seen her car go. In the distance, he saw a woman hugging a child. Another woman in a brightly colored smock stood very close to them. She was looking around nervously and held on to the child's hand while the other woman kissed the child's face several times.

As he got closer, he heard the nervousness in the voice of the woman wearing the smock. "Please, I could lose my job." She continued to hold on to the child's hand as if the other woman was about to abduct her.

"Moriah?" he called with a note of questioning in his voice. The childcare worker pulled the little girl out of Moriah's embrace and scuttled back behind the fence of the playground.

"No, please. It's okay." She pleaded following the woman who ran into the building. She quickly shut the door, and closed the blinds. Laughter and squeals of other children filled the air from behind the building. Moriah dared not enter the establishment.

She turned and faced Tyro. "Are you happy now?" Her eyes squinted in irritation. "Why are you following me?"

Sheba barked to greet her. "Quiet, Sheba," Tyro demanded as he guided her by the leash in the direction Moriah had stormed away.

"What was that all about?" he asked while he and Sheba trailed behind her toward her car.

"I don't need you to be in my business." She turned and fixed her eyes on him, holding back the tears threatening to fall.

"What about our bond, Moriah? Trust, remember?"

She swiped a lock behind her ear and glanced at her watch. "I need to go. I'll be late for my next client," she said as she tried to side-step past him to get into her car.

"So," Tyro began to broach the subject, dragging on the word *so*. "This is one of your clients?" He narrowed his eyes.
Moriah shifted her eyes to the door then to her feet.
He lifted her chin. "Is there something you need to tell me?"
"What is it you'd like to know?" she said boldly looking at him as if to remind him that it was none of his business. Folding her arms, she glared at him. "What are you doing here anyway? Are you following… spying on me?" she asked incredulously.

"Don't do it… Don't try to change the subject." He pointed his finger toward the grassy area a few feet away. Sheba whined but immediately trotted over and lay on the grass. "You know very well I'm not. Why, do I have need to? Obviously, you've been keeping something from me." He paused. Turning back toward the daycare, he erupted. "Is this it? Is this the big secret?" He stumbled over his words. "You… you have a child and you didn't even have the decency to tell me?"

When she didn't respond, he lifted his head toward the sky. "Great," he said sarcastically. "I guess this is your definition of trust." He ruffled his hand through his hair. "Moriah, please. Talk to me. What's going on? Who's the kid?"

"I got to go." She opened the door and looked back at the building where the child had been swept away. "You wouldn't understand. This is not the time nor the place." She turned the key in her ignition and sped away. He threw up his hands, whistled for Sheba to come along as he crossed the street and headed back to his car.

A woman had watched the whole scene unfold behind the smoked window of her white limousine. Moriah had been too preoccupied to notice the vehicle conspicuously parked across the street.

Petra shooed with her fingers motioning for her driver to follow the white Range Rover with the license tag that read, "LAINO2."

Chapter 27

Parker helped his little Rosey out of the black Lincoln town car. They sang her favorite nursery rhymes while he opened their front door.

"Is that why you've been insisting on picking her up every day?" Petra handed him a folder of pictures the PI she hired had taken before he could get completely in the door. "You've been double crossing me!" She fumed behind him, gritting her teeth with a low growl. "She's been seeing our grandchild all along, hasn't she?"

Ignoring her, he led his granddaughter to her closet by her tiny fingers. "Let's find you something you can play in," he said, picking her up to explore her options. "We're going to the park to have a picnic."

"A picnic," Amelia repeated in delight.

"For heaven's sake, Parker, why do you need to take her to the park, again? She has a big enough play set right here in our back yard," Petra complained.

"I wanna wear the yellow dress with the big purple flower in the middle," Amelia sang.

He smiled and removed the outfit his granddaughter had chosen out of the closet dresser and helped her into it.

"Are you listening to me?" His wife pulled his free arm.

"No. I'm not," he responded in a gentle but firm tone. "Are you coming, or not?" he turned and asked his wife and headed for the door when he received no answer.

Two men got out of a Fed car. "Sweetie," he said, kneeling in front of his granddaughter, "go play in your room for a little while.

Your granny and I want to talk to these gentlemen for a few moments, okay?"

"Okay, but don't take too long. I don't want our cupcakes to go bad." She carried her bunny in her arms and skipped around the corner.

"Obstructing and tampering with evidence in a Federal investigation!" Petra raised her voice while reading the charges among the other papers she'd just been handed.

Parker knew what he had to do.

Petra read her husband's proposition and slammed the papers on the kitchen island. "You want me to grant Moriah full and final custody and only visit our granddaughter on holidays and occasional overnight visits on some weekends?" The papers fell to the floor. "You must be out of your mind!"

"You'll be lucky if you're even granted home visits from the looks of it." Parker turned his attention to the subpoena at the far end of the island. A warrant for her arrest lay under it. She had been given until tomorrow to turn herself in.

Petra slapped her hands against the counter. Lifting herself up she stared him straight in the eye. "You had this all worked out, didn't you?" she raised her brows in suspicion. "You knew this was coming, didn't you, Parker? Why didn't you say something?"

"Honey, once you sign this," he picked the papers up off the floor and slid them quietly in front of her, "I will be at ease to take care of this whole situation you got us in. But for now, I don't know what's going to come of it." He placed a pen on top of them.

She scribbled the pen over the lines in the designated places, scratching her signature on his dreaded contract. She shoved it in his direction. They toppled off of his desk. Petra had stewed over the matter for hours. Having her hands tied, she conceded. She knew Parker wasn't going to help her get out of this mess if she had not done so.

"It's for the best," he'd said. He picked up the signed papers and locked them in his safe. She knew he'd already changed the combination. He'd told her so, in the event she'd change her mind overnight.

Lovingly, he gathered her in his arms. "I couldn't be a full time parent, run the business in your absence while engaged in a long term legal battle, now could I?" He kissed her forehead. "Now you get some rest. I have a few things to tie up. We have a long day ahead of us tomorrow."

She pulled away and marched out of the room.

The next morning when they dropped Amelia off at the daycare, Petra hugged her granddaughter in her usual two-second hold. Nothing special. No explanation as to why she wouldn't be there when she came home. No talks about not being around for a while to go with her and Poppy to the parks. Nothing. She just smiled, tapped her on the nose, and sank back in the shadows of her limo.

She hadn't given her granddaughter a special, *good-bye* hug. The thought of not seeing her for a long time caused her pain. But it was incomparable to the grief she was up against. Still, she was not sorry she'd done it. She counted it a blessing to have had the time they had her all to themselves. *Without having that Moriah in the way.*

As they drove away, she watched Parker drum his fingers on the top of the briefcase he held on his lap. Without a doubt, he'd combed over every word, every jot and tittle. Everything was in order. She looked at him with remorse. He wouldn't be there to hold her at night. To assure her everything with the business, their family, their life would be okay. She shoved the thoughts of sleeping in a strange place out of her thoughts. She wanted to hold on to her pleasant memories. She'd have plenty of time to fume over her stupidity of getting caught later. *That incompetent Casillas!* If only he hadn't removed the entire camera, just the videodisc like she told him to, she wouldn't be in this mess.

She was glad he no longer worked for them. She'd fired him days before he'd stolen one of their helicopters. She had no idea he'd do something so stupid, no idea he was insane. And how had he figured out Moriah's whereabouts to go after her when he'd abducted her. Crazy. Still, she'd thought Parker had informed Moriah that he'd been fired. The secret, second background check they ran on him didn't add up to the one they'd originally gotten. Guess he had someone working on the inside to have forged the first one for him.

She thought of her disdain for Moriah. It's true, ever since her son granted her full custody and not them—his own parents, she saw the girl in a different vein. But she would have never wished the things she'd been through on anyone. Petra thought about the times Casillas had actually flown her to and from her own destinations. Frightening.

But she didn't end up petting with the psycho either.

She wiped her brow with her Swiss woven handkerchief and immediately flung it to the floor. She was going to have to get used to doing without the niceties, the finer distinctions of life for a while. Still, she was relieved she wouldn't be going to one of those overcrowded rat holes either. Where she was heading for her crimes would definitely be better than most upscale hotels. She was sure Parker would see to her extreme comfort. After all, it was one of the stipulations she'd added to his preposterous proposition.

She stared out the window the entire ride downtown. "Why don't you read through these while I go in and talk to our lawyer?"

She shoved them to the side. She'd seen them before. He didn't need to remind her of her promise to relinquish custody of Amelia. What did he think she was going to do, protest it from the inside?

He vacated the limo, headed up the steps to the historical building on Twelfth and French.

Several minutes later, Parker came out with their lawyer and headed toward a Fed's car that had just pulled up in front of hers.

367

"What's going on?" she called. The driver pulled her limo from the curb and stopped at Parker's signal.

Parker walked over and kissed her cheek, reminded her of her promise about Amelia, and turned and walked away. Without looking back, Parker waved his hand once to signal for her driver to pull away. She watched in disbelief as he was handcuffed and placed in the back of an unmarked car. The car peeled out of sight.

She'd barely heard the words he'd spoken to her when he'd whispered in her ear. She remembered them now. *"I told you I'd make everything all right."* His words resounded in her ears amidst her tears.

Chapter 28

"I don't mind the fact that you have a child." Tyro walked out on his balcony and stared out over the Delaware River. It was quiet with not much activity going on to distract his mind, his anguish. Moriah had only stopped in to explain. She owed him that much. He ran his fingers through his hair. He looked worn. She gathered it had been a sleepless night for him just as it had been for her. "It's your never-ending secrets that keep popping up that I don't like. I'm always finding out things about you the hard way or through someone else. Important things you should have told me." He kept his hands stowed in his pockets. He avoided looking at her.

"Oh, like you tell me everything." She was convinced the conversation wasn't going to go like she'd hoped. He was beyond reason. She didn't blame him, but she at least hoped he'd listen and try to understand.

He turned his head in her direction but avoided looking at her. "What have I not told you about me?" His sudden curtness made her react.

"What about you being wealthy?"

"What did I need to say about that? You could see well enough for yourself."

"You led me to believe it was your dad's..." She changed course; that fact wasn't completely true. "You... you destroyed my truck." She knew it was a stupid thing to say. She couldn't think straight. None of the things she said made any sense. She didn't want to argue. She hated when they had disagreements. She was sure that this was the last straw for him. She felt it in the cold manner he now looked at her. She couldn't bear it.

"Why didn't you tell me you had a child?" He quickly spun around and faced her. His face was hard. His eyes fixed. Cold. Boring into her soul, cutting her heart out. "I trusted you," he grumbled. "I thought you were different. Who's the father?" He peppered her with questions.

Moriah fidgeted with her hands. Her voice trembled as she spoke. "Amelia is my niece. I've had her since she was eight months," she said quietly.

"What?" Tyro turned and faced her. "You expect me to believe that?" he said incredulously, convinced his father and Roy had been right about her having a hidden agenda.

"Anaya was my twin. She suffered with a severe form of postpartum that led to schizophrenia and ultimately, suicide." Her eyes trailed off into the distance. "We didn't see the signs. When she died, I became Amelia's primary caretaker. Our parents had my sister and me at a late stage in their lives." Her heart wrenched against her chest.

She wanted to tell him everything. Tell him that both of her parents had mental challenges. She wanted to tell him how they'd met in a mental institution, got married, and had her and her twin sister. How they weren't in any condition to raise their own children, much less a grandchild. The words choked her. She was too ashamed to say it.

Tyro stood staring at her, calculating every word. This was another part of her dark history she prayed he'd never know about.

"Go on." He crossed his arms and glared at her.

Moriah swiped tears from her cheeks. "When my sister died, her husband's parents were busy sailing around the world. They didn't have any interest in taking care of Amelia. Moriah looked down.

"What about the child's father?" He was convinced she would trip her own self up in her web of lies.

370

"I tried to help Kenny, but he had his own share of grief. I had mine too. We tried to balance taking care of her between the two of us. But when his parents thought that we were spending too much time together taking care of Amelia," she added for clarification, "they all of a sudden had a change of heart toward wanting her.

"They began to stay home a lot and wanted Amelia to visit with them. Each visit turned into longer visits. They insisted that she stay overnight, and then it became for days at a time, weekends, and holidays.

"Well, you should have been happy that they wanted to spend time with their grandchild, relieve you of some of the burden," he said unapologetically. He continued to stare out over the water.

Moriah peered incredulously at him for his insensitivity.

"Can't you see?" she said pleadingly. "They wanted to take her from me. I had her for two years; they wanted to take her away from me."

"Were you two becoming an item?" Tyro whirled around. He narrowed his eyes, studying her face carefully. It was as if he hadn't heard a word she just said.

Moriah stared harder into the distance. She shook her head. "He killed himself within a month after Anaya died." She sobbed. He kept his distance and waited for her to finish. She dried her eyes. When she looked up, Tyro was looking at her as if she were a complete stranger.

He jabbed his hands in his pockets. "Did you fall in love with him?" His words were cutting, terse.

Moriah looked up at him like he had lost his mind. She couldn't believe his ruthless insensitivity. "Kenny loved my sister. He was good for her." Not that she felt she owed him an explanation as far as this particular matter was concerned; still, she continued on. "I was very fond of him, for her. I thought that my sister was the luckiest girl, despite all they had gone through to be together." Her voice trailed off. "I know my sister would have wanted us to be a family for Amelia's sake. She'd even hinted at it before she died." Moriah fought to maintain control, to keep from losing herself. "It was as if she knew she was going to die. Oh God, why didn't I see it?" She wept bitterly.

"Moriah, I told you trust is very important to me. You should have told me. I can't be in a relationship with you wondering what else you're keeping from me."

"And what about you?" She wheeled around to face him. "Is that why you didn't tell me we were being watched… to save me like you did the first night we met… to clear your conscience about not being there to save—" Moriah had almost said it. Though she hadn't said it completely, he knew exactly what she meant. Not that she had wanted it to come out this way; it was too late to pull her words back.

He turned away from her. "You should leave now. I've heard enough."

"Maybe I'm not ready for a relationship," she rebutted. "Not with you… or anyone."

Without saying another word, he stepped aside for her to leave.

Moriah conceded and quietly closed the door behind her.

Quincy just happened to pop in as Moriah was leaving. Tyro stood with his fists balled at his sides. His face was flushed and his eyes were full of anger. Quincy patted his son on the shoulders. "It's best to let her go, son. Give yourself some time."

"Dad. Please." Tyro brushed past his father. "Just leave me alone." He trudged into his bedroom. The hat Moriah had lost the night they first met lay on his dresser. After the incident yesterday, he'd planned to give it back to her. He'd already determined it was over. His mind whirled with the anguish of unanswered questions, disappointment. Anger. He tossed the hat back into the drawer and grabbed the bottle of blue and yellow pills.

He stared at the bottle. It'd been a long time since he'd taken any. *I didn't need you then, I don't want you now.* He dumped them into the trash. As he turned from the receptacle, he heard Sheba let out a distressing yelp. Tyro rushed to her side. She was showing early signs of premature labor.

Chapter 29

That same day, Petra thought long and hard about her promise. Sitting outside of Amelia's daycare, she removed the papers she'd shoved aside earlier, before the Feds took her beloved Parker away. She'd planned to keep her promise, but since fate had knocked at her door, what was the hurry?

She was able to intercept the package he'd left in their office for the carrier to deliver to Moriah. *He's so predictable sometimes to his own detriment,* she mouthed to herself. She wasn't as concerned about his present predicament. She was sure he had that situation all worked out, too.

She had her secretary to shred the entire package. She advised her not to even open it. "Just shred it to pieces." She popped back into the area where her secretary was working. "Just remove the address label and place it on my desk," she commanded before leaving to pick up her granddaughter. Dinner would be served at five-thirty, a bath and bed by seven. Just the way she liked it. She was in control, for now.

She was sure Parker would be home in the morning.

Parker indeed came home the next morning. Waiting out of sight, he watched as Petra commanded Amelia to get in the car. The child had been crying for her Poppy. *Hang in there, little Rosey, things will get better soon,* he promised softly to himself.

When her limo exited out of the iron gates and turned the corner, Parker entered his home. He opened the safe and took out the original signed documents and placed them inside a courier envelope. He addressed it to Moriah on Terminal Avenue, Wilmington,

Delaware. He then placed that envelope inside a box and addressed it to Seattle. He then nested that box inside of two other boxes, each having different delivery locations as well. He routed them to ship around the country with the original package to arrive back at Laino Enterprises, for Moriah.

Each package contained a note to one of his colleagues to assure that the package inside was delivered to its own destination immediately.

It was a lot to risk being sent all over the country like that, but he had to keep a step ahead of his darling wife. She had too many connections and he couldn't chance her intercepting it.

And no, he couldn't go to Moriah in person. It had to be done this way. He knew the Feds were watching and he couldn't risk being seen with her. The final courier would be one of his own personnel. He was sure he'd get the package to its final destination. After mailing the package from a faraway location, he returned home.

He rearranged his granddaughter's room back to the way it was before he left. The way Amelia liked it. He ordered his chef to fix a special meal, and requested grilled cheese for his Rosey, and to place the picnic basket in the refrigerator. He reminded her to trim the edges off of the grilled cheese sandwiches; just the way Amelia liked that too.

After that, he swam several laps in the pool, showered, and dressed in a casual jogging suit. He sat in his favorite chair and waited patiently. He owed his granddaughter a picnic. And a picnic she would get.

Chapter 30

A package had sat in Moriah's office for several days now. It had been marked personal and confidential. Mickey saw that a Parker Smythe had sent it. She felt it was of a personal nature. She placed it on her desk for when she'd come in the office.

Quincy just happened to be around when it arrived. One of their company's competitors had delivered it. He eyed the sharpness and efficiency of the carrier. He'd validated Mickey's signature and spit her out a receipt from his hand-held itron.

"Well La-di-da. " Quincy said under his breath. Wondering if his own company was as up to date with that particular technology. He grimaced for a moment. He'd been the one who'd always argued about not chasing after the latest technology. In his mind things were running fine just the way Laino had run things. He could finally see just how wrong he'd been.

"I'll take this to Ms. Styles," he told Mickey, reaching for her delivery. Not that he felt he owed her any explanation; after all, it was part of his business, his office. But he knew Mickey was a force to be reckoned with. There'd be no pulling any wool over her eyes.

"Oh that's okay, Mr. Simmonds. Moriah said she'd stop in to sign some papers before the movers show up this morning." She politely removed the package out of his hand and put it away at another location for safekeeping.

He could have pulled rank. He was itching to get his hands on the delivery. He was familiar with Parker Smythe. He'd read about him in the report his informants had provided him. But he also knew that he was Moriah's former boss. Not knowing what was up was eating him up on the inside.

"Did you say she's moving today?" he called out to where Mickey had stationed herself outside of Moriah's office.

"Today's the day," she sang in reply.

"Oh hockey puck!" He'd forgotten that he was to send a crew over to move Moriah's belongings from her storage location into her new home. He removed her set of keys from the board, the job spec from the printer, and headed out to the yard. He tracked down the foreman. "The trucks needed for this job are all out on out of town runs. The soonest we're scheduled to have one back is tomorrow. Night," The foreman added cautiously. He rechecked the clipboard twice. He'd seen the dissatisfaction on Quincy's face. "The forty-footer would be too big.

"We'd have a lot of breakage if things shifted while en route."

"Well pack it right!" Quincy barked.

The foreman removed his cap and scratched his head. He looked at the street address. Tilting the clipboard for his boss's review, he braved to ask, "Do we know if this street will even accommodate a forty-footer?" He gazed up into the white haired man's unhappy face. "Uh, let me have that. I'll gather up a crew to take care of it."

"Never mind." Quincy snatched the job from his hand. He stormed toward the east side of the yard. He grabbed Orlando and a few other guys. "Come on, we've got a job to do."

He marched into the office, picked up Moriah's package, and headed to where a twenty-eight foot moving van just happened to be pulling out from one of the bays.

"Ironically, this truck just happened to be in," the foreman explained nervously to Quincy.

"After this job is done, be sure to be in my office first thing in the morning," he demanded of his foreman. "And bring your shop steward with you.

377

Chapter 31

Moriah stood on the balcony and looked over the river from her new home. She and Nettie had just waved good-bye to Quincy and his moving crew after filling them full of cola, subs, pizza, wings, and chips. A bittersweet mixture of emotions coursed through her like a shot of adrenaline. She had her own place now. But the overwhelming sadness that Amelia wouldn't be there with her weighed heavily on her soul.

Her mind slumped in deep thought. It wasn't an easy decision to make. She had to choose between using the money toward settlement on her home or giving it to her lawyer for the appeal. Still, he couldn't guarantee her she'd win. Fifty-fifty chance his last email had said.

Tyro had offered to help her financially before their big blow up. She wouldn't accept his money. She couldn't. She hadn't been totally honest with him about the case. How could she when the appeal had really been about custody for a child he didn't even know existed?

Even still, she wouldn't have accepted his money, period.

When she prayed about it before making her decision, she felt the Lord leading her to trust Him. She remembered the bird that had landed on the balcony when she was at Tyro's. *Faith and courage*, He'd reminded her.

She had the faith, but she didn't know it was going to be so hard to trust Him. That's where courage came in. Courage to act on what she felt she was to do even though it didn't seem to make any sense, at all.

She walked back inside of her 2,500 square foot, four-bedroom, four-and-a-half-bath townhouse.

She thought about the package Quincy had given her. Consumed with the move, she had tucked it away for later. She was reminded that she had it when she saw the corner of it sticking out of her computer bag, a few moments ago. She picked it up and held it steadily in her hand. She looked at the label of the sender. The Smythes had sent it. Well actually, Parker's name was noted as the sender. She figured it was more legal mumbo jumbo. She placed it back to where she removed it from. She was too exhausted to deal with that right now.

She thought of Tyro. Emptiness gnarled at her core. Tyro hadn't been back to his condo much since their last conversation. She sighed thinking about it. It hadn't gone too well. They'd argued. It was over between them. No need to remind herself.

Quincy had told her that he spent a lot of time in the apartment unit above the office at the yard. He was using Sheba as an excuse, being that she was so near her due date. He told his father he needed her to be in a quiet and uneventful environment. Now exactly what he meant by that, she could only guess. She'd be the last person to bother him ever again.

She had a funny feeling Quincy blamed her for their break-up although she was sure he had no clue as to why they were no longer together.

A ship passing through the drawbridge got her attention. Her mood mellowed out as she praised God for blessing her and Nettie with such a beautiful home and the gorgeous view. It had been the perfect day for moving. It was a crisp November day and the sun was still beaming spectacular colors off of the water. She was enamored of the view and ecstatic that she'd get to experience it every day. She took in the beauty of the tree-lined street across the water. The leaves had already started turning colors. The sun beamed a gorgeous fall-ish glow off of the Delaware River. "I just love the fall." Moriah took a deep breath.

"I love that we's out of that hotel-motel… rat trap." Nettie had said and instantly froze as soon as the word *rat* flew out of her mouth. From the corner of her eye, Moriah saw Nettie peeking at her.

Nettie stretched her arms wide in praise to God. "Home sweet home and right on time for Thanksgiving. Thank you, Jesus." She did her little happy dance as she turned and looked over all of their furnishings, boxes, and crates from storage.

She tried her best to cheer Moriah up. She'd been in a somber mood all week. Well, actually, it'd been a few weeks since she and Tyro had their falling out and all her joy seemed to have evaporated. "Gurl, Lawd knows you sure gave them a good workout today. They carried all your stuff up three flights of stairs!"

"Don't you even try it, Nettie. You have just as much stuff as I do." They laughed and plopped down on the sofa and breathed.

"I sure don't want to have to do this again. No time soon anyway." Moriah chimed.

"Not even when you and Prince Charming kiss and make up, get married and have some—"

"Now see, there you go meddling again." She threw the dishtowel she was holding at her.

"Me Meddling. I'm not going to be going through the holidays with you moping around like some sick puppy." She was glad her friend seemed to be coming around and was beginning to enjoy their progress. "Ya'll just ought to kiss, make up and get it over with!"

"You mind yours and I'll mind mine," Moriah said as she leapt from her seat.

"Speaking of which," Nettie inquired, "what ever happened to that thang of yours anyways?"

"What *thang*?"

"Oh no you not trying to play dumb with me. You know what *thang* I'm talkin' bout." She chuckled in between her teasing. "The Shrek mobile… carnival comes to town on 18 wheels." She followed

Moriah into the kitchen. "That one, or have you forgotten all about it already?"

Moriah shrugged. It had been over a month since the media had broadcasted any inkling about the Green Monster fairy tale saga. A blurb here and there, but no one was interested in it anymore. Moriah learned what had really happened to her hideous vehicle. She saw a scrap of the evidence one day while she was walking Sheba around the yard.

Tyro never denied it. But he never admitted to it either. She decided to let the matter go and agreed that the truck she bought very cheaply from him settled the issue.

"Oh no you don't... There's something you not telling me, isn't it?" Her best friend accused.

"I think Tyro junked it."

"Good for him. All the more reason why I think he's a keeper." She paused on a serious note. "Moriah. What about the Rat man?" She steadied her by her arms. "I never pressed the issue, even though you'd promised me you'd tell me. But to be honest, I'm kind of concerned, now with Amelia—"

Moriah took a deep breath. "If you must know, I agreed to allow Tyro to have his personal private detectives keep a close eye on her. It's the only thing we've been able to come to terms on. I won't take a chance that he... Fletcher..." she shuddered at the thought and shook it from her mind. Amelia was in good hands. She was sure of it. She and Tyro may not be in good standing as far as a relationship, but he could be trusted to look out for Amelia. There was no doubt that he had her watched over as well.

"And what about you?" Moriah spun around as if in great revelation. "Are you worried, concerned he might come after you? If you are, I'm sure Tyro would have you guarded too, if he hasn't already."

"What, you mean I could be being followed, watched? Sure hope he's tall, dark, good looking, and a doctor."

"How about him being saved and sanctified," Moriah quipped.

Nettie soughed and threw a decorative pillow at her best friend. Moriah ducked and they both let out a hearty laugh.

Chapter 32

Sheba was very close to her time to deliver. Tyro stayed by her side night and day, pampering her to ensure she had everything she needed. Living at the unit in the yard was closer to the vet's office and would allow him to get her there faster when the time came. Tonight, he'd stayed up all night with her. She was in labor. But something didn't seem right. Tyro called the clinic and the doctor on call came right over.

After examining her, he said she was doing fine, but to bring her into the clinic in the morning. She would be ready to deliver within the next few days and she could have her puppies there under their care. Although Sheba had her previous pups under Tyro's careful watch, he didn't argue with the doctor's recommendation.

He couldn't shake that gnawing feeling in his gut. Something was not right. Something wasn't right with Sheba's gestation period and something wasn't right about Moriah's well-being. He lay on the couch and drifted in and out of sleep. He'd dreamed of Moriah and had awakened suddenly. He tried to push her out of his mind, but he couldn't. He twirled the hat that she had left behind around his finger. He'd planned to give it back to her when he saw her again.

Maybe he'd do it tomorrow and get it over with. He reasoned it was best to give it to her in person rather than to just ship it to her. He'd hoped that giving it to her in person was the right decision. He didn't want her to get worried that this Fletcher guy had found it and was stalking her. He wasn't sure what to do about the piece of torn clothing Sheba found on the deserted island. He hadn't asked her, but he was pretty sure it was hers.

He placed both items in a bag and stowed it by the door. He'd be sure to put it in his truck so that he wouldn't forget it. No use prolonging it. He wondered what his reaction would be once he saw her. It was easier for him to stay away. It made it hard to resist pulling her into his arms whenever he laid his eyes on her.

He thought of the child he'd seen her with at the daycare. He hadn't been spying on her on and whenever he thought of the love she had for the child, he couldn't help but to think of what a great mother she was.

If only she would have trusted him.

"Why didn't you tell me?" he yelled out into silence. He was still appalled that she hadn't. Why didn't she trust him? So many secrets, too many and Tyro never could tolerate being deceived. He'd told her so when he first brought her to his island.

He lay his head down on the arm of the couch. He'd hoped that she didn't think he was rejecting her because of the child. The little girl had nothing to do with it. As far as he could tell, she was so adorable. He'd love to be in her life, but Moriah had already made the decision to keep him out by lying to him.

Tyro appeased his despair. He'd warned her how important truth was to him and that's that. She made her choice.

But weren't you the one who had been dishonest with her? The thought rose swiftly in his mind. *But I apologized, numerous times.*

Apologizing and being remorseful for your actions are two different things.

He knew this to be true from the many clients he'd helped through his former law practice. Many were sorry only because they'd gotten caught. There was no remorse for the crimes they'd committed. They were sorry about the consequences and not the actual wrong they'd done. He closed his eyes with his newfound assurance. She made her choice. Once he'd give her back her belongings, it was over.

Tyro tossed and turned in a fitful sleep. Suddenly, he bolted straight up. He glanced over at the clock. It was a quarter past four in the morning. He'd had the dream again. His heart raced. He wiped sweat from his brow; again he dreamt that he couldn't save his mother. Images of her sinking into the murky waters, her hand outstretched to him, calling to him, haunted him. He had been swimming as fast as he could. He pushed through his tiredness. It seemed as if he'd been swimming for hours. When he finally reached her, it was too late. She was gone.

He heard a cry in the distance. He spun around. Moriah was trapped in a fire. She screamed in agony, calling out his name to have him help her. His feet were on dry ground now. He ran with all his might, but something was holding him back. He was running in place. He could see her. He was so close. His hands almost touched her fingers. He thought he had her, but she crumbled like grains of sand when he grabbed her.

He'd had a similar dream a few nights just before he'd met Moriah. But in his dream he hadn't been able to see the woman's face. The night that he first saw her when she was stuck in the middle of the intersection in that hideous truck of hers, he knew immediately it was her, the mysterious woman he saw in his dream. It's what propelled him, pushing him harder toward her truck, ignoring his own plight of danger. That night, the dream had scrolled through his mind like a clip from a movie. It caused him to run faster than he had ever run before in his life.

He'd determined he'd stop at nothing to save her. At the time, for a split second, he considered the danger. He'd made up his mind that if he died trying to save her, he was willing to die. After he'd gotten her safely out of her truck, he cradled her in his arms, carrying her to safety. He felt an impulse to kiss her. It was like he knew her, had seen her before. It was clear to him now that the woman in his dream was Moriah.

Tyro sat up on the couch. The images of his mother and Moriah lay fresh in his mind. He blinked to focus in the still darkness of the room. It had only been a dream. A dream he'd had before. Another image from the dream popped into his mind. Sheba. He remembered now. Fear taunted him. Reality seized him. In the dream, he hadn't been able to save his Shepherd either.

He covered his face with his hands. He wanted to get up to rinse his face with cold water. Maybe it would help to bring him out of the stupor. But he couldn't move. He was paralyzed by the images of Sheba falling from the mountain they'd been climbing. Suddenly, he was at the bottom. His arms outstretched, his feet steadied, ready to catch her. She'd been falling for a long time. His arms grew weary from being lifted outward. His legs became like lead. He called to her, assuring her that he had her. But he hadn't, she'd fallen right through his arms and was instantly swallowed by the ground. He focused to block the images from his mind.

The sun was now peeking through his window as it rose. He could hear the men in the yard stirring, preparing for the day's work. He caught a glimpse of his bible sitting on the night table. He'd been meeting with Willie on several occasions now. The talks had been helping. He was glad that Willie finally went home to his wife. A smile of satisfaction peeked briefly from his face. He was starting a new church. Tyro was glad that he could help, as much as Willie had allowed him. He'd told him that this was God's work and that he didn't want to be depending on man as his source, only as the Lord led. That impacted Tyro. He thought about the lesson Willie taught at Wednesday afternoon Bible Study. He looked up the passage in Isaiah 43:2 and read it out loud.

When you passeth through the waters, I will be with thee; and through the rivers, they shall not overflow thee: when though walkest through the fire, thou shalt not be burnt; neither shall the flame kindle upon thee.

But what did it mean? He thought of his dream. He pondered about his life. He held his head between his hands. Moriah. What did any of this have to do with her?

He wanted to be with her. But she didn't want to be with him. She'd told him so, at least her actions had. He tried to block out the confusion. It was no use. What was it going to take to get her out of his mind? His system. But he couldn't live without her. He was sure of that now. What did it matter if—.

"Yes, I love her," his voice blurted out into the stillness of his room.

Sheba whimpered and let out a loud yelp. It broke his train of thought. He didn't like how she looked. Her outer nose dripped with sweat. The pads on her paws were wet as well. She was panting profusely. She turned her eyes and looked pitifully up at Tyro.

"That's it. You're going to the clinic, now!"

Chapter 33

It was 6 a.m. when Tyro sped into the veterinarian's parking lot. "Today's the big day, huh?" Nettie commented while she held the door for him to carry Sheba inside. Tyro's no nonsense demeanor and curt forwardness told her he was worried.

"Come on, dad... she'll be fine," Nettie said as she put the finishing touches on the generous sized whelping pen for Sheba. It was set up in a private room large enough to allow Tyro to sit with her as well as room for the attending doctor and assistants as needed.

Dr. Croix was in the midst of relieving Tyro's concerns when Quincy and Mario burst through the door. "I have been calling you for the past three hours," Quincy barked. "Where is she? Let me see my dog," he demanded.

Dr. Croix extended his hand towards the irate white haired man. Quincy ignored it. Mario received the doctor's hand immediately. "Sorry. We're just a little anxious."

"You can go in to see her as soon as you calm down. Dogs are very sensitive and you will upset her calm state of being if you go barging in like that." He looked Quincy straight in the eye and smiled. "I know it's stressful, but the best thing for Sheba is that everyone remains calm and level headed."

The doctor furrowed his brows. Tyro could only imagine what he was thinking. After all, this wasn't Sheba's first time having pups. "I'm aware of everyone's anxieties," Dr. Croix said, trying to lighten the air.

"Please," he said pointing to a family waiting area. "Help yourself to some coffee or tea while you wait."

Quincy stared at him as if he had two heads. Mario calmed him by patting him on the shoulders. He guided him to the waiting area.

A few minutes later, the doctor returned. "I do have something I need to discuss with you." He turned to Tyro. "I assume you'll be making all the decisions since she's your Shepherd?"

"Yes. I will. Is there a problem?" He rose and looked toward his Shepherd's pen.

Indignant, Quincy jumped to his feet. "She is your mother's dog and you know that, Tyro," he spat.

Tyro fixed his eyes on him. "Dad. Please. Not now." It was true that his dad had bought Sheba for his mother's birthday over six years ago. But it had been Tyro who'd trained and took care of her. Ever since, Sheba went everywhere with him and his mother hadn't minded. Even when he had moved out of the family home, Sheba had come with him. So yes, for all intents and purposes, everyone knew she had become his dog for a long while now.

Quincy sat and leaned forward and rested his forearms on his legs. He motioned with his hand for the doctor to continue. "I recommend that this be her last litter. She is having some complications—"

"Complications?" Quincy bounded to his feet. "What kind of complications?" His voice echoed as he overly stressed each syllable.

"Mr. Simmonds. I'm going to ask you to leave my clinic if you don't calm yourself. I have patients here and they don't need to be around your—"

"Dr. Croix, please come quick!" Nettie said as she rushed back out of the room.

Quincy lunged forward and burst through the door ahead of the doctor before anyone could stop him. If there was something wrong with his wife's dog, he would be the first to find out.

"SURPRISE!" The doctor's staff sang, then their voices quickly fell off. The man who'd barged through the door was not Dr. Croix. The lanky assistant holding a birthday cake full of lit candles tried to get out of the way, but the wild haired man who'd just careened through the door was still charging toward him. Quincy hadn't seen him standing there with the double layered, extra frosted birthday surprise until it was too late.

"You can use this to keep us updated." Mario gave Tyro his cell. Tyro had been almost to the clinic when he realized he'd left his cell at home.

Trying not to laugh, everyone watched as Mario escorted Quincy out of the clinic. He was covered from head to shoulders with chocolate icing and candles still flickering. Good thing they were battery operated candles.

Nettie worked with Dr. Croix and Tyro to keep Sheba calm. Still, she wasn't doing so well. The doctor discussed the consideration of a caesarean for Sheba. But before he'd do so, he had to get her temperature regulated.

Chapter 34

A man disfigured beyond recognition, checked his trunk to assure he had all his gear. Rope, cloths, a mirror, and a deplorable cot folded haphazardly were the only things occupying the space, besides the spare tire that was void of any treads.

He shoved the items from the glove compartment fitfully to the floor with one swipe of his better hand. He placed the bottle of the homemade lethal substance, rag, and plastic baggie in the now uncluttered compartment. After limping around to the driver's side, he finagled himself up into the seat. The metal door protested as it creaked badly when he slammed it shut.

He caught a glimpse of his face as he backed out onto the dusty road and headed north. One side of his face drooped from third degree burns. He struggled to shift the column gearshift with his defective hand and cursed profusely when the jalopy resisted picking up speed.

"She will pay for what she did to me," he vowed as his spit entwined with the pouring rain. He spat again through the broken window.

Fletcher, in a delusional state of mind headed north. When he got to his destination, he pulled his rusty truck around the back of the run down motel. He parked behind the dumpster and peeped around to ensure that no nosey neighbors lingered or were peeping out of their windows. He poured chloroform into the rag and stuffed it in the plastic bag before he jammed it into the outer pocket of his cruddy old military jacket.

He had come to finish what he'd started. He hadn't liked that she had escaped the last time. She had something he wanted back badly. After he got it, he'd have no further need of her. He glanced in the rearview mirror one last time and sneered at his appearance. His teeth showed through the decaying flesh of his jaw. She definitely had her debts to pay.

Moriah had just finished packing the remainder of her and Nettie's belongings. They'd planned to go back to the motel together, but Nettie had to go into the clinic to help with Sheba's delivery. Moriah was torn. She wanted to be there. She just didn't want to be in the way. Truthfully, she couldn't bear to see Tyro. Her heart ached for him.

The few items that remained were neatly packed and stowed underneath the window by the door. Moriah looked at the few bags of things that needed to be thrown in the trash.

She contemplated whether she should take them out back to the dumpster or wait for Tyro's crew. Although they hadn't been on the same level of relationship as they formerly had, occasionally he'd email her just to check up on her. She'd received one from him last night asking how the move went. When she told him she still had a few things to get from her old place he was adamant about sending a few of his guys over to help.

"Please Wait For Them," he'd emphasized in big, bold letters.

Although he'd insisted that she wait until they got to her new place and could drive behind her, where they could load the rest of her belongings while she finished cleaning up the motel room, apparently, with all that was going on with Sheba, he'd forgotten to send them.

She looked at the four grocery bags she had neatly tied up that contained spoiled food from the frig, paper towels they had used to clean with, and other useless items. "I could have thrown them in the dumpster by now." She complained to no one in particular.

She received a text from Nettie's that Tyro was at the clinic with Sheba. He had left his cell phone home, but he wanted to remind her that his crew should be there shortly to move the remainder of their belongings. "He's a keeper!" Nettie concluded adding her own two cents to the dialogue.

Moriah blew out a quick breath. She didn't know what was taking them so long. She reasoned that she could handle taking out that small amount of trash as well as loading the boxes in her car. Before she wasted any more time thinking about it, she grabbed the bags and bounded out the door. In her impatience, she had left her cell phone on the bed.

Moriah headed around the building toward the garbage receptacle when she noticed a dilapidated truck parked by the dumpster. She barely paid it any mind other than she hadn't remembered seeing it there before. She figured it had been abandoned since it seemed no one occupied it as she strained to see inside from a distance.

After tossing the garbage in the dumpster, she be bopped back around the building and closed the door quickly behind her. "Now that wasn't so bad."

Just as Moriah closed her apartment door, she thought she heard Tyro's crew clambering toward her door. She grabbed her cell phone and stuffed it in the side pocket of her hoodie.

Glad to have gotten the task completed, she swung the door open. Her lungs gave way to any breath that remained as she stared into the eyes of the man who confirmed her fears were true: Fletcher had come for her.

Nettie's phone had been chiming all morning with texts and voicemails. She hadn't had time to answer them. There were two other dogs in labor and the clinic was still receiving incoming patients.

This was Nettie's scheduled day off, but she was called around 5 a.m. to come in for the growing and anticipated patient load, along with her favorite patient. Today would be her first time delivering puppies on her own.

393

She had received strange calls from Moriah all morning, but she was too engrossed with her patients' care. When her cell rang again, she quickly told Moriah she couldn't talk, but to hold on for a moment. She trekked over to Tyro and shoved her phone in his hand. He'd taken a quick break from being by Sheba's side while the doctor examined her.

Tyro took the phone and placed it up to his ear. He was about to say hello, but he could hear Moriah carrying on about something. Her voice was panicky.

"Help me." Moriah whispered as loud as she could without her abductor hearing her. "He's going to kill me... he's not dead...we're at some gas station RT 13 south.... He's not dead!" She was now screaming into the phone. "He drugged me..."

"Who's not dead? Where are you?" Tyro asked as he turned his attention to the doctor waving for him to come immediately.

"Moriah!" Tyro hollered into the cell as he walked outside so he could speak louder. He tried to get her attention but the phone suddenly went dead. One of the assistants popped her head out the door. "Come, quick. The doctor needs to see you right away. We're losing Sheba!"

Tyro raced back into the clinic. Nettie's cell chimed. It was a text from Moriah's phone. "HELP ME. FLTCHR. BCK SIT"

A 2nd text chimed: "TIED CNT GET LOOSE. MY LOCK ON"

"Mr. Simmonds," the assistant said, "as Dr. Croix advised, you have to make the decision." She handed him the clipboard with the consent form. Check here if you choose for us to save the puppies or here to save your dog.

"The decision has to be made quickly or we could lose them all." She reminded him of the urgency of the decision he needed to make. There was no time to spare.

"What?" Tyro responded in a daze.

Chapter 35

Tyro had signed the consent forms simultaneously as he called Mario and rushed out the door.

"What do you mean, she needs a caesarean?" Quincy snapped as he snatched the phone from Mario's ear.

"Dad, put Mario back on the phone."

"We're clear." Mario said as he watched his brother-in-law storm out of the room.

"Where are you?" Mario asked after receiving the phone back and placing it on speakerphone. "Yes, I'll call Sable and the detectives."

"Mario, take me off the speaker phone. Can you get back to the clinic without my dad knowing about it? I had to sign a waiver to save either Sheba or the litter."

Mario looked over his shoulder to ensure Quincy wasn't lingering. "I'll head over there as soon as I make the contacts. I'll get Roy to keep him occupied." Mario hesitated for a moment. "Which did you sign to save?"

Tyro paused. "I don't remember." He tried to control his anguish. He needed to think straight. Clearly. "I left as soon as I got Moriah's call on Nettie's phone."

Tyro's voice trembled. "I listened to Moriah's voicemails. She's in trouble, Mario. Moriah's in trouble. I'll never forgive myself —"

"Listen, we'll find her. I've already texted the detective. They put a trace on her cell locator as we were talking. It pinged her heading below Rehoboth, still heading southwest."

He headed back to the condo to retrieve his cell to see if she'd tried to call him and hoped she'd left him more clues to locate her.

"Four hours ago…" Tyro anguished that it had been over four hours since she'd been abducted. His heart failed as he thought of the hopelessness she must have felt when she couldn't get a hold of anyone.

"I'm sorry, Moriah. I've failed you." He cried in despair. He grabbed his phone and smart watch. Both had wedged between the cushions where they had fallen as he drifted in and out of sleep last evening. Frantically, he searched through his messages as he raced to the rooftop. Slinging himself in the helicopter, he ignited the engine. He took off immediately upon getting air clearance to fly.

Chapter 36

Ebbing backwards into the loneliness of his bedroom, Quincy shrugged from what he'd been able to hear. Somebody was in danger. He'd been listening trying to determine whom Tyro and Mario were talking about. He couldn't tell who it was. Since Tyro was on the other end, it wasn't him. Had this Fletcher character—the one that had murdered his wife, hurt someone else? That's all he could make out other than the authorities had been alerted. But what did it concern Mario and Tyro; what could they do about it?

He remembered overhearing that the perpetrator was last known to have been in Rehoboth. An idea came to mind. He could help. After all, he reasoned, he needed something to do to ease his mind, calm his nerves until he'd heard that Sheba's pups were there and all was well.

He reached for his briefcase to pull out his map. He wasn't up to par using these newfangled gibber jabbering navigational apps, and such. But he could read a map like the back of his hand.

He snapped opened the briefcase. A red and gold bag had been neatly folded and placed on top. Whoever placed it there like that had done so intentionally so that he wouldn't miss it.

He recognized it. Moriah had given it to him. Well, actually, she'd left it on Tyro's kitchen counter for him on the morning he'd ordered her flown off of his island. At the time, he didn't trust her. Since spending time with her, helping her move, he thought better of her. In some ways, she reminded him of his Laino. He pushed the memories of the foolish way he'd treated her aside.

He focused back on the gift. He'd never opened it; in fact, when he saw it he'd scowled and thrown it in the trash. He hadn't cared what it was. He felt a ting of remorse. Mickey must have retrieved it. The more he thought about it, it had to have been her. He plopped down in his easy chair by his bedroom balcony. His mind wandered down memory lane of when Laino had bought the chair for him to relax while he took in the view on rainy or snowy days.

"She was a good woman," he mused but quickly ignored the sadness that threatened to distract him.

Now curious, he unfolded the meticulously packed package and removed the item still wrapped in tissue paper. He started to complain about people going through such nonsense, until he caught himself. He used to grumble about it when his wife used to painstakingly wrap gifts. He just didn't get it.

"It's part of the surprise," she had many times told him.

He gripped his lips together. He'd never thought to do the same for her, or any one. Had he done so, she would have smiled. He could imagine her petite fingers reaching to accept his gift with such poise and grace. He imagined in his mind now, him presenting it to her, wrapped all pretty with a large gold bow on top. He knew it wouldn't have mattered to her what was inside as much as the thought, if he had done so, presenting it to her. As he thought about it, he regretted it now. Oh why, why hadn't he… There were many things he'd done, or hadn't done he regretted now. He lowered his eyes. He reached for the card that had fallen in his lap when he had emptied the contents out of the bag.

He removed the card from the envelope and read the handwritten note.

Time may not heal all wounds, but God is the One Who mends broken hearts. Thanks for letting me be a part of your son's life. Moriah.

He removed the wooden case from between the tissue paper. His eyes fell on the vintage silvery watchcase. He allowed its long chain to cascade between his fingers and dangle from his hand.

He pushed the small clamp on the side of the watch; its top snapped loose. His fingers trembled as he pried it all the way open.

He stared at the opened masculine, ornate pocket watch. He ran his finger over the inside of the lid. A picture had been affixed there. It was a picture of him and Laino. In the picture they were holding each other as if madly in love. His face brightened at the way she smiled.

His eyes shifted back to the card. He read Moriah's last remarks aloud.

Thanks for allowing me to be your family's 'house guest.' With love, Moriah Styles.

He repeated the part that read "With love, Moriah Styles." He sat in silence. She was good for his son. He'd hope they'd make amends.

He heard Mario calling out to him. It burst through his thoughts. He'd told him he was leaving and that he couldn't stay to join him for the lunch Roy was preparing. *Mario seemed in a hurry now.* Quincy's mind snapped in alarm. Something was up. He heard the urgency in Mario's voice. He tried to think through his cloudiness. Had something gone wrong with Sheba? He leapt from his chair and trekked into his great room. He caught Mario just as he was closing the door. The door jolted out of his brother in law's hand when he grabbed it. "Is it Sheba?" His brows connected together.

Mario looked away. "No puppies yet." He returned his attention back and stared at his weary looking brother in law. "Relax. I'll call you as soon as I hear something."

Quincy didn't like the feeling. Neither did he believe him. He paced the floor. His mind churned, straining at various possibilities. He went back over the snatches of conversation he was able to hear between his son and Mario. No, all of a sudden, he was leaving. Something was up; he wasn't buying that it wasn't. He thought through what he gathered.

He pulled the pieces to the puzzle together. He remembered hearing Mario saying something about *someone being abducted... finding her...calling Sable.*

Find whom? Quincy couldn't make sense of it. Then it hit him like a ton of bricks.

Tyro.

Moriah is in trouble and his son had gone to save her. He was sure of it. His adrenaline rushed through him at the very thought that his son may be placing himself in danger.

He placed a call to one of his contacts and told of the urgency. A few minutes later, he was bounding towards the reserved private indoor garage; the map held tightly in his hand.

He uncovered the Bugatti Veyron Super Sport —2010 World Record Edition. It had never been driven. Well, maybe once... twice. Several times. He grinned slightly thinking about. It. He'd bought it for his wife's last birthday. He smiled as he remembered her teasing him that he had really gotten it for himself. Well, he had tried to beat the world's record of 267.8 mph. It was the only car on record to have done it. He wanted to put it to the test. And last year he certainly had.

Even though she never got to drive it, she had loved driving fast cars around the private track they'd built on their island. She was concerned that the car's 0 to 60 second speed might get away from her.

Quincy read the text that chimed on his phone. As his old war buddy hopped in the passenger seat, Quincy peeled out from the garage. He reached his destination in 30 minutes flat. According to the latest report from his inside contacts, Moriah's cell locator placed her 30 minutes north of the Chesapeake Bay Bridge.

Chapter 37

Moriah faded in and out of consciousness. She fought to ward off the drowsiness. Both her hands and feet were tied. It was pitch dark where she laid. The smell of pee reeked heavily. Out of the eerie darkness and silence, she assumed she was where Fletcher had been hiding from the authorities. Where was he? Her heart was beating so loud it sounded as if it echoed around the room. She strained to see around her environment, anything that would give her a clue of where she could be. And escape.

The feelings of death lingered all around her. Her adrenaline soared beyond control. She struggled wildly as she fought to get her hands loose. Flashes of the last time she was in his grasp seized her mind. Her strength failed her. She thought about the messages she was able to send before he'd pulled over to the side and bound her hands, feet, and mouth. Why hadn't they answered her plea for help? she wondered.

Had Tyro blocked her number? Did Nettie get her messages? Did anyone even know she was missing? Fear, desperation, and feeling destitute stabbed at her heart. Sweat coursed down her spine as her fitful rages seeped out of every pore in her body.

She couldn't reach her cell. She wasn't even sure that it was still in her pocket. Then she remembered, Tyro had placed a locator on her cell when he learned of her attack. He promised he'd always protect her.

"Where are you?" she cried out in distress.

She heard a sudden movement as if she had awakened a sleeping giant. Staggering footsteps pounded in her direction. Fear seized her. Her body fell still. A heavy breathing told her someone was there in the room with her. Standing over her. Looking down at her.

Something shiny reflected on the wall as it flashed in the small glint of light stealing through the mud-smeared window. Her heart thumped so loudly, she was sure he heard it.

She felt the gut wrenching pain as a heavy piece of tape was ripped from her mouth. A rag long enough to tie around her mouth suddenly gripped her and was heaved in between her lips. It was snapped in a short, quick and tight knot behind her head with swiftness as if he had done it before… many times.

Moriah's head, body, and mind flailed, gyrating wildly, uncontrollably with everything in her as she attempted to ward off her assailant from gagging her.

Her head snapped back as he grabbed her hair. "I've waited so long for this." His putrid breath sneered over her. She turned her head to keep from vomiting. "Remember me?" He let her head fall from his grasp as he struck a match to light an oil lamp that hung at the foot of the bed.

His monstrous shadow lurked on the wall. He leaned closer for her to see his face. The stench of his ill cared for burns smelled of rot and infected flesh. She held her breath and prayed not to gag beneath the cloth he'd tied tightly to her mouth. She fought to hold it down. If she puked, she would asphyxiate on her own vomit.

Chapter 38

"Do you understand the risk of taking your dog from this clinic?" Dr. Croix said incredulously. "She just gave birth to seven pups, for heaven's sake."

Tyro didn't stop to debate. He scribbled his name on the liability release form and dashed out the door with Sheba tightly in his arms. He'd wrapped her in a blanket to keep her warm.

"Sorry to do this to you, Girl," he muttered and finished loading her in the back seat of the helicopter. He'd landed it in the backfield and kept it running. "We got to find Moriah." He strapped her in tightly.

Sable jumped out of the car that had just peeled into the parking lot. She headed his way. Just as she was about to lift the helicopter, she saw Nettie running toward the craft. Sable glanced back at Tyro for instructions. "Let her in," he'd said.

She leaned over and helped her into the front seat. "Strap in and put these on," she commanded in one short breath. Her accent was thick, but Nettie nodded at each command. "Don't touch nothing. If you have to hold on, use the hand strap." She jutted her head towards the strap above Nettie's head. "Don't look down if you're squeamish." She paused to ensure Nettie was grasping what she was telling her. "No yelling, no screaming, and no puking." She turned back to her controls. If you can handle that, we're good to go." She slapped a barf bag on Nettie's lap as they lifted from the ground.

"One more thing," Tyro added. "You must stay in the helicopter at all cost. He leaned up to make sure Nettie had heard him.

"Got it," she responded to assure him that she understood. Her hands quickly folded into a prayer. He wasn't sure if it was for Moriah, or the fear of flying. Maybe both, he reasoned.

"I gave her some pain medication before you left." She shifted in her seat enough to observe Tyro. He repeatedly petted Sheba on the head. The anguish was prevalent. He loved his dog. She knew he loved Moriah too. "She should be good for another hour or so, depending on the flying," she said, glancing over at the pilot who had swiftly veered the helicopter away from the grassy field.

Tyro lifted the silver shimmery hat he had of Moriah's for Sheba to smell. He was glad he'd held on to it. She slowly lifted her head and sniffed.

Twenty minutes later, Sable set the craft down in an empty field. "This is where we last had a signal. It held steady until two hours ago. We assume her battery died or…" She glanced at Nettie.

"She must have turned it off to keep him from finding it. Moriah charged her phone fully last night, as she does every night," she said. She knew it was risky being there. But there was no way she was going to abandon any hope of finding her friend alive.

Sable nodded. "Remember, you stay put. We don't need to be searching for the both of you," she commanded gruffly.

Tyro backed the motorcycle down the ramp from the back of the helicopter. Once he got Sheba situated in the attached sidecar, he checked to ensure that her belly band was secured. He strapped her in, securing her with support belts that looked like seatbelts. He tucked the blanket snuggly around her.

He held the hat and the torn piece of clothing to her nose again that he—actually Sheba—had found on the island. He knew when she had found it that she had brought it to him because it had Moriah's scent on it. Now, he could only hope that she was able to detect the perpetrator's scent as well. She raised her head as she sniffed into the direction of the wind. She whined and let out a low growl and barked.

"Here." Nettie handed him two pain pills after looking across the rugged, rocky field he was about to travel. She also handed him a savory doggie snack and had him give her a drink of water. "It'll help hold down the nausea from the pills."

Sheba lapped the water from his hand taking the tiny pills down with it. "Good girl." Tyro whispered as he rubbed her behind her ears like Moriah always did. "Let's go get our girl," he said as he started the muffled engine and raced across the field in the direction Sheba had indicated Moriah's scent.

Sable drew her gun as she heard crunching from behind a line of tall trees in the distance. She waved for Nettie to get back into the helicopter and to get down on the floor.

"Sable. Put that thing down 'fore you hurt somebody." A gruff voice called as he marched her way. Quincy clambered from out of the wooded area. He and Detective Smith appeared from upstream twenty yards away.

"The place is swarming with operatives," Detective Smith proclaimed. "If he's here, we'll get him. I only hope we're not too—" He stopped abruptly as his eyes followed Sable's head nod.

"Who... what...?" he questioned, seeing Nettie's wide eyes peering out of the open door of the helicopter. "Her best friend. I'll explain later," Sable said as she waved at her in an irritated manner for her to get back down.

Nettie's cell chimed. Her fingers typed feverishly across the lighted screen in response to the text that flashed across her screen.

U THERE?

"YES. WE'RE COMING TO GET YOU. WHERE R U?" She replied back to Moriah's text. For a long time, there was no response. Ever since Moriah's last ordeal, she'd had anxiety attacks whenever she thought too deeply about how the detectives, the ones who were to have protected her, never came.

Nettie texted the secret code they made up. "WGU" She wanted to assured Moriah that help was on the way. She hoped she remembered that WE GOT U meant that help was definitely on the way.

"Give me that!" Quincy demanded and snatched Nettie's cell away from her. "Are you out of your —"

"Ma'am. Please let us do our job. Do you have any other means of communicating with Ms. Styles?" Sable stared hard at Nettie waiting for her to answer.

"I sent her this text earlier today... before I came with you."

"He knows we're here," Detective Smith said, reading the corresponding messages." He turned and tossed the phone to Sable.

"These are his texts. He's baitin' us," she confirmed, giving the phone back to Smith.

"That is exactly why you should have stayed home," Quincy barked. "It was asinine for you to have brought her," he scowled.

"What ya got now?" Sable asked peering down at the screen in the detective's hand.

"Broken Covert," A voice boomed coming from behind them. Neither the detective nor Sable heard him coming as they spun around, alarmed with weapons trained at the intruder.

"Aww, put your weapons down. He would have killed the both of you and the stray kitten by now if he'd wanted to." He nodded to Nettie as their faces puzzled regarding his remark about a kitten.

"That is exactly why I called my guys in." Quincy glared at Sable and the detective, daring them to say a word. "Incompetent fools. That's my son's life out there."

"That's all you're concern about... is your boy?" Smith smirked. "Yeah, yeah, and the girl too. She knew what she was getting herself into."

"What do you mean?" Nettie charged out of the helicopter. "You think she put herself in this position to be brutally assaulted by a psychopath?" She stepped close to Quincy's face. "Let me tell you one thing—"

"We don't have time for this, little lady," Quincy said, turning his head toward the darkening sky. "You have done enough with your meddling." He headed across the field surrounded by a team of men dressed in combat gear.

"I hope the rain holds off long enough to pick up the trail." He stopped briefly and turned. Pointing his shotgun in Nettie's direction, he barked a command to one of the men with him.

"Get her out of here. Now."

Chapter 39

Tyro's motorbike bounced mercilessly as he barreled across the field. He'd noticed the storm clouds rolling his way. He prayed that he'd find Moriah in time. He had to.

A billion thoughts rumbled in his mind. What if he was too late? What if he lost her? He'd promised he'd protect her. He blamed himself for not being there for her.

Now was not the time to be hard on himself. He pushed the crippling thoughts out of his mind. He had to focus on the task at hand. He had to get to Moriah.

Periodically, he'd glance over at his Shepherd. He knew she was in pain as she whimpered when they rode over a rough patch. But the further they drove, the bumpier the ride had become.

He noticed blood seeping through the blanket wrapped around her. His heart ached. He found himself in a dilemma. His Shepherd could bleed to death. He was torn between the two of them. He'd never forgive himself if something were to happen to her—to either of them.

Sheba was getting weaker. She struggled to lift her head. Her head snapped to the right. Her ears pointed straight up. Her heavy growl told him they were getting closer.

Tyro saw a flash of light coming out of the woods to his distant left. The rain had come suddenly, blocking his vision. He pulled to a stop. He didn't want to leave Sheba unprotected in case it was a trap.

He heard a familiar whistle. He was relieved to see his uncle as he stepped out from the brush.

A burning smell brushed past their noses. Tyro killed the engine and pointed to a contraption to their left. From the distance, it appeared to be a dilapidated house. As they moved closer from out of the trees, the rain pounded harder. They realized it was a good chance it was where Moriah was being held captive. Tyro's adrenaline soared at the very thought of her being in that maniac's possession. If he as much as touched one hair—

He noticed Mario signaling for his team to proceed. It snapped Tyro's mind back to the task at hand. "No. I must go," he insisted.

Mario looked up at the shack. There were no lights burning, only a small stack of smoke wafted through the chimney.

"Are you out of your mind? I'm not letting you go in there alone," Mario said in a low, heavy voice.

"He knows we're here," Mario said. He signaled for his men to circle the house and wait for his command. He looked Tyro in the eye. "This is not about her," Mario insisted. "It's about me. This whole thing has been about me. Your mother's... my sister's death, Moriah's first abduction, and now this. The whole thing has been about revenge. Somehow in his twisted mind, he thinks he's paying me back.

"What?" What do you mean?" Tyro asked as he pulled back on his uncle's arm.

Mario sighed. "Long story and we don't have time for details." He looked Tyro soberly in the eye. "Moriah looks like a girl I dated... I didn't recognize it until after you told me her story and I saw her face to face on the island."

Tyro thought about the fact that Mario had actually met her at his restaurant, but now was not the time to get into that. "The look of fear on her face when she was at your house," he said as if he could read Tyro's mind. "That's when I put the whole thing together. Your mother's death was an accident. He'd planned to kidnap her to get back at me. It was never about the ransom or being fired." Mario was sure of it.

When we were stationed in Tokyo, he accused me of stealing his girlfriend. I thought he'd gotten over it. So, I hired him. I knew he was a top-notch pilot and aircraft mechanic."

Holding Tyro by the shoulders, he looked him sternly in the eye. "I know you mean well; but please, let me... let us handle this." He let go of Tyro and began checking his clip in his weapon. "They're well trained for this." He gave him a stern look. "I can't risk losing you."

Tyro realized what his uncle said made sense. He didn't want to get in the way, and he certainly didn't want to cause things to go wrong either. He thought about it further. Somebody could get hurt because of his pride. He looked back at his Shepherd.

He commanded Sheba to stay put as he pushed his vehicle behind the trees. Two of Mario's men crouched near the door. It was strangely slightly ajar. One of the men threw a rock to hit against the floor inside. They listened for any reaction. Nothing. Mario and a few others crouched up behind them.

Tyro signaled to his uncle that he was going back to his bike when he heard rustling in the woods coming from Sheba's direction. She was growling now. His heart raced as he thought about his Shepherd being in imminent danger. If she leapt from the bike, she would rip herself and bleed out. He'd left her unattended. What if... he shook the notion from his head. "STEADY GIRL. STAY." Tyro commanded rushing to her side. He resented bringing her. He realized he hadn't thought it all the way through. All he knew was Moriah was in trouble. But only Sheba could have led them to her since the signal on Moriah's cell location device diminished several hours ago.

"Well, well, well." The ominous voice called. He stepped out of the brush holding a death grip on Moriah's arm. Sneering in Mario's direction, "If it ain't my old Navy Seals brother," Fletcher teased. "You think you gonna take her away from me again? Oh, no.

410

Not this time. I'd kill her first before I'd let you do that, brother." He flashed to show he held a weapon at her side.

Mario stepped out into the opening ahead of the others.

"Look like your canine ain't gonna make it." Fletcher taunted nodding his head toward the two-car cycle Tyro had ridden.

Tyro looked at the blood soaked blanket. Sheba lay limp. Her head hung lifelessly over the sidecar, her eyes closed.

"I guess you think you gonna take her away from me again, huh?" Fletcher grabbed Moriah's hair and positioned the sharp instrument at her neck. It was dark. Too dark to see exactly what it was.

Tyro's dream flooded back to him. He saw his mother laying still. In his dream, he'd lost the first round. Now the final round, he had a choice.

No way was he going to leave without Moriah. For the first time, he prayed sincerely for God to spare them both. He knew he'd be lost without his Shepherd, but there was no way he could go on without Moriah.

"Tyro, Sheba's bleeding. Get her out of here... Take her to the hospital, please!" Moriah's voice trembled as she pleaded.

"I'm sorry I let you down, Moriah. I promised I'd—"

"Get out of here, or I'll end all of this right now!" Fletcher demanded. He pressed the sharp object into her tighter. She cried out in pain.

"Do as she says! Get Sheba out of here." Mario commanded. "We got this. She's coming back with me. Alive. You have my word." He kept his eyes trained on Fletcher. His rifle aimed for a sure shot.

"All right... okay, I'll take Sheba to get some help." He looked from Moriah to his Shepherd. If Sheba had any chance of surviving, he had no choice. He kept his hands combat ready. He crouched backward to the motorcycle. He backed the cycle out until he was out of sight before turning it to drive forward.

Chapter 40

"This is between me and you, Fletcher. Let the girl go," Mario demanded.

"You want her? You gon' have to take her from me and the only way you gon' do that is if I'm in a body bag." His mouth drooped on one side of his face.

"Why Fletcher? Why her?" He nodded toward Moriah. "Why my sister?" he paused. "Why any of this?" he stalled for time.

Tyro raced the motorcycle across the field toward the helicopter. When he was a half mile away from where he'd left the woman he loved in a life-threating situation, he turned his cycle around and headed back toward her.

He saw movement in the bushes off to his right. Quincy and three other men stepped out in view. His father waved his flashlight to get his attention. "My son, are you—"

"Dad, get Sheba back to the helicopter, now!" His tone was short and urgent. "She's losing too much blood. Tell Nettie to get her back to the clinic. Call ahead, let Dr. Croix—"

"Just what do you think you are doing?" Quincy demanded when Tyro jumped off the bike and headed back in the direction he'd come. "I won't stand for you putting your life in danger needlessly. Now you listen to me—"

"Dad." He stared at his father in his worried, strained eyes. "I need you to do this for me." He looked at Sheba. She was unresponsive, but breathing in small, shallow breaths. He looked to his father who hadn't budged. Tyro peered back toward the shed. It would take him at least five minutes to get back there if he ran. He turned his head in the direction of the helicopter. He walked over to

Sheba, "Hang in there, girl, it might be a rough ride, but I'm going to get you——"

"Are you going to just stand there or get out of my way?" Quincy quipped. He shoved Tyro aside and hopped on the cycle and sped off toward the helicopter.

Tyro ran with all his might to save the woman he loved. He hoped… prayed that he would get there in time. His mind churned with regret. How could he have let his tiff between him and Moriah go on for so long. He knew he should have never let her out of his sight. Why hadn't he forbidden her to go back to that place by herself?

His pain, his regrets, his fear for her life fueled him. His feet barely touched the ground. Again, he found himself speeding through the air like Flash Gordon. He remembered the first time he'd met her; he'd risked his own life to save her. Only this time he knew she was the woman in his dreams. Her face came clearly to him now. He pushed his body forward with lightning speed.

His woman was in trouble and he'd stop at nothing to save her.

Everything was on the line. Tyro didn't have much time. He'd anguished over having to choose between saving Sheba, or the woman he loved. His dream——he dreaded that it had come to fruition. He seethed in anger.

Sneaking up from behind, Tyro swung the heavy branch at Fletcher's head. Dazed from the impact, he spun around and lashed out at Tyro. Tyro drove the branch into his gut causing him to lumber to the ground.

Holding his weapon tighter, he raised his arms and was positioned to swing again. "Tyro, no!" Moriah cried out.

He stopped. His hands held onto the branch in midair. If it hadn't been for Moriah, if he hadn't heard her voice he would have delivered the final blow. Still, at that moment, he waned between obeying her and his regret of not finishing him off.

It was only when Mario had pried the branch from his hands that he realized he'd gone too far. He had been out of control. And that scared him.

Chapter 41

"I'm sorry, there's nothing more to be done," Dr. Croix said in a compassionate tone. He'd come to the animal hospital as soon as he'd gotten the call about Sheba. As if they hadn't heard him the first time he repeated, "We've done all we can. You may see her in a few minutes." He offered this final word of encouragement, gently squeezed Tyro's arm, and excused himself.

Tyro, Moriah, Quincy, and Mario were swiftly escorted back to Sheba's room. She was hooked to an IV secured around her arm with bandage tape.

Her tongue lay to the side, her eyes barely open. She gave no sign that she was aware that they were there.

Sheba was dying.

Tyro sat on her gurney and scooped her up in his arms. He nestled his face to her head. "I'm sorry, girl. I'm so sorry."

Moriah kneeled and began stroking her behind her ear. "Come on, Girly Girl, you can make it." Tears formed in her eyes. The feeling of hopelessness loomed in the air. Looking around the room, she cried out, "We have to hope…pray that she pulls through."

She bowed her head. "Father God, we know you have a heart for mankind and animals too. You said so in your Word." She swiped the tears that ran down her cheek. She looked up at Tyro. Dazed, he held Sheba, his faithful friend in his lap, staring down at her.

Continuing on with her prayer, "Please find it in Your compassion and mercy to help her pull through. I believe it is with the stripes of Jesus that You've healed all sickness, diseases and had conquered death when you raised Him—"

415

"Hog wash!" Quincy's words bellowed in the air interrupting Moriah's prayer. He'd been pacing back and forth, mumbling. His words had been all jumbled together and she really hadn't paid them any mind until now.

He looked from her to Sheba and then back at her again. She hoped he wasn't blaming her for Sheba's predicament.

Guilt gripped her heart. If it hadn't been for her, Sheba wouldn't be in this condition. She lifted herself from the floor. She wanted to get it out in the open, but now was not the time. *Dear Lord, give me the words, the wisdom to handle this situation in the right way. Please God, don't let me say anything that I'll regret.*

She took a deep breath and gingerly approached Quincy. She tenderly reached for his arm. "That animal… did that to you?" Quincy asked just as she was about to speak. His eyes scaled over the cuts and bruises on her arms, face, and neck where Fletcher had just a few hours ago attacked her.

He raked his hand through his hair. "I am sorry you had to go through that. If we had caught that—"

"It's okay, Mr. Simmonds. I survived it, that's what matters." As soon as the words came out of her mouth, she wished she could suck them back in. Reality hung in the air. His wife hadn't survived it and now Sheba's life hung in the balance. Again, she felt the sting of guilt.

She braved to look up into Tyro's face. He must have felt her looking at him as his head raised. His gaze met hers, but only for a moment. His eyes were their normal gray in color, sad, but not blue from anguish. She silently sighed with relief.

She turned her attention back to Quincy. "I'm so sorry about your wife," she whispered. "For all it's worth, she loved you." She braved to hold him by his arms, "You were her only true love." Moriah released his arms and walked over to Mario.

"Your sister would've been proud of how you've helped to hold this family together."

He nodded.

Taking her place back near Sheba, Moriah couldn't contain it any longer. "Dear Lord," she cried out. "Thank You for hearing our prayers."

"Amen." Mario, Tyro, Moriah, and Quincy responded solemnly. Moriah smiled inwardly. They were all on one accord.

Chapter 42

An hour passed since Sheba's emergency surgery to clean out the infection and to re-stitch the sutures that had come undone in the woods. Dr. Croix, Nettie, and several nurses had come in to check on Sheba at various times. They offered beverages as well as their encouragement and support to the family.

Tyro finally had laid her back on her bed after Nettie had convinced him she'd be more comfortable lying flat. Still, he remained by her side.

Two hours later, Tyro awakened after drifting in and out of sleep. Moriah had fallen asleep by his feet. They were hanging over the side of Sheba's bed. He noticed the small area of dried blood at the top of her head. He surmised she must have gashed her head during her struggle. He leaned forward and separated her hair to take a closer look. Although it didn't look deep, it still needed to be cleaned and protected from becoming infected.

He removed his cell from his belt. A few moments later Nettie came in with cotton balls and an antiseptic cleanser spray.

"OW!" Moriah complained.

"Sorry!" Nettie chimed. "Gotta clean this up. You have dried blood all tangled in with your hair. I could do it the easy way, you know." She winked at Tyro and whispered, "I'll be right back once I find me some scissors."

"Oh no you will not cut my hair!" She covered her head with her hands as she struggled to remove herself from the floor. "Are you crazy!" she exclaimed more loudly then she realized.

Sheba must have heard her voice. She licked her lips and whined. She tried to raise her head until Tyro gently massage her back and kept her still. Sheba whined again and sniffed in the air.

"I'll get her something for pain." Nettie swiftly cleared away the supplies she used to help Moriah. "You's lucky she saved your behind, this time. But if you start bleeding again, you're going to the hospital." Nettie hurried out of the room to get the doctor.

Moriah rushed around Tyro and began rubbing her behind her ears. "Girly Girl! I knew you'd pull through! Thank you, Jesus!"

"She's not out of the woods yet." Dr. Croix said bidding for space to examine her. "We're going to have to keep her sedated. That's the only way she has a chance to recuperate."

"Sedated!" Quincy bellowed. He leapt from one of the chairs the staff had provided for them. "How long will she be here... can't we take her home to rest... we can keep her still better than some ole drugs," he barked.

Amused, Dr. Croix looked at the white headed man. His wiry hair now protruded all over his head. Maintaining his professional mannerism, he responded, "If she has any chance at all I suggest only one or two of you stay here at a time.

"What?" Quincy yelled stepping too closely into the doctor's space. "I'm not going any—"

"We must trust her into the hands of the good doctor," Mario said, pulling Quincy to sit back down. He remembered their last encounter when Dr. Croix had politely asked Quincy to leave his facility because of his irrational behavior.

Quincy must have remembered it too. He shook his head but conceded to the doctor's recommendation and took his seat.

Nettie insisted on taking Moriah to the hospital to get her wounds checked out. She hadn't like the way her head was healing. Mario took Quincy to the clinic to see Sheba's puppies. "Seven, huh." Quincy commented. They'd almost forgotten about them. The clinic had found a surrogate Shepherd to nurse them.

Tyro was left alone with Sheba who was now in an induced coma. He repeatedly stroked her head and alongside her body. His mind was in a state of flux. Did he do the right thing? Should he have taken her to find Moriah? He smiled after reading Mario's text that her puppies were doing well.

Several seconds passed before Mario texted again. "She is an amazing woman," he stated. "But I'm not telling you anything you don't already know." His thoughts immediately trailed back to Moriah.

Her love was unselfish. When Sable had seen Tyro and Moriah below in the woods, she landed the helicopter to pick them up.

His eyes swelled with moisture.

Moriah had insisted on holding Sheba the entire flight back. Nettie assured her it was best to let her lie on the floor and to give her space to breathe. If only she was breathing. At the time, he couldn't tell. He remembered feeling lost. He kept his eyes trained on his Shepherd during the entire flight. If only he hadn't brought her there, what if she died? As if Moriah read his thoughts, she had touched his arm. "Pray, Tyro. Pray that she'll make it." He mindlessly rubbed the place she had touched him.

He texted Mario back, "Yeah, I know, if only..." he sent the message just like that.

Chapter 43

After taking out the last of the clutter from moving, Moriah looked around her new home and smiled. For several weeks, she'd spent her days emptying boxes, opening crates, and organizing her home.

She was in her own home, and right on time for Thanksgiving.

She settled on the couch to rest for a few moments. She'd determined as part of her healing, she'd allow herself to dwell only on good thoughts, and good feelings from her past, even if things had changed and people were no longer around. She had learned not to allow it to stop the process of moving on with her life. For those few moments, she settled her thoughts on Sheba. She'd pulled through and was even well enough to have come home. She sighed in relief.

She thought of how she'd been rescued. Tyro. He had been so brave. She appreciated what everyone did, risking their lives to save hers, including Nettie. Of course, she hasn't let her forget that! Every chance she got she'd clip her fingers like scissors toward Moriah's hair. They'd laugh and end up hugging each other. She was indeed a good friend. The best anyone could have.

She thought back over the latest chain of events that had taken place in her life.

"Are you gon' open this or do I have to die from the suspense?"

"What?" Moriah opened her eyes. Nettie towered over her, one hand on her hip; the other shoved the carrier envelope toward her. She had totally forgotten all about it.

Moriah tried doing that neck roll thing again. "You open it since you care so much about it," she told Nettie.

She'd forgotten all about it with everything that had happened. She sighed. Nettie was not letting the matter go. She stood there with one hand on her hip and the other jabbing the envelope in her face. "All right!" she conceded. "I might as well read and see what else I need to add to my prayer list." She glanced up at Nettie. But Nettie paid her no mind. She stood her ground. Moriah sat up and ripped it across the top.

Her eyes scanned over the note that had been clipped to the papers that had been stamped ORIGINALS. She couldn't believe her eyes. She shot up from the couch. "Nettie! Nettie!" she screamed.

"I'm right here, gurl, you don't have to—"

She shook her friend by the shoulders. "I'm getting my Amelia back! She's coming home... Nettie, Amelia's coming home!" Moriah leaped around like a schoolgirl being asked out to the prom by the football captain, but this was better than that. Oh yes, much better!

"Let me see that!" Nettie grabbed the note from her and read out loud.

"Originals," Nettie said, reading the word with emphasis.
My Dearest Moriah,
I'm sorry for allowing this matter to go on for too long. Somehow I wish there was a way to make it up to you. But for now, I hope the contents of these papers will in some way make amends.
Enclosed you will find the original signed affidavit granting you full and unconditional custody of Amelia Rose Smythe.

Moriah couldn't believe her ears. Her eyes had not deceived her.

Nettie continued reading.

"I suspect that this may take a few days than normal to reach you. I had to do some fancy rerouting, if you know what I mean. Petra wasn't so willing to let go. I'm sure you can understand a mother's love.

We hope that the enclosed check for $540,000 will serve as restitution for back pay and damages done.

Also, please note that the check has been endorsed as "payment in full." Upon your signature and cashing this check any monetary disputes between you and TSMA and its owners will be settled. You may wish to see your lawyer regarding this matter before doing so.

One more thing. I hope... pray that you will find it in your heart to forgive... well, you'll see the request for visits to see our granddaughter as written in the affidavit. Please see the photo enclosed.

Best Regards,

The Smythes

"Boy he sure is cautious in choosing his words. Why didn't he just come out and say they were wrong and this is what you get—take it or leave it," Nettie said, doing her infamous head and neck roll.

"For one, you never admit anything in writing. And second of all, he knows that I know full well what *payment in full* means. I've sat through enough litigation to know that I will seek legal counsel and I will also write on the back of the check *without prejudice* before I sign it. That way it's not a done deal."

"Well, you go on with yo' bad self!" Nettie pushed her hand off her friend's shoulder.

A photo of a smiling Amelia sitting in front of Parker and Petra was attached to the papers. A note requesting Moriah to please frame it for Amelia's room with a smiley face was attached.

423

"Aww, that's so cute," Nettie said, referring to the smiley face he'd drawn on the paper.

"Well, after you see your lawyer friend," she said signifying, "what you gon' do with all that money?" she asked seeing that Moriah had ignored her comment about consulting her *lawyer*, Tyro.

Moriah hadn't paid her much attention. She was too busy flipping through the papers.

"No, I don't think I want to go after any more money. After I see a lawyer before signing anything," she lifted the forms up in declaration of her blessing, "most likely I'll set this up in a trust fund for Amelia's college fund, make prudent investments, and allot a monthly stipend from an interest bearing account for her living expenses while in college, or something along those lines."

"Umph! Nettie exclaimed. "She'll be a billionaire by the time she finishes college if you invest it right."

"Yep, that's the plan," she chirped as she pulled Nettie out the door. "Come on, let's go get my Amelia!"

Chapter 44

"God, You are so good!" Moriah bellowed, reaching for the handle to go inside of Dango's Studio. Dango had a few thoughts about Moriah's newest client and she wanted to see what she thought about it. Dango was in the back on the phone with another client. She could hear her going through numerous suggestions from where she stood.

While she waited, she sighed in contentment of her life's recent turn of events. All was well, except her heart ached in one area. Tyro. Still, there was one last thing she needed to do as far as he was concerned, then she would force herself to move on without him. She knew it would be for the best.

Her phone chimed. She smiled when she read Mickey's text that she'd picked Amelia up from her preschool since it was closing early for the day. She reminded her that she would be taking her to Quincy's condo.

Quincy's place! Can you imagine that! Quincy was still a force to be reckoned with, but when it came to Amelia, that little girl had him wrapped around her little finger. He was tickled beyond the stars that Amelia had asked him if she could call him Pop Pop since she already had a Poppy. From that point, he insisted that Moriah call him by his first name. "We are family now," he'd mumbled.

"Somebody's happy!" Dango said, sashaying from out of the back. "Sorry to keep you waiting. I was finishing up on a piece. I made five changes already," she complained. 'I wish more clients were as decisive as you. "Oh well," she waved off, "that's not what you came for!"

Moriah smiled and received her in a warm embrace.

"Come with me. I want to run some things by you." Moriah followed her to the back. She wasn't surprised at the extremely tidy workspace. Everything was in order and neatly stowed in its place as usual. There were no globs of paints, water jars filled with dirty brushes, splatters of colors, or evidence it was an art studio anywhere. If she hadn't known better, she never would have guessed it was Dango's space where she actually did her artwork.

A thought crossed her mind. "Have you heard of an artist by the name of DeBorah? She had... or has a studio by that name."

She pulled up the picture of Laino from the card she had snapped on her phone. "This was taken from a piece she did."

"Let me see that." Dango handed Moriah back her phone. "Send it to me, I'll pull it through a vector file and blow it up." She walked over to her 30-inch computer screen. "Extraordinary!" she exclaimed a few minutes later. She waved for Moriah to come look over her shoulder. "I ran it through a vector file so that I could blow it up. You see these brush strokes?" Dango made intricate strokes with her fingers in down, upward "U" shaped motions along the front of the screen to demonstrate her point. "Very few people have learned to master this technique. Until recently, it had only been taught in Europe. It takes years to perfect it." She turned to face her friend. "DeBorah, you say?"

"Yes, DeBorah's Studios. The "B" is capitalized. At least that's how it's noted on the back of the Christmas card. Apparently the cards were made from the original painting."

"And the painting was done recently?"

"It seems so. It's a painting of Tyro's mother. We're looking for the person who painted it. I'm sure it would mean the world to Quincy if he could acquire it."

"I'm sure." Dango closed the file. "I'm sorry, but I haven't heard of DeBorah... did you say what her last name is?"

426

"No," she sighed. That's one of the issues that make it harder to locate her. Believe me, we've tried every avenue. She's not registered anywhere. We assume it's her pseudonym name. Well, one thing that came out of this, it's given Quincy a new outlook on art. He's subscribed to various art publications. He even does extensive search on the web looking at paintings and different artisans. And don't get me started on his sudden love for museums." Moriah chuckled. "He's been taking Amelia to a museum every chance he gets. She's always loved art." Moriah thought of her box filled with Amelia's collections since she was coordinated enough to hold a crayon. Yep, she'd kept them all "She'll color, draw, and paint for hours if you let her. And now, she has a partner in crime to cheer her on."

"That's so cute. How is the little darling doing? Has she readjusted well?"

"Pretty much. She misses her grandparents, but she'll be able to see them soon." Moriah looked at her watch. "Speaking of the little blessing, I got to get home soon. Quincy will be bringing her back around two."

"Quincy, huh?" She couldn't contain the wicked smile from crossing her face. "You tell Quincy to let me know if he ever wants some company —as mutual friendship and not a date, of course—when he takes his next trip to the museum. I would love to give him some pointers, you know," she teased, batting her eyes in a seductive matter. "Art wise, that is!" she thought she'd better clarify even though she knew Moriah knew that she had only been teasing.

"Well, you know where to reach him. He's there most evenings during the week. You tell him yourself. I ain't going down that route again."

They chuckled and proceeded on with the business for which Moriah came.

"Love it," Moriah said, looking at the proposed changes to the sign for Willie's church, "HOUSE OF REFUGE." The sign was set on a deep purple backdrop and beamed with arrays of gold, yellow, and white graphics. The sun was displayed rising in a glistening orange. Dango recommended doing the tag line: "Where No One is Left Behind" in the same orange. Moriah was pleased. Amazing how that little detail made the cheery sign pop even more.

Willie. Pastor Willie Stubbleton. A smile bubbled up on the inside just thinking about him. When he'd told her he had his own place, she had no idea he meant his own home. Willie had gone home. When Tyro had told her, it did her heart good to know that. He'd called to commission her to do the sign for Willie's church. *God was up to something good,* she thought. After they finalized the details they hurried out the door. She had enough time to meet with another client before dashing home for Amelia.

Chapter 45

Moriah had barely gotten in the house when her cell rang. She smiled as Quincy's white wiry haired picture she'd recently snapped of him showed up on her display. They weren't what you would call "chummy" per se, but things certainly had gotten a whole lot better between them. She knew there was only one reason for that. Amelia. He adored her.

She and Tyro's dad had come a long way. He was still Quincy, and it didn't take much for him to go from zero to one hundred, but she noticed he was much calmer when Amelia was around.

There was no denying it, the little stinker had stolen his heart.

"Hello, Quincy," Moriah chirped.

"Hi, Auntie, it's me. Can I come home now?"

"Of course you can, sweetie. You don't ever have to ask if you can come home." Moriah heard her giggling over the phone and as well as outside her front door. She opened the door.

"Quincy, don't you be teaching her your little *"conniveries*," Moriah said using a word Quincy had made up.

Nettie popped out of the kitchen. "Amelia Rose!"

"Aunt Nettie!" Amelia broke from her auntie's arms and bounded into Nettie's embrace. "Look how big you're getting." She twirled the four-year-old around. The child beamed with pride. "I just made lunch. You hungry?"

Amelia shook her head no. "Mr. Quincy bought me a hamburger."

"He did, did he?" Moriah eyed Quincy who was beaming bright red.

"You're sure you're not hungry? I made your favorite." She sweetly cupped Amelia's chin in her palm. "Grilled cheese with no crust," Nettie said, pulling her into the kitchen.

"Thank you for bringing her home." Moriah tenderly touched his arm. "And thanks again for having your guys move us!"

Quincy stretched his neck to see into the kitchen. "I just want to say goodbye." He fidgeted with a small bag he held in his hand.

Moriah recognized that it had come from a pet store.

"What's this I hear about you giving her one of Sheba's puppies?" Moriah folded her arms across her chest. "And just who do you think is going to take care of *this* puppy. And what about when she stays with her grandparents?"

"We have plenty of help," he quipped.

"That may be so, but—"

His cell chimed.

"I will be there in a minute," Quincy stated. He placed his phone back on his belt clip.

"Is everything okay?" She suspected it was Tyro. Other than speaking with him about the notarized documents Parker and Petra had delivered to her when they granted her full custody, she and Tyro hadn't talked much at all. He never broached the subject of their relationship, or lack thereof. Neither had she.

"May I?" Quincy pointed the bag toward the kitchen.

"Of course you can."

When he returned, he had the biggest grin on his face. It fell to its usual solemn state when he noticed Moriah looking at him.

He walked to the door and turned before he pressed the handle. "I know it is certainly none of my business," he glanced into her face and paused. "And I promised my son that I would stay out of it, but I cannot stand to see him so miserable. It drives me bonkers." His face remained in its usual expressionless pose. "I do not know why he cannot see that you are good for him. You are so much like…"

Quincy stopped midsentence. He rustled his hand through his thick, white mass. "She would have liked you." His red face was evidence he was uncomfortable mentioning his wife. *Imagine that.* Moriah mused within herself about his apparent nervousness.

"Why can't you two—"

"Quincy. Please," Moriah said as respectfully as she could muster.

He shook his head to affirm that she was right. "Well, I sure appreciate you." His words may have been muffled, but she certainly heard what he said.

She contained her surprise and amusement. "Look, I know you mean well, but Tyro has to come to terms with himself. He needs to decide what he wants and what he wants to do. Amelia and I are a packaged deal."

She reached for a small package she'd placed on the table in her foyer. It contained a letter she'd written to Tyro. She apologized for not returning the necklace sooner. She explained it was what she'd tried to give him when they were on his beach. She said nothing about their relationship. She did add a thank you for helping her get Amelia back. She ended her note by stating that for that, she would be forever grateful.

"He knows that! Did he not help you to get her back?" Quincy said interrupting her thoughts as if he could read her mind.

"He knows what?" she questioned. She shook her mind from the fogginess. She'd drifted into deep thought.

"Have a good day. Thank you again for picking her up from the Smythe's."

"You already said that." He opened his mouth to say more but closed it. "Well," he said holding his hand out toward the package. "I do not know why you two will not just kiss, make-up, or something and get it over with." He had held it in long enough. He may have changed in his feelings toward her, but he was still… Quincy.

431

He kept his hand on the door handle. "Don't make a habit out of this." He shook the package her way, opened the door, and closed it behind him.

Moriah leaned her back against the door and smiled. *Did he just thank me? Mmm. He actually appreciates me!* She thought about his words. Exactly what he was referring to she wasn't sure. Maybe for bringing his family together... allowing him to be in Amelia's life... helping his son get out of his despair over the loss of his mother?

He'd also hinted that she reminded him of Laino, although he hadn't come right out and said it. His words hung in her mind. "I knew it would only be a matter of time before that son of mine would man up."

She surmised he was referring to the heated conversation she wasn't supposed to have heard. She was proud of Tyro. He'd put his dad in his place and had given him an ultimatum. She smiled at the thought of it. "Don't think you're giving me a choice between you and her," Tyro had said. "As far as I'm concern, there's no choice. I love her, Dad. It's up to you whether you're going to accept it or not."

She prayed for guidance and left the matter in God's hands.

Chapter 46

Moriah stood outside the building to Tyro's office. She pondered that her townhome was just on the other side of the drawbridge from his penthouse suite on the Riverfront. Still she hadn't heard from him since he helped her with the legal issues regarding Amelia and the check. Neither had she bothered to call him even though she thought about him every day. She sighed thinking about what Quincy had recently told her. "You two just need to kiss and get over it."

Oh how she wished it were that simple.

She tapped lightly on Laino's former office, but got no response. She knocked again, this time a little louder, with more sass. She'd made up her mind what she'd come to do. There was no use prolonging it.

She knew he was in there. Quincy had nodded in this direction when she'd asked if Tyro was around. He also added it was where he'd been spending most of his time.

"There you are," Moriah said solemnly when she opened the door. She hadn't bothered to call ahead. Part of her hoped that he wouldn't be there when she came while the other half of her desperately needed for him to be.

He stood looking out the window. "I came by to thank you for everything." She placed the key to the office she'd been leasing from him on his mother's desk. "I won't be needing this any longer. The office I'm renting in the building near my home will be perfect. It's only a few minutes' walk from Amelia's..." She stopped abruptly when she noticed his seemingly melancholic and unresponsive demeanor. He continued to stare out the window.

"Goodbye, Tyro." She'd done what she came to do. She headed for the door.

"Goodbye? Is that it? Is that all you came to tell me?" He pivoted to face her. "Just like that? Goodbye?" Silence filled the air. "What if I'm not willing to let you go?" His eyes were his normal gray in color although his face showed his anguish. He wasn't despondent after all. She was relieved about that.

"But I won't stand in your way if this is what you want." His gentle but determined tone broke her train of thought. He turned back to the window and let out a deep breath. He stared at the few leaves remaining on the trees. His eyes fell on those scuttling around on the ground beneath in the sporadic gusts of wind.

"I'm tired of feeling like I'm not good enough for you." He jammed his hands in his pockets. "I can't make you——"

"What are you talking about?" She spun around interrupting him. Tears filled her eyes. "How could you not be what any woman would want? If only our circumstances were different."

His head snapped up, her words pierced his heart. He walked over to the desk and stared at the key. He picked it up and coiled his fingers around it as if it were the key to his heart. "My mother told me that love would come one day." He glanced at her. Moriah wondered what he was leading to.

"She warned me I'd have to choose whether to hold on to it or let it go. If it was true love, it would come back to me."

He glanced back at the leaves falling from the tree. "That's what I thought I was doing, Moriah, giving you your space. Isn't that what you wanted? Time?"

She didn't answer. What was she to say? This wasn't what she'd come for, was it? *Is he trying to tell me he loves me?* She shook the notion from her head. How could he? Their last conversation came to her mind. She tightened her lip.

His attention gravitated back to the window. From where she stood, she could see the few remaining leaves swaying in the breeze clinging to the branch for dear life. He seemed to focus on the leaves that had fallen. Some were scuttling around with the wind, others huddled around the trunk of the tree. Seeing them whirl around like that reminded her of her complicated life. *Is that it? Is that what he thinks of me, that my life is too complicated for him? Am I just a pile of leaves that have fallen from a tree?* Her imperfections were what they were. She may not have told him about her niece beforehand, but she'd shared what she'd been through, her pain... at least a good part of it. She'd shown him her true colors... of her own *fall* and just like the trees, through all of it she was still standing.

She spun on her heel and headed toward the door conceding to what she'd already known to be true, it was over between them. He followed behind her and lightly took hold of her hand and closed the door before she'd passed through it. Keeping her hand in his, he kneeled on one knee. He kissed her palm. "Moriah," he pressed his forehead onto the back of her hand and then, he looked up at her. "Please forgive me? I know I said I was sorry for abusing your trust, your feelings toward me for my own selfishness. But I don't think I ever asked you to forgive me."

Moriah weighed her feelings. Her scars ran deep. He'd hurt her. Still she had forgiven him. She thought about what God told her a few months ago when she'd been on his island, she gave a thin smile. "One thing I've learned is that forgiveness is not about the person who hurt me." She tugged for him to stand. She spoke slowly. "Of course I forgive you. I believed you when you said you were sorry. And I really do appreciate you trying to make it right between us, at least on this issue. As I said before, 'trust takes time.'" Her gaze fell from his.

"Please, don't make this any harder than it needs to be." She hadn't meant for it to end this way between them, but it was for the best. He turned around and shuffled papers on the desk. It was obvious he was hiding his disappointment. She watched him stare at nothing in particular. Methodically, his fingers moved to straighten the corners of the papers to line them up. His hand was trembling now. He looked up and met her eyes that were fixed on him. "If you would have come into my life before now…" He paused. "I don't think I could have appreciated you like you deserve."

"And you feel as though you do now?" Her voice quivered.

"We've been through so much together," he reminded her. "Both of us have our own pain; so far we've been able to come through it together. Suddenly his face gleamed with a hint of hope. He stepped toward her again. "Why throw it all away now?"

Her mind remained on the encounter in the chapel. Her stitches had come undone. God had showed her He had always been right there with her. She needed to trust Him.

But Tyro was not God. And she was far from perfect too. In all, there was just as much to gain, as there was to lose. She lowered her eyes. "I can't. If I couldn't trust you with my secrets… my shame…" Her eyes fully closed now to shutter away the memories that threaten to pull her under. "You had to find out about Amelia some way other than me being honest with you. She was the reason I was pressing forward with the appeal." She observed his reaction. "There is so much you don't know about me. I didn't… I can't trust you or anyone with my pain."

"Let me try. With so much out in the open we have a better chance now, if we work at it." He took a deep breath. "Please, hear me out. I should have listened to you the day you came by to explain. I was too busy blaming you, accusing you. I thought… I couldn't get past the suspicion that there was another man in your life, the child's father. At the time, it was the only thing that made sense to me why you had not told me about her. I assumed you were still involved… in love with her father. I was stupid. I was jealous."

His words pulled her inside his point of view. She hadn't thought of it from that perspective. It made sense now, the way he acted, it was no excuse, but she understood his reasoning.

He continued. "When I thought I'd lost you, I knew I would never forgive myself if something happened to you." He touched her arm. She stiffened but didn't pull away. "I've been foolish. I see that now, and I'm not proud of it. I'm just seeing it for what it is. But when that murderer took you I blamed myself. I'd promised to protect you, Moriah. I failed." He beheld her face. Although she believed him, there was something else in her eyes. She was resolved.

"God!" he cried out. "I can't stand to think about what he might have done to you. What he did to my mother. What he did to you the first time."

Moriah's face flexed with indecisiveness. She wanted to get it out in the open. She reasoned she'd feel better. It would be the last of her secrets that stood between them. But she felt so shamed. She swallowed the little courage that tried to rise up, causing it to sink back down into her hidden box. It was a forever secret. She couldn't risk the pain of telling him. Besides, there was no need to. When she walked out of that door, she had no intentions of seeing him again.

And she knew why.

He couldn't possibly want her if he were to find out. It was better to leave well enough alone. She was willing to make the sacrifice now and spare them both the pain bound to erupt later. She was damaged goods. Defiled. He caressed her face. His gentle touch brought her mind back to the present. Tears stung her eyes. She clamped them shut in desperation to keep them from falling. There was no getting around it, she couldn't tell him. She wouldn't.

But for some unexplainable reason, her lips began to move on their own. Before she could pull back what her heart wanted... needed to say, small puffs of breath escaped carrying the forbidden words. They tumbled from her lips.

"I was raped." Her words, barely audible but she could tell by his demeanor he'd heard her. She felt the need to make him understand. "Fletcher raped me."

Chapter 47

Outraged, Tyro tried to contain his reaction. The night when she had told him about Fletcher kidnapping her and taking her to that island, he'd wondered if she had been. And now, he was hearing for himself, it was true. *"Moriah, raped? God!"* he called silently. His heart sank at the reality. He pulled her close and folded himself around her. She needed him, not his reaction. This was not about him, not about how he felt, or the revenge he wanted. It was about Moriah, the woman he cared so much about. The woman he loved. He'd been foolish before with his rash reactions.

He grimaced thinking about the time he'd gone along with his father to have Sable to take Moriah back to that despicable place. He remembered her anxiety attack. He sighed in relief now that they hadn't actually landed there with her. He admitted that at the time, all he had in the forefront of his mind was what she knew about his mother's killer. He hadn't considered how it would affect her to go back there. He had no idea. And if he was totally honest, at the time he hadn't cared. It was yet another thing he wasn't proud of.

"When I left you on my beach that morning, I thought going there would bring answers. I was wrong. The moment I stepped inside that cave and saw what you had lived through, survived, I felt so ashamed of my selfishness. Seeing what you had to endure pierced my heart, Moriah."

He struggled to rein in his turmoil. His anger toward the perpetrator made his blood boil. The disappointment in his own selfish actions toward her, weighed on him so heavily. All of it made his stomach churn. He struggled to subdue it. *Not now!* He got a grip

438

and held on with everything within him. Willie's words burst through his mind. "Vengeance belongs to the Lord. Let Him and the law handle him. God has entrusted her to you. What are you going to do about it? Are you going to step up and do what you got to do to protect her from you?" Tyro remembered being stunned by those words: *protect her from me?* But Willie was right. Now he understood. Until he was able to put his own needs aside... his anger... in order to give her what she needed; if he truly loved her... *No! he seethed inside. I can't let her go. I won't!* He swallowed his pride.

Her eyes slowly rose to meet his. His eyes softened as he gazed into hers, but only for a moment. She recoiled and pulled away. He wanted to be there for her, but his rage, the pull was too much for him.

He hadn't realized she'd slipped from his embrace. His mind churned in consideration. When he realized he was no longer holding her, he reached for her.

"Don't," she pleaded softly. She stepped back further. "Now that you know, can't you see that everything between us has changed? How do you think we can go forward with that hanging over our heads?"

"We start over."

"There's no need to fool ourselves. We know what the issue is, now don't we?" She raised her brows. He didn't answer. He couldn't. She was right.

"Goodbye, Tyro. I pray all the best for you." He let go of her hand.

She moved away. Laying a small black object on the desk next to the keys, she sighed. "It's what the Feds have been looking for."

His eyes glanced over it, then he gazed into her face. She tore her eyes away from his puzzled stare. Hugging her arms she said, "It's the video recording from the helicopter that everybody's been all up in arms about."

Before he could ask, she answered him. "Yes, I had it all the time." The muscles in her face tightened. "I never said that I didn't or that I did have it." She turned from his confused look. "It was my only leverage; I had to keep Fletcher from killing me. He knew I had it."

"How did you get it?" he asked.

"He gave it to me," she sighed. "Long story, but everything Sable and her goonies want to know… what they've been looking for is on this disc." She turned and walked toward the door.

He glanced quickly over at the videodisc. "But why give it to me? Why turn it in now?"

"He's no longer a threat to me or Amelia." She sighed in relief that it was over. He'd be incarcerated for a long time.

"Look at it if you want. Or you can turn it in. Do what you want with it." She studied his demeanor but didn't let it weaken her. "One more thing. I kept a journal… it was my only way of holding on to my sanity…" She studied the floor. "I'd buried it on the island before I was rescued. Everything that happened, what he did, what I did while held against my—"

"Shhh…" He cupped his hand over hers. He stared into her eyes. "I know." He reached and opened the drawer and pulled out a small book. It was weathered on the ridges and smelled of musk and mold, just like the cave she had been contained in.
Her eyes filled with tears and spilled softly down her cheeks. He laid it on the desk when she didn't reach for it.

"Don't worry. I haven't read it." He hadn't wanted to. Now he was glad that he'd chosen not to. He lifted her chin with his finger. "No one has. Sheba led me to where it was buried when she brought me the piece of your clothing that had been torn off." He wiped her tears with his thumbs. He wanted so badly to take her into his arms and sooth all her pain away. He wished to God that such a horrendous act had never happened to her. Not to his mother or anyone.

Reaching for the door handle, she shrugged her shoulders. She hadn't responded to the fact he'd mentioned he'd found her torn skirt.

440

"What's done is done." She cupped her hand over his face, smiled faintly, and closed the door, leaving the journal and the love of her life behind it.

Tyro stared at the closed door. He couldn't believe he let the woman of his dreams, his lifeline, walk out of his life without putting up a fight to keep her. But the truth was, he didn't know how to get past the hatred stirring inside.

He glanced at the videodisc. He was certain it held the answers to many of his questions, maybe some insight into how to help her. He was tempted. But what if it contained something he couldn't handle? He was still working on his rage whenever he thought of Fletcher, what he'd done to his mother and Moriah. Could he handle any more?

He held it in his hand. For a split second, he thought about destroying it like he'd done with the Green Monster. His former partner had taken care of the claims and legal issues that may have occurred the night they met. They were free to move on with their lives, if only they didn't let their disappointments get in their way. Her pain. His too.

He shook his head. The longing for her intensified, but reality took its place. His dream about her had come true. It was her pride, her shame, and the unwillingness to forgive herself that were the flames consuming her. He glanced again at the empty space where she had just stood. He went numb. Moriah had slipped through his grasp in the dream. She'd slipped from his fingers on the night they first met, and now, she'd slipped through the door between them. She was gone. This time it would be for good.

Chapter 48

Moriah lay in bed that evening with Amelia snuggled next to her. They'd settled into their new home and routine with ease. Amelia loved her room, but she was making up for lost snuggle-time. Moriah had missed their snuggles just as much as her niece had. So for tonight they'd make another exception, the same one as every night since she'd been home.

Her mind folded back to her conversation earlier that day with Tyro. It was too painful so she forced her thoughts to skip along. She smiled as she thought about Quincy. Just as she'd suspected he had been eavesdropping on their conversation. Yep, he was up to his old tricks again. But this time, she knew why. She'd been willing to oblige him on the one account. Amelia. The other, well, unless a miracle happened, her relationship with Tyro was a closed deal, just like the closed door he'd been listening through. There would be no reconciling between her and his son. The damage was too great.

A quaint smile crossed her face. When she'd left out of the office from seeing Tyro, she'd walked over to him. He'd pretended he was looking at a painting on the wall.

"You know you can bring… what's the puppy's name again?" she asked. She couldn't remember what Amelia said she would name it although she talked about her all the time.

"Casey B." Quincy tried to contain his enthusiasm, grinning like a schoolboy.

"Well, you can bring Casey B over anytime to visit Amelia. You have my number. Call me. If she's not scheduled for any activities, you're more than welcome to spend some time with her. After all, it is her puppy, right?"

"Uh, right," he responded after clearing his throat.

Before she left, she gave him a surprise peck on the cheek. She had left the office before he had a chance to meddle any further.

Amelia squiggled in her arms, wooing Moriah back from deep thoughts. She lovingly gazed at the sweet child, lulling herself back to sleep. She sighed in appreciation and thanked God for getting her back. It was a few weeks ago when Tyro had reached out to her. Quincy told him about the affidavit. She appreciated his insight regarding the custody. He'd helped her to secure her rights in the event the Smythes had a change of heart. Of course she wouldn't hinder Amelia from visiting them and perhaps spending the weekend sometimes.

Moriah said a "thank You, Jesus," that they had signed the affidavit to relinquish full custody of Amelia to her before everything came to light. She was certain that was all Parker's doing.

She thought of the tremendous love he must have for his wife that he was willing to spend ten to fifteen years in prison. She said a prayer for him, for her, for the both of them.

Her mind stumbled back to Tyro. She sighed. "All right, Lord, I do appreciate him." She twisted her bottom lip and closed her eyes. "Yes, I love him." There. She'd said it. She'd admitted it. She turned and gave Amelia another kiss on the cheek and covered her with the comforter.

More thoughts of Tyro waded in the background. He'd been the one who'd gotten Detective Smith and Sable off her back. He'd threatened to incite charges against them for their wrongful act in the manner in which they'd removed her from his premises. He also threatened to file charges for kidnapping, harassment, and wrongful detainment without an arrest. They knew he was legally well versed with such proceedings.

The man had some very impressive persuasive skills for sure. She wondered if he'd stepped away too soon from practicing law.

Sadness had its way as she thought of him. She gazed back over at her sleeping child. He would have made a great uncle. Dad.

But none of it was her concern anymore. She'd moved on with her life and so had he. She removed the book Amelia had fallen asleep with. It was her favorite. Moriah picked up the book. She smiled back at the big purple elephant and wondered how many times Amelia had read the book.

"You're a very good reader," she remembered telling her earlier. She had Amelia to read her several of the pages. Like any good Mom, she'd pointed to several words out of sequence just to assure that she wasn't reading by memory. Moriah was impressed.

Kissing her on her sweet face, she couldn't help but kiss her again… and again. She'd promised her she could go back to her old school on Monday. Moriah was pleased that her life was getting back to some kind of normalcy. If only…

Chapter 49

Today was Pastor Willie Stubbleton's opening day for his newly established church, House of Refuge. It was the perfect time for celebrating on the Sunday before Thanksgiving. Moriah stopped briefly to take a glimpse at the sign over the entrance. *What a beautiful display and a fitting name for his church,* she thought.

A few minutes before service was to start, Moriah slipped quietly into the back left row. She settled Amelia next to her. She was pleased to see the 300-seat capacity was mostly filled. She'd done an okay job marketing... getting the word out to the community, as Pastor Willie had redirected her choice of words in their initial discussion.

She was glad she was able to contribute something to the cause, especially since Tyro had insisted on paying for the sign.

Her niece pointed to the front. "Auntie, is that the man on your phone?"

"What man, honey?" She set her purse beside her and followed the direction to where Amelia's little finger was pointing.

Tyro was seated on the far left in the second row from the front. He stood to shake Pastor Willie's hand. Moriah's heart stilled at the very sight of him. It was unbelievable for him to be even more gorgeous than when she'd last seen him. Or was it that she missed him so?

She peeled her eyes away and took in the view of her surroundings. Willie and Ethel had done a remarkable job converting the old Sultry Sin Supper Club—former downtown theatre on Second and Orange—into a vibrant inner city church.

"Look Auntie, he's coming over here."

"Shhh, darling. We have to use our indoor—"

"Well, who is this adorable young lady we have here?"

"She's my auntie," Amelia said with the biggest smile.

"Mmm," Tyro leaned back with his fingers cupped over his chin. He stooped to her eye level. "Well, yes, your auntie is very cute, but actually, I was talking about you." He tickled her nose with his finger.

"Are you going to kiss him, Auntie, like you do his picture every night before—"

"Sweetie. That is not something you should be saying to someone you've just met."

Amelia retreated behind her aunt's back as far as she could fit. She peeked out, not wanting to miss anything that was happening.

"You're looking great as always, Moriah."

"Thanks. You don't look so bad yourself." Her gaze fluttered off into the far distance. "I think they're about to get started." She nodded toward the front.

"Oh, yeah." He stood. Gazing at the empty seat next to her, he raised his finger. "You mind if I—"

"Tyro, please. Maybe—" he turned and headed back to the front before she could finish speaking. She wanted so badly to run after him. She wanted him to hold her and promise her that everything would be okay between them, but she couldn't. She wouldn't.

She shook it off and turned her attention to the preliminaries that were about to begin.

A young couple, in their early twenties approached Moriah. The woman extended her hand and introduced herself as Pastor Willie's daughter and also introduced her husband. They were the Children's Church and Youth Associates. Moriah asked Amelia if she'd like to go to the children's area where they had service and activities for kids. Amelia squeezed her aunt's neck before hopping down and skipping along with the other children being gathered to join them.

She turned her attention back up front and was mindful not to look in Tyro's direction. She felt a pang of guilt for being so rude and cutting him off like that, but being there with him would have only made her heart ache even worse. They would leave at the end of service and be distant. She wasn't up to having salt poured into her wound.

After the opening prayer, the praise team, which consisted of Pastor Willie's wife, a few members from his former church, and a homeless gentleman whose apparel told of his state of being. Willie had befriended him while he was in his own time of living on the streets of Wilmington. But the man had the biggest toothless grin that would warm any heart. She thought it was a nice touch that the pastor had allowed each of them to give their testimonies before praise and worship started. It was a nice segue to understand their praise.

Now, as the First lady put it, "it's time to get your own praise on!"

Just as the music started, the church doors burst open and an influx of twenty or more people poured in. Some of them sat in the far back, as she had, while others marched their way up the aisle to sit as close to the front as possible.

One of the ladies that sat directly in front of her turned and smiled at her. "Is this your first time hearing Pastor Willie?" Moriah responded with a slight nod. "You're in for a real treat. He's a fiery preacher and I've been a member, well, I have been a member of his old church for over five years."

Moriah didn't know what to say. She was taught not to talk in church during service. She smiled politely and mouthed sweetly a thank you to the woman. The woman got the hint and shifted herself back to face the front. She bobbled her head and said something derogatory to the woman that came in with her. Moriah had offended her.

She didn't let that move her; although she was grateful when the praise team encouraged everyone to stand to his or her feet. As the worshipper said, "It's time to get your praise on!" Moriah hopped to her feet. It felt good being in the House of the Lord, again.

Chapter 50

During the pastor's sermon he began giving his testimony. He asked the people to be patient with him, God was going somewhere with it. God had restored his family, his passion for ministry, and his church. His wife had never given up on him. She'd held all night vigils, fasted, and prayed for his protection and restoration to his family for over twelve years. She let out a hearty "hallelujah!" and jumped to her feet and did a happy dance. The congregation exploded in praise.

Moments later, she retook her seat on the right front row. She straightened her Sunday hat and wiped the tears that flowed freely down her face. They were tears of joy and jubilation.

Moriah was happy for what God had done in their family. She thought of Tyro. Her eyes shifted away quickly. Her heart ached. If she had known he was going to be there, she would have had second thoughts about coming. But as she thought further about it, she wouldn't have missed Willie's opening day for anything in the world, including having her heart ripped open at the sight of Tyro.

She then wondered if God would work the same miracle in her life. She recognized that God wasn't the issue. He never is.

Moriah listened intently to every word Pastor Willie said.

He continued on with his testimony. "It took me twelve years to realize what the problem was. I wasn't running away from life. I wasn't running away from my church, my wife, or my child." The evidence of his pain trembled in his voice. "I was running away from God's Righteousness to worship my own self-righteousness. I thought

I had a right to be offended at God. I thought I could maintain my stance. I said to God, 'After all I've done, the fasting, praying, baptizing, marrying, funerals, baby dedications, and visiting the sick even when I was sick myself.

'Sometimes I was tired in my bones, yet I pressed on, and You still let them take the church right from under me?'"

Pastor Willie slapped the podium as he made his next point. For twelve long, unnecessarily hard years, I stood on my own stance, my own righteous indignation against my offenders, and against God."

He shook his head and gazed out into the congregation. "The truth is, I walked away from it all because I didn't stand in the power of His Might, but on my own stupid, self-righteous, selfish pride."

Moriah sat straight. She'd asked similar things about her own situation. Her mind race back to her own words she breathed when she'd cried out to God in the chapel. As clear as a mirror wiped clean from a steamy shower, her words stared back at her.

"I've been faithful... How could You...? I thought You loved me—God, where were you?"

She had accused God for the wrong that had been done to her.

Was she being self-righteous? Her heart shuddered at the mere thought of it. She tucked the thought away until she could deal with it later. She wondered about her own life. What had she walked away from?

Tyro came to mind. Was that it? Was that part of being self-righteous? She didn't want to be with him because she couldn't... wouldn't forgive him, yet she wanted God to forgive her?

"But this doesn't have to be you." The Pastor's voice broke through her thoughts. "Don't let the devil fool you. Don't let your deceitful heart fool you. First John chapter one, verse eight through ten says:

If we say that we have no sin, we deceive ourselves, and the truth is not in us. If we confess our sins, he is faithful and just to forgive us our sins, and to cleanse us from all unrighteousness. If we say we have not sinned, we make him a liar, and his word is not in us.

He walked out in front of the congregation.

"I stand before you today, my friends, in the presence of God and confess before you all that I have sinned."

Sudden gasps of surprise erupted from the congregation.

Moriah drew in her breath. Not because of the pastor's shortcomings, but because of her own sin. As she listened to his confession, she believed he was sincere. She considered Tyro's apologies. They meant something to her, but they weren't enough for her to get past it and move on in their relationship. Well, she forgave him as much as she thought she could. But the forgetting part was another issue. That was the one thing she was brutally honest with herself about. She wanted to forgive but couldn't forget. Or was it she wanted to forget but couldn't forgive? Her thoughts became jumbled.

She felt God nudging her. *Let it go, all of it. Forgive completely, unconditionally just as I have forgiven you, Moriah.* She recognized His voice. She remembered the encounter she'd had at the chapel. *Lord, I have forgiven, haven't I?*

Although it was a struggle, she finally was able to focus her attention back to Pastor Willie. He was standing in front of Tyro. Tyro had come to the front. She'd missed that part of the service; her mind had wandered away.

Disappointed that she had no idea what was going on and why he was on his knees, she kept her mind on what was going on with him, looking for some clue of why he was the center of everyone's attention.

She wished now the girl in front of her would whisper something to her friend. Say something, anything, to give her a clue of what was going on. But she only heard her express interest in having a man like

451

that and that she didn't see a ring on his finger. Moriah rolled her eyes as she watched the woman pat her hair into place, as if that would make him notice her.

Chapter 51

Pastor Willie's hand remained on Tyro's shoulder. His other hand rested on his head. When he finished praying for him, he helped him to his feet. Tyro discretely wiped his eyes while his back was still toward the congregation. He squared his shoulders, turned, and walked back to his seat. She couldn't help but recognize the joy, the peace, the expression of feeling free that shone from his face.

He didn't look her way. In fact, he hadn't looked anyone's way. It was as if he was giving his undivided attention to what was going on inside of him, she surmised.

Pastor Willie extended his hands outward. "When you've been forgiven, God does not want you to live in shame of what you've done. Should there be remorse, yes. Understanding that your actions will have consequences, yes."

He wiped his own eyes now. "I needlessly missed watching my daughter grow up. I brought her pain and shame the times she'd run across me when I was living on the street." He paused to remove a handkerchief from his pocket and placed it back when he was done with it.

He looked out over the congregation. "But God is rich in mercy and grace, He is always perfect in His timing." His eyes settled on Moriah. She shifted in her seat. *Is he talking to me? How does he know?* Her eyes fell. She smoothed down the front of her dress with the palms of her hands. *I've never told him. I've never told anyone. Not even Nettie knows.*

She lifted her head and held the pastor's loving gaze. He smiled tenderly. She felt something tugging at her heart, compelling her to open up. Face it. She couldn't undo what had been done. In order for her to realize her own freedom, she would have to put the shame of her life aside. She could no longer hide behind the wall of it and expect to move on, to be happy. Free.

Pastor Willie stood back at the podium. "Come all that are heavy laden. Let Jesus give you rest just like our brother Tyro has done."

Her eyes peeled away from the pulpit. She wet her lips. She swallowed hard but the lump in her throat wouldn't disappear. She knew God moved on Willie in the prophetic. It was years later after she'd first met him that she found this to be true. It was Christmas Eve and temperatures had plummeted to the low teens that evening. She saw a homeless man sitting on the curb. He fixed his eyes on her as if he was waiting for her. "Is this the one?" he had mumbled to himself.

He told her his name was Willie. He said that the Lord had been trying to tell her something.

When he refused her offer to buy him something to eat, she gave him a hundred-dollar bill, hoping it would help his situation, at least for the next few nights. She insisted on taking him to a shelter. Thinking back, he probably only agreed to get in her car so that he could tell her what the Lord wanted her to know.

He'd warned her then her world would soon be turned upside down. He urged her to take heed, to surrender her life and completely depend on God. She ignored him. She couldn't imagine how such a thing would ever be possible. She'd been attending church often. She prayed. She didn't remember God telling her anything like that. And besides, things were going extremely well for her. She was at the top of her game.

She remembered now how her heart burned within her to take heed. Still, she paid him no mind. Why should she? Her career was at its peak, and she was making more money than she'd ever imagined.

She'd just left the hospital from seeing her newborn niece and she was in high spirits. She wasn't going to let some homeless man spoil her joy. It was four years later when she realized how right he was. Her life had indeed been turned completely upside down.

She focused her attention up front. Pastor Willie had just called another member from the congregation to come forward. He was moving in the prophetic. The woman was nodding her head to whatever she was being told. Moriah watched as the woman bowed over, wailing in grief. He signaled for his wife to lay hands on the woman and pray through with her.

Willie looked Moriah's way. Their eyes locked. Moriah's heart thumped rapidly. *God, you told him?* She bowed her head, avoiding eye contact. The disgusting, degrading thought flashed in her mind. The whole scene was as real as if she were still there. She breathed in shallow snatches. Her head began to spin.

She remembered the video recorder Fletcher had removed from the cabin of the helicopter. One of his multiple personalities, the kind, gentler, and compassionate one gave it to her after he'd cut her free from the cot she'd been tied to. "Quick," he'd urged. "Hide it so he won't know you have it."

He'd told her to keep it in a safe place, and trust no one with it. She remembered the kind voice also telling her it would save her life one day. She recognized it had been this personality who was the most reasonable one. The chance to survive had presented itself. It was the only way. She coaxed him to get in the helicopter, to go get help. She promised to wait for him. She urged him to hurry.

She knew the helicopter had been doused with fuel. She'd watched him do it just several hours ago. Fletcher had told her earlier that she would never get off of that island alive. "There'd be no way to get away from him."

She tried to push the horrible scene out of her mind, but she couldn't. She had to face it. She could no longer hide from the truth if she wanted to be free of it. Her mind tumbled back to watching Fletcher climb in the helicopter. It took off several feet in the air before bursting into flames. It hovered and sputtered in the air for seemingly a long time before it finally crashed into the ocean. She heard him screaming for her to help him. She watched him thrash around engulfed in flames. He kicked repeatedly on the door trying to get it open. But she had been the one who had removed the pin so it wouldn't open once closed. He couldn't escape. And no, she didn't even try to help him. She didn't want to. She wasn't going to. She remembered standing there filming the whole scene. She could still hear his cries for help; smell his burning flesh. She remembered wanting him to die. *Yes! I wanted him dead for what he had done to me!*

"Someone here is dealing with shame." A hush swept over the congregation. Moriah's mind snapped back to the present. The pastor continued, "Someone here is dealing with pride. Shame is pride." He paused to allow the words to settle in. "God hasn't shared the particulars with me and it's really none of our business." His eyes drifted back to Moriah. "He just let me know that there is someone here whose pride has them all bound up. God wants you to know that He loves you. And the truth is, you have to come to grips with that. You must realize that your sins have been thrown into the sea of forgetfulness. If you've asked God to forgive you and you meant it, then you're forgiven. It's only you who have not given yourself the permission to be forgiven. Let it go. Let go of your pride, the guilt, and the shame of what you've done. Let His Word wash you, renew your mind, and cleanse your soul."

Moriah heard the keyboard playing in the background. She felt faint. Her conscience was getting the best of her now. The sin of her past had caught up to her. She was ashamed. But he's not dead. I didn't kill him. *But you wanted to. You thought you had.* Her inner self reminded her. I've asked God to forgive me. She argued with herself.

If she didn't do something about her guilt, her shameful secret, it would overcome her. *But God, You said that we're more than overcomers. Help me. What should I do?*

"Until you fall into the unconditional loving arms of your Heavenly Father, the burden will consume you. It will sabotage,

456

destroy you and everything God has planned for you. No my friend, it's not God destroying you. It's not the devil. It's you. Forgive yourself." His eyes found hers again. "Forgive yourself and be free."

The pianist began playing a soft tune. A tightness rose up in her throat. She felt the grip of death, and torture. *God, help me. I want to forgive. I want to…*

"Why don't you come… come to the altar and lay your burdens down? Refuse to drink of the devil's poison any longer." His voice was assuring, and comforting. "God has so much more for you, but you can't receive what He has if you insist on holding on to your pain, your guilt, your shame, and unforgiveness."

A few people meandered to the altar. "Repent of this sin," Pastor continued. "Don't let it take you to rock bottom. Turn your burden over to Jesus before you're devastated and feel hopeless like I was. For twelve years I lived like that. For what, because folks did me wrong and stole every penny I had?" He shook his head. "No, you don't have to wait until you get to your lowest point like I did. Come now while God is pulling on your heartstrings. I know you feel Him."

Moriah hadn't realized that she was on her feet and had stepped out into the aisle. Within a split second she thought of her options. She shifted her eyes toward the door. It was only a few feet away. She could slip through it without being noticed. Except God was pulling her in the opposite direction.

She looked up at the front. She didn't see Tyro. Her eyes raced around the room. She couldn't spot him anywhere. She became anxious. *Where is he?*

Where. Are. You? Again, she heard the undeniable voice inside of her. She knew what He meant. Would she rebel? Did she feel as though she had a right to not let it go?

Her heart fluttered. She knew she couldn't stay in the condition that she was in. She knew what she had to do. Bowing her head, subconsciously, she moved forward. Her arms lifted spontaneously toward her Heavenly Father. Her lips quivered as her words tumbled over each other, echoing from her soul.

She'd reached the front but hadn't remembered getting there. She stood frozen. Her eyes settled on the back of a man's head full of sandy hair. He was bowed completely over, his face in his hands. His shoulders shook uncontrollably. She recognized it was Tyro. She was surprised to see him in such a state. Others were kneeling amongst him, some prostrated across the altar. All were crying out to God for forgiveness.

She realized that it was her heart that had moved her forward. She fell to her knees and surrendered everything completely to the Lord.

Chapter 52

Several minutes ago when Pastor Willie was giving his final invitation to come to Jesus, Tyro had also been wrestling with his own inner turmoil.

"If you're feeling like you've got a burden on your back and no matter how hard you've tried, you can't seem to lay it down. Or maybe you have, but the temptation has been too great and you find yourself picking it right back up. You lay it down only to pick it up over and over again."

Tyro's eyes were closed. His mind was grasping to hold on to the peace and serenity he felt when he'd come to the altar earlier. Only now he was feeling heavy inside. He couldn't concentrate on what the pastor was saying and neither could he ignore his thoughts, the feelings of guilt, pain, and bewilderment swirling around on the inside of him.

He thought about his recent actions. How had he been so willing... so ready to strike—to kill at the first opportunity? Didn't his mother teach him that God hated revenge?

His jaws tightened. He thought about his mother. He imagined her struggling, fighting for her life. He vividly remembered the pool of blood she'd lain in. He could still see her face as she struggled to survive.

Wasn't he justified in his actions for revenge? After all, the opportunity had presented itself. At that moment, he'd tuned out what Pastor Willie was saying. Still, he felt the tug on his heart to go forward.

Repent. The word resounded again in his ear. He looked up. He couldn't tell if the pastor had said it or if it was his own conscience.

Repent. He'd heard it again, this time it was louder. He couldn't deny it. Nor, could he ignore it.

He glanced up to the front. He saw the pastor's mouth moving, but it took a while for the words to sink in. It was like he was far away, in a tunnel. The pastor's hands remained outstretched to the congregation, giving the call to come to Jesus.

He wondered what was going on. *God, is that You?* Tyro waited for an answer. But there was nothing. He turned his attention to the pastor.

He was looking over his congregation and had paused. He gestured with his arms. "I'm going to offer the invitation again. I know there's somebody the Lord is speaking to specifically. "Will you come today, give your life to Him?"

Reading from the King James in the book of Matthew chapter eleven, verses twenty-eight and twenty-nine, the pastor said, "Jesus said, '*Come unto me, all ye that labour and are heavy laden, and I will give you rest. Take my yoke upon you, and learn of me; for I am meek and lowly in heart; and ye shall find rest unto your souls.*"

He remembered hearing that verse before. It may not have been put quite like that, but he was familiar with it and he understood what it meant. He wondered if God would forgive him. He'd blamed God. He'd accused Him of letting his mother die. He'd turned his back on God. *Will God forgive me for doing that?*

"I was there once, consumed in my own pain," the pastor began. "I was so full of hate, hurt and disappointment that I isolated myself from society, my family." He paused. "I had even turned my back on God."

What? Tyro's head shot up. *Willie? Turned his back on God?* He listened more closely giving him his full attention.

The pastor looked at his wife and gave her a loving smile. "I thank God for grace."

460

Turning back to the audience, he picked up where he'd left off. "So, you see my friends, no matter where you've been or what you've done, God is calling you now. He's giving you a chance to get it right. Give your burdens to the Lord: Every hurt, all your pain, failures, and disappointments. Let Him throw your sins as far as the east is from the west into the great sea of forgetfulness. Once you turn your burdens over to Him, He won't remember them anymore. So, I'm asking you, why should you continue to carry your burdens?"

He walked back up to the altar and raised his arms. "You know whether it's you the Lord is speaking to. Right now, you're feeling uneasy. Your heart's pounding like it's going to beat right out of your chest. Your palms may even be sweaty."

Tyro's heart was pounding. His mind wandered back to Fletcher. He liked the way he'd felt when he had hit him, although he hadn't intended to strike him so hard. Or had he? The satisfaction he felt seeing the perpetrator, the monster who'd mutilated his mother and left her to die from his ruthless act. Yes, he felt justified. His vein bulged in his neck. He felt like bolting to his feet. He wanted to shout it out to the whole world. *That maniac got just what he deserved.* And if he had his way about it... The overwhelming feeling, the urge he had when he'd wanted to hurt Fletcher burst through his mind. Just that quickly, the nasty feeling had crept up inside of him. He thought about when he was in the woods standing over the guy with his ready-made weapon.

The feeling, the impulse that had swept over him back in the woods. The hate, anger, and need of revenge burst out of him like a rabid beast. He wanted to kill him. At the time, he hadn't cared. Fletcher had taken his mother away from him. And once he knew what he'd done to Moriah, he felt justified for having the urge, the unstoppable force that drove him to want to kill him. It had been festering in him since the day he'd found his mother brutally stabbed. This hate had consumed him... his life... his peace, and his better judgment and feelings about Moriah. About everything. He was angry with God. God hadn't stopped that savage beast from killing his mother. Neither had God stopped him from hurting Moriah. Why should He stop him from his revenge?

He gritted his teeth. *I want to kill him!* His fist balled until his knuckles turned white.

He hadn't realized how much his thoughts were raging inside of him until Pastor Willie placed his hand on his shoulder. Tyro looked up. Anger shot from his eyes.

Pastor Willie sat next to him and spoke slowly and low enough for only him to hear. "Let it go, man. Give it to God. Whatever is eating at you will consume you. It will overpower your better judgment. To harbor hate in one's heart, to want to kill someone is from the heart and mind of a murderer."

What? He wanted to shout out. *You calling me a murderer?*

He was so consumed in his thoughts, he didn't notice when Willie removed himself from his side.

A gnawing scratched at his inner being. He tried to shake it off. It intensified until it rose into a lump in his throat. The words *murderer... hater,* pounded inside his head like thunder and lightning.

He felt the tug in his heart to yield to God. The thunder clashed louder. "This burden is too heavy for you." He remembered Willie's words. He knew the preacher was right. His heart convicted him. He wanted to hold on to his *right* to hate; yet at the same time, he felt smothered by it. He couldn't breathe.

Suddenly, by divine intervention, he realized he was at a crossroads. If he didn't deal with it right then and there, all the hate he felt, the guilt and pain that consumed him would overtake him. He would become just as much of a monster as his mother's killer. He needed God's forgiveness. He wanted it. He stumbled to the front and fell to his knees.

The rage built up inside of him was ready to blow. The pastor laid a calming hand on his head and began to pray. It was as if the Lord had reached down and touched him Himself. "That's right, my friend, give it all to the Lord."

Tyro wanted to surrender. Doubt tried to seize his mind, but he was tired of feeling like he'd lost control. He realized how deeply he needed the Savior. He bowed his face to the ground and covered his head with his hands. His fury gushed out like the rushing of mighty waters. His cries were heard in the heavens and God began filling him with His all-consuming light where darkness had once reigned.

Chapter 53

It was the Wednesday evening before Thanksgiving. Tyro had his own idea for holiday festivities. Feasting with family and friends at Mario's wasn't part of his plan. He'd spent it alone with his Shepherd and her pups. His door chimed. He sipped his coffee having no intentions of answering it. The door chimed again. He could tell by the way his bell rang that it wasn't who he'd hoped it would be. He couldn't quite describe it, but when Moriah rang the bell, it sounded… different. It had more of a singsong, cheery jingle to it. Maybe it was just his imagination. But he suspected whoever it was, that it wasn't her. It chimed again.

Reluctantly, he answered it. He was right.

"I thought I was being ignored," Sable said, stepping inside the room before being invited. She glanced back over her shoulder at Tyro. "You alone, huh? Thought I'd find everybody here." She considered his solemn expression. "Oh." She waved a package in his direction. "Thought I'd catch you good folks here. Got some updates—"

"They're at Mario's restaurant on the Riverfront," he said abruptly without saying anything further. He stood at the door and kept his hand pressed down on the handle. He wasn't up for any company. She was the last person he wanted to talk to right now, although he tried to hide his disappointment. He was kind of expecting… hoping… although he had no valid reason to believe she'd come. She wanted no part of him. She'd made that clear in the way she acted toward him Sunday.

Sable wished him a happy Thanksgiving and started to leave. "I'll just hop on over there." She patted him on the arm. "They can fill you in later."

Suddenly, an idea popped in his head. He quickly closed the door and rushed toward his desk. He turned his head over his shoulder and asked if she'd do him a favor.

In a hurry, he tore off a piece of paper and scribbled a few lines. He sealed it in one of the envelopes from the greeting cards Moriah had left behind.

He reached in his desk and removed a bundle of something wrapped in tissue paper and set the note on top of it. "Would you please give this to Miss Styles, if you don't mind?" He handed it to her like it was one of his prized art projects from elementary school.

When a strange look crossed over Sable's face, he nodded to Sheba who was in her whelping pen by the fireplace nursing her pups. A grin crossed her face. "Proud Papa, huh?"

He nodded in response.

"I know. It's difficult to leave them when they're so young. How many?"

"Seven." He answered as politely as he could without extending an invitation for more annoying questions.

As if right on cue, Sheba slowly lifted herself up, careful not to step on her puppies and gingerly walked out of the room. When Sable heard the sound of a flushing toilet, a sudden gush of water running and Sheba coming back around the corner, her face puzzled in amusement. "Is that...? Did she...? Oh, I got to see this!"

"Go right ahead," he offered. But the detective had already turned the corner by the time he finished speaking.

"Would you look at that!" She jutted her head toward Sheba's bathroom. "You did all this yourself?"

He nodded. The proud grin quickly faded. Moriah hadn't seen it completed. She would have been impressed. He followed Sable to the door.

"I'll see what I can do." She held up the note. His shoulders dropped and he sighed.

"Relax, I'll see that *she* gets it," she commented and watched his demeanor lighten.

*

Before leaving his condo, Tyro ensured Sheba had everything she needed. A buddy of his just happened to stop by and agreed to sit with her. Tyro instructed him to give him a call right away if anything were to come up.

He'd been pacing back and forth for over an hour since he'd reached his destination. It was only a short span that he'd been trekking in front of the bench he used to meet Willie at on the Riverfront. He stopped a few times to glance at his watch before observing the perfectly shaped sphere hanging low in the starless night.

He glanced at his watch three times within a minute's time. It was already thirty minutes past the time that he said he'd wait in the note Sable was to have delivered. Could he assume that Moriah didn't want to come since she hadn't by the appointed time? He understood if she didn't.

Well, he wouldn't like it, but still it was her choice. He'd written that in the note too. He wondered if he should have left that part out. He hoped that he hadn't given her an excuse, a reason not to come.

Someone whizzed past him on a bike causing his mind to surface back to the present. Ignoring the fact that he'd just done so, he checked his watch again. He ruffled his fingers through his hair and continued to pace.

His mind wandered onto the dream he'd had that morning. It comforted him. Thinking of it compelled him to wait a little while longer. He wanted to. An hour had gone by. He checked the time again. He checked his cell and his smart watch for any messages. Nothing.

He thought again about the note he'd sent by Sable. *Had Sable forgotten to give it to her?* He sat on the bench where he used to find Willie when he lived on the street. He pondered on the dream he had of his mother that morning. She was smiling. He remembered the peace emanating from her whole being. She glistened with a joy he longed to have.

He was drawn toward her. He'd wanted to hug her even if it would have been just for a moment. In a loving gesture, she had raised her hand for him to stop. She then pointed behind him. Peace washed over him as an overwhelming feeling of love passed from her fingers and brushed past him. An explosion of happiness coursed through him like lightning. He began to radiate with everything he was feeling, seeing, experiencing. It was like the feeling he'd had Sunday during service. It was then that he'd released the murkiness, the need for revenge, and his hatred toward the Lord.

He realized he needed to forgive. He thought it was interesting the way dreams sometimes worked. In this particular dream, he knew he was dreaming. Maybe that's why he heard Moriah's voice interjecting that forgiveness was for him. As he stood there, he knew the Savior was with him, just as He was also there with his mother.

He pivoted to trace where her finger pointed. Somehow he knew that he was to turn around and go back. He didn't want to. Every fiber of his being wanted to be where his mother was.

He'd heard sweet singing behind him. It was Moriah. He turned and looked but didn't see her. Still, he knew the voice.

He was torn.

Was he to go with his mother even though she'd forbidden him, or should he follow the singing? He turned back to glance at his mother. She was walking away. Her gown glowed with light as if adorned with rays from the sun. She held on to her Savior's hand. He was guiding her. Tyro watched as they disappeared, engulfed in a splendor of joy. It was a joy that gave him peace, comfort. As the dream ended, he knew what he was to do.

A gentle breeze caressing over him helped his mind to settle back to the moment. He breathed easily. He tapped his foot and kept himself occupied with positive thoughts. Confusion, guilt, and doubt tugged at his emotions, but he refused to let his mind wane. He allowed the negative feelings to blow away with the evening wind.

Remembering the lesson Willie had taught on Wednesday at Bible Study, he was grateful for his new lease on life. Repentance. Forgiveness. Freedom.

He realized he had a long road ahead of him. He'd have to work at giving things over to God and not be so quick to take matters into his own hands. He'd spent the past few days, reading passages Willie had recommended. He also spent a lot of time praying. Sending that note to Moriah like that was risky. It could backfire on him and set them beyond any possibility of mending their relationship.

It was a chance he was willing to take. Whether she came or not, he did what felt right. Whatever the outcome, he knew he had to trust God. Gazing into the silent and cloudless sky, he assured himself that he'd made the right decision not to go to Mario's for dinner that evening. He knew Moriah would be there. He didn't feel like going through the motions, forcing himself to be polite, and pretending that they were getting along while in the company of others.

He could only hope that his newfound faith and relationship with God would guide him to his destiny.

Chapter 54

Moriah hadn't eaten much. She tried, but she was too jumbled up inside. Why had she been so unkind to Tyro? What would it have hurt for him to sit next to her Sunday? She knew why and there was no need to go down that road again. Self-righteousness. Okay. She couldn't ignore it. The word had been coming up in her spirit since Sunday service. She didn't feel condemned, but she was wise enough to recognize when God was trying to show her something.

A few days ago, when the reality had set in that she indeed had been so, she was shocked. *Me... self-righteous?* She finally had swallowed her pride and recognized her Heavenly Father wanted to expel this stronghold from her heart, her soul, and free her from her self-destructive behavior because of it. She willingly yielded to His guidance but not without resistance. She had been just as wrong as Tyro.

"Are you all right?" Mario asked, bringing her thoughts back to the present. She'd been pushing her food around her plate. The lamb, sweet potatoes, peppered zucchini and squash medley, along with other items looked like a pre-school art project. She hadn't realized she'd been making such a mess. "Sorry." She gave a tight smile.

Mario and Roy had collaborated and prepared the perfect meal fit for a king and queen. It was obvious to everyone she wasn't feeling very festive.

She gazed around the room. Everyone's eyes averted from hers, except for Quincy's. He started to say something, but closed his mouth and shook his head. He kept his eyes trained on her as he stabbed a piece of meat and jabbed it in his mouth. He chewed slowly. His eyes did not move away. Finally, he broke the silence. "Bull headed. The both of you are just plain stupid and—"

Amelia tugged on his arm to whisper something in his ear. He leaned to hear what his sweet new grandchild had to say. Of course, she hadn't perfected her skills in the whispering department. "Pop Pop, it's not nice to say potty words. Especially at the table." Her little finger wagged giving him the business as she spoke.

The table erupted in laughter. Thank God. It helped lighten the mood.

Moriah took in the various aromas and choice spices wafting through the air. Several of the dining tables had been lined up together and adorned with lit tapered candles. It created the perfect atmosphere for a cozy family and friends gathering. A hint of excitement fluttered within her. She would be hosting a big dinner tomorrow at her new home.

She was relieved that Mario decided to hold the dinner tonight instead of on Thanksgiving. She was looking forward to having Thanksgiving dinner in her new home. Of course they all were welcome.

Moriah wasn't surprised that Tyro hadn't come that evening. She was disappointed but knew how awkward they both would have felt. They hadn't spoken to one another since the service on Sunday.

During dinner, many thoughts bombarded her mind. She restrained herself from shoving food around on the fresh plate the server had brought her. This time, she made a better effort to enjoy her meal. She took small bites and raved about the delicious food.

She'd caught Roy eyeing her on several occasions. There was no fooling him. But she appreciated him not saying anything. Well, at least his Athena had distracted him by feeding him a forkful of sweet potato soufflé, or Mario's famous pumpkin croissants. He'd fuss that he was stuffed and she'd comment he hadn't eaten enough. Watching the two of them was entertaining to say the least.

Surprisingly, it helped her to push her troubles, thoughts of Tyro aside into a reserved place until she was alone. She'd already determined that Amelia wouldn't see her cry herself to sleep again and having a meltdown in front of everyone was not an option. She managed to push through the evening. She'd already made up her mind to go on without him. It was evenings like tonight that provided the challenges she'd faced in doing so.

She'd gone to see a plastic surgeon about the scar on her inner thigh. He assured her that he could remove it although it would be visible to anyone who looked closely, but not as intrusive. She hadn't made up her mind whether she'd go through with it or not.

Everyone knew Tyro was using Sheba as an excuse to isolate himself even though she was recovering nicely. She had been able to nurse her pups since the drugs had been completely flushed out of her system.

Quincy had beamed proudly when Amelia insisted on sitting near him. Moriah saw as he quickly wiped the tear from his eye. She'd met Roy's wife for the first time and immediately liked her. Just as Roy was about to serve his famous desserts, someone tapped on the restaurant door. Moriah's head popped up. Her heart thumped in anticipation. She forced herself to refrain from showing her disappointment when the short, sandy-blonde detective stepped into the dining area.

"Is that seat for me?" Sable pointed to the empty chair across from Moriah.

"You're welcome to join us if you'd like." Mario pleasantly gestured for her to have a seat.

"Nah, I just came by to share some news with you and to wish you all a happy Thanksgiving."

"Good news, I hope?" Mario asked.

Sable smiled at Amelia. "Well aren't you a cutie pie?" Nettie rose, politely excused herself, and took Amelia to help uncle Roy and his wife with the desserts.

"We've located the black box from Mr. Casillas—the helicopter he'd stolen."

"Stolen?" Moriah repeated alarmed.

Looking around the room, Sable announced, "I'm sorry, I think I've come at a bad time," she addressed Quincy and Mario specifically. Turning back to Moriah, "There are a lot of details we need to weed through. I don't think this is the time to get into it." A heaviness rose in the air. It was obvious what everyone was thinking.

Mario shook his head at Quincy. He noticed the rising red flush in his face. "Then may I ask, exactly why are you here?" he said before Quincy had a chance to blow his top.

She swiped her brow. "I thought that perhaps I could put your minds at ease to know that he has confessed."

"Confessed what?" Mario said with a little more agitation.

She pushed a crop of her hair behind her ear. It didn't stay. "Like I said, there's a lot of information we can discuss later, but we do have a signed confession by Mr. Casillas for the murder of Mrs. Simmonds." She cleared her throat.

Mario handed her a glass of water. She guzzled it down in two seconds. "He's pleading insanity," she said, spitting her words out. "We can go over what this means as well as the details when you come downtown... let's say on Friday, since tomorrow is a holiday."

She faced Moriah. "I just want to say it was wrong what they... Mrs. Smythe did to you." She cleared her throat, again. "It's a shame that it's not a crime, but unfortunately, it's not." She swooped a mop of hair back with a swift move of her head. "Mr. Smythe has confessed to tampering with evidence, although it was found in Mrs. Smythe's possession. Not sure what the judge is going to do with that. But we still haven't been able to locate the missing video recorder." She waited for Moriah to respond. "Having the information from that tape would help clear up a lot of loose ends."

Moriah kept her eyes fixed on the detective. Her expression remained blank.

As if she needed to explain herself further, Sable continued, "A company has a right to protect their assets even though they took it to the extreme. The judge would not indict TSMA for any wrongdoing on that account. But he did warn them that it was definitely unethical and he wouldn't think twice about charging them if they were found doing it again."

Moriah tried to follow what she was getting at. *Tyro hasn't turned in the video.*

Sable gazed around at the somber faces. "Can ya come down to the station on Friday?" she asked again, glancing at Quincy and Mario. She waited for their responses. "No need spoilin' your dinner." Her face contorted in realization from the somber stares that perhaps it really wasn't such a good idea for her to have come tonight. "There's something to be said about one being overzealous in one's work. I hope I haven't ruined—"

"We'll be there," Mario responded to her request."

Moriah's mind had wandered off as she tried to remember where she'd heard the name before. *Casillas.* It sounded familiar. Then she remembered. Sable had asked her about the name at Tyro's after barging in like she was the big bad wolf. Hearing the name in full made sense. She had only known him as Leroy Fletcher. He had insisted everyone at TSMA call him by his last name. When Sable said that they had everything they needed to convict him, it hadn't made Moriah feel any comfort. It couldn't erase her past nor would it bring their loved one back. *Is this the news she's come to tell us?* But, she was relieved that he wouldn't be getting away with his crimes.

She thought again about her perpetrator. The overwhelming cleansing and freedom she experienced on Sunday had birthed compassion for his soul. Should he have to pay for what he's done? *Absolutely,* she thought. Was she totally free from the pain and scars he'd caused? Not at all, but she no longer blamed herself. And that in itself was a blessing. She wasn't responsible for someone else's actions. Still, she pitied him.

She slouched back in her chair and began picking at a few crumbs on the table. She felt sorry for the real Fletcher trapped inside his own mind in a world warring against itself amidst confusion, control, and evil. She felt relieved to no longer feel the pangs of bondage for having wanted him dead.

For now, she had to trust God to help her to forgive... to totally forgive him for what he had done, as well as forgive her own sins.

Chapter 55

Moriah's attention returned to the present. She noticed that the package Sable once had under her arm was now in her hand. *What now?* She held her breath and stared curiously at the woman. Sable walked around the table to address her as if she didn't want anyone else to hear what she had to say.

Surprisingly, she spoke so that everyone in the room could hear her. "I owe you an apology, Miss Styles." Moriah noticed the detective fidgeting with the package in her hands. *She's nervous?*

Moriah shifted and sat straight. "Apology? For what?"

"I doubted you."

You mean you used me, Moriah wanted to say but thought better of it. She thought about how Sable had put her life in danger. She was the one who reached out to her. Yes, at the time Fletcher was her pilot. Then it dawned on her. Was it her idea to install the video camera in the first place? Was that why it was a federal crime for her to have it?

Still, she held her peace. She'd find out what she needed to know later. *Looks like Mario's sources will come in handy after all.* She didn't want to ruin the mood any further than it had been already.

Sable stepped closer, intruding in Moriah's space. "Because of you and how you used your head to... well, to survive, we were able to catch him." She let out an anxious chuckle. "You led him right into our lap."

Isn't that exactly what you wanted?

Sable slowly shook her head as if her thoughts were catching up with her. "You knew he'd come after you. You were the one who outsmarted him... Heck, you outwitted us all."

Moriah thought about it. Yes, she knew he'd come after her. And she definitely knew why. She wondered if Tyro had turned in the disc. *Does he know what happened to me?* His mother? It was all on there: Fletcher's guilt ridden conscience confessing what he'd done to her; and his failed kidnapping attempt that led to him brutally murdering Mrs. Simmonds. Did Tyro watch the videotape?

"Oh, by the way," Sable said, "that photo of him kissing you, seems like your boyfriend... Mr. Simmonds," she corrected herself, "seems like he's a very smart man." Moriah restrained the smirk rising to her face. She wasn't telling her or anybody who knew him anything different. "Come to find out, the judge will allow it to be used as evidence of offensive touching." A sober look crossed her face. "You do plan to press charges, don't you?"

Moriah didn't answer. Her eyes shifted around the table.

"But of course, having the video recording would help clear up a lot of things. It may just help to assure his conviction."

She leaned in and whispered to Moriah. "Guess it's no use asking you for it, huh?" Her British accent was thick as usual.

Moriah had had just about enough of this woman. She wanted to be polite, but Sable really was getting on her last nerve. She was trying to make light of her impatience; after all, she and Nettie were invited guest. And as for Amelia... well, she was family as far as Quincy was concerned. Mario too.

She leaned her shoulders back and replied to the detective in a playful southern drawl. "Why detective, whatever do you mean?"

Sable stepped back and straightened her posture. "Thought not. Well, you know where to find me if you—"

Moriah shifted her eyes to the package in Sable's hand. "Is that for me?" she asked, intentionally interrupting her as politely as she possibly could.

Sable grinned sheepishly and handed her the envelope. "Yes, I believe this belongs to you." Moriah leaned back in her chair and stared at it.

"Go ahead. Take it." Moriah hesitated but reluctantly took the brown envelope into her hand. It was marked, FEDERAL EVIDENCE ITEM # 1. She gave a quick glance over at Nettie who had just come back with Amelia and Roy from the kitchen with a serving cart full of sweets. She gave Moriah a quick hunch with her shoulders and then nodded for her to open it.

"Should I be concerned?" Moriah asked, turning her attention back to Sable. Sable crossed her arms and gave her a coy grin.

Amelia skipped over to Quincy and whispered loud enough for everyone to hear. "I made something special just for you, Pop Pop!"

"This little lady right here," Roy pointed to Amelia who propped herself on Quincy's lap, "she done gone and stole Mr. Simmonds' heart."

"I did?" Amelia gasped and placed her head on his chest. "His heart's still in there. I can hear it!"

The room bloomed in laughter.

Sable cleared her throat and shifted to stand evenly on both feet. The package dangled from one hand. She rested her fingers on her chin with the other. Rocking back and forth on her heels, she looked up to the ceiling.

"I don't know. You might want to open it before it melts." She grinned.

Moriah took the package from her and lifted the self-sealed edges. Everyone watched with just as much curiosity. She removed the heap of neatly folded tissue paper. It covered something soft. When she tried to unfold it, something shiny fell into her lap. She covered her mouth in surprise.

"Where did you... how did you...?"

Sable was now standing by the door. She had no idea what was in the package. She had stuffed the tissue paper and note that

477

Tyro had given her in place of the report she had come to give. She pointed to the note that had fallen on the table. Moriah hadn't noticed it until then.

Her eyes raced over the words. She read the note again. In one swift move, she bolted from the table. She rushed toward the door. She held up the note in Quincy's direction too speechless for her words to come out. She paused only for a moment to ensure he understood her unspoken request. He nodded and grinned and crooked his eyebrows. Of course he'd watch after Amelia until she returned. She flung the door open. Praying she wasn't too late, she ran down the Riverfront. She was already a couple hours past the designated time Tyro said he'd wait for her.

Chapter 56

Tyro had wandered away from the appointed place to where he hoped Moriah would come. It was two hours past the appointed time; he needed to get back to Sheba. Another breeze whisked past him and he thought he heard a voice. Her voice. He paid it no attention. It was only his wishful thinking playing tricks on him.

"What, you going to give up and leave so soon?" A voice sailed in the wind, this time wrapping itself around his heart.

He spun around. His eyes shifted from the sequined hat sparkling in her hand to her eyes. He froze. All the things he'd planned to say... wished to say... needed to say, blew away with the wind.

Moriah stopped a few feet in front of him and caught her breath. Her hand trembled, she held up the scrap piece of paper. "I. Got. Your. Note." She sucked in air between each word. She searched his face for meaning.

"It was the quickest thing I could find. I didn't want to hold Sable up. I wasn't even sure if she would deliver it."

"It was sweet." She blushed and lowered her eyes. He pushed toward her and lifted her chin with his finger. Their eyes met.

Tyro took her by the hands, "I didn't know if you would come."

"How could I not? It's not every day that I get such a proposition on the back of a church bulletin. It's like God had written it Himself."

"He did." Tyro pointed as he spoke, "From my heart, to yours."

Realizing it was no use skirting around the reason he'd requested for her to come, he cupped his hand around her hand. She held on to the note tightly. He began to recite what he'd written. "'If you're as miserable as I am without you... if you're ready to forgive and put the past behind us... if you're willing to take a chance with a guy full of imperfections,'" he improvised bringing the past tensed of what he'd written into the now, "'then your destiny awaits,' here and now."

Tears filled her eyes. He wasted no time concluding the final words he'd written. He nudged her forehead with his. "I love you, Moriah Styles."

She fell into his arms. "Oh Tyro. I'm so sorry. I used my shame to blame you for everything. The truth is, I was afraid if you knew the truth about me... about my past and..." And with that, she spilled over with words she'd held locked deep in her soul.

She choked on her words. In one breath, she tried to tell him everything. She wanted him to know about her mother being diagnosed with lead poisoning and that she had lived in a mental facility since the age of two. She told him that her father had been admitted to the same institution shortly after he had been discharged from the military thirty years ago. They met there, fell in love, and married shortly afterward.

Tyro tried to listen attentively. He'd give her all the time she needed to get it all out. He heard pieces of her story about how she and her twin, Anaya had been raised by their aunt Rachel. He caught snatches of details about her sister's death and Kenny's, whom he gathered was Amelia's father. She trembled in his embrace as she continued on about Fletcher and the things she had to do to survive, things that she hadn't told anyone. She was babbling so fast it was too much for him to follow, and a bit much for him to take in. But he assured her they had a lifetime to pray and work through it all.

He was pleased she was being freed from the walls she erected. Her false sense of security was being exposed. He knew he would need God's help to handle the matter delicately. He was glad that Willie had come along at this time in his life. His counseling and praying with him had helped him face his despair.

Tyro breathed deeply knowing that she trusted him.

"Shh," he finally admonished her. She collapsed in his arms, exhausted yet free from the guilt and shame that had weighed upon her, sabotaging their relationship. Her life. Her sanity. He kissed her on her forehead and enveloped her in a warm embrace. He remembered the first night he'd held her in his arms. He couldn't resist the urge. He swooped her up in his arms. The moon cast their silhouette against the still waters. Tyro breathed deeply as he nuzzled his nose to hers.

He thought about what his life would have been like if he'd never met her. And now that he had, he couldn't imagine living without her. He had been miserable over the past lonely weeks.

He placed her down to stand on her feet. A feeling of joy bubbled over him. Lifting her from the ground, he swung her around. She squealed in delight. He enjoyed the glow that shined through her tear stained face. She was free. So was he.

"So, who's the fellow in the picture you've been kissing at night?" he said referring to what Amelia said when he spoke with them in church on Sunday.

She cocked her eyes over at him. "What? Oh... that." She grinned.

"It's been brutal without you these last several weeks." He squeezed her shoulders a little tighter. "You know, I've always wanted to have a girl first when it came time to start a family."

"Is that right," she commented matter-of-factly, holding in her excitement.

"Mmm hm. I have the feeling that Amelia's going to be the perfect child to teach me all about this parenting stuff." He peeked at her. "That's if the two of you will have me."

"Oh, I don't know. We kind of have our own thing going right now," she teased.

"Well, I'd say, we should ask her how she'd feel about it."

"Tyro, that's not fair. Ever since she saw you at church all she's been asking about is 'when is he coming over?' 'Auntie, don't you like him? He really likes you, I can tell'." Moriah chuckled. "She hasn't stopped talking about you since.

"At least she knows a good man when she sees one." He leaned away to escape her playful slap on his arm.

"Tyro, why'd you say that I needed to be here by 7?"

"No, what I said was that if you weren't here by then that I'd understand. Isn't that what I wrote?"

"Uh-huh." She gestured with her head. "You also wrote that you wouldn't bother me again if I didn't show."

"I didn't say that."

"It's what you meant."

"What I was trying to say was if it took you longer than that to make up your mind, then you weren't ready. Besides, I knew I'd be kind of anxious to get back to Sheba, but one of my old buddies from the yard just happened to show up. He agreed to stay with her until I got back. That's after I'd sent the note."

"Uh-huh." She leaned her shoulders back. "So, if Orlando hadn't showed—"

"How'd you know it was him?"

"I'm not telling you my sources, or my ways," she added for emphasis to sound like Mario. "But I figured you were using Sheba as an excuse, so I texted him to check up on you. I wanted to make sure you were all right."

They chuckled and held on to each other. He gazed into her eyes and smiled back at her. He could see it on her face; this time, she meant it. She was willing to push past the pain. To forgive, *really* forgive him. She'd said, "Yes." Yes, that she wanted to start over. Fresh. They made a promise they'd hold back nothing. If their past

482

got in the way, they'd work through it, giving the other the time and support needed. But to never isolate from the other.

The evening atmosphere was pleasant and full of promise. He remembered that Moriah loved the fall. He'd grown to appreciate it too, because of her. All those hours he spent watching the leaves turn colors and fall from the tree, made him think about life, and God. The leaves were like life's little lessons. He accessed his playlist on his smart watch and lifted her to her feet. After placing the sequined hat on her head, he wrapped her arms around his neck as he embraced her. They swayed slowly to the salty, jazzy tune.

"So, my hero. She gazed into his eyes. "You had my hat all along?"

"I did."

"And you didn't tell me?"

"I did not."

"Are you always this blunt."

"I am... not always." He couldn't refrain from laughing. "It gave me hope that I'd find you again. When you disappeared on me, I was glad to have found it. I kept it knowing that one day I'd find you."

She leaned her shoulders back. "And that was how many months ago?"

He pulled her closer. "Ah, do you always need to know so much? I had to make sure it was returned to its rightful owner. She is my destiny, you know."

"Uh-huh." She laid her head back quietly on his chest. "Well next time, don't let her get away."

A refreshing wind blew off of the water. He wrapped his jacket around her shoulders as they sat back down. Placing his arm around her, he held her gently. She leaned her head on his shoulder. He kissed her forehead. Her love had guided him from a world of despair to destiny, God, and His great and immeasurable love. And Moriah, he was not about to let her get away from him again. Ever.

483

But there was one more thing he needed to iron out. He felt for the videodisc in his pocket. He considered if this was the right time. He didn't want to spoil the moment; yet, he yearned for her to understand... she could trust him. Really trust him this time and for always. He hadn't watched it. Whatever she wanted him to know, he wanted it to come from her. He placed the disc in the palm of her hand. "Whenever you're ready to talk about it." She stared in his face.

"I haven't watched it." He studied her closer. "It's your call what you want to do with it. Whatever and whenever you want to talk about it with me, I'll be right here."

She folded her hand over it. "I'll let you know. But, in the meantime, I'll turn it in when I meet with the *good* detective on Friday." She laid her head back on his shoulder. A soft sigh of relief escaped.

"So, you're going through with it, huh?"

"Yes. I'm ready to get the whole ordeal behind me. I know it'll be a long drawn out process, which I'm not looking—" she peered up into his face. "What about you? Are you ready?"

He pulled her closer. He didn't want to think about that right now. "We're in this together, right? On both counts."

"I wouldn't have it any other way."

His mind slipped back to when she'd crossed over the threshold with him on the island. As if she could read his mind, she said, "I'm ready for the journey we started the night I saw the real you." She observed his face. Specks of gold glistened through his beautiful steel grays. There was no sadness peeking or hiding behind them.

"No turning back?"

"Not this time," she replied.

He cocked his head to the side and eyed her.

"Or ever," she said and ruffled his hair. "I love you, Mr. Tyro Hernandez Simmonds. I love you very much."

Facing the river, Tyro and Moriah sat silently for an undetermined amount of time on Willie's old bench. Drenched in the fullness of the moonlight, they held each other. They gazed upon their silhouette casting upon the water as if they were larger than life. What they each were about to face was bigger than the both of them, but there was God. And they had each other.

He thought about his mother. If she hadn't requested for them to work undercover, he would never have met her. The night he'd first met her he'd just finished tracing the routes his carriers took that were the longest. When he'd finished, he felt so discouraged. His mother had been right. Some of his crew was skimming on the job. She'd laid heavily on his mind. Her death, the dreams, everything had started closing down on him. He didn't know where to turn. He didn't know what his future held. His dad had been in no position to help him. He needed help himself.

"I felt so alone," he said out of the blue. She looked up at him as he continued. "That night, I'd been driving around for hours in a daze. I felt so alone, Moriah and I didn't care whether I lived or died. And then I saw you. I knew at that moment, when our eyes met that you were my destiny. I don't know how, or why, I just knew."

"Yeah, the whole thing was pretty scary. But when I saw you running toward me, I knew everything was going to be all right." She settled back into his arms and they stared into the deep-purplish sky.

The dream of his mother from that morning floated across his thoughts. He'd share it with her someday. Soon. But for now, he wanted nothing more than to relish the peace and joy radiating from Moriah's face. It reminded him of the serenity that surrounded his mother as she faded into the glorious light. It had made her smile even brighter.

He felt his mother was pleased that for him, love had come. He'd let it go and it had come back to him as it was meant to, in perfect timing.

Discussion Questions

1. What pulled you into the story? How did you feel about Tyro and Moriah's relationship in the beginning? Who was your favorite character, and why? Did either of them have valid reasons not to trust each other?

2. What were your thoughts about Laino? Do you know someone who is like her? How does she impact your?

3. What did you think of Roy's perspective about women wanting men for their money? Do you think most Christian men have this perspective? Do you think women in general who make a significant amount more money, intimidate most men? What has been you or your friends' experience that face this issue?

4. Why do you think Parker went to such extremes to get Moriah the papers for the full custody of Amelia? Do you agree with his method of having Petra sign over custody of their granddaughter? Why do you think he gave Moriah full and not joint custody?

5. What was your favorite part or chapter of the book? Where did you pause to reflect on a character, scene, or where the plot maybe going?

6. What was the difference between Moriah's sin and Tyro's? Does God look at these sins differently from one to the other—as in one is not as bad as the other? What is God's perspective on forgiveness? How does unforgiveness impact our relationship with God and each other?

7. Moriah was shocked when she realized she had been self-righteous in her judgment of Tyro. It wasn't as easy for her to recognize this sin as compared to Tyro's sin of hatred and unforgiveness. Why do you think that is? How does this point of view cause you to look at others faults differently?

8. How was Fletcher's character depicted? With all the evil and craziness in the world, should Christians live in fear? Explain.

9. Moriah knew her perpetrator would one day catch up with her. How do you feel about her keeping federal evidence? Why did she feel she could not trust the government to protect her? What were your thoughts about Sable? Did she always seem to have Moriah's best interest at heart? What was her motive?

10. Do you know anyone who had been living on the street and God restored them? What do you think about Willie's faith? His wife? Do you think it was too soon for him to have begun a new church? Why?

11. Why did Tyro put up with his father's tyranny? Why did Quincy have a   change of heart toward Moriah regarding her relationship with his son? How did it impact their relationship? Can you think of a time your act of love and continued kindness helped make a relationship better?

12. The next book in this series will feature Mario's story. How do you think he   will find the love of his life working as an undercover boss? How do you perceive his character? What do you hope will happen in his story? He had broken the family tradition of the firstborn son giving the necklace to his bride. Instead, he'd given it to his sister. Does it give you an indication of his outlook on marriage?

Join in our group discussions on Bev's Facebook page about In Perfect Timing and other Christian work of fiction.
Facebook: https://www.facebook.com/BevjPowers/

LOVE FOR THE HOLIDAYS
A Love Undercover series
Coming this fall

beverlypowers author page amazon

Other books published by Bev Powers, aka Beverly Powers

Children's Books
The Fourth Little Piggy
Peaches Gets a Pet
The Crooked Ole Tree
Birthday Present for Homer

Bio

Beverly Powers is an author and speaker who loves to write stories that are fun, encouraging, and transformational. She has been featured in local newspapers and newsletters for the reading program she has established in her community.

Beverly is a member of the SCBWI as well as a few writers' and critique groups. She has written and produced several plays, puppet skits, and skits for children. She is the author of several children's books including The Fourth Little Piggy, and Peaches Gets a Pet. She also is the author of a Christian romance, suspense novel called In Perfect Timing. It is the first book in her Love Undercover series. Beverly teaches writing and puppetry techniques to children, young adults, and adults. She loves to travel, spend time with family, friends, and creating characters for her stories and puppets.

Please visit her blog at www.BeverlyPowers.com.
You may follow Beverly on
Twitter at: https://twitter.com/BevPowersII

www.ingramcontent.com/pod-product-compliance
Lightning Source LLC
Chambersburg PA
CBHW051532250626
47157CB00001B/10